Far Star Crystal

Nicholas Marselos

VORDERLAKE PRESS

ISBN 979-8-9871725-1-3 Paperback

Dedication

To Rose and Davis, Amelie and Adele.
Your greatest adventures are ahead of you.

ACKNOWLEDGEMENTS

Chuck Eaton and Beth Hoffman offered their time and many valuable suggestions to make this book better. To them, I own many thanks.

Everyone benefits from having a cheerleader, and mine was Kay Eaton. My everlasting thanks for your continued support.

To my wife Leslie, for her encouragement and support, and for being my best critic. I credit her for what is best in this novel, blame me for the rest.

CHAPTER 1

The hauler bucked violently as it skipped across the atmosphere.

"Watch what you're doing. I don't want the cargo to tear loose," Troden yelled at the pilot.

"The atmosphere is denser than I thought it would be."

"It's breathable air. Of course, it's dense."

Troden turned from his co-pilot's seat to the three crewmen sitting with the cargo. They were checking if any cargo had come loose. They indicated it hadn't.

This was Troden's seventh trip to the moon as the Veluxin's Cargo Chief, but the first time with this new pilot. He should cut him some slack since the moon had unusual atmospheric currents. It was just that Troden didn't like this pilot.

Their old hauler pilot was fun. He was a good-natured guy who loved to play cards with the crew, despite losing most of the time, loved his drink, too much as it turned out, since he fell down drunk as the hauler's cargo door closed, crushing his leg.

The new pilot didn't drink, wasn't interested in playing cards, and kept to himself most of the time. He was no fun to be around.

"There, see the runway," Troden pointed to a thin strip of asphalt two kilometers north of the compound.

"I see it." The pilot brought the hauler around to line up with the runway. He landed the big hauler smoothly, then rolled it up to the large hangar at the end of the runway.

"Continue on the roundabout. It's easier for the colonists to unload the cargo."

The pilot did it. After he stopped the hauler, he said, "What colonists? I don't see anyone." He was looking out the cockpit window.

"Don't worry. They'll be here."

The fact they hadn't acknowledged the Captain's signal when they entered orbit wasn't surprising. This was a colony of scientists who felt they were too almighty busy to monitor a ship entering orbit. Troden only guessed that they were scientists. He didn't know what they were really doing here. The Veluxin crewmembers were paid well not to ask questions or say anything about the colony. It wasn't just the pay that kept them quiet. It was the threat if they told anyone, they would be killed along with anyone they told.

Troden walked back to the cargo area. He opened the hauler's side door and scanned the area. He didn't see anyone either. He stepped out onto the tarmac to look for a greeting party. Even if the colonists weren't interested in monitoring to see the Veluxin enter orbit, they couldn't miss a hauler landing. This was their six-month supply of fresh food. They were always eager to get it. A dozen or more would come out in trucks to help the crew unload and bring the food back to the compound. Today, there was no sign of them.

He was about to curse the colonists when he heard screams coming from the compound. The pilot, with the three crewmen, had joined him. They heard the screams.

"Is this normal? I mean, it sounds like wild animals," the pilot said.

Troden had no idea what was making these horrific screams. He didn't believe wild animals were on this moon, but he wasn't sure there weren't.

"What do we do?" The pilot asked.

"We go see what's making those noises," Troden answered.

"Who?" The pilot said.

"You and me." Troden could fly a hauler. If there were wild animals, he'd toss the pilot to them to give himself a chance to escape.

"You stay here to guard the hauler," he told the three crewmen. They looked happy to stay there because the sounds from the compound were growing louder.

Troden gave the pilot a push in the direction of the compound. The pilot reluctantly walked with him. The compound was a configuration of Quonset huts arranged around a large open space. Once they got near the compound, they hugged the side of one of the Quonset huts for cover as they approached the open area where the screams were the loudest. What they saw there made no sense.

The colonists were screaming wildly as they fought one another. They weren't just fighting. They were trying to kill each other. They were attacking each other with any weapon they could find. There were bodies on the ground, some with energy burns, most had been bludgeoned. The ones with plasma rifles must have run out of ammo because they were using their rifles as clubs.

The pilot whispered to Troden, "Why are they doing that?"

"How would I know!"

"What do we do?"

"We tell the Captain what's happening." Troden had no idea what he was seeing, so he would make the captain decide what to do. The pilot eagerly agreed. They crept back to the hauler, careful not to be seen.

Troden called Captain Rolund from the hauler. "The colonists are attacking each other, actually killing each other."

"Are you drunk?" was the Captain's response.

"I'm not drunk. I mean it, they are killing each other!"

Troden heard the Captain give an order to scan the compound. After a long delay, the Captain said, "Whatever in Klatan is going on down there, bring as many live ones back to the ship as you can."

"How am I going to do that? They're killing each other. They'll kill us, too."

"Knock them out, I don't care. If all of them die, the Emperor will skin me alive. I'll do the same to you if you don't save all you can. So do it!" The comm went dead.

Troden stood in the hauler as he considered how he would get any of these crazed killers back to the Veluxin. The hauler was full of supplies. There wasn't any room for colonists.

He turned to the crew, "Empty the hauler. Leave the cargo on the runway."

They had been listening in on the Captain's order. They knew the Captain wasn't making an idle threat when he said he would skin Troden. He would skin them as well. They began to empty the hauler.

With the hauler empty, Troden had to deal with capturing these insane colonists without being killed. He remembered there was a fully stocked medical facility in the colony. If they could get there without being attacked, maybe they could find something to subdue the colonists.

The hauler crew armed themselves with anything they could find as a weapon. They took wooden boards torn off pallets, a pipe used to tighten pallet straps, and a large wrench. Troden took the wrench for himself.

Troden led them to the colony's Medical Quonset hut, ensuring the battling colonists didn't see them. It was in shambles. Drawers were pulled out, cabinets overturned, and contents spilled onto the floor.

Searching through the mess, they found vials of anesthetic agents used for surgery. Troden had them load syringes with the stuff. He could only guess at the dose that would put someone to sleep, not kill them. Armed with loaded syringes plus their weapons, they went out to capture colonists.

The colonists were fighting each other ferociously. It seemed that everyone was trying to kill everyone else. Troden recognized a few of them from his past trips. These were intelligent scientists, quiet people, people you'd never expect to kill an insect, much less another person. Yet they were using anything they could find to attack each other.

Troden figured the only way to capture any of them was to wait until they could find one of them alone. It took four of them to hold the first colonist down so they could inject him with the anesthetic. They subdued a few by whacking them on the head. Troden killed one when he hit him too hard. He justified that it was kill or be killed.

They found a few colonists already beaten into unconsciousness but not dead. Just to be safe, they injected them as well. They had fifteen unconscious colonists lying on the floor of the hauler. It was getting too dangerous to attempt to capture anymore. Troden decided that if the Captain wanted more of them, he could capture them. They flew back to the Veluxin.

Captain Rolund surveyed the unconscious colonists now lying on the deck of the Veluxin's cargo hold. "This is all you could get?" he asked.

"All we had were clubs to capture them," Troden said, hoping Rolund wouldn't send him back for more colonists.

The cargo bay comm unit buzzed. Roland picked up the mic, "What do you want!"

"Captain, we are scanning the compound but don't see any movement. Either they're all dead, or the fighting has moved inside the buildings."

"Crap!" Rolund said. "I'm taking us back. Let the Imperial Fleet deal with this. Meanwhile, you keep them alive." He left Troden standing there looking at the fifteen sleeping, some maybe dead, bodies.

CHAPTER 2

Troden rubbed his scruffy chin as he watched for movement from the fifteen bodies sprawled across the deck. It had been ten hours since he brought them aboard. The lack of a ship's doctor was no reason for the Captain to assign him, the Cargo Chief, to nursemaid these crazed colonists.

Movement in the center of the room caught Troden's eye. He hoped it was the twitch from a fitful dream, not a sign he was waking up. It was eight hours since the Veluxin had come through the wormhole. They were back in Imperial space. Soon, they should rendezvous with the ships coming to relieve him of these killers.

The man moved again. It was more pronounced this time. He was awakening from the sedative they gave him.

Troden yelled to Willis at the other end of the cargo hold, watching the sprawl of bodies for signs they were awakening. "That one there, give him another knockout shot!" His voice echoed in the two-story cargo hold.

"What?" Willis yelled back.

"That one is waking up." He pointed to the man moving in the middle of the deck. "Give him another knockout shot!"

"Got only one dose left."

"Use it, dammit!"

The knockout shot was the anesthetic they found in the Medical Hut that was meant to keep a patient unconscious during an operation, not to keep them unconscious for hours. It worked to keep them out, or maybe it killed some of them. Troden wasn't sure which, and he didn't care. This one was alive and waking up. Troden feared more of them might be waking soon. That meant trouble.

Willis stepped over the bodies until he reached the moving colonist. He jabbed a syringe into his neck. The man quickly went quiet. The feeling of relief didn't last long. Troden could see more movement.

Troden said, "Great Klatan, they're waking up!" He had no more knockout drug to keep them unconscious. What was he going to do?

He yelled to Willis. "Get rope, lots of rope to start tying them up."

"Which ones?"

"For Klatan's sake! All of them!"

Troden grabbed the comm to get another crewman to help tie up the colonists. He prayed it wasn't too late.

CHAPTER 3

Troden worked frantically with the two crewmen to tie up the reviving colonists. He told them it would get ugly if one of the colonists got free. They bound each colonist's hands and feet to immobilize them. When one of the tied-up colonists became fully awake, he screamed. Troden had him gagged. Troden told his men to gag all of them, afraid their screams would awaken the others. All the tying and gagging was hard work. Troden would sooner have bashed them in the heads to knock them out. The captain would never accept that because most of them would end up dead.

The ship shuddered. It meant the ship was breaking hard. They must be approaching the rendezvous with the other ships. Troden began to relax. He would soon be rid of these demented colonists. How they would get fifteen crazed, partially awake, bound people to the other ship was a problem for his superiors.

The next person to be tied up was a small, spindly old man. He had a deep gash on his forehead. Troden remembered finding the man lying unconscious in the dirt. He was too old and frail to look like he had put up much of a fight. Troden thought he was lucky he went down without being killed.

The man was reviving. Troden leaned over him to see if being knocked out had dispelled the insane drive to kill. The man slowly opened his eyes. He stared up at Troden for a couple of seconds without showing any reaction. Then he let out a blood-curdling scream as he tried to push Troden away.

"Shut up!" Troden yelled, trying to put a gag over the man's mouth. For his size, the man was strong. He fought off Troden's attempt to gag him while he continued to scream. Troden had enough. He stood up and kicked the man in the head with the metal toe of his boot. The man went quiet, as his dead eyes stared up at Troden.

"This one was dead when we brought him aboard," Troden told the other two crewmen. They nodded. They had no reason to say otherwise. They only cared about getting rid of these colonists as soon as possible.

There were only three colonists left untied. Troden recognized the next man. He was the colony's security officer. The Veluxin brought him to the colony six months ago. Troden had spent time talking with this man during the trip. He remembered his name was Collins.

· · · · ● · ● · · · ·

Collins was reliving the nightmare. He was asleep in the barracks when screams from outside awakened him. He ran to the door. The colony was filled with ugly beasts with grey, gelatinous, pus-colored masses for heads on bodies that pulsated in and out of focus. The monsters were everywhere, and they were fighting each other.

Collins couldn't see any of the other humans. He guessed they were hiding. That was good. It was his job to ensure their safety.

He went inside to get his plasma rifle. Stepping outside, he was confronted by one of the monsters running at him with a garden spade over its head, ready to crash it down on Collins's skull. A single shot brought the beast down.

Collins kept killing the monsters until the rifle ran out of ammunition, then he used the rifle to club them to death. He fought until four monsters grabbed him while another stabbed something into his neck. Everything went black after that.

He could hear screaming. It shook him out of his nightmare. Opening his eyes slowly, he saw one of the hideous creatures standing over something lying on the floor. It was another monster. He was trying to tie it up as it continued to scream wildly. He kicked it in the head until the screaming stopped.

The floor was littered with these monstrous creatures. Most were tied up, some fighting to free themselves from their bindings, others were unmoving. None of this made sense. Why were the monsters tying up their own kind? For that reason, why were they fighting each other in the human compound?

The only rational explanation was that two factions of these creatures must be at war. They must have landed at the colony, where a battle ensued between them. If that was what happened, why did they take him?

Three of the monsters were approaching him. He closed his eyes to make them believe he was still unconscious. He could sense one of the monsters was standing over him.

• • • ●• ●• • •

Troden stared down at Collins. "This one killed a lot of colonists. Better tie him up good. I imagine they will have a lot of questions for him when he gets to Klatania. I'm going to call the Captain to tell him we have them secured."

Collins could hear the monster talking. It was gibberish except for one word, Klatania. The planet Klatania was the seat of the human Empire. They must have tortured the colonists to tell them about Klatania. If these monsters learned where Klatania was, they could launch an invasion against the human Empire. He had to do something to stop them.

Collins could feel a rope being wrapped around his wrists. One of the monsters was tying his hands while another was beginning to tie his feet. Opening his eyes, he kicked the monster at his feet in the head. It dropped to the floor, either unconscious or dead. He grabbed the rope not yet tied around his hands and threw a loop around the monster's neck. He squeezed the rope as tight as he could until the beast let out a gurgling sound before going limp. He let it fall to the floor.

As Collins finished with the second monster, the third monster came running at him. He whipped the rope low so that it wrapped around the monster's legs. He pulled the rope hard knocking it down. He ran over to it and kicked its gelatinous head repeatedly until the monster stopped moving.

Collins couldn't see any colonists among the monsters tied up on the floor. Only two of the monsters on the floor were untied. They were not moving. He kicked them repeatedly in the heads until he was sure they were dead.

The room was quiet. He heard the unmistakable throb of a Quantum Drive Engine. He was in a spaceship. These creatures used the same propulsion technology as humans.

Collins raced to the door. Cautiously, he opened it. The passageway was empty. One thought raced through his mind, *stop this ship at any cost*. He staggered out of the room. He was familiar with Quantum Drives. He had to get to the reactor.

CHAPTER 4

Admiral Dunkun nervously watched the screen as the long-range scans showed the Veluxin approaching. His orders had been to bring a hospital ship with four cruisers to this location. He was to wait there to rendezvous with the freighter. They told him the Veluxin would transfer fifteen patients to the hospital ship. It was imperative these patients be handled carefully and then returned to Klatania. There was nothing about who the patients were, their origin, or their condition.

This was rebel territory. The longer they stayed here increased the chances the rebels would find them. He didn't want to fight his way out through a rebel fleet. Despite having four cruisers, he couldn't guarantee they could save the hospital ship or the freighter if the rebels attacked.

Dunkun's communications officer called out, "The Captain of the Veluxin, Sir."

"Admiral Dunkun here."

"This is Captain Rolund of the Veluxin. I'm transmitting a log of the events when we collected the cargo. We should be at your location in ten minutes."

"The sooner the better. We have the ship ready to receive your cargo." It was code in case the rebels broke their encrypted communications. He was told the Veluxin would refer to their patients as cargo. He should do the same.

"We are eager to transfer our cargo as soon as ..."

"Captain. I didn't hear your last statement."

"Sorry, Admiral. We seem to have a problem aboard. The cargo has gotten loose. I will call back when the problem is ..."

The line went dead. The Admiral turned to his communications officer, who was working to reestablish contact. Suddenly, their ship shook violently. "What in Holy Klatan was that?" the Admiral yelled out.

The communications officer said, "The Veluxin just exploded."

CHAPTER 5

The human body suffers a miserable death if unprotected in space. All those who enter the void of space in spacesuits know this. They also know the thin layer of cloth, a heating and cooling system, and a supply of oxygen is the only thing keeping them from this horrible fate.

Space fever is the name given to the panic someone experiences when they have spent too long in a spacesuit. They begin to believe their spacesuit has a tear, or their oxygen is depleted. Neither is true if they've succumbed to space fever, but they can't be convinced. They desperately seek to get inside and out of the void. Once space fever hits, it is hard to get someone to put on a spacesuit and again go out into the void.

Almost anyone can experience space fever if they work in a spacesuit too long. Everyone but Seth. To him, the void of space was the only place he could truly relax. The only place the thoughts of the others weren't constantly bombarding him, trying to creep into his head. He cherished these moments when he could forget he was a rogue telepath.

Seth sat in the open cockpit of the UVac as he floated above Rocket 272. He could relax in the velvet blackness punctuated by stars, thousands of miles from the Trumulian star and the planet Trumul. He could let his mind drift and relax from the thoughts of those he worked with. Here, he was truly free to be himself.

"Boss, are you okay?" His helmet speaker ended his tranquility. It was time to get back to work.

Seth withdrew the articulated arm that jutted from the front of the UVac. He had just used it to test that Rocket 272 was securely attached. The automated probe's visual inspection had identified what appeared to be a potential weakness in the bolts holding the rocket in place. Seth decided to check it himself. The rocket didn't move when he tugged on it with the articulated arm.

"Rocket 272 is good. Begin the tests when everyone is in place," he told the controller.

"We will be ready as soon as Reilly gets his butt to Rocket 270."

"Tell him to get moving. I'm coming to oversee his test."

"Will do Boss."

Seth smiled to himself. When he first came to the Trumulian project three years ago, they called him many things, none of them Boss, though he was hired to be that.

• • • ●• ● ● •• ••

The Trumulians learned their system would enter a massive cloud of space dust twenty years ago. Their star's energy reaching Trumul would be reduced by fifty percent. The planet would begin to freeze. It would take over 100 years before they exited the dust cloud. By then, the entire population of Trumul, over half a billion people, would die.

The Trumulians would have to relocate their entire population, farm equipment, and animals to a different planet. Except they couldn't. Trumul was an outer planet on the fringe of the Empire. There were no other planets for them to relocate to. Even if they could find some planet, the money they would need to borrow would put them in debt for centuries if they ever could clear that debt. Their only option was sticking it out, believing some would survive. The odds were against it.

Robert Harthset, the greatest planetary engineer of all time, heard of Trumul's problem. He proposed a solution that would allow them to stay on their planet and survive the diminished energy from their star. He proposed they build a lens that would focus the reduced star's energy on the equatorial region of Trumul. It could keep that region from freezing, possibly even warm enough to grow crops outside.

The Trumulians didn't believe a lens that large could be built. Robert Harthset said it wouldn't be one huge lens but thousands of small lenses, acting in unison as if they were a single lens. They challenged the idea of building a structure large enough to hold thousands of lenses. A structure that large couldn't be lifted off the planet. If they built the parts for the structure on Trumul, it would require too many expensive launches to move the parts into space.

Robert Harthset's answer was to build the disk in space, for that is what it would be. Robots would mine metals from the nearby asteroid field and manufacture the disk components there. The robots, under human guidance, would construct the disk in space.

They agreed to do what Robert Harthset suggested. It was that or face death. He designed the disk. Eighteen years ago, they began constructing it.

Robert Harthset never got to see his invention beyond its initial phases. Six years into the project, he was killed when his spaceship collided with a meteor. The Empire honored the great inventor by erecting a twenty-meter-tall statue of him in the center of Klatania's Capitol City. Next to his image was a scaled representation of his greatest invention, the Habitation Engine, which had been used to transform fifteen planets for humans in far less time than the centuries it usually required.

Three years ago, Seth was viewing the Imperial Planetary Commission's board for job openings when he saw the posting for a manager of the Trumul project. He applied for the job, sure they wouldn't select a twenty-five-year-old Planetary Engineer who was only four years out of university. However, they did. He believed his last name had to do with his selection.

Seth was Robert Harthset's son. Robert abandoned his wife and son when Seth was five. Seth's father never talked to his son or wife again. Seth admired his father, and despite his father rejecting him, Seth chose to become a Planetary Engineer like his father.

Seth vowed he would make sure his father's last invention succeeded. That turned out to be more difficult than he anticipated. The crew, most in their forties, many of whom worked on the project from its inception, revered Robert

Harthset. Having his twenty-five-year-old son, an inexperienced Planetary Engineer, foisted on them as their project manager was an insult. They called him Boy, or Sonny, to his face and other more derisive names behind his back.

The biggest problem Seth faced wasn't the crew. It was the state the project was in when he arrived there. The previous project manager quit working when the Imperial Planetary Commission was late paying him. The Commission was notorious for paying late, and sometimes not paying at all. The project was a half year behind schedule when Seth arrived.

They only had three years to complete the Beanie before the dust cloud engulfed the system. Beanie was the nickname they called the disk after one of the crew remarked its parabolic shape reminded him of the beanie skull caps popular with the children of Trumul.

Seth worked harder than anyone. He devised many creative innovations to bring the project back on schedule. He also instilled in the crew the belief they would have the Beanie ready in time. He went from being called Sonny to Boss. They meant it when they called him Boss.

· · · ● · ● · ● · · ·

Seth glided his three-meter UVac along the face of the Beanie toward Rocket 270, the first rocket they would be testing today. The Beanie was a disk over 1570 kilometers in circumference. It was made of concentric circular rings held together by crossing beams tied together by steel cables. The interior of the disk had over twenty-four thousand lenses. The lenses were not yet aligned. As Seth flew over them, they reflected the star's light like thousands of diamonds.

To reduce the fuel necessary to keep the Beanie in position, it was built at the L1 LaGrange Point, the place in space where the planet Trumul balanced the star's gravity. There were 360 rockets mounted evenly around the Beanie's outer ring to maintain its alignment in space. Each rocket could be rotated three hundred sixty degrees on a horizontal plane and sixty degrees up and down. The rockets needed to be fired carefully in groups not to put undue strain on the Beanie. Though the Beanie was a massively large structure, it was quite fragile.

Everyone worked hard to bring the Beanie back on schedule. The original schedule was for the dust cloud to reach Trumul in three months. A scouting mission sent to inspect the dust cloud found it had changed shape. The cloud had formed a leading finger that extended ahead of its main body. This finger of dust would reach Trumul not in three months but in ten days. When it did, the planet would begin to freeze.

Before the Beanie could be put into operation, they had to ensure all the rockets worked correctly. Once that was completed, they could align the lenses. Each of the 360 rockets had to be tested separately, otherwise multiple rockets being fired together could shift the Beanie's position. The tests consisted of firing each rocket once in opposite directions parallel to the plane of the disk, then once in each direction at right angles to the disk's plane.

To ensure each rocket performed properly, an observer in a UVac had to see it. If a single observer did this, it would take 10 minutes to watch the rocket test, then 11 minutes to fly to the next rocket to watch its test. The time to test 360 rockets would take 5.25 days of around-the-clock testing. It wouldn't leave them enough time to align the lenses before the dust cloud engulfed the system.

Seth devised a leapfrog approach to speed up testing the rockets. It used six observers in six of the eight UVacs the Beanie had. Seth's approach was to have observers at three consecutive rockets on one side of the Beanie, then three more observers at the three rockets across the Beanie from the first set. The first observer would watch the first rocket being tested, then fly to the fourth rocket on that side of the Beanie while the other five rockets were being tested. The first observer would be ready to watch the fourth rocket test when the other five rockets had been tested. It reduced testing all 360 rockets to sixty hours if everything worked perfectly. It was rare when everything worked that well.

"Reilly, are you in position yet!" Sandar called. Sandar, a crusty veteran of the Trumul project, controlled the rocket tests. He was running the tests from the control center called the Hub, a box structure attached to the disk's outer rim that also served as the crew's living quarters. The Hub controlled everything from firing the rockets to aligning the lenses.

"Keep your pants on, Sandar. I had trouble getting my UVac to start," Reilly said.

"The Boss says he will be there to check on you."

"Fear not, Boss. I will be there in the blink of an eye."

Seth was listening in but said nothing. Reilly was the Beanie's clown. He was the second youngest crew member, four years older than Seth. He was short and slightly built and loved playing pranks on his fellow crew members. Some of which they hated, others they enjoyed.

The crew decided on a lottery to choose who would observe the first rocket test firing. Reilly won. The crew joked the first rocket would be the only one to fail. He countered, saying the citizens of Trumul would erect a statue in his honor to recognize his contribution to saving the planet.

"Boss, we're ready to start testing the rockets," Sandar called to Seth.

"Then let's do it." Seth was still too far from Reilly to see his UVac as anything more than a speck floating next to the Beanie.

"Commencing Rocket 270 test," Sandar said.

"The first test is good. Begin the second test," Reilly called out.

"Wait. Something is wrong." It was Reilly speaking. "The rocket didn't shut down. It's starting to wiggle. I can see a bolt holding it to the beam coming loose. Turn the rocket off!"

"I did," Sandar responded.

"It hasn't stopped firing!" Reilly shouted back.

"Reilly, are you sure it's still firing? According to my panel, Rocket 270 is off."

"Your panel is full of crap. The rocket is still firing. It's beginning to bounce around like a Goewallian belly dancer. Kill the fuel to it!"

The fuel for each rocket came from tanks mounted around the disk. They fed fuel through pipes that ran throughout the Beanie. Above each rocket was a fuel shutoff valve the Hub controlled.

"I've already cut the fuel to Rocket 270," Sandar told Reilly.

"It's still firing. I can see something tore loose from the rocket and damaged the fuel valve. It must be stuck open. I'm going to have to shut the fuel off manually."

Seth was too far away to see Reilly, but he could see the rocket's exhaust plume gyrating erratically. Reilly would have to leave his UVac to manually shut off the fuel valve on the beam just above the rocket—a dangerous maneuver with the rocket firing.

Seth was about to tell Reilly to wait until he got there when his mind flooded with an image of Reilly holding on to the beam above Rocket 270. The rocket was vibrating as it twisted. The rocket's gyrations were causing the steel cable securing the beam to whip back and forth. Reilly held onto the beam with one hand as he reached for the fuel shutoff valve with the other. He began pulling the shutoff lever down when the cable broke free above him. It whipped down, crashing through Reilly's helmet and killing him instantly.

This was a premonition. It was like the premonition he had when he was a teenager. He saw the mine disaster, but he let himself be convinced nothing would happen. It did. People died. But this premonition was stronger and more vivid than that one. Seth was sure Reilly was going to be killed.

Seth shook his head to clear the vision. There were only seconds before the cable would break and kill Reilly. He was about to push the UVac to full throttle to reach Reilly when he realized he had already done it. While he had the vision, he unconsciously set the UVac to its top speed.

Seth was close enough to see that Reilly was already out of his UVac. He was moving to the fuel shutoff, avoiding the still firing rocket. Seth called over his comm, "Reilly, get out of there!"

Reilly replied. "Can't receive ... think rocket br...king up comm...about to shut off fuel."

Seth wasn't sure he could get to Reilly in time. He could just make out Reilly grasping the beam. The cable securing the beam was vibrating violently. It was about to snap. There wasn't time to warn Reilly.

He aimed his UVac above Reilly, rotated it so the bottom was facing up towards the cable, and threw the UVac's thrusters into full reverse. Timing was crucial. If he arrived too late, the cable would kill Reilly. Too early, he would fly by before the cable came down, still killing Reilly.

Seth couldn't see the cable. He was flying upside down to Reilly's position. He could see Reilly's startled expression just before everything went black.

CHAPTER 6

In the darkness, the cable was coming at him. It was no longer a steel cable. It was a huge snake with its mouth open, fangs showing, as it bit down on him.

"Boss, Boss, wake up!"

Seth slowly opened his eyes. He was looking up at the ceiling and realized he was lying on the bed in the Hub's med bay. Someone was standing over him. He tried to turn his head, but a sharp pain in his back stopped him. He moved slowly, turning enough to see Crandon, the crew's medic, standing next to him.

"We thought we lost you for a bit," Crandon said.

Seth blinked to make sure he wasn't dreaming. He wasn't. He wasn't sure how he got there. What he said was, "How's Reilly?"

Reilly stepped out from behind Crandon. "If not for your crazy stunt, I'd be mashed up by that cable."

Seth tried to get up. As he did, every muscle in his body screamed in pain, stopping him. Crandon gently pushed him back onto the bed. "You have a concussion plus bruises over half your body. I think you better stay still."

"What happened?" Seth asked.

Reilly answered, "You drove your UVac right over my head just as the cable came down. Your UVac was cut in half right behind your seat. It would have cut you in half if it hit a little closer. The impact tossed you out of the UVac., and you bounced against the beam. It was a miracle your spacesuit didn't rip open. I thought you were dead when I grabbed you. We didn't know you weren't until we got you here. I can't imagine how you knew the cable would break because

I don't know how you could have seen it in time, but somehow you did. Thank you for saving my life. Let me add that my wife and children thank you, too. They will when I tell them what happened."

Seth smiled. He wasn't going to tell them about his vision. "I had to save you. We're shorthanded as it is." Seth's mind was coming into focus. "What about Rocket 270?"

"Frank came out in the UVac. He replaced the fuel shutoff valve circuit board. He also replaced the cable. The rocket was okay. He only needed to retighten the bolts attaching it to the beam," Reilly said.

"How long have I been out?"

"About five hours," Crandon said.

"What about the rocket tests?"

"Frank tested 270 after he fixed it. It's fine. They completed tests on 29 rockets so far. We stopped when Crandon said he wasn't sure you were going to make it. They came in for your memorial service. That seems a bit premature now," Reilly laughed.

Seth propped himself up on an elbow. The entire crew was standing there looking at him. "We can't fall behind. We're one UVac down, so we need all hands on deck to finish the rocket tests. I should be A-OK in an hour or two."

Crandon shook his head. "No, you won't. You need to rest today, possibly for a couple of days. You're too beat up to do anything. Just lie here."

Crandon was right. His body wasn't interested in moving, no matter how much he willed it. Seth laid back on the bed. His head rang, and his back felt like a mule had kicked him. "All right, I'll rest. Go back to work."

"Boss, Don't worry. We'll get the rockets tested in plenty of time," Reilly said.

"Keep in mind, if we don't begin aligning the lenses in five days, we won't be ready when the dust cloud gets here."

Reilly smiled, "We will. You heal. We'll take care of the rest." He turned to look at the crew. "Come on boys, we better get back to work before the Boss kills himself trying to do the entire job himself."

The crew began to disperse when someone said, "What in Klatan is that?"

Seth turned to see what was happening. They were all looking out the large window that faced Trumul, except Trumul had disappeared. The window was black.

Seth struggled to get a better view. He could see the black was moving. It was a ship. A huge black ship that was passing between them and the planet.

"Holy Klatan, that's one mother of a ship," someone said.

The ship moved slowly across the window, eventually uncovering Trumul. The ship was the biggest spaceship Seth had ever seen. Even more unusual was its non-reflecting black color, making it virtually invisible against the background of space."

The entire crew, except Seth, ran to the window to look at the strange ship. Crandon said, "I think it's a Viper."

"What the hell is a Viper?" Reilly asked.

Crandon kept looking out the window as he said, "Some freighter jockeys who came through here a bit ago said they heard rumors of a new stealth warship called a Viper. They said it was the biggest warship in the Imperial Fleet, it could make three or four jumps in a row and was invisible to scans. I asked if they ever saw one, they said no, they had just heard about it. I wrote it off as another freighter jockey myth. Though from what they described, I think this is a Viper."

The comms speaker came alive, "This is the Imperial Command Ship Delaigo. I want to speak to Seth Harthset." Seth pulled himself up painfully to a sitting position on the bed. Crandon brought over the comm microphone.

"This is Seth Harthset."

"I have orders to bring you to Klatania."

Seth thought this must be a joke. It would take weeks to travel to Klatania. "You've got to be mistaken. I'm the manager of this project. We are at a critical phase in its deployment. I have no time to travel to Klatania."

"There is no mistake." There was authority in his voice.

"Contact the Imperial Planetary Commission. I have a contract to finish this job."

"You have been released from your contract. We will be docking at your station in the next few minutes. Be ready with your belongings to come aboard."

"What if I refuse?"

"You will come with us either voluntarily or by force."

Crandon said, "Boss, you better go with them."

"We are shorthanded here as it is. I can't leave you now."

"It doesn't sound like he's giving you a choice," Crandon said.

Reilly spoke up. "Don't worry. We have your plans for completing the Beanie. Trust us. We'll finish this job on time. After all, our families on Trumul are depending on us."

CHAPTER 7

Seth could hear the black ship dock with the Beanie as he finished packing his belongings in his duffle bag. He'd learned how to get by with few possessions due to his mother's paranoid belief the Imperial Guards would come for them. She constantly moved them from one outer planet to another, always as far away from Klatania as possible. This nomadic lifestyle resulted in Seth having few friends and no attachments. Working the past three years on the Beanie had felt more like home than any place in his past. He would miss the Beanie's crew.

Two crew members, one of them Reilly, insisted on accompanying Seth to the Beanie's airlock. As they got there, the inner airlock opened. Three men dressed in black uniforms stood facing them with weapons raised.

"No need for weapons," Seth said. "I'm coming with you peacefully."

One of the black ship's crew grabbed Seth's arm. He began pulling him into the airlock. Seth turned to face Reilly. "Keep the morale high. Meet the schedule."

"Don't worry, Boss, we will."

Seth hoped he was right. Seth suddenly had a feeling he would never know if the Beanie was successful. Whether this was another premonition or pessimism, he didn't know. If it was a premonition, was it telling him he wouldn't learn the outcome of the Beanie because he would be dead? That thought was unnerving.

The black ship's crewman pulled him into the black ship. Another closed the airlock hatches between the ships.

Seth was still feeling rocky from the concussion. His back hurt with every step. Once the airlock closed, Seth staggered. He'd pushed himself to look strong for his crew. His body wouldn't be pushed any further.

The one holding Seth's arm kept him from falling. He yelled, "Get the doctor!"

Seth didn't remember anything after that. When he woke up, he was lying on a bed. He could hear the pulsing sound of a Quantum Drive. His head felt better. Even his back didn't hurt as much. He brought himself up to a sitting position to check his surroundings. He was in a cabin larger than he had ever been in on a ship. There was a table with three chairs. A comfortable looking padded chair was pulled up to a desk. On the desk was a large-screen VID player. The cabin even had its own bathroom.

Seth stood up. The dizziness he'd felt when he came aboard was gone. He went to the door. It was locked. He was a prisoner of sorts. A prisoner with exceptionally good accommodations.

Seth sat on the padded chair. He found it was quite comfortable. A luxury after sitting on the hard metal chairs they had on the Beanie. His duffle bag was on the rack next to the bed. All his things were there. There was a pitcher of water on the table with three glasses. He poured himself a glass of water and drank it.

"Good, you're up," said a young man with red hair wearing a pitch-black colored uniform as he opened the door and entered the room. The insignia on his uniform identified him as an Imperial Fleet Crewman Second Grade. The young man smiled as he introduced himself, "My name is Tiller. I'll be taking care of you on this trip."

"How long was I unconscious?"

"Two hours."

"Where are we going."

"To Klatania."

Klatania, the Imperial home world, was a long way from Trumul. "It will take weeks to get to Klatania," Seth said, frustrated at the thought of spending so much time on this ship when he should be directing work on the Beanie.

Tiller smiled, "Not on this ship. We will be there in four days."

"How is it possible to get to Klatania in four days?" Seth never heard of any ship that could do that.

"I shouldn't say. Well, you will see. The ship can make multiple jumps in a row." He said it with pride.

The only way a ship could make multiple jumps in a row would be if it had multiple Quantum Plasma Drives. It meant the Delaigo would have to be an incredibly huge ship. "I've never heard of a ship that could make four jumps in a row. What kind of ship is this?"

"We are a prototype warship. The fastest, best equipped in the fleet. Soon, we'll have a fleet of these babies. Once we do, the rebels won't bother anyone anymore," Tiller said with a prideful smile.

"Then the Delaigo must have multiple Quantum Plasma Drives."

"Yeah, four of them. Although, that's supposed to be a secret that I shouldn't talk about." Tiller said it somberly, then he brightened, "But you must be important. You have our best cabin. We call it the VIP cabin." Reassuring himself that telling a VIP guest details about the ship was not a big deal.

"Why am I being taken to Klatania?"

Tiller shrugged his shoulders. "I don't know. All I know was we were told to get you. We used two of our four QP drives to get to Trumul. It means we'll have a minor delay for them to realign while we use the other two."

Seth pointed to Tiller's uniform. "Your insignia shows you are part of the Imperial Fleet. So, why are you dressed in black when Imperial uniform colors are red?"

Tiller smiled. "All I can say is we're a special part of the fleet. I really can't say more. How do you feel?"

"I feel better than I did."

"You can thank our doctor for that. You passed out when you came aboard. The doctor found that you had a concussion, and your back looked like someone beat the heck out of it. He patched you up. He says you should be fine."

"Can I go thank your doctor?"

"Sorry, my orders are to keep you in the cabin for the entire trip. I will pass your thanks along to him. If you want anything, I'll bring it to you. That includes your meals."

This confirmed he was a prisoner, though a pampered one. "Can I get news VIDs?"

"No problem."

"If you have any recent news VIDs, I'd like to see them. I've been working on the station at Trumul for three years. We didn't get news VIDs."

"We have a fully stocked library of news and the latest entertainment VIDs. I'll bring you the news VIDs for the last month. If you want any further back or entertainment VIDs, just ask. One more thing. Are you hungry?"

Seth hadn't eaten since the morning meal before he went out to test the rocket. "Yes, I am."

"I'll bring some chow right away."

With that, Tiller left the cabin. Seth tried the door. It was locked.

Seth sat at the table, contemplating why anyone would want him in Klatania. Why would they need to send this unique Imperial Fleet ship to get him there in four days instead of the four weeks it would take for a normal transport ship?

His mother's obsessive fear returned to him. She moved them from one outer planet to another, never staying on one planet for more than a year. When he complained about all the moving, about never being able to have friends, she said one day the Imperial Guard would come for them. He couldn't get her to elaborate on this. Eventually, he wrote it off that she had a paranoid fixation about the Imperial Guard.

During the sixteen years he lived with her, the Guard never came. Now that she was dead, they had come for him. Maybe she wasn't paranoid, just protective. All he could do now was go along with what would happen once he reached Klatania.

Tiller returned carrying a tray of food. He set it down on the table in front of Seth. He pulled off the warming cover to reveal a savory cut of beef. It was a real steak surrounded by chunks of real potatoes with an unfamiliar vegetable. Seth had only eaten a steak once before. It was at a party sponsored by the President of Klatania University for those receiving their doctorate degrees. Meals in the outer planets consisted of synthetic or plant-based protein and any local vegetable growing there.

Tiller said, "I hope you eat meat."

"Where did you get this?" Seth asked, clearly showing his surprise.

"We come fully stocked with the best food. We also have white or red wine for your meal. Sorry, no hard liquor, it's not allowed aboard the ship. Although, if you want some, I can get it for you."

"No thanks. I don't need the wine either. This meal looks great just as it is."

Tiller smiled. "I'll bring the news VIDs when I pick up your dinner plate. Just press that button when you're done with your meal or whenever you need something." He pointed to a button next to the controls for the VID player.

Seth nodded, and Tiller left. Seth spent the next thirty minutes enjoying his meal and thinking they were indeed providing him with VIP treatment.

CHAPTER 8

S eth had just finished his meal when the ship began a jump. A jump always made him feel queasy. It was even more pronounced now with a full stomach. He sat back to allow his stomach to adjust.

Seth's stomach finally settled down. He pressed the button to summon Tiller. Tiller came in almost immediately carrying a container filled with VIDs.

"How was the meal?"

"It was the best meal I've had in a long time." Seth meant it. "I felt we just entered a jump. Are we still on schedule to get to Klatania in four days?"

"On schedule, according to the captain. I brought some of the latest news VIDs for you. As I said, if you want more, just ask. If you've lost track of time, it is night watch aboard the ship. I'm going off duty now. Someone else will come if you ring. I'll bring you breakfast in nine hours. Have a good night." Tiller put the container of VIDs down next to the VID player before leaving with Seth's dinner plate.

Seth sat back to consider what happened to Reilly. The memory of his vision of Reilly being killed came to him. Was it a premonition or just his intimate understanding of the Beanie? Would it have happened as he saw it in the vision? Reilly thought it would. The difference was that he changed that outcome.

It brought back memories of the mine disaster. He had a premonition that it would happen, but after it did, he convinced himself that it was a coincidence and that he had no insights into future events. He never had another one, until today.

• • • • • • • • • • •

He was thirteen when his mother moved them to a planet with a small mining colony. Most of the people in the colony worked in a deep underground mine digging platinum arsenide ore, while the rest worked on the surface extracting pure platinum from the mined ore.

She was their only physician, the sole person working in their clinic. The first week after they arrived, Tramr Willon, a foreman for the mine, came to the clinic with a hairline fracture of his hand caused when a piece of equipment fell on it. He returned to the clinic several times to have his hand checked. After it was healed, he continued coming to the clinic. He would bring sweet rolls so he could visit with her over coffee.

Seth could see Tramr had a romantic interest in his mother. He wasn't sure she felt that way about Tramr. She liked him, and so did Seth. Tramr was a frequent dinner guest at their house. He was cheerful with an abundance of funny stories to tell.

Seth was eating breakfast one day when he had a vision of the mine ceiling crashing down on the miners. It was as real as if he were there. He had no idea why he had this vision, but he was sure it would happen.

He found Tramr as he was about to enter the mine for his shift. Seth told him about his vision. He begged Tramr not to go down in the mine. Tramr just smiled. He assured Seth the mine was safe. Tramr left him standing at the mine's entrance. He continued feeling upset about his vision, but now he was unsure if it was anything more than a delusion.

A few minutes past noon that day, Seth felt the earth shake. A terrible sound came from the mine. He ran to the mine's entrance to see smoke billowing out of it. People were yelling there was a collapse in the mine. It took hours before they heard that the mine ceiling collapsed on the men when they were eating their lunch. In all, sixteen miners died and another twenty-four were injured. Tramr was one of the miners who died.

• • • • • • • • • • •

Seth sat back in the padded chair as he remembered the mine disaster in light of what happened to Reilly. He was a telepath, yet no one ever said a telepath could foretell the future. Was that what he did at the mine, did on the Beanie? Was it a premonition that he would never know if the Beanie was successful? If he was capable of having premonitions, it wasn't showing him what was waiting for him in Klatania.

He was too tired to continue ruminating about these events. His body demanded rest to heal. He took off his shoes and pants, then laid his shirt over one of the chairs. He crawled into the bed and fell asleep immediately.

CHAPTER 9

S eth was up and showered before Tiller came in with his breakfast. It was another feast with real eggs, sausages, and freshly baked bread. Seth was beginning to feel like himself. The Delaigo's doctor had done a good job. The pain in his back was reduced to a little stiffness. The knot on his head was the only reminder he'd had a concussion.

After breakfast, Seth began watching the VIDs. He was woefully behind in current events since news on the Beanie was limited to gossip about the happenings on Trumul. VIDs were the principal source of information for the human-occupied planets. The distance between the planets was such that sending electromagnetic communications was too slow. Cargo ships using jumps to travel between planets could deliver VIDs containing the news much faster.

The Empire controlled the news. What wasn't propaganda or outright lies were stories adjusted to show the Emperor's or the Empire's actions in the best possible light. Those like Seth, who lived on the outer planets, had learned how to interpret the news.

Seth rifled through the container until he found the oldest VID. A single VID could hold hundreds of hours of video and written articles, of which there were occasionally a few. Everyone had access to VID players. Seth carried a portable VID player with him. Today he would enjoy watching the VIDs on the large screen player on the desk.

He planned to watch them in chronological order. The oldest VID was a month old. Seth put the small cylindrical VID rod into the player. All the videos on this VID were about preparations for the 350th anniversary of the Great Migration. In two months, it would be 350 years since the first ships left the dying Earth for new planets that Karl Klatan found for humans.

Seth's mother didn't like using the New Era calendar. She taught him how to translate New Calendar years into the old Earth calendar. The first ships of the Great Migration left Earth in the year 2234. The 350th anniversary meant it would be the year 2584 on Earth, if Earth still existed, which it didn't.

Seth pulled out the next oldest VID. This one was about Emperor Wuden Klatan's 95th birthday celebration. He was shown at the celebration, a 95-year-old man looking more like someone in his early 50's. Seth's mother bristled when anyone remarked about the Emperor's youthful appearance. She never explained why it bothered her so much. He considered it just another manifestation of her hatred for the Empire.

The VID continued with the Barons giving celebratory speeches for Wuden's birthday. Seth had never seen the Barons other than on VIDs. They were hand-picked by the Emperor to be his representatives on the nineteen Core Planets. These planets, along with Klatania, were the earliest planets first populated by humans. The Core Planets were within one or two jumps of the center of the Empire's seat of power, Klatania, home of the Emperor.

The Barons enforced the Emperor's edicts on the Core Planets. They also collected taxes for the Empire. Since the Core Planets had large populations with major industries, the taxes collected from them were significant.

Seth had lived his entire life on planets far from Klatania, collectively called the outer planets. The forty-two outer planets were under the Empire's control, and they didn't like it. The Emperor once sent Barons to the outer planets only to have them run off the planets. The outer planets rankled at Imperial laws. However, they had to be careful. If the Emperor felt an outer planet was too rebellious, he would send Imperial troops. That would often end in people being imprisoned, sometimes in bloodshed. Since the Empire couldn't control all the outer planets, they were allowed to govern themselves as long as they paid the taxes the Empire imposed on them.

The outer planets differed in how they were run, much of it depending on the size of their populations and relative wealth. Planets with large populations chose to elect officials to govern them, a democratic system on the surface, though the Emperor controlled those elected. Planets with smaller populations, or ones that were not wealthy or in their early stages of being settled, were typically small mining or farming colonies, often both together. On these planets, the individual colonies were governed by committees. The Emperor didn't have much influence on these planets. There wasn't enough wealth to make it worthwhile for the Empire to station a garrison on them, however, these planets were still expected to pay taxes to the Empire. Imperial Guards would be sent there to collect them if they didn't. The planets the Empire had the least influence over were the lawless planets. Warlords ruled these planets, often multiple warlords who battled each other for supremacy.

The last story on the oldest VID was about delays for the ships landing on Klatania. It said the delays were to ensure ships were not carrying contraband. What piqued Seth's interest was that these inspections were conducted in orbit.

If the ships were being checked for contraband, it could be done after they landed. Conducting these inspections in orbit could only mean they feared a rebel attack. The rebels had been operating for years to gain independence for the outer planets. Many outer planets secretly supported the rebels, but to do it openly would bring down the wrath of the Emperor on them.

The news never mentioned the rebels, but it was generally considered the rebels were more of a nuisance than a serious threat to the Empire. Living on the outer planets, Seth would hear stories about rebel ships attacking freighters delivering goods to Imperial bases on the outer planets. They were pirates, stealing the ship's cargo, then reselling it to support their cause.

All the time Seth spent on the Beanie, he never heard anything about the rebels. If he was interpreting this news story correctly, the rebels must have become more of a threat if it forced ships going to Klatania to be searched in orbit.

CHAPTER 10

Senior Commander Freedom sat in front of a lineup of monitors. He was surrounded by resistance members tracking the movements of the Imperial fleet. They were at the base called Liberty, the logistical command center for all rebel activities. Liberty was hidden inside a moon orbiting a dead planet within an asteroid belt. A perfect hiding place to direct attacks against the Empire.

Freedom wasn't his real name. No one in the rebellion's leadership used their real names, nor did they share details of their former identities. This anonymity protected the resistance if any of them were captured. Knowing the Emperor's boundless thirst for revenge, it also protected the families of those in the resistance.

He was waiting for three of his commanders to arrive. As he waited, he reflected that this day was an anniversary. Not one to be celebrated, though it was an event that dramatically changed his life. Thirty years ago, he was a young lawyer presenting a case before the Empire's High Court. He was one of twenty other lawyers, all advocates for the outer planets, who presented a petition to the High Court demanding the outer planets be given their independence from the Empire.

The petition for independence culminated a long legal battle through the courts to have the Empire reduce the onerous taxes they extracted from the forty-two outer planets. Since the Empire wouldn't budge on reducing the taxes, their only recourse was to demand independence for the outer planets.

The High Court listened to their arguments. They said they would deliver a decision in a few months. None of the petitioners believed the High Court would grant independence to the outer planets. The petition was a statement to show how serious the outer planets were to have more reasonable taxes.

The High Court never made a ruling. Four days after they presented the petition, all the advocates representing the outer planets were rounded up and imprisoned. Freedom was fortunate, some of his friends heard what was happening and hid him from the Imperial Guards. Those they imprisoned were never heard from again. Everyone believed the Emperor killed them, but they could do nothing about it.

The Empire didn't stop with those who petitioned the High Court. Imperial Troops went to the outer planets to seek out anyone who supported the petition. Many were killed. All the Empire succeeded in doing was to create an underground rebellion.

The petition presented to the High Court took place thirty years ago today. Freedom chose his name when he devoted his life to a rebellion against the Empire. They began by pirating cargo ships that supplied Imperial outposts and using the funds to buy more ships. Thirty years later, the rebels were stronger and becoming a substantial threat to the Empire.

The landing pad monitor began sounding to indicate activity. Freedom watched the monitors as a section of the mountain slid sideways, revealing a landing pad. Three rockets landed simultaneously. Once all three rockets had cut off their engines, the floor of the landing pad descended into the ground. The mountain slid back, returning the moon to its barren appearance.

Freedom left the command center for the conference room to wait for his Senior Commanders, who had just landed. Twelve minutes later, the three principal leaders of the resistance entered the conference room.

Commander Nightmare was first. Freedom thought his choice of this name would have been comical if not for the fact by deed and appearance he lived up to the name. He was a big man with a scar that ran down the front of his face from his right eye to his chin. The scar helped sell his name's legitimacy. Nightmare claimed it was a battle scar. Others said he got it long ago in a bar fight.

Commanders Impulse and Hider followed Nightmare. These were names they also chose themselves. Impulse was tall and thin. He was an excellent strategist known for driving the crews on his ships to do their jobs better. Impulse was Freedom's best attack commander.

Hider was small and wiry. The name Hider not only seemed to fit his stature but was also appropriate for what he provided the rebellion. He was head of the rebel's spy network. His spies were their best source of information about the Empire. He even had spies in the Imperial Palace. More than anything, Hider's spy network kept the rebellion alive.

All three joined Freedom at the table. Nightmare spoke first. "I hear new planets have joined us."

"The leadership of four more outer planets have pledged their support to us. That puts the number at fifteen planets giving us financial aid."

Nightmare shook his head. "Fifteen planets secretly supporting us is a pitiful number compared to twenty-seven outer planets that still pledge their loyalty to the Empire."

"We have some support from all the outer planets. The leadership on many outer planets fear openly supporting us. They know they have spies among them. If they openly express that they are backing the rebellion, Imperial Guards will be sent to their planet to root out and kill all those who support us. Meanwhile, they secretly give us money to support the cause," Freedom said.

"This isn't as big a problem as it once was. We eliminate any spies we find. It seems the Empire is running low on EYE Corps spies," Hider said with a chuckle.

"I called this meeting to tell you we have added more ships to our fleet."

"How many?" Nightmare asked.

"We just added seven freighters. That brings our fleet to seventy-eight ships," Freedom said.

"Freighters are no match for Imperial battle cruisers. We need warships," Nightmare said.

"They may be freighters now. Once we refit them with the latest weaponry, they will be able to stand toe-to-toe with any Imperial Fleet Cruiser. Consider that at seventy-eight ships, we have more concentrated firepower in our sector of the galaxy than the Empire does."

"We won't have much chance if they bring the entire fleet against us."

"That's why I've started another cell in a sector on the other side of the Empire's Core planets. They have twelve ships ready to raise hell in that sector. If the Imperial fleet has to protect itself on two fronts, it can't focus all its attention on us. I know we can't engage in a conventional war with the Imperial Fleet now. I want to plan an attack on the Imperial Fleet as soon as we have enough warships. If we can win a substantial victory over the fleet, it will force them to pay attention to our demands for independence."

Nightmare let out a disapproving groan. "And when do you think we will be ready for that? It's more likely the Imperial spies will learn about our plans long before we can be ready to take on the Imperial Fleet."

Hider spoke up. "Don't be such a pessimist. We have more leverage than you think. My sources say the Emperor is clearly showing signs of dementia. If he becomes unstable or dies, there will be disruption in the Empire's leadership. The Barons are uneasy about Prince Victor becoming Emperor. They don't trust him. If the Emperor dies, it will be a perfect time for us to stage an attack. It will give us leverage to negotiate with the Barons or the Prince. We can see which of them will support our demands for independence."

"By joining one side in that power struggle, we might be trading one master for another. The only way we can get independence for the outer planets is by making the Empire understand they can no longer control us. That will only happen through force. It is the only way to guarantee independence for the outer planets." Freedom checked the others to assess their support for his bold statement. They showed no reaction. He had hoped they would agree with him.

Freedom continued, "There is another reason I called you here. We have another sighting of Imperial ships in the Reagis sector. A freighter was mining asteroid QR56233 when they detected five Imperial Fleet ships entering the sector. The freighter captain is a sympathizer. He sent a shuttle to find out where these ships were going. The ships stopped in the region just beyond the Reagis gas cloud. The shuttle pilot hid in the rings of a nearby planet and recorded what happened. Here is that recording."

Freedom turned on the conference room's VID player. The image showed five bright dots in the middle of the screen. The camera zoomed in to show there were four Imperial Cruisers along with a larger ship. The image focused on the larger ship. It was a hospital ship.

Hider said, "That's crazy. Why would they have four warships plus a hospital ship in a region where there's nothing?"

No one had an answer to Hider's question. That region of space was empty except for a gas cloud. They continued to watch the recording. A ship appeared. It was a freighter heading to the Imperial Fleet ships. The freighter was still far away from the Fleet ships when it blew up. The explosion vaporized the freighter, a clear sign the freighter's reactor must have gone critical. It was an unlikely accident since there were safeguards to keep it from happening. The recording continued until the Imperial ships left.

Freedom turned off the VID player.

Impulse said, "There's nothing in that part of space. Where did the freighter come from? What made it blow up?"

Nightmare leaned back in his chair as he drummed his fingers on the table. "There have been other Fleet ships seen in that sector. It was always a single ship. We considered they were on a scouting expedition. Since there is nothing of value there, no one paid much attention to them. However, having multiple ships in the sector is suspicious, not the least of which is having one of them blow up."

Hider leaned forward, both elbows on the table. "We've been suspicious the Empire has a secret base in that region from the occasional reports of ships seen there. If there is a base, I can't find where it is."

Freedom said, "Something important must be there. Without a reason, they wouldn't have a small fleet with a hospital ship waiting for a freighter. If they have a base there, it could launch attacks against us that we would never expect or see coming. I want that region patrolled for any activity. If there is a secret base in that sector, we need to find it. We also need to make sure the Imperial fleet knows this is our territory."

CHAPTER II

By his third day on the Delaigo, Seth's pants were getting tight from the rich food they were serving him. He laughed that maybe they were fattening him to be killed and eaten. The thought they would eat him was ridiculous. The idea they might kill him lingered until he considered it didn't make sense that they would be taking him to Klatania in these lavish accommodations just to kill him.

Seth was finishing the VIDs from the last month when he saw an ad for the EYE Corps. This heinous organization of telepaths served the Emperor. They acted as human lie detectors that could probe minds to learn a person's deepest secrets. Everyone feared them. Bending to the fears of the public, the Emperor had an eye tattooed on the forehead of those in the EYE Corps. No one trusted that all the EYE Corps members had been tattooed. It was a common belief that untattooed EYE Corps telepaths acted as the Emperor's spies.

The VID ad was for recruiting telepaths. It extolled the benefits of joining the EYE Corps, including a free education at EYE University that would lead to a well-paid career providing an important service to the Empire.

Seth thought the ad was strange, since a couple of years ago, a credible news source said no new telepathic children had been found in the past eight years. If there were no new telepaths, why make this ad?

Everything about his abduction from Trumul became clear. They must have learned he was a telepath though he never used his ability, nor had he told anyone he was a telepath. If they were bringing him to Klatania to force him to serve in the EYE Corps, he wouldn't do it, even if it cost him his life.

• • • ●• ● ● • ••

Seth was eleven when his mother moved them to the planet Graddian. This was the fifth planet they had moved to in four years. As a famous physician, Seth's mother was welcomed on any planet she went to. She was treated as a celebrity after finding the cures for two major diseases while still a student at Klatan University. Colonies on the outer planets were always in need of physicians. They gave her free housing and paid her generously because she was often their only physician. That was also true on Graddian.

For Seth, Graddian was just another planet of the many he'd already lived on in his young life. Constantly moving from one outer planet to another never allowed Seth to make lasting friendships. Eventually, he gave up trying. Seth's teachers would describe him as a sullen introspective boy, though he was smart, having advanced through school well beyond his peers. Seth was eleven years old in the ninth grade. Most of his classmates were thirteen and fourteen. The age difference between him and his classmates was one reason he rarely made friends.

Today, that changed, and Seth's life would never be the same.

The class assignment was for everyone to read silently at their desk. Seth was reading his book when he heard Jol Groden, the boy sitting at the desk next to him, speaking. Jol said Clerin Conlers was sexy. He was pondering if she would go to the flicks with him this weekend if he asked her.

Seth turned to tell Jol to stop talking because it was bothering him. Jol's face was planted in his book. His lips weren't moving. He wasn't speaking. Despite that, Seth could still hear him. Now Jol was saying, "Why is this new guy looking at me?" No sound was coming from Jol's mouth. Seth returned to his book. As he did, he heard Jol speculating if Clerin was the kind of girl who would kiss on the first date. A quick look at Jol found his face was still planted in his book, his lips not moving.

Seth didn't understand what was happening. How could he hear Jol when Jol wasn't talking? Then the deluge came. It wasn't only Jol talking, it was the entire class. A cacophony of chatter. Everyone had their faces planted in their books, yet Seth could hear them all.

Seth put his fingers in his ears. The sound didn't stop. The din was overwhelming. He felt like running out of the room until he heard someone shouting his name. "Seth, focus on just one!" Everyone was looking at their books except Tovar. He was a short, dark-skinned boy sitting on the opposite side of the room. He was staring at Seth. Tovar was someone no one in the class paid much attention to. Tovar was a loner. In that way, he was a lot like Seth.

Seth didn't know what to do, so he did what Tovar said. He focused only on Jol's voice. Jol was now musing about Clerin Conlers' morals. The voices of everyone began to fade. Now all Seth could hear was Jol.

Tovar was still staring at Seth, now he was smiling. Seth heard Tovar's voice in his head say, "Welcome to the club."

Seth waited for Tovar after school. They went behind the building. Once alone, Tovar asked, "Didn't you know you were a telepath before today?"

Seth shook his head. "Is that what I am, a telepath?"

"You can read people's minds, so you're a telepath. I am too."

"How? I mean, I've heard that some outlanders are telepaths. How did I get to be one? How did you become one?"

"It happened to me almost a year ago. I was in a shuttle station with my parents on our way to visit my grandmother on a nearby planet when I suddenly began hearing the thoughts of people sitting around me. I panicked, like you did today. A guy in his twenties was sitting next to me. He must have read my panicky thoughts because he talked to me in my mind. He told me he was a rogue telepath, one the EYE Corps hadn't found out was a telepath. He told me to focus on just his thoughts. I did, and it calmed me down. He explained that anyone who is a telepath discovers they have this ability sometime after puberty. In my case, I was a late bloomer. He said it takes time to learn how to control it. He asked me if I planned to join the EYE corps. I said no. He warned me the EYE Corps has checkpoints for travelers on the Core Planets. The checkpoints are looking for contraband or something else criminal. But they can also discover if you are a telepath.

"I asked him, still talking through my mind, how he kept from being discovered by the EYE Corps. He told me all it takes is to think of something that terrifies you, but to make sure that the terrifying thing isn't having them find out you're a telepath. If you can generate enough fear about something that isn't criminal enough for them to arrest you, you can block an EYE Corps agent's probe from seeing your thoughts clearly. That was how he kept them from finding him all these years."

Seth and Tovar became close friends, closer than most friends could be. Outwardly they played together as normal kids do, while secretly carrying on telepathic conversations. Tovar convinced Seth he shouldn't tell his mother about his ability.

"She will either send you to the EYE Corps or be fearful they will get you when they do the sweep."

"What's the sweep?" Seth asked.

"A member of the EYE Corps comes here every year to interrogate each student in the fourth through ninth grades to see if any of them have become telepaths."

"Did you go through the sweep?"

"I wasn't a telepath when they came the last time. You don't want to join the EYE Corps, do you?"

Seth had to think about it. VID ads for the EYE Corps promised an education and a job in one of the most respected positions in the government. All the ads would end with, 'Being in the EYE Corps means you have joined Emperor Klatan's elite force that safeguards the Empire. Long live Emperor Klatan.'

The idea of having an eye tattooed on his forehead was distasteful, serving as a spy for the Emperor was even worse. He was an outlander, living his entire life on Imperial outer planets. When the Empire found outlanders supporting the rebellion, they were imprisoned and then killed. When Imperial spies were discovered on the outer planets, they were quietly killed. It was the reason outlanders were not welcoming to strangers, Seth's mother the exception.

"I don't want to join the EYE Corps," Seth told Tovar.

"Then we have to practice seeing if we can fool them when they come for the sweep."

They began testing each other to see if they could block the other from reading his thoughts. Tovar was good at it, but Seth was not as good. Over time, with constant practice, each learned how to block the other from reading their thoughts.

The day came when the class was informed that a member of the EYE Corps was there to ask each student a few questions. Seth read the teacher's mind and learned she supported the EYE Corps. She was excited that they might find telepaths among her students. She believed the Emperor was nearer a God than the tyrannical dictator most outlanders, including his mother, claimed he was.

Students were brought into a room one at a time to be interrogated by the EYE Corps agent. He was a young man in his early twenties. He had an open eye tattooed on his forehead. He smiled when a student came into the room, possibly to put the student at ease, though the tattooed eye was disconcerting. He had the student sit down on a chair at the table opposite him. A folder on the table had the student's picture and some written notes. He came right to the point, "Are you a telepath?"

Most students stumbled as they answered. Not being a telepath, it was difficult for a student to say no, after all, how did they know for sure?

The EYE Corps interrogator asked, "Have you ever felt you knew what some-one was going to say before they said it?"

That was a leading question. What kid didn't know what a parent was going to say when they knew the question would be, 'Have you done your homework?' or, 'Did you clean your room?'

The kids would lie and say no. The EYE Corps interrogator would know they were lying. He would read their thoughts and know the lie was nothing more than the fear generated by the interrogation, not a lie to hide they were a telepath.

He would ask a few more questions before releasing the student so the next one could be ushered in to be interrogated. This went on all day. He met with all the fourth, fifth, and sixth graders on one day. The next day he continued with the higher grade classes. Finally, it was time for Seth and Tovar's class.

Tovar went in before Seth. When he came out, he didn't send Seth a telepathic message that the interrogator might overhear. He just smiled, signaling he had been successful.

When Seth went in, he had worked on blocking the interrogator by focusing on the fear that his mother would beat him for stealing some money from her purse. He had stolen the money to make this realistic, though his mother had never, would never, beat him. Seth focused on his fear of being found out as the interrogator asked his questions. Seth wasn't sure if his ploy worked until the interrogator said he could leave, giving no indication he detected Seth was a telepath.

The interrogations ended. Later that day, their teacher said she was sorry that no one in her class was a telepath. Tovar winked at Seth across the room.

Seth was awakened early the next morning by his mother. She told him the EYE Corps had taken Tovar away. She told him what happened.

Tovar's eleven-year-old sister saw him take a beer from their refrigerator. He wasn't allowed to drink alcohol. Their parents were out of the house, but she planned to tell them about Tovar taking the beer when they returned.

Tovar returned before their parents. His sister said nothing to him about the beer, she was sure he hadn't seen her when he took it. He gave her an odd look, then he said she better not tell their parents about the beer. How could he know she was planning to do that? The EYE Corp representative had interrogated her. All she could think of was that Tovar read her mind, that he was a telepath.

When their parents came home, she told them what happened. His parents confronted Tovar, not about the beer, they wanted to know if he had telepathic ability. He denied it. They wanted to be sure. They called the EYE Corps Interrogator, who was still in the area. The Interrogator came to their house in the middle of the night. He tested Tovar for over an hour. At the end, he announced Tovar was a telepath and took him. Seth's mother said she learned of this from Tovar's parents. They were delighted that Tovar was a telepath and didn't understand why he wanted to hide it.

Seth was afraid Tovar would tell the EYE Corps Interrogator that he too was a telepath. Later that morning, Tovar's parents gave Seth a note. They said Tovar wrote it before he left, and he asked them to give it to Seth. The note simply read, 'I will always be your friend'.

Months passed without Seth hearing from Tovar. When he asked Tovar's parents if they heard from their son, they said they hadn't. They were worried since he promised to write often. The EYE Corps Interrogator said it would be fine for Tovar to write to them. Five months after Tovar was taken, Tovar's parents received the news of his death in a short message that read:

Your son attempted to climb Klatania University's steeple as a prank. He lost his grip and fell to his death. EYE Corps University expresses its sympathy for your loss due to this unfortunate accident.

They shared it with Seth. It was a lie. Tovar was deathly afraid of heights. There was no way Tovar could be convinced or even goaded into climbing anything taller than three meters. Seth feared that Tovar may have taken his own life. More disturbing was thinking he did it to protect Seth's secret.

Seth vowed never to use his telepathic ability again. He worked hard not to read people's thoughts. He was eventually successful at doing it, though it was stressful. For that reason, he avoided being around people whenever possible. Working on the Beanie was a test of his resolve. The crew of the Beanie lived in tight quarters. At times Seth would have liked to know what the crew of the Beanie were thinking, especially when they were rejecting him as their leader, but he didn't break his promise to himself. He never read anyone's thoughts on the Beanie, or anywhere else. Even now, he wouldn't read Tiller's mind to learn if he knew more about why they were taking him to Klatania.

Chapter 12

The Delaigo came to a stop on the morning of the fourth day. Shortly after the ship stopped, Tiller came into Seth's cabin. "You're going to be transferred to a smaller ship that will take you to Klatania. It isn't good to show off this ship, at least not yet. Rebel spies are everywhere. We can't let them see this prototype."

Seth was transferred to a Runabout, a small pleasure craft used for short hops between nearby planets. The Runabout had a pilot and copilot. Seth was the only passenger. The pilot initiated a jump as soon as Seth was seated. When they came out of the jump, Klatania loomed outside Seth's window.

Klatania was the first of the four planets discovered by Karl Klatan that could support human life. He named this planet after himself. Over centuries, four planets became sixty-two. Throughout the expansion to other worlds, the planet Klatania continued to govern all humans.

Seth's mother told him a story about how the Empire grew that conflicted with what he was taught in school. Seth learned in school the Empire was needed to keep humans from falling into chaos as they moved out to other planets. Since the Klatan family had made it possible through the invention of the Quantum Plasma Drive for humans to move out into the galaxy, they were the obvious choice to sit on the throne as the Emperor for all humans.

Seth's mother's version was that when humans first began to colonize the planets, they formed a governing organization called the United Federation. It was a democracy that had elected representatives from the planets who met at

Klatania to make laws to govern all humans, no matter what planet they were on. In the generations that followed, and as humans expanded to more planets, the Klatan family used their wealth and position of power to leverage control over the planets. Eventually, they became so powerful they dissolved the United Federation, substituting an Empire where a Klatan was installed as the Emperor. During the following generations, humans had all but become slaves to the Klatan family.

An alarm rang, and a voice message sounded on the Runabout's speakers. "Prepare to be boarded for inspection."

The pilot picked up the mic. "We have urgent business on Klatania. We were told we didn't have to be inspected."

"Prepare for inspection or be shot out of the sky."

Seth could see a ship approaching them.

"We will comply," the pilot said. He turned to the co-pilot. "Damn these rebels for all this security."

The ship coupled with the Runabout's airlock. Two burly Imperial Guards came through the hatch with their hands resting on their sidearms. One of them asked for everyone's papers. The pilots gave them theirs. All Seth had was his contract for Trumul. He handed it to one of the Imperial Guards.

"What's this?" The guard asked Seth.

As he explained that this was his contract, the pilot whispered something into the other guard's ear. "They're OK. Let's leave," the guard said.

The guard holding Seth's papers looked confused as he handed them back to Seth. The guards left, the airlock link was broken, and the Runabout descended into Klatania.

"What did you say to the guards?"

The pilot turned to face Seth, "You'll find out soon enough."

Seth watched the Runabout slowly descend. Klatania had only two continents on opposite sides of the planet, separated by an ocean. One of the continents was named Genesis I, and the other Genesis II. Seth attended Klatania University on Genesis II. Capitol City, the seat of the Klatan Empire and home of the Emperor's palace, was in Genesis I. In the five years Seth attended Klatania University, he never went to Genesis I, but as the Runabout left orbit, he could see they were heading to Capitol City.

Capitol City was huge, the biggest city Seth had ever seen. The media referred to Capitol City as the grandest place in the Empire. Tall towers of glass and steel glittered like jewels in the sunlight. From what Seth could see from the Runabout's window, he agreed this city was exceptional by every standard.

Seth could see a busy spaceport in the distance. Nevertheless, the pilot turned away from it. In front of them was the Emperor's Palace. It was called the Light of the All, considered one of the most beautiful structures in the Empire. He thought the pilot would fly over it as a friendly gesture to show him this spectacle most humans in the Empire only saw on VIDs. The pilot didn't fly over the palace. He landed at it. He put the Runabout down on a small vertical landing pad on the palace grounds.

The pilot told Seth to disembark, someone would be coming for him. Seth grabbed his duffel bag. He stepped outside. It was warm, the sun high, the sky brightly blue. It was the first time Seth had been under a sky in three years. He breathed in the moisture-laden air as he smelled the nearby ocean, so different than living on the Beanie.

He scanned the tarmac to see who was coming for him. A lone man was running towards him from the palace. As the man approached, Seth saw he was wearing a kaftan. One of the VIDs Seth watched said kaftans were the palace fashion. The more ornate the kaftan, the more important the wearer. Kaftans lavishly embroidered with designs stitched in gold or silver thread indicated a person of high status. The man approaching Seth was wearing a less than lavish kaftan.

When the man finally reached Seth, he stopped to catch his breath before saying anything. He was a short man, a bit overweight, obviously not used to running. He finally wheezed out, "Are you Seth Harthset?"

"I am."

The man took a couple of deep breaths and said, "Follow me."

Seth followed the man back towards the palace. Seth had seen pictures of the palace, but none accurately conveyed its incredible size or beauty. It had many ornate spires that reached high into the sky. Some were actual towers, others only elegant artful spires. None of the pictures Seth had seen did justice to the palace's incredible golden color. It looked as if it were made of solid gold. The sun's reflection off the gold was so brilliant he had to shield his eyes.

The little man led Seth to a door at the side of the palace. A guard wearing a plasma pistol stood outside the door. The little man nodded to the guard. The guard returned the nod as the little man guided Seth into the palace.

The little man led Seth down a hallway, up two flights of stairs to a door that opened into a large garden. There was a pond in the middle of the garden with a fountain shooting water high into the air. Flowering trees sat amidst beds of colorful, exotic plants. People dressed in more lavish kaftans than Seth's guide sat on benches that surrounded the pond. Others in equally lavish kaftans strolled about the grounds.

The little man stopped. The quick walk through the palace and up the stairs had added to his oxygen deprivation. Breathing hard, he sat down on one of the benches to recover. He gestured for Seth to sit next to him. After a couple of minutes, his panting returned to normal breathing. He turned and looked up and down at Seth. The muscular young man had a face with sharp, well-defined lines, intense brown eyes, and thick black hair. However, his clothes were totally inappropriate.

"Great Klatan, what are you wearing?"

Seth wore a pair of rugged wool slacks with a camel-colored cotton pullover top. He had a nearly identical outfit in his duffle bag. These were practical clothes worn by those on the outer planets. Sturdy clothes for hard-working people.

Before Seth could answer, the little man shook his head disapprovingly, "It's too late to do anything about your wardrobe now. You'll have to wear that. Come, you are late."

Seth wanted to ask late for what, but the little man pulled Seth off the bench and led him across the garden to a door. The door opened into a long hallway. Seth followed as the little man raced down the hallway to a set of stairs at its end. They rapidly walked up two flights of stairs. The little man was breathing hard again when they reached the top of the second flight. He hesitated, then took a couple of deep breaths before opening the door on the landing.

It opened to another long hallway. Seth saw a man sitting at a table at the end of the hallway. Standing behind him were two guards cradling plasma rifles. These were not ordinary guards nor ordinary humans. Seth was 1.9 meters tall, tall by human standards. These guards were at least 2.3 meters or taller. Seth had heard rumors that the Emperor had made genetically modified guards to protect him. Information about what happened inside the palace was scarce, often no more than false rumors. The stories about genetically modified guards were considered a myth. The guards here confirmed it wasn't a myth.

As formidable as the guards were, the man sitting at the table sent a chill through Seth. The man's forehead had an eye tattooed on it. This was an EYE Corps checkpoint. The telepath was there to check the mind of anyone who went beyond this point. The last time Seth encountered a member of the EYE Corp was when he was in school with Tovar.

Seth's fear the EYE would learn he was a telepath surged through him. He would be discovered as a rogue telepath if he continued letting this fear play in his mind. He forced himself to settle down. He remembered the drills he practiced with Tovar on how to hide his telepathic ability. He focused on something that might block the EYE's probe.

The little man stopped at the desk in front of the EYE Interrogator. He said, "Hurry up. We are late."

The EYE Interrogator was unmoved by the little man's appeal for haste. He turned to face Seth. Seth brought up the fearful thought he hoped would protect him from the mind probe. He focused on this fear, letting it rage through his body until he began to shake. He could see the EYE Interrogator focusing hard on him. Seth could sense the interrogator's probe in his mind. It felt like fingers sifting through his thoughts. He didn't betray that he could feel the probe as he focused all his attention on the fearful thought. After three or four minutes, the EYE Interrogator stopped his probe.

The little man said nervously, "Are you done?"

The EYE Interrogator turned away from Seth. As he faced the little man, he said unpleasantly, "Go on."

The little man led Seth through the door next to the EYE interrogator's station. On the other side of the door, Seth stopped to let the adrenaline dissipate from his body. The little man was three meters ahead, insisting Seth follow quickly. Seth was standing on a floor of mosaic tiles depicting scenes of people frolicking in a woodland setting. The three-story ceiling above him was covered with frescoes of mythical gods from ancient Earth. Seth had visited museums, but he had never seen anything like this. He stood there as he took in the incredible beauty surrounding him. The little man beckoned him to come. Seth followed him as he marveled at the magnificent art in the hallway.

He led Seth down two more hallways as beautifully decorated as the first one. Finally, at the end of the third hallway, he stopped before a large set of double doors. Two normal-sized human guards stood in front of the doors. Seth's guide nodded to them. One of the guards opened the doors. Seth's guide indicated he was to enter. When he did, his guide stood outside as they shut the doors behind Seth.

He was in the entryway that led to a larger room. A false wall blocked his view of the room beyond. He was about to walk around the false wall when he heard voices.

CHAPTER 13

S eth followed the voices. As Seth rounded the false wall, he could see it was part of a large room. A round table that could seat thirty filled the center of the room. Four people were sitting together at the table facing a standing thin, dark-skinned man. Seth knew this man. He was Doctor Rashid Vishendzia. He was one of the Empire's most eminent epidemiologists. He had also been Seth's guidance counselor when he was a student at Klatania University. He was wearing a kaftan more ornate than the one worn by the man who had brought him here.

The wall's partition partially hid Seth as he listened to what Dr. Vishendzia said. "If I can characterize what we know, we are not sure why we are here. We also have little in common as far as our areas of expertise. Does that summarize our situation?"

No one spoke up to disagree with what he said.

"Young man, do you know why we were brought here?" The man asking was older than the doctor, heavy set, slightly balding, dressed in a more opulent kaftan than Dr. Vishendzia's. Everyone turned to look at Seth.

Seth stepped into the room. "I agree with what Doc said. I don't know why I'm here or why any of you are here."

Doc was what everyone called Dr. Vishendzia on campus, primarily out of respect but because students often mangled his last name.

Wearing a big smile, Doc walked over to Seth and shook his hand. "Mr. Harthset, it has been a long time. How are you?"

"I'm fine, though I'm as confused about being here as the rest of you are."

A young woman was sitting at the table. "Harthset, this can't be Robert Harthset, he's too young. Besides, I heard Robert died years ago."

"I'm Seth Harthset. Robert was my father."

Doc said, "Let me introduce you to the group." He gestured to the man in the opulent kaftan who first addressed Seth. "This is Professor Siegfried Howton, the Randolph Klatan Professor of Human History and Alien Studies at Klatania University."

The next man at the table was a big, broad-chested, square-jawed man with closely cropped blond hair, wearing black slacks with a black leather jacket buttoned to his neck. The clothes gave him a military appearance. "This is Gunther Voltig. Mr. Voltig is a weapons expert."

Voltig's eyes appraised him with the intensity someone might use to determine if Seth was dangerous.

Doc smiled at the young woman sitting next to Voltig. "This is Jana Walkner. She is Professor Thomas Kleinfeld's assistant. Professor Kleinfeld is an expert in poisons, as is Ms. Walkner. She says they came for Professor Kleinfeld. He had come down with the Vishendzia flu. I wish they would stop calling it that. I created the vaccine cure, not the flu. That aside, unfortunately, or possibly fortunately for him, Kleinfeld was only two weeks into the six weeks he needs to be quarantined, so they brought Jana here in Kleinfeld's place."

Jana Walkner was in her mid-twenties, dressed in serviceable, outer planet clothes of slacks and a beige blouse. She gave Seth a slight smile.

"This is Alan Daiton. Mr. Daiton has a particular skill. He is a linguistics expert." Alan Daiton was younger than Seth, lean, with delicate features and a pale complexion. He wore a kaftan with simple embroidered designs of colored thread, not gold or silver.

Jana spoke up. "And you, Mr. Harthset. What is your specialty?"

"I'm a Planetary Engineer. Just starting, not the expert my father was."

"You are too modest, Mr. Harthset." Came a voice from the rear of the room. The person who spoke was a tall, lean woman standing at the corner of a false wall in the rear that mirrored the one in the front of the room that Seth was still standing next to.

She was in her early forties, tall, muscularly lean. She strode into the room with authority. She was followed by a tall man in his fifties. Both wore dark red military uniforms with buttoned-up jackets. The outer colonists joked that the military wore red so they wouldn't faint from seeing their blood during a battle. The man had a fixed, stern expression with a Major's insignia on his jacket. The woman had no rank insignia, only a gold emblem on the left breast of her jacket's pocket and three black stripes that ran diagonally across from the right shoulder of her jacket to her left hip. They were followed into the room by two guards carrying plasma rifles.

The Major stood in the rear with the guards as the woman walked to the front of the room. As she did, everyone at the table stood up and bowed. Seth didn't know who she was, though it was apparent she was someone this group felt they should show deference to. Seth had never bowed to anyone. No one in the outer planet colonies received or required such an action, yet he thought it prudent to follow those here. He bowed slightly. The woman walked around the table to the front of the room.

"Prime. We are honored by your presence," Doc said.

Seth thought *This is Prime!* Leader of the Empire's military. The outer planets referred to her as the Butcher or the Death Witch. She was considered the most dangerous person in the Empire, second only to the Emperor.

Seth was attending Klatania University when Andraia Gretler was made Prime. She was a Guard Captain when she was sent to Guiez to quell a strike by workers at the Imperial mine. The workers argued they had not received pay in months, while their only source for basic food was the Empire's store that charged them unreasonably high prices. The man who was Prime at that time advised her to find a peaceful resolution to the strike. She followed a different path. She had her troops slaughter ten percent of the strikers. She threatened the rest of them and their families with a similar fate if they continued the strike. The strike ended. The Emperor was so impressed by her forceful tactics he made her Prime. Seth could see that bowing to her had been a prudent decision.

Prime said, "Everyone sit." It was said calmly, yet the underlying authority in her voice made it clear she expected immediate obedience.

Doc returned to his seat. Seth sat next to Alan Daiton.

Professor Howton asked, "Are you the one who brought us here?"

"You were brought here at my direction, and now I will tell you why you are here."

Prime walked over to the wall. She pressed on a wood panel that opened to reveal a small remote control. She picked it up. Pressing a button on it, a three-dimensional image of a space probe appeared above the center of the table.

"This is a Finder Probe. Emperor Richard commissioned 100 Finder Probes to be launched randomly into space 180 years ago. They were designed to last for centuries as they searched for additional planets that could support human life. Professor Howton, you must be aware of these probes."

Professor Howton nodded. "I am. I also know none of the probes ever reported finding any habitable planets."

"That isn't entirely correct. One of the probes found something more interesting than a habitable planet. That probe fell through an Einstein-Rosen bridge, commonly called a wormhole." She smiled at the confused looks of her audience. "Wormhole is an old term long forgotten once ships could travel long distances in space using jumps. A wormhole is a tunnel to a distant place in the galaxy. Imagine a door that allows a ship to pass from one location in space to a very distant location without using a Quantum Plasma Drive jump. Wormholes are exceedingly rare, virtually almost impossible to find. Anytime one has been found, it was unstable. One hundred years ago, an exploratory ship was sent through a wormhole only to have the wormhole close. The ship was never heard from again." She addressed Professor Howton, "You are familiar with these events, are you not?"

"Yes, I am familiar with why we abandoned searching for wormholes. However, I was never informed that any Finder Probes were successful."

"There was a reason that knowledge was kept secret. The Finder Probe that fell through the wormhole did so forty years ago. The wormhole exited 25,000 light years from Klatania. The probe found a viable planet that could support human life. We would have never learned of this finding since the signal from the probe will take 25,000 years to reach us. The entrance to the wormhole is invisible. It was only discovered by accident thirty-three years ago when a scout ship detected the probe's signal as it flew across the wormhole's entrance.

"I don't see why finding another human life-supporting planet would be a reason to bring us here, especially one so distant it would take decades to reach it using jumps," Professor Howton said impatiently.

Prime gave him a stare that looked like amusement as she continued, "Maybe this will interest you, Professor." She pressed a button on the remote. The probe's image was replaced by one of a gas giant planet girdled in colored bands. The image zoomed in on a moon orbiting the gas giant. As the image of the moon grew, it showed it had a liquid ocean. The image continued zooming in on the moon as it rotated. A continent came into view. It was roughly rectangularly shaped. On one edge of the continent, a coastal plain was green with vegetation butting up against a mountain range. Beyond the mountain range was a vast expanse covering most of the continent that looked bleakly arid. As the image approached the other edge of the continent, there was another mountain range. This coastal plain looked as arid as the continent's center, except that the ground was not brown but gray. The image began zooming in on this coastal plain. As it did, a regular pattern became visible on the ground.

Prime froze the image. "Professor Howton, you wrote a book on how to communicate with an advanced alien species. However, you have not encountered advanced aliens to prove your theories."

"I did write that book. It is also true we have not encountered advanced beings. This does not support the thesis that we are the sole advanced beings in this galaxy. It simply means we haven't gone far enough into the galaxy to find intelligent aliens," Professor Howton sounded as if he were delivering a lecture.

Prime said, "What if we have." The image continued to zoom in on the regular pattern until they became thousands of square shapes. Closer yet revealed they were buildings. The image froze.

Professor gasped as he sat upright. "Are these structures built by aliens?"

Prime had the smug look of a fisherman reeling in a fish that had just taken her bait. "A little more history about the discovery of this planet, first. After detecting the probe's signal, my predecessor Prime sent a military scout ship through the wormhole to see if the probe's information was accurate. The scout ship found the wormhole was stable. That itself was peculiar since most are not. The scout ship confirmed this moon could support human life. It also discovered advanced beings had once occupied the moon."

Professor Howton rose, yelling, "Advanced beings were discovered thirty-three years ago, but no one thought of sharing this information with Klatania University or with me. That's outrageous!"

Prime flashed him a predatory stare.

There was a murmur from the others indicating challenging Prime was unwise, even if you were an esteemed university Professor.

Professor turned pale before sheepishly sinking back into his seat.

"All the information about Alenia has remained on that moon," as she said it, she scanned the rest of the group with an intensity that quashed anyone else who might consider making an outburst or even asking a question. She continued. "Observations from the scout ship identified these structures had been built by intelligent beings, though they could see no movement around them. My predecessor sent a military team to explore the moon. The moon has a human breathable atmosphere that supported the intelligent alien creatures who once lived there. He established a permanent research colony on the moon thirty years ago to study these creatures."

Professor Howton seemed to be boiling over with questions but remained silent.

It was Doc who spoke up, "Forgive me for interrupting. I don't understand why you are revealing this to us now?"

"As I said, a research colony has operated on this moon for thirty years. The intelligent alien creatures there called themselves the Alenians, so we call this moon Alenia. They were a primitive farming culture that used minimal technology, yet they had a spaceport, but it could only support a single ship. We have learned that approximately seventy years ago, the Alenians vanished."

Regaining some of his composure, Professor Howton asked, "Have you brought us here to evaluate information about these advanced beings?"

"No."

"Then do you want us to determine why or how they disappeared from the moon?" Doc asked.

"You are here because two weeks ago, eighty researchers and five military support personnel on Alenia began to kill one another. A supply ship landed as this was happening. The crew of that ship was able to capture fifteen of the colonists, which they described as being violently insane. Before they could return the captured colonists to Klatania, one got free and blew up the supply ship."

"Am I correct in assuming you have gathered us here to try and determine why the killings took place?" Doc asked.

Prime walked over and stood behind Doc. "Yes, I want you to determine why the members of the research colony began to kill one another, but I want you to go to Alenia to do it."

Professor Howton was flustered. "I can't go. I have responsibilities. People depend on me. I'm sure the same thing is true of Dr. Vishendzia."

Prime didn't respond as she extinguished the image in the center of the table. She turned to face the group. "I have a simple proposition for you. You can go to Alenia to determine why the colonists began killing each other, or you can have a brainwipe to remove all memories of this meeting. I offer this alternative to all of you. Either you all go, or all of you have your memories removed. You have one hour to make your decision."

She left the room, followed by the stern looking Major and the two guards.

CHAPTER 14

There was silence for a few minutes after Prime left the room. Jana spoke first. "I don't want my memories wiped. We all know it's an imprecise process. I heard of a woman who wanted them to remove memories of her ex-husband. They did. They also removed all the rest of her memories. Now she's a vegetable."

Doc said, "You're correct that a brainwipe is not a precise process. Memories are sometimes inadvertently destroyed. Your example would be an extreme case that I suspect is a myth."

"No one is going to fiddle with my brain. I've been putting things in there too long to have someone hack at them," Professor Howton said emphatically.

Doc nodded, "I agree with Professor Howton. I'm not eager to have any of my memories removed, even the ones from today. Nonetheless, Prime said we all go, or we all undergo a brainwipe. I say we put it to a vote. Who doesn't want to go?"

Each person looked at the others. No one indicated they wouldn't go.

"Well, that's it," Doc said. "We are all going to Alenia. The only question is, why us? If you will indulge me, let me give my opinion on why each of us was selected."

He paused to see if somebody was going to object before he continued. "I'm a virologist and an epidemiologist, which means I have some familiarity with epidemics caused by bacteria or a virus. It is possible the colonists were driven into a killing frenzy by either a virus or a bacterium. It explains the reason I was selected. If the problem is not caused by something viral or bacterial, the source could be some form of poison. A hallucinogenic substance from a mold that might have originated from a mushroom-like source. That would explain selecting Ms. Walkner as a substitute for the ailing Professor Kleinfeld."

Jana Walkner nodded her agreement.

"Professor Howton is an obvious choice for his theories regarding how to deal with intelligent aliens, though they are as yet untested theories." Professor Howton gave him a scowling look.

Doc continued, "Ideally, over thirty years, the research colonists would've thoroughly documented all they learned about the Alenians. Having a linguistics expert like Mr. Daiton would be valuable to interpret what they learned."

"Mr. Voltig, you say you are a weapons expert. If the colonists' insanity resulted from a weapon, possibly an alien weapon, your inclusion would be extremely valuable."

Gunther Voltig grunted. It was unclear whether that meant he agreed, but he didn't say he disagreed.

"That leaves you, Mr. Harthset. The moon Alenia has a breathable human atmosphere, making the need for a planetary engineer seem unnecessary."

"I agree. I have a question. Will each of you say when you were collected for this meeting?"

Doc said, "I was having a coffee with Professor Howton at the University this morning when the Imperial Guards came for us."

Alan Daiton went next. "An Imperial Guard brought me here from the Linguistics Research Library this morning."

"I was already on Klatania," was Gunther Voltig's gruff answer.

"Yesterday they came to our site. When Professor Kleinfeld wasn't available to come, they put me in a Runabout that traveled overnight. I arrived here this morning," Jana Walkner said.

They were all relatively close by. None of them had to travel on a secret military ship for four days to get here.

"And you, Mr. Harthset. When were you collected for this meeting?" Doc asked.

"They came for me four days ago." He decided not to mention he was on Trumul, or that they came for him in the Viper. One thing was apparent. If they needed a planetary engineer, they could have found one much closer than Trumul.

"Since we have all agreed to go on this mission to Alenia, I will inform the guards. Now let's hope we've made the right decision, and we are not putting our heads in the lion's mouth," Doc said. He left the room.

CHAPTER 15

Prime had just exited the conference room with Major Krugar when one of the Emperor's female servants approached her. Bowing deeply, she said, "The Emperor wishes to see you."

Prime turned to the Major. "Are the preparations ready to transport them?"

"Are you sure they will accept?"

She didn't answer. He quickly added, "Of course, they will accept. I will prepare a shuttle to take them to the freighter."

"A freighter is slow. It would be faster to put them on a cruiser."

It wasn't wise to disagree with her, though this was too important not to speak up. "That sector has seen increased rebel activity. A common freighter can get them there unnoticed. It will rendezvous with four of our light cruisers in that sector that will take them the rest of the way."

Prime was about to respond to the Major when she noticed the Emperor's servant hadn't left. She snapped at her, "Why are you still here?"

The girl said fearfully, "The Emperor insisted you should come immediately." She made a quick bow and left.

Prime let out a breath of impatience as she thought, *What stupid thing does he want now?*

She turned to the Major. "You know what to look for in Alenia."

"Is that why we are taking Seth Harthset?"

"The Emperor believes Harthset will lead you to more of the purple powder."

The Major understood the purple powder was important to the Emperor. He didn't know what it was used for, nor what it had to do with Harthset. He also knew asking questions about the purple powder could be dangerous.

"Now go prepare. I want them on their way today. Remember, what you will do there is too important to fail."

Major Krugar bowed, then walked quickly away.

Prime went to the Emperor's wing of the palace. He called it his study. It had become his sanctuary. One of the few places he felt safe as his paranoia grew that someone was planning to kill him. Few were allowed into the study. Besides her, he only allowed two doctors, who came there constantly to check on his health.

In the past, the Emperor had many advisors. They made the fatal error of giving him advice he didn't want to hear. She was one of the few he still listened to. For now.

Two genetically modified Zinder guards stood at the entrance to the Emperor's study. These large, freakish creations had moronic intelligence. They were programmed with the single purpose of protecting the Emperor.

She stopped in front of the guards. She waited impatiently while one of the guards pressed a panel to inform the Emperor she was there. Finally, the panel showed green. The giant guard said, "You may enter."

She walked into the study. It was a long room twenty meters wide by seventy meters long with a three-story ceiling. At one end was a desk on a raised platform. Behind it was a door that led to the Emperor's living quarters, which she had never seen.

Walking down the length of the so-called study she passed by some of the most important art in Earth's history. On each side were ancient statues from the Sumerian, Roman, and Greek periods, alongside Michelangelo's Pieta, Rodin's Thinker, and all interspersed with modern sculptures. The layout had no organization she could see, but it was what the Emperor wanted.

If the statues didn't represent enough art from Earth, the walls were adorned from floor to ceiling with priceless paintings. One was a red disk cut out from the wall of the El Castillo Cave in Spain, considered Earth's oldest painting. There were paintings from the earliest periods to Dutch Masters, Impressionist, and modern abstracts. All of them hung in no specific arrangement or by period or type.

Prime didn't find this collection of much personal interest. She recognized these were important paintings and sculptures from Earth. Art treasures citizens of the Empire had been told were lost. Few knew they had been brought here to become part of the Klatan family's private collection.

The Emperor sat at the desk on the platform a meter above the floor, his paranoid substitute for a throne, watching her. There were rumors about automatic weapons built into the walls that he could direct to kill anyone he deemed dangerous as they approached. She believed they were more than mere rumors.

She stopped in front of the platform. The Emperor looked down at her from behind his elevated desk. She wondered if he used this perch because it made him feel more powerful. How much more power did he need than being the Emperor of all humans?

He was wearing a green kaftan with brocade designs in gold thread. Three years ago, he decided that kaftans should be the dress code in Klatania. Being in the military, she was thankfully exempt from his whim.

"You wanted to see me?" Prime said, with a slight bow of her head. She hated bowing to anyone, even to him. However, she also wanted to continue living.

"I have been waiting for you Andraia."

Prime cringed at hearing her first name. She gave it up when she became the Prime. To everyone she was Prime. He used her first name to remind her to whom she owed her position.

"I'm sorry. Your servant did not say it was urgent."

He shifted angrily in his chair. "I will punish her for that. I want to know if the boy is here?"

"Seth Harthset is here" It was silly calling this twenty-eight-year-old a boy. There were younger members of the palace he never called boys. To him, Seth Harthset was 'the boy'.

"Has the EYE checked him? What did the EYE learn?"

"The EYE found nothing of value in his probe."

She wasn't going to tell him that all the EYE could see in Seth Harthset's mind was an overwhelming fear he would be punished for taking money from the

Imperial Planetary Commission, money he used to attend his mother's funeral. A trivial matter at best, unimportant since he repaid it. It would send him off on a tangent speculating why Harthset was worried if she told him that. She didn't need that now. The mission was too important to have it put in jeopardy by this old fool.

"Maybe the EYE needs to do a better job of probing him. He must know where there is more of the purple powder."

She feared that any delay could jeopardize the mission. "You wanted Harthset to go to Alenia. He will. We put him with a team of specialists leaving for Alenia now to learn why the researchers began killing one another."

"Are they dead? All of them on Alenia, dead?"

"We don't know. That is why we are sending experts to learn what happened there. At your request, we included Seth Harthset on this mission."

"Harthset is going to Alenia. Good. She will find more of the purple powder."

Prime was confused. "Who is the she you are referring to?"

"Anna Harthset."

Prime held back as her frustration grew. She said calmly, "Anna Harthset is dead. You requested we send her son, Seth, to Alenia."

"I said Seth Harthset, not Anna!"

"My mistake."

He began staring at the wall. Prime looked at the place where the Emperor was staring. It was a section of empty wall. Nothing was there.

"The boy is going to Alenia?"

"Yes. Seth Harthset is going to Alenia."

"He will find more of the purple powder," he said without shifting his gaze from the wall.

"If there is nothing else?"

"Go," he said.

As she left, he continued staring at the wall.

Prime walked back down the long hallway of the study. The purple powder was the Empires most tightly held secret. A small amount of the powder mixed with a liquid became a purple serum. The Emperor had this injected into him daily. He had been doing this before she joined the Imperial Guard. It was what kept a man of 95 looking like a healthy 50-year-old. It kept his body youthful. It didn't do that for his mind.

What she learned about the purple powder came from rumors or what she could infer based on them. Anyone who had firsthand knowledge of the purple powder had been killed. The powder came from Alenia. No one understood what it was used for until it was given to Anna Harthset.

It was not surprising Anna Harthset was given the purple powder to analyze. She was by all measures a genetic genius. While still at the university, she developed cures for two genetic diseases that had plagued humans for centuries.

Anna Harthset discovered the purple powder when mixed into a solution and injected into someone, would cure them of almost any injuries or diseases, and it would extend their life. That someone was solely the Emperor.

One of the first orders the Emperor gave her as Prime was to watch Anna Harthset. That was difficult. Harthset moved constantly from one outer planet to another, places where strangers were not welcome, where Imperial spies would disappear.

Prime did what she could to keep track of Anna Harthset. They searched her things many times looking for information about the purple powder. They never found anything. Prime was sure Anna Harthset neither had more of the purple powder nor a formula to make more of it. She could never convince the Emperor of this.

Anna Harthset's death sent the Emperor into a panic. He was sure the purple serum had stopped working. He was adamant he was rapidly aging. His doctors ran every test to show he was not, but they couldn't convince him. He had sufficient purple powder to last for years. However, he was determined they needed to find more of it. He ordered Prime to send a small army to Alenia to search for more of it. They found nothing. Now they might all be dead.

CHAPTER 16

Prime left the study. As she rounded a corner, she saw Prince Victor Klatan at the far end of the hallway waving for her to come to him.

Prince Victor was the third son of the Emperor and the only child of the Emperor's second wife, who died giving birth to the Prince. The Emperor's first wife had given him two sons, the next two in line for the throne. That was true until six months ago, before an accident killed the Emperor's first wife and her sons. They were in a Runabout on a trip to Genesis II to visit her mother. Their Runabout crashed into the sea. The pilot's last message was that his controls were not responding. It took time to confirm no one had survived. An exhaustive investigation reported the crash was due to a mechanical malfunction, without any proof to substantiate that claim. Those investigating reported it to save their lives from the Emperor's wrath. They were successful. The Runabout maintenance crew was not so lucky.

Prime was there when the Emperor's family had lifted off in the Runabout. Prince Victor was there too. She was surprised to see the Prince looked unusually stressed. She was also with the Prince when they received news the Runabout had crashed into the sea, though it was believed the royal family survived. She saw the same stress reflected on his face then.

When they learned that there were no survivors, she saw him momentarily relax, before he joined the Emperor to mourn their loss. But that instance where he seemed to take pleasure when he heard they were dead bothered Prime. She believed the Prince had something to do with their deaths.

Her suspicion was bolstered by knowing Prince Victor's driving ambition to become the Emperor despite being third in line for the throne. With their deaths, he was now the only heir. All that stood in his way to the throne was his father's incredible longevity, made possible by the life-extending serum.

Prime decided to spend more time with Prince Victor, though she detested him. Removing his father from the throne was not out of the question if he killed his brothers to become the Emperor. The more time she spent with the Prince, the more she was sure he was planning a coup. He had all but admitted it to her at times, though never directly.

If he became Emperor by killing his father, she had to protect herself from the upheaval that would follow. Having the Prince believe she was his ally would protect her if he succeeded. But she knew she was playing a dangerous game. If the Emperor found out what the Prince was planning, it would mean the Prince's death. If the Emperor learned she was associated with this plot, it would mean her death, too.

Prime walked up to the Prince. He grabbed her by the arm, pulling her into an alcove. "You just spoke with him. What did he say about the people you are sending to Alenia?"

It was no surprise the Prince knew about what happened on Alenia and who she was sending there. He had spies everywhere. However, neither the Prince nor the Emperor knew everything about Alenia. She had to make sure they never did.

"He wants those going to Alenia to search for more of the purple powder used to make the serum," she whispered. The Emperor had his spies too, not to mention the palace was filled with the Emperor's listening bugs.

"The serum, always the serum. If he finds a way to make more of the serum, he might live forever!" the Prince said angrily.

Prime whispered, "He doesn't remember that we have searched Alenia exhaustively. There is no more purple powder. Despite that, he has enough of it to last another fifty years."

"I won't live another fifty years! You can see he is losing his mind. I can only imagine what will happen in ten more years. By then, he will have completely lost his mind and the Empire will collapse under his insane policies."

Prime leaned closer to Victor's ear. She said, "I expect you're right. The serum may keep his body alive while eroding his mind. It might not be long before he is dangerous. Do you have a plan to deal with it?"

"I have something."

Prime whispered, "We need to have this conversation in a more secure place. Come to my headquarters in two days. It will be safer to discuss this in greater detail there."

"Yes, of course. The walls have ears." Without saying another word, he quickly walked away from the alcove. Prime stood there watching him, as she thought, *This fool may get me killed*.

CHAPTER 17

After Doc informed the guards they accepted Prime's offer, they were hustled off to a room at the far end of the palace. Each was given a set of gray coveralls with a tag for a freighter called Cauloten Six. They were told to put them on.

"Why are we putting on these ridiculous coveralls?" Professor asked one of the guards.

"To blend in," was his answer.

"As a freighter crewman?"

"Exactly. Now hurry up."

"What about our clothes," Professor said.

Seth could see why the Professor was complaining. He was wearing an expensive kaftan. He undoubtedly wanted to be sure he got it back.

"You'll get your clothes back when you get back. Now, get moving." The guard stepped away, indicating he was through answering questions.

Professor put on the coveralls. He then neatly folded his kaftan before placing it in the container they gave them for their clothing.

Gunther Voltig grumbled as he struggled to get into coveralls barely large enough to accommodate his large, muscular body.

Seth and Jana were given coveralls, too. They were allowed to bring their duffle bags containing their clothes since a duffle bag was something a member of a freighter would have with them.

Once everyone was in the coveralls, they were taken out of the palace to a waiting shuttle. It flew them to Klatania's cargo port. Dozens of haulers from orbiting freighters were there unloading or loading cargo. They were directed to a hauler at the far end of the congested loading area. Anyone observing them would think they were a freighter crew returning to their ship.

Once in the hauler, they were directed to sit on the seats along the walls. The hauler took off immediately. It was in orbit within minutes.

"I don't understand all this subterfuge," Professor Howton said to no one in particular.

Doc answered, "I suspect the reason for it has something to do with the rebels."

"It's bad enough we are going to a place where people are killing one another without considering problems with the rebels," Professor said.

Twenty minutes later, the hauler slipped into the loading bay of the freighter Cauloten Six. They waited in silence for the loading bay atmosphere to normalize. Once it did, they were led to the freighter's bridge.

Two men were on the bridge waiting for them. One was the stern-looking Major from their meeting with Prime. He was dressed in the same coveralls they were wearing. He had the hard look of someone it would be unwise to challenge. The other man, shorter by a head than the Major, looked in his late forties and bore a more pleasant demeanor.

The Major addressed them, "I am Major Krugar. This is Captain Hollinsky. We will be leaving orbit in a few minutes. You will travel in the Cauloten Six for three days until it rendezvous with four light Imperial military cruisers. We will transfer to the cruisers, and they will take us the rest of the way to Alenia. I will accompany you to Alenia to direct your investigation."

The Captain said, "We will be making several jumps, so those of you who feel upset by a jump, we have some pills that can help."

No one took the Captain up on his offer, so he continued, "We will be traveling through rebel space. You are disguised as members of my crew in case the rebels stop to search our ship. They have been searching freighters to find ones carrying supplies or weapons for Imperial Military outposts. It is unlikely they will stop us. If they do, you have an information packet in your cabins that explains your duties aboard the ship. Memorize it. Once you have, then destroy it."

Gunther Voltig spoke, "Are you expecting us to work as the crew on the ship?"

"You are our guests. Learning your role as a member of the crew is a precaution in case the rebels board us. If they ask you, you better be able to tell them what you are supposed to be doing on the ship."

Doc spoke up next. "I'm assuming you're not carrying weapons for the Imperial military, and we are the only contraband aboard the ship."

"Our cargo hold is filled with food for a colony in the outer rim. We have papers verifying our destination."

Major Krugar added, "There are ten Imperial Marines on the ship dressed in crew uniforms. They are for your protection on Alenia."

Imperial Marines were the best trained, most vicious fighters in the military. Seth thought this only added to the idea Alenia would be dangerous.

The Major continued, "You have a monitor in your cabin that will give you access to ship's files. These files will provide you with background about Alenia. Remember, your mission is to learn what happened to the researchers. Read the files immediately. They will be deleted if rebels board the ship. Do you have any questions?" The Major asked it in a tone that didn't invite any questions.

Not taking the hint, Doc asked, "Are our movements restricted aboard the ship?'

Captain Hollinsky answered, "You are free to go where you please, though I ask you not to interfere with the crew as they perform their duties."

"You know what you need to know," the Major said. "Now, you will be taken to your quarters."

Members of the crew led each of them to their cabins. Seth found his cabin was a tiny room with a cot for a bed, a single chair, and a pulldown shelf on the wall that served as a desk. A small monitor sat on the shelf-desk. It was a far cry from the luxurious cabin on the Delaigo.

He dropped his duffle bag on the bed. As he did, he felt the freighter leave orbit. For good or bad, they were on their way.

CHAPTER 18

Seth was reading what his crew duties were supposed to be when he felt the ship make a jump. He was supposed to be a pilot plus a cargo handler. It wasn't unusual for the crew of a freighter to have multiple jobs. What surprised him was selecting pilot as one of his jobs. Seth was a trained pilot. Was it just a coincidence they chose pilot for his job, or did they know he was a pilot? Knowing what he was supposed to do on the ship, he tossed the information packet in an incineration chute just outside his cabin.

Seth considered he might be able to determine where the wormhole was based on how they got there. The Cauloten Six was an old freighter. At most, it could make two moderate long jumps in a day. Counting the number of jumps the freighter made would give him a rough estimate of their distance from Klatania. Knowing they would be in rebel territory gave him an idea of which sectors they would be traveling through. If he could estimate how far they traveled in the Imperial cruisers, he should have a rough idea where the wormhole was, though he wasn't sure what he might do with that knowledge.

Seth turned on the monitor and brought up the ship's database on Alenia. A quick scan of the information showed it was a collection of files that must have been hastily put together. There was no organization to them, nor a table of contents or an index.

Scanning the files, he found one with a physical description of the Alenian star system. The system had five planets orbiting its moderate-sized star. The two nearest planets to the star were airless rocks. The next two planets were relatively

Earth-sized with liquid water. Earth metrics were still used as the planet's comparative standard despite the Earth no longer existing. A note for these two planets stated *the planets had a human breathable atmosphere but were uninhabited and lethal to humans.*

Lethal to humans, but they had a human breathable atmosphere. This was an odd description that begged additional explanation. He couldn't find any.

The fifth planet orbiting the star was a gas giant. Alenia was a moon orbiting the gas giant. The information on Alenia was that it was Earth in size, with Earth-norm gravity and a human breathable atmosphere.

There was a statement that caught his attention. The Alenians had transformed the moon's atmosphere. The Alenians needed to breathe the same air as humans. They were able to change the atmosphere of this moon for their needs. Until recently, humans found transforming a planet's atmosphere a difficult, centuries-long task. His father's invention of the Habitation Engine made it easier and faster to transform a planet's atmosphere into one suitable for humans. He would be interested in learning how the Alenians did it.

He went on to read about the physical characteristics of Alenia. An ocean covered the moon with only a single large continent. The climate was temperate enough to keep ice from forming at its poles. A note stated the moon's temperate climate was due to its molten core intensified by gravitational friction from the gas giant. If not for this, the moon would be covered in ice.

A photograph was taken from space with an accompanying description of the single continent on Alenia. The continent was rectangular in shape, six times wider east to west than north to south. Tectonic pressure from the ocean plates sliding under both sides of the continent raised tall mountain ranges on each coast.

The planet's rotation caused the wind to blow predominately from west to east. The western mountain range blocked rain from falling on the continent's center. It made the western coastal plain lushly green. Beyond the western mountains, the lack of rainfall made an arid, lifeless region that covered two-thirds of the continent. Humans named it the Great Desert.

The Alenians lived between the mountain range and the ocean on the eastern coastal plain. The photographs showed the coastal plain as arid as the Great

Desert. Seth didn't understand why the Alenians chose to live there when the other side of the continent looked lush with vegetation. Their physical nature might have dictated the choice of living there. He searched the files for a physical description of the Alenians but couldn't find one.

Seth was interrupted by a knock on his cabin door. A crewman outside the door announced the evening meal would soon be served. Seth followed the crewman to the dining room. It was a small room with a single table. The table had ten chairs, but there were only six place settings.

Doc was sitting there alone. He smiled as Seth entered the room, "How is Mr. Harthset?"

Seth smiled. "Now I'm Mr. Harthset. I remember you calling me other things at Klatania University, like lazy, unfocused, or wait, I remember, wasting my time."

Doc's smile broadened, his white teeth shining against his dark skin. "I do remember pushing you hard that first year. You were sixteen, too young to be at the university. I felt I needed to keep you motivated. I guess it worked. Look at you now."

"Indeed, look at all of us here now."

As he said it, Jana Walkner and Gunther Voltig came into the room, followed by Alan Daiton. They sat down as Professor Howton entered, led by a crewman. Professor Howton seated himself next to Doc.

Doc asked the crewman, "Is the Major going to join us?"

"The Major is eating in the mess hall with the Marines." He left, closing the door.

Professor grumbled, "I am a cook according to the job they assigned me on this ship. I have never cooked other than to boil an egg. It is ridiculous that I could convince the rebels I am a cook."

"I'm a kitchen helper, a dishwasher. I can help Professor Howton when he cooks," Alan Daiton said, with a grin splashed across his face.

"They made me the ship's doctor. I won't have a problem with that," Doc said. He continued, "We might as well get acquainted, considering what we are undertaking. Let me start. I have been the Head of the Virology Department at Klatania University's Research Center for the past ten years. I began working at the University in various research roles that over time became more administrative." He turned to Professor.

Professor Howton accepted he should go next. "You heard my title at Klatan University and that of my book. I have spent my life studying all we know about the planets humans have explored or colonized. I am still angry that they discovered an alien species over thirty years ago but didn't inform me of the finding, nor have they shared what they've learned about these aliens. Although I initially objected to going to Alenia, I am delighted to be going there. I am sixty-five years old. I had given up hope I would live to see the day we found an intelligent alien species. I am excited to have firsthand experience seeing how these aliens lived."

"Ms. Walkner, do you mind sharing your background with us?" Doc asked Jana.

"There isn't much to tell. I went to a small college on one of the outer planets. After I graduated, I was looking for a job when Professor Kleinfeld came to investigate toxic plants that grew on our planet. He was looking for assistants. I applied, and he hired me. He invited me to join his team as he traveled from planet to planet, cataloging exotic, poisonous plants. I've been working with him for six years. I eventually became his Lead Assistant. He came down with ..." she paused, "the flu. They brought me instead."

"Thank you for remembering my aversion to having that flu given my name," Doc turned to Alan Daiton, "Mr. Daiton, you are a linguistics expert yet so young."

"I have a gift for languages, had it from an early age. I have been working for the Linguistics Research Library cataloging old Earth Native American languages." He stopped as they waited for him to say more. He didn't.

Doc smiled as he said, "A friend of mine who works at your Library once bragged about the young man whose translation skills were unprecedented. It was you he was referring to."

Alan Daiton gave an uncomfortable nod.

"Mr. Voltig, you said you are a weapons expert. What surprises me is that you are not in the Imperial Guard. I didn't know we had weapons experts who weren't in the military."

Gunther Voltig stared at Doc for a long moment before answering. "I'm an independent contractor. I assist the military when they need my services." He didn't explain or say anything more.

Doc turned his attention to Seth. "Mr. Harthset, besides being the son of our most famous Planetary Engineer, can you give us some of your background."

"I graduated from Klatan University seven years ago. My jobs have mostly been servicing Habitation Engines on several outer rim planets." He decided not to mention working on the Trumul project. It would force him to tell how he got to Klatania in only four days. He had no interest in hiding the Viper's existence, but he didn't know these people, and living on the outer planets taught him to be cautious with strangers.

"Well, I am glad to see you again," Doc said.

Two crewmen came in carrying trays of food. One tray had meat that resembled chicken. Since chickens were rare, if not nearly impossible to find, it was most likely some other kind of fowl. The other tray had vegetables with boiled potatoes. It was hearty food for a freighter crew, nothing that would compare to Seth's meals on the Delaigo.

They ate in silence. When everyone finished eating, Doc said, "I propose taking blood samples from each of us before we arrive. Each day we are on Alenia, I will do the same. This way, any changes in our blood might indicate we are about to go insane." Doc gave a smile as he said it, but it was a weak smile without humor.

"Ms. Walkner, will you assist me in drawing blood?"

"I will, Doc, but please call me Jana."

Doc smiled at her. "Jana, it is."

Seth said, "I think we can all go by first names. After all, to quote Doc, we might be putting our heads into the lion's mouth. A little camaraderie would be a good idea."

Seth noticed Professor Howton had a scowl on his face. Doc must have noticed it, too. He said, "You can call me Doc. It's what they call me around the campus. I might suggest our esteemed Professor Howton would prefer to keep his title. We might leave it as only his title. Is that acceptable, Professor?"

Professor Howton let out a sigh as he nodded his head to agree. He never liked the name Siegfried. It was his mother's father's name, one he wouldn't have chosen for himself. Just being called Howton lacked showing him respect, or that would be how he would perceive it at the University, though they were not there. Professor was the thing most people called him for more years than he cared to remember. "Yes, please feel free to call me Professor as if it was my name. Since I am the only Professor here, it won't be confusing to anyone."

Doc turned to Gunther Voltig. "Is Gunther acceptable?"

"Yah. You can call me Gunther. I have been called worse."

Everyone at the table laughed. It wasn't the laughter of humor, more the release of the tension each of them was feeling, though trying not to show.

Professor stood up. "I'm returning to my cabin to see if I can learn anything from the data they've provided us on Alenia."

Everyone else got up to leave the dining room. As they did, Jana tugged at Seth's sleeve to indicate she wanted him to stay behind.

CHAPTER 19

Seth sat back down at the table next to Jana. "You want to say something to me?" Seth asked.

"Do you remember being on the planet Taynor?"

He remembered his mother moving them to Taynor when he had just turned fifteen. They were only there four months, one of the shorter stays in his mother's endless moves from one outer planet to another.

"I remember we only spent a brief time there."

"Do you remember the clinic your mother worked at?"

Seth remembered it was a small clinic. One his mother said was woefully ill equipped.

"Yes. I remember the clinic."

"Do you remember a woman brought in after being pinned under a tractor? Her arm was badly broken, her chest nearly crushed. You probably don't. Do you remember her eleven-year-old daughter sitting in the waiting room crying?"

A memory of a little girl sitting alone in the waiting area flashed into Seth's head. "Were you that little girl?"

Jana smiled. "I was. Do you remember sitting with me, even holding my hand? You told me your mother was a great doctor and that she would help my mother?"

"I remember."

"Well, you were right. Your mother saved my mother's life, even her arm."

"I'm glad."

"I've never forgotten what you did for me that day." She leaned over and kissed Seth on the lips. "Mark this as a long overdue thank you."

She left the room. Seth sat there stunned as he watched her leave.

CHAPTER 20

B ack in his cabin. Jana's kiss did more than surprise him. It awakened a desire to find someone to share his life. He had a few relationships with women in his last few years at the university. He found it difficult not to listen in on their thoughts. It wasn't the only reason these relationships were short-lived. It wasn't the women's fault. It was something else, something fixed in his mind. It was the image of his ideal woman. She was blonde, dressed in all white, with incredibly blue eyes. Sometimes, he dreamt about her. Sometimes, he saw her during the day when he let his mind wander. She was always there, lingering in his thoughts for years. Who she was, or even if she was a real person he once saw, was a mystery to him. What wasn't mysterious was how he felt about this fantasy image. She was to him the ideal woman, the person he wanted to one day find, possibly to marry.

He admonished himself to be realistic. Wherever he got this image of the blonde woman in his head, she wasn't real. He wanted someone real. Maybe Jana could be that someone. She was smart, attractive, comfortable working on the outer planets, everything he could ever want.

Before he allowed his hormones to cloud the situation, her kiss might have just been the thank you she said it was, nothing more. Even if it was an invitation, this wasn't the time to pursue a relationship with her. After they returned from Alenia, it might be.

He shook off thoughts about Jana. Now was the time to learn about the Alenians. He turned on the monitor. The Alenians were farmers. They had extensive irrigated fields, which they planted and harvested only using hand tools.

Another file briefly described the Alenian's technology. There was only one spaceport on the moon. It could handle a single ship that landed vertically. The Alenians had electricity, of sorts – the file didn't explain why there was a qualifier. They had a laboratory with a sophisticated genetics machine.

This didn't make sense to Seth. If they had the technology for a spaceport and an advanced genetics laboratory, why were they farming the land only using hand tools?

Maybe he could guess the answer. On his first job out of the university, he was repairing a Habitation Engine on a planet that was near a farming community. Those farming the land were doing it without using machines. When he asked why they farmed in this primitive way, he was told they believed that is how it should be done. The Alenians may have been motivated by similar beliefs.

The next file Seth read destroyed his assumption that the Alenians used hand tools to farm based on their beliefs. It stated the moon was a penal colony. The Alenians were prisoners forced to farm the land with primitive tools as punishment. The spaceport with a single space pad was for a supply ship.

It didn't make sense that a penal colony would have a sophisticated genetics lab. A more important question was if the two inner planets in the system were uninhabited, then where did the prisoners come from who lived on this moon?

Seth quickly scanned the other files for an answer to these questions. He couldn't find an answer to either question.

Seth's eyes were beginning to burn. The clock in his cabin showed it was 2 a.m. Time varied on ships according to their home origin. This ship was running on Klatania time. He stood up and stretched. He didn't feel tired. He left his cabin in search of a cup of coffee or tea. He figured the ship's galley would be near where they ate dinner. He headed that way.

CHAPTER 21

Seth walked to the room where they ate dinner. The door was closed, but he could hear familiar voices coming from inside. He peeked in. Doc and Professor were sitting at the table. There was a half empty bottle of brandy sitting between them. Each had a glass half filled with the brown liquid.

"Sorry, I didn't mean to interrupt. I was looking for the galley to get some tea or coffee."

Doc smiled. "You're not interrupting us. Forget your search for caffeine. Come help us finish this brandy."

"Be glad to." He took a seat at the table.

Doc grabbed a glass from the rack on the wall. He poured it half full of brandy before handing it to Seth.

"Where did you get this?" Seth asked.

"One of the crew has a stash of liquor. I convinced him with a few Imperial Crowns to give us a bottle."

"More like highway robbery. You could have bought two cases of this stuff with what you paid," Professor said.

"Money will be useless to us on Alenia, and possibly afterward. We are discussing what will happen to us at the end of this adventure. I use the term adventure facetiously, of course. It is my opinion if we don't succumb to what drove the researchers mad, they will perform a brainwipe on us when we return. Professor is more optimistic. He believes we will emerge unscathed to keep this secret for the rest of our long, prosperous lives," Doc said, with a light touch of sarcasm.

"They can't do anything to us. I am a distinguished member of Klatania University. You are the head of Virology at the university's Research Center. Just the fact we've disappeared without notice will have raised alarms. If we return as mindless shells of our former selves, there will be an investigation."

Doc took a sip from his glass. "You think we will be missed, my dear friend? Note that no one in our group has someone waiting for them. Alan and Jana are young, unmarried, and from what they told me, neither has living relatives. Gunther says he never married and has no family. I am a widower of three years. You, my dear friend, are a widower of five years. Neither of us has children. Is anyone waiting for you, Seth?"

Seth shook his head.

"Well, there it is. No one will miss us except for a few colleagues. If we don't return, they will be informed that each of us, or all of us, had a fatal accident. We might even be given lavish funerals at the Empire's expense."

Professor emptied his glass. He stood up. "I don't believe our situation augurs your depressing view of the outcome. Besides, I am tired. I am going to get some sleep. Good night, Doc. Good night, Seth." There was a little weave in his step as he walked out, shutting the door as he left.

Chapter 22

Doc's glass was empty. He poured more brandy into it, waving the bottle in front of Seth. Seth shook his head. His glass was only down a sip.

Doc swished the brandy around in his glass before taking a drink. "I've wanted to talk to you in private since you joined us. First, I heard your mother died. You have my condolences."

"You know I didn't like my mother."

"I do. However, there are things about your mother you don't know that I think you should."

"I know she was paranoid, fearing the Imperial Guard would come for us. I also think she drove my father away, so he never wanted to see or talk to me. I don't think she ever really cared about me."

"Some of what you think you know is wrong."

Seth drained his glass and stood up. "Thanks for the drink. I don't think you can tell me much about my mother that I don't already know."

"Wait. Please let me explain. I don't want to be confrontive. Do you know your mother and I were classmates at Klatania University? Or that I was the one that introduced your mother to your father?"

Seth sat back down. "You never mentioned you knew my mother or my father."

"Then let me tell you."

Doc poured more brandy into Seth's glass. Seth took a drink as he waited for Doc to continue.

"I met your mother in medical school at Klatania University. We never met in our undergraduate studies. Not surprising with 200,000 students attending the university. It was in our first class in med school. Your mother and I were paired as lab partners. She told me she was going to be a general practitioner. I told her I wanted to specialize in virology. We became friends. It didn't take long to recognize how brilliant your mother was. I encouraged her to become more than a simple physician. I said it would be a waste of her talent. She said she had signed up for the genetics program a few days later. I was excited for her. It was the first time we went out to celebrate at a local bar."

Doc took a big gulp of brandy before leaning back in his chair. "I'm going to be perfectly candid with you. I don't imagine it will make any difference now, but you should know that I loved your mother. I would have asked your mother to marry me if the Heritage Laws weren't in effect then. You may not be familiar with those laws since they disappeared into the black hole where they put all stupid policies. However, at that time, Emperor Wuden issued an edict that no one could marry someone who didn't have an eighty percent genetic heritage match. It meant I could not marry your mother. As it turned out, I found my wife, Simana, while in medical school. We had a happy marriage until she died three years ago."

Doc got a faraway look in his eyes for a second. He took another sip from his glass.

"You said you knew my father."

"Robert and I were on the same rugby team. Looking at me now, you can't imagine I could play rugby, though I was rather good at it. I invited Robert to attend my and Simana's engagement party. It was at our engagement party Robert first met your mother. I introduced her to him. It was apparent from the start that there was chemistry between them. I wasn't surprised when they married within six months."

Seth was listening intently, sipping his brandy. "What kind of man was my father?"

"Robert Harthset was a man of purpose. He took planetary engineering seriously, although he liked to call it by its old name of terraforming. He postulated a planet's environment could be made habitable for humans in a far shorter time than the centuries it often required. He was right. He proved it by inventing the Habitation Engine. He also had a high regard for integrity. I would say, an obsession for it. I remember once he learned a professor was selling test answers. Robert made it his mission to bring that professor to justice, which he did."

"Do you know why my mother and father separated?"

"Your parents graduated a few months after they married. I lost track of them after that. More precisely, I couldn't find them. Some mutual friends told me that they had signed up to work on a new colony on an outer planet. Seven years passed before I heard from your mother. She contacted me. She told me she was separated from your father. When I asked her if she would explain what happened between her and Robert, she wouldn't say, other than she had a five-year-old son named Seth, and she needed a job. I told her to come to Klatania University. I was sure I could find her a job there. She insisted it had to be on one of the outer planets. She was looking to be a basic physician on an outer planet. I pressed her on why she wanted a job so far beneath her. She wouldn't explain.

"I found her a job as she requested. She said she would contact me when she got established in her new job. She didn't contact me again for three years. When she did, it was only a VID. She said she had moved on from the job I got for her to four similar jobs on other outer planets. She said she enjoyed working as a physician in the outer planet colonies because it gave her a chance to help people who needed it."

"She moved us a lot in those years. I don't think we stayed in one place for over a few months. She was obsessed that the Imperial Guard would be coming for us."

"I tried to communicate with your mother many times. She never responded. Years went by when I didn't hear from her. Then she sent me a communication saying you were coming to attend Klatania University. She asked me to help you. I did."

Seth said, "You mean as my student counselor."

Doc swished the brandy around in his glass for a few seconds before answering. "It makes no difference now, though I promised your mother I would say nothing to you. You would've never gotten into Klatania University without your mother's help."

"That isn't true. It was my last name that got me accepted. I would say it had more to do with my father than with my mother."

Doc smiled. "You were sixteen. A bit young to be admitted to the university despite having fulfilled the necessary admission requirements. I was outside the admissions office watching you meet with the admissions agent. He rejected you, didn't he?"

"Yes. When I told him I was the son of Robert Harthset, he accepted me."

"Do you remember the agent was called away to answer his phone as you were pleading your case?"

Seth nodded.

"That was me. I called him. I told him to ask you for your last name, and after he did, he should accept your application."

"I don't understand. Why did you do that?"

"When I told your mother you had arrived at the university she asked if I would intercede on your behalf to make sure you were admitted."

"I ran away from my mother after I told her I wanted to attend Klatania University. She said I couldn't trust anyone there. She was adamant that I attend one of the colony colleges. I wanted to be a Planetary Engineer, like my father. There are no Planetary Engineering programs in the colony colleges. It is one of the reasons, not the only one, that I left her."

"You made it clear to me then, as you are now, that your relationship with your mother wasn't good. What you don't know is that she was protective of you. She did all she could to ensure you succeeded at the university."

"That isn't true. She never contacted me when I was at the university. You were my counselor. You helped me."

"Did you ever consider where the money came from that paid your way through Klatania University?"

"You told me an academic achievement scholarship paid for my schooling."

"The scholarship only covered your tuition. Your mother gave me the money to pay for your other expenses."

Seth took a big swig of brandy. "She never said anything about helping me get through the university. That was like her, never explaining. When I asked her why we moved so often from one outer planet to another, her answer was it was safer if I didn't know. I badgered her to tell me why she and my father divorced. All she would say was my father was a good man, nothing more."

"You may have grievances with your mother. I believe it is important for you to know she did what she could to help you get through the university. She loved you, no matter how you felt about her."

Seth drank the last of his brandy. "Thanks for the drink. I'm not sure how I feel about what you've told me, or if it makes any difference about how I feel about my mother." Seth left.

Doc poured more brandy into his glass as he pondered how Seth would deal with what he just told him.

CHAPTER 23

Seth returned to his cabin. He sat on the cot to consider what Doc told him. Had she been in the background helping him at the university? He went to his duffel bag. He pulled out the last VID she made for him. He turned it over and over in his hands. He remembered her lawyer giving him this VID at her funeral. He said this was a message your mother made for you just before she died.

The first contact he received from her came shortly after he graduated from the university. Somehow, she knew where he was to send him a VID. There was a handwritten note saying he should play the VID to its end. That was odd. A VID could hold five hours of video recordings and hundreds of text articles. Assuming all she had on the VID was her video message, it would eject at the end of that recording. So why did she say he should play it to its end?

He put the VID into his player. The video showed her sitting in front of the camera. She congratulated him on graduating from Klatania University. She said he would be an excellent Planetary Engineer, like his father. Another surprise, since he didn't know how she knew what profession he had chosen.

The VID message ended. He was about to pull the VID out of the player when he remembered the note. He let it play on. All that appeared on the screen was static. Normally, the screen would go black at the end of a recording, followed by the VID ejecting. Her camera was still on, but only static showed on the screen.

Seth watched the static for a few minutes. He reached to eject the VID when a mechanical voice said, "Place of birth?" It surprised him. He stood there watching the static. The question repeated. He answered, "Digeria." It was the planet where he was born.

The VID screen lit up with her image. She smiled. "I'm glad you understood my message. I know this may be odd to you as so many other things I do may seem. This is the only way I can be sure the Imperial spies or other prying eyes don't see this message." She continued to say where she was and described what she was doing. She ended with, "I know you have questions, questions you've asked many times about your father and why our marriage ended. I will tell you all you want to know someday, but not today. For now, take care of yourself. There may be those who wish to do you harm." Her image faded and then the VID ejected.

It was just like her, so paranoid she needed to send him a secret message with nothing more important than where she was. He wanted more information about his father, about their divorce. Her vague offer to tell him sometime in the future only angered him.

In the following years, she would send him a VID about every six months. It always began with a simple message followed by the mechanical voice asking for his place of birth. Once he answered Digeria, it unlocked her secret message. In all those secret messages, she never mentioned the reason for their marriage breakup, nor did she discuss his father. The fact she wouldn't answer these questions continued to fuel his anger. He never responded to her.

It wasn't long after he got the job on the Beanie that he received a message from a person who said he was her lawyer. The message said she had died on the planet Gardolay. The lawyer was asking for instructions on what to do with her remains. Seth was only one jump from Gardolay. He hadn't received pay for eight months. He didn't have enough money to go to Gardolay to give her a proper funeral. He took money from the engineering fund of the project he was working on to travel to Gardolay.

Arriving there, he met with his mother's lawyer. The lawyer gave Seth a small bag with his mother's belongings. She didn't have much. The only thing personal was a small handmade pendant with an unusual design she always wore. He once asked her about the pendant. She would only say it was important to her.

There was a VID in her belongings with his name on it. The lawyer said she made it shortly before she died. She told the lawyer to make sure Seth got it.

Seth arranged for her cremation. The colony's council leader asked Seth if he would come to a gathering they held in his mother's honor. Gardolay was a new colony, mostly a farming community with some light manufacturing. The people of Gardolay arranged a memorial service for his mother in the public meeting hall. Everyone in the colony must have been there from the group's size.

Seth stood at the door, dutifully greeting everyone who came. He listened to them praise his mother for being an excellent doctor and a wonderful person. He politely accepted what they said when all the time he wanted to argue that she wasn't the person they thought she was, at least not to him.

Seth agreed when the council leader asked if they could bury her ashes in a place of honor in the Gardolay cemetery. Once that was done, he left feeling guilty that so many people loved her when he couldn't find it in his heart to forgive her.

He returned to his job. A month later, he received his back pay, and he reimbursed the engineering fund for the money he took. Three months passed before he decided to view his mother's final VID. She appeared drawn and pale. Her lawyer told Seth she had died from Boxtonaire disease. She caught it from one of her patients. The patient came into her clinic complaining of a fever. Before his mother diagnosed that the patient had the highly contagious Boxtonaire's disease, she too was infected. Boxtonaire had a 98 percent mortality rate. Seth's mother wasn't one of the two percent who survived it.

She was extremely thin. She struggled to speak as she greeted him. She began speaking about trivial things, not once mentioning that she was dying. The VID ended. The usual static appeared before the secret message. Seth waited for the prompt to hear the real message she sent on this VID.

The static was finally interrupted by the mechanical voice asking its question. This was a different question. The mechanical voice said, "Origin?"

The normal question was the place of his birth. Why a different question? He didn't know why it was asking origin or what origin it was referring to. He answered Digeria, as he always did. The static continued. After a minute, the mechanical voice repeated the question, "Origin?" Seth cycled through the process several times, giving his place of birth without anything happening. He answered the question saying Gardolay, the planet his mother died on. Still nothing. He answered where his mother was born, where his father was born, he even answered

Klatania, none of it made a difference. The VID continued showing static as the mechanical voice repeated the question, 'Origin.'

Seth finally gave up. Maybe she died before she could record an additional message. He tossed the VID in his duffle bag. It stayed there ever since.

He sat on his cot holding her last VID. There was no reason to frustrate himself further by trying to find an answer to the question "Origin." He put the VID back in his duffel bag. Whatever secret message she left for him, assuming there was one, would be lost forever.

CHAPTER 24

S eth woke early. The crewmen who guided him to supper last night said the cook had fixed times for every meal. Anyone not there for the meal would have to wait for the next one. There would be no exceptions.

With plenty of time before breakfast, Seth turned on the monitor to continue reviewing the files about Alenia. He found two audio files from the supply freighter that had come to Alenia when the fighting took place. One was between the captain of the freighter and his Cargo Chief. The Cargo Chief had just landed on Alenia. He described the mayhem he saw at the compound to his disbelieving captain.

The second audio recording was between the captain of the freighter and an Admiral waiting with a few fleet ships to receive the colonists the freighter brought back from Alenia. Seth didn't understand why the colonists blew up the freighter when they were safe. It would take an incredible level of insanity to do that.

It was still too early for breakfast when Seth headed for the dining room.

Doc was there alone.

"Did you get to bed?" Seth asked, seeing the empty bottle of brandy in the trash bucket.

"I did, for a while. I'll have time to catch up on any missed sleep in the next two days. I hope what I said last night didn't offend you."

"I appreciate that you shared your history with my parents. My mother never told me how she met my father. Thanks to you, now I know. My father left us when I was five years old. I don't remember him. When I came to the university, I tried to contact him. I thought he might talk to me. He never responded, and then he died in my sophomore year.

"Your father may have been driven by his goal of making planets more habitable. At his core, he was a good man."

"I'm trying to understand why my mother helped me get through Klatan University. She didn't want me to go there. Knowing she made it possible with your help to be accepted into the university makes me feel cheated. I wanted to make it on my own, while all the time she was still pulling the strings."

"What she did, she did out of love for you."

"I've harbored resentment so long for my mother driving away my father, I have trouble seeing her in a better light."

"When I was around your parents, they were deeply in love with each other. Their divorce surprised me. Your mother was among the kindest, most thoughtful people I've ever known. I find it hard to believe she drove away your father."

"My guess is she drove him away by her hatred of the Emperor and her paranoid fear the Imperial Guard would come for her. I'll never know now since they are both dead."

Alan walked into the room looking more tired than Doc. He quietly took his seat.

Gunther came in bristling, "They have no exercise facilities on this ship! I had to go to the cargo hold to use cargo crates as weights to exercise."

As Gunther sat down, Jana walked in. She smiled at everyone without singling out Seth. He felt relieved. Maybe the kiss was nothing more than an expression of her gratitude. If it was meant to be an invitation for something more, she may have reconsidered it. Either way, it was better to keep anything between them on a professional basis until this mission was over.

Professor was the last to arrive. "The bed in my cabin is lumpy," he grumbled, as he sat next to Doc.

The cook brought a large bowl filled with a synthetic substitute for oatmeal. Synthetic food was supposed to be nutritious. It failed to be tasty.

They ate in silence. After they finished the meal, Doc said, "We need to guard ourselves against encountering whatever caused the colonists to go mad once we arrive on Alenia. The vector that infected them could have come from their food or water or be an airborne agent. If it was the food, they would have all had to eat the infected food at or about the same time since the supply ship noted they were all participating in the killing spree. Food is a possible source, though I think it is unlikely to be the cause. Water is a more likely culprit. In either case, we can guard ourselves against being contaminated by not eating or drinking anything on Alenia until Jana and I have a chance to make sure both are safe. That leaves the possibility of an airborne agent. If it was an airborne agent, we might succumb to it the minute we step off the ship."

Professor gave Doc a hard stare. "Now that you've frightened us, do you have anything we can do to save ourselves other than not leave the ship?"

Seth said, "I don't think it was in the air unless it dissipated rapidly. The crew of the freighter arrived there during the killings. They spent a lot of time capturing some of the colonists, and then more time with them as they returned to Imperial space. If the agent that drove the colonists insane was airborne, I would expect the freighter crew would have gotten infected. All indications are they hadn't."

"A good observation. That would rule out an airborne agent unless it took a long time before it caused the people to act in the way they did. It reaffirms my idea of taking blood samples daily on Alenia. We need to take samples before we land. If you don't mind, I found blood collecting equipment in the ship's medical supplies. I'd like to take the samples now," Doc said.

No one disagreed. Jana and Doc went around drawing blood from each of them. Once that was done, they returned to their cabins.

CHAPTER 25

Shortly after Seth returned to his cabin after breakfast, there was a knock on his door. He opened the door to find Alan standing there.

"Are you busy? Am I interrupting something? Mind if I come in?" Alan stood there looking sheepish.

"Not at all. Come on in."

Alan stepped into Seth's cabin. He stopped inside the doorway. "This is small. My cabin is twice the size. I have a free-standing desk plus a table with three chairs." He looked at the cot. "I also have a regular bed."

"I guess you're special.".

Alan shook his head. "All of us have the same cabin. Except you."

Seth said, "They must have run out of the more luxurious cabins." He knew that was a lie. They came for him before everyone else. There was another reason to put him in this tiny cabin. Maybe they wanted him to be uncomfortable.

"Did you come to check out my cabin?"

"No. I'm here about something else. Can we talk?"

"Be my guest."

Alan took the chair. Seth sat on the cot. He waited for Alan to say what he came to say. Alan was nervously rubbing one hand over the other. He finally said, "I didn't want to come. I was going to vote against coming. I didn't. I was more afraid of having my brainwiped than coming. Now that I'm here, I'm not sure I made the right choice."

"None of us are happy to be here, except possibly Professor. We didn't have a choice. No one wanted to have their memories erased with a brainwipe."

Alan said nothing for a few seconds as he continued wringing his hands.

"When the Captain asked if anyone wanted pills for jump sickness, I didn't say anything, though I wanted to. I've never experienced a jump before. I couldn't sleep last night after the ship went through its second jump. It upsets my stomach, and it scares me. During a jump, they call what we are traveling through Dead Space. What if something happens during the jump? We could be stranded in Dead Space."

"You did look a little out of sorts this morning. I can assure you that no ship has ever been stuck in Dead Space. They only call it Dead Space because they don't know what else to call it."

"But I've heard there is nothing in Dead Space, not even the stars."

"They don't see stars when a ship makes a jump, that's true. There is a theory that the jump is traveling outside our known dimensions, but that is only a theory. They don't know. As far as the upset feeling you get when we make a jump, everyone gets it. Eventually, you get used to it. Just lie down after a jump to let your body adjust."

Alan continued nervously rubbing his hands together.

"Is there something else you want?"

Alan blurted out, "I'm only twenty years old. I've never been anywhere off of Klatania before this. I'm afraid I will die on this mission."

"I'm twenty-eight years old. I'm afraid, too, though I don't plan on dying on this mission. I'm sure none of the others do either."

That didn't stop the hand wringing.

"You've never been to another planet?"

"No, I haven't. I don't know why they chose me for this mission. The information they gave us about Alenia says they couldn't translate the Alenian language. They've had thirty years to do it. What do they expect me to do there?"

"Well, Doc says you are an incredible linguist. Maybe they think you can do what no one else has done."

The handwringing continued.

"Do you have someone waiting for you back on Klatania?" Seth asked.

"I have no one. My family died in the Mandilton Accident when I was ten years old."

Seth remembered the Mandilton accident. He was at the university when it filled the news. Two Runabouts were instructed to land at the same place simultaneously. They crashed. Everyone on both Runabouts died. The accident was blamed on a computer glitch compounded by human error.

"That must have been traumatic."

"Everyone thought I should be crushed by it. I wasn't. My parents were emissaries for the Emperor. They traveled a lot. I didn't see them much because they were rarely home. A nanny raised me. When they died, the nanny continued. She died a year ago."

"So, no one is waiting for you on Klatania."

"I have no one. Can we spend some time together? I mean, to talk."

Seth was feeling uncomfortable realizing where this was going. He'd avoided close relationships ever since Tovar. Living in the close quarters of the Beanie, he'd gained greater control over not reading their thoughts. He was more confident in his ability to shut out the thoughts of people, but having Alan constantly around him didn't feel like a good idea.

"You can talk to Doc, he's friendly enough."

"Doc has a history with Professor."

"What about Gunther or Jana?"

"I don't think Gunther likes anyone. As far as Jana, I'm uncomfortable with girls."

"Are you more inclined to men or boys?"

"Oh no, I like women. I've just never been comfortable around them. I've never even been on a date."

"What about school? Weren't there girls in your school?"

"Most of my education was at home. My parents hired tutors. The tutors continued even after my parents died. Only when I went to Klatan University did I have any contact with girls. That was almost none."

"Wait. When did you go to the university? You told us you've been working at the Linguistics Research Library for four years. You're only twenty."

"I entered Klatan U. when I was twelve."

Seth let out a low whistle. "Twelve! I started when I was sixteen. I thought I had problems attending Klatan U. since I was younger than everyone else. You were only twelve! That must have been infinitely harder."

"Everyone treated me like a kid. The other students didn't accept me as an equal. Even the professors were skeptical I should be in their classes, despite showing them that I could handle the work, even handle it better than most of the other students, still they didn't show me much respect."

Seth could empathize with these feelings of not being accepted by the students or the staff when they considered you too young to be in college. "You have my admiration at surviving Klatan U. at twelve. How old were you when you graduated?"

"I got my PhD in the Comparative Linguistics of Ancient Languages when I was sixteen."

Seth gave out a laugh. "Sorry for that. I went to Klatan U. at sixteen and graduated with my PhD at twenty. I thought I broke every record they had for the youngest Ph.D. You shredded my record."

Alan shrugged his shoulders. "Sorry."

"Don't be. You are a genius. That may explain why they put you on this team. They probably couldn't translate Alenian writings the past thirty years without someone of your caliber there."

They continued sharing their teenage experiences at Klatan U. After a while, Seth felt more comfortable with Alan. Alan was so open there was no fear he might read Alan's thoughts, there was no need to. Alan shared his every thought. Maybe Alan and he could be friends. If so, it would be his first friend since Tovar.

CHAPTER 26

They spent the rest of the morning swapping their experiences at Klatan U. It was only realizing they would miss lunch that broke it up. They were the last to arrive in the dining room. When they arrived, Alan described how small and primitive Seth's cabin was to everyone.

Doc said, "I understand this freighter would carry paying passengers for additional income. These passengers used our rooms. They must have run out of the nicer rooms when they included Seth on the team."

Seth shrugged. He wasn't about to complain. His room on the ship was twice the size of his space on the Beanie.

Doc continued, "I learned there is an observation deck on the ship. It has a window where the paying passengers could idle away their time watching space."

"I found it last night. It's the door next to the cargo bay," Gunther added.

"You could have told us," Jana piped up. "We might have wanted to see it."

Gunther just grunted.

Jana said, "I was talking to some of the Marines. One of them said Alenia has a code name. They call it Far Star."

"It seems an appropriate name for something 25,000 light years from the nearest human planet," Doc added.

The door opened, and Major Krugar came in. "I have received orders that you will have three weeks to investigate what happened on Alenia."

"What is the reason for such an abbreviated schedule?" Doc asked.

"The wormhole to Alenia will be closed in three weeks."

Seth asked, "How do you close a wormhole."

"We will blow it up. Explosives were placed around the Alenian side of the wormhole years ago to protect it from anyone unauthorized passing through it. Prime has ordered the wormhole closed in three weeks. Once that is done, there will be no access to Alenia."

Professor sputtered as he said, "There will be no way to return to Alenia! We were told everything they learned about the Alenians has remained on the moon. Does that mean we will bring everything they learned about the Alenians back when we return?"

"I have no orders to do that."

"We can't lose thirty years of research about the only other intelligent species ever discovered!" Professor said, as wrinkles of frustration appeared on his forehead.

"You have one objective. It is not to study the Alenians, it is to learn what happened to the colonists on that moon. You will have three weeks to do it." With that, the Major left.

Professor blurted out, "If we can't bring back what they've learned about the Alenians, there is no way I can absorb thirty years of research about them in just three weeks!"

The discussion continued about what the Major said. In the end, there was nothing they could do. The Major was in control.

They left the dining room together to check out the observation deck. It wasn't a deck so much as a room with a large window looking out to space. There were several benches facing the window. Three monitors faced the benches. Two of them showed images of space, the third was turned off. One monitor was labeled forward view, another aft view. The third monitor was off and had no sign stating its purpose. Forward, aft, or through the window, the views were similar, There was nothing near enough to even judge the ship's motion.

"Isn't this entertaining. We can see where we are, where we're going, and where we've been," Professor said sarcastically.

The next two days dragged on. The team, as they began referring to themselves, used mealtime to discuss what they learned about the Alenians from the ship's files. They concentrated on the Alenians since there was no useful information about what motivated the killings.

What they could understand from the files was that in all the time on Alenia, the researchers were unable to determine the physical appearance of the Alenians. Based on their living units and the tools they used, they believed they were human-sized creatures, but that was all. The problem was they never found any images of the creatures nor any burial sites or graves. Nor did they find any crematoriums. It was a mystery what the Alenians did with their dead.

The obvious answer was their dead were returned to their planet of origin. That fit with the assumption the moon was a penal colony. The question then was where did they take them? Since the Alenians changed the moon's atmosphere to one it turned out humans could also use, it was logical to assume they came from a planet with a similar atmosphere. The two inner planets had a human breathable atmosphere. The problem was they were said to be uninhabited and lethal to humans. Then if the Alenians didn't come from one of those two planets, where did they come from?

The files gave the team another mystery to deal with. What happened to the Alenians? The researchers determined that forty years before humans arrived on the moon, the Alenians disappeared rather quickly. They couldn't have all left the moon by rocket, since their population was estimated to be around thirty thousand. A single spaceport capable of supporting a single, small rocket would not be able to take all of them off the moon in the time it was estimated they disappeared.

There was one thing in the files that Seth found humorous. The researchers stated that based on the hand tools the Alenians used to farm, they must have either had hands or tentacles. Seth found it funny that they couldn't determine the physical nature of the Alenians any better than having to guess if they had hands or tentacles.

Seth was the only one who found humor in the files. Professor ranted that the files were more remarkable in what they had left out than what they included. He railed that this was a pathetic collection of information if it was all the researchers had learned about the alien species in thirty years.

Doc reminded Professor since the information about the Alenians had remained on the moon, whoever put these files together may have done it from memory and apparently hastily. Undoubtedly, there would be more information about the Alenians once they were on the moon. He also reminded Professor the Major was adamant their mission wasn't to learn about the Alenians but to find out what happened to the colonists. Professor didn't accept that was going to be *his* primary mission.

Aside from the meals, the members of the team spent most of their time in their own cabins. All except Alan, who spent much of his time with Seth.

Though Jana was pleasant to Seth, she never mentioned the kiss or acted as if it had ever happened. The kiss continued to bother Seth more than he thought it would. Maybe by Jana ignoring that it ever happened, he was making more of it than she intended.

The Major was invisible to them. He spent his time in his own cabin or with the Marines.

Gunther preferred spending his time in the cargo hold exercising. Gunther came to the meals but never volunteered any personal information about himself, and only rarely expressed his opinion on any of the topics being discussed.

Alan didn't turn out to be as much of a pest as Seth feared. Alan was keenly interested in hearing about Seth's work as a Planetary Engineer. Having never been away from Klatania, Alan was enthralled listening to Seth tell him about his work on the outer planets. Alan wanted to know what the landscape was like, what the people did, how they dressed, how they spoke, even what they ate. He was even interested in the Habitation Engine repairs, even though to Seth it was long hours of dirty, grueling work.

When not with Alan, Seth decided to explore the ship. He learned the Cauloten Six normally had a crew complement of thirty. To make room for the six of them plus ten Marines and the Major, the ship's crew had been stripped to a dozen, the barest minimum necessary to operate the ship.

Seth wanted to see if the Marines knew anything more about this mission. He wanted to know why they were limited to only three weeks, and also why they were blowing up the wormhole. The ten Marines were a hard-looking lot, not the people you wanted to be around if they suddenly became insane killers. The

Marines kept to their quarters and the ship's galley. Seth came upon a Marine in the galley and tried to strike up a conversation with him. The Marine made it clear he was not interested in talking to Seth about anything. That was true for all the Marines. It seemed they were only interested in talking to Jana. Not surprising, since Jana was the only woman aboard the Cauloten Six.

The ship's crewmembers were more talkative. They believed the team's members were spies. Knowing they would be handed off to Imperial ships in rebel territory, they conjectured the team members would be dropped off on different planets where they would spy on known sympathizers of the rebel's cause. In short, the crew had vivid imaginations but no insights into their actual mission.

After exhausting what he could learn from the ship's database, the useless information he got from the crew, and no information from the Marines, there was nothing more he would learn until they reached Alenia. All he could do now was deal with his own concerns about what to expect when they got there.

CHAPTER 27

They were eating breakfast on the third day when a Marine came in. "The Major wants you to assemble on the observation deck. Wait there to be transferred to the other ship."

"When do you want us there?" Doc asked.

"Now," was his curt response.

Seth and Jana went to get their duffle bags. The others had no personal items other than the coveralls they were wearing. Duffle bags in hand, they joined the others who were sitting on the benches staring out the window. There was no sign of other ships.

Captain Hollinsky's voice came over the ship's PA, "We will be rendezvousing with the fleet ships in thirty minutes."

"Thirty minutes! This is truly a military operation. They hurry us out of breakfast, only to have us sit here and wait," Professor said with a groan of frustration.

They shifted their gaze to the monitor showing the forward view.

"Does anyone know how far the wormhole entrance is from where we're meeting the other ships?" Alan asked.

"One of the Marines told me the wormhole's entrance is a day's travel from where we will rendezvous with the other ships. He didn't tell me if it required a jump," Jana answered.

Professor tugged at the neck of his coveralls. "I'm ready to get out of these uncomfortable work clothes. I hope they have some real clothes for us on the other ship."

"The Major says they have a change of clothes for us aboard the cruiser. He also said our accommodations will be a little more spartan on the cruiser than they are here," Jana said.

"I hope they won't be worse than Seth's," Alan added.

Everyone let out a laugh knowing how Seth's cabin compared to theirs.

"What is that?" Doc pointed at the ship's forward monitor.

It looked like an explosion in the distance. They stood up to move closer to the monitor. It was an explosion.

Doc went to the comm. "Captain, there is what appears to be an explosion in the direction we are heading."

He got no response. Doc was about to repeat it, when the speaker in the observation deck exploded to life with Hollinsky's voice, "The fleet ships are under attack!"

They weren't sure if he meant to keep the comm open or forgot it was open when they heard him yell, "Magnify that image!"

Then they heard the Major say, "Rebels are attacking our ships!"

Hollinsky yelled, "Thrusters, full reverse!"

The ship shuddered and everyone was thrown to the floor.

"What happened?" Alan yelled.

"The ship's artificial gravity inertial dampening system could not react fast enough to compensate for the hard stop. This is a commercial freighter, not a military craft. Captain Hollinsky should know better than to engage reverse thrusters that hard," Gunther said.

"Is anyone hurt?" Doc asked.

Professor answered, "Nothing is broken, just a few bruises." Seth helped Professor get up. Everyone else said they were all right.

Doc pointed to the monitor as a bright light filled the center of the screen. "It was an explosion on one of the Imperial cruisers."

They stared at the monitor that showed eight small craft raining energy blasts down on the hulls of four Imperial cruisers. One of the cruisers had a hole in its side that was venting huge plumes of fire. Another cruiser fired missiles at the attacking ships, destroying two of them. The remaining six attackers fired on that cruiser. Their barrage on it continued until it erupted into a huge fireball.

The remaining two cruisers were firing on the six attackers. Everyone watched as the six attackers were reduced to four, then to three, and then one of the cruisers exploded. The last undamaged cruiser fired on the three remaining attackers. Two of the attacker's ships were destroyed. The last attacker's ship fired continuously as it dove at the cruiser. The cruiser fired back but missed the attacker's ship. The attacker's ship didn't pull up. It crashed into the cruiser generating a blinding flash. When the team could see again, the last attacker's ship had destroyed the remaining cruiser. All that was left was the cruiser venting fire from a hole in its side.

Doc said, "Let's go to the bridge to see what's happening!" They followed him as he jogged to the bridge.

When they arrived, the Major was talking on the comm, "How damaged is your ship?"

"Our captain is dead. Three decks have decompressed, and our jump drive is down."

"Can you continue with the mission?"

"No, we can't. Our ship is too damaged to travel that far. We will be lucky to get away from here before more rebel ships find us."

The Major was steaming with anger. He grabbed Hollinsky. "You will take us to Alenia."

The Captain stammered, "I...I'm not prepared to go there. I've never been."

The Major stared at him with his cold, black eyes. "This ship is going to Alenia. The only question is will you continue as its captain."

Hollinsky gave a meek nod.

"I will guide the ship there. Now order the crew to proceed on my directions to the wormhole."

Hollinsky gulped. He turned to the navigator. "Follow the Major's directions."

The Major noticed the team standing in the doorway. "Get out of here! Go back to your quarters. Stay there until you are told otherwise."

CHAPTER 28

The team waited impatiently in their cabins. When any of them attempted to leave, they found a Marine standing guard at their door, ordering them to get back inside.

Late in the afternoon, the freighter made a jump. There hadn't been sufficient time for the freighter to fully recharge for a long jump, which indicated the wormhole had to be relatively close to where the battle had taken place. It substantiated what the Marine told Jana. It also confirmed Seth's belief the entrance to the wormhole was in rebel territory.

They were kept in their rooms the rest of the day and into the night without meals. It was 5 a.m. when Seth felt the ship begin to vibrate. As the vibrations grew, the ship began to creak under the stress. This was an old freighter, not in good condition. Seth was worried the old hull of this ship might crack.

The chair in Seth's room began to bounce around as the monitor crashed onto the floor. The cot was bolted to the floor, and Seth got under it and held onto one of its legs as the ship continued vibrating, causing things to fly around the cabin.

When the vibrations stopped, Seth stood up and opened the door. The Marine guarding his cabin seemed unhurt. He held his hand to his ear. He was listening to someone on his personal comm. He saw Seth and said, "The Major wants you on the observation deck." Then he walked away.

Seth met the rest of the team on his way to the observation deck where they found the Major waiting for them.

"What was all that shaking about? I thought the ship was going to fall apart," Professor said with a touch of fear in his voice.

The Major's eyes wandered over everyone, looking for injuries they might have sustained. Finally satisfied they were uninjured, he said, "We have just passed through the entrance to the wormhole. We will be orbiting Alenia in less than an hour. Get ready to depart." He left the observation deck without offering to answer their questions.

The observation window's view of the star-studded blackness of space had changed to something milky white. It was as if they were flying through a cloud. Dark swirls moved violently through the white, milky substance, as a storm might churn through clouds. This must have been the turbulence they experienced when the ship entered the wormhole.

"It appears as if we're traveling through something dense. It almost looks as if we are traveling through a liquid. It's incredible to think we are traveling thousands of light-years," Doc said.

Professor scoffed, "Incredible! I thought the ship would be shaken into scrap."

"I have traveled a lot in space but never encountered anything like this. It is invigorating," Gunther said.

Doc padded Gunther on the shoulder. "Well, good for us that we can enjoy this novelty."

"Novelty! I think you are both mad," Professor said.

Abruptly the ship began to shake again, but only briefly, before the white clouds disappeared and they could see normal space outside the window. What they also saw were large metallic cylinders floating near the ship.

"Those cylinders must be the explosives to blow up the wormhole," Gunther commented.

"Let's hope they don't go off while we are still on this side of the wormhole," Professor added anxiously.

The freighter left the cylinder field behind as the front-facing monitor showed a star. The ship was heading for a gas giant with layers of colored rings.

"This must be the gas giant that Alenia orbits," Jana said.

Seth could see bright objects nearer the star. These had to be the two mysterious uninhabited planets that had human breathable atmospheres but were lethal to humans.

Jana pointed to the monitor at a bright object above the gas giant. "That must be Alenia."

The Major's voice came over the intercom, "We will be orbiting Alenia in less than twenty minutes. I will send a contingent of Marines down first to ensure the area is secure. We will transport you to the surface once it is safe."

CHAPTER 29

S eth returned to his cabin to fetch his duffel bag. As he headed back to the observation deck, Jana came up behind him with her duffel bag. The rest had stayed on the observation deck. They sat on the benches watching the forward viewing monitor as the ship approached Alenia.

Professor was complaining he would have to live in these uncomfortable coveralls until they returned to Klatania. It made Seth smile. Professor was more concerned about his uncomfortable coveralls than the unknown dangers they might soon face on the moon.

"Don't worry. One of the dead colonists may be your size. You can use his clothes," Doc said with a sly grin.

"You make light of it, although I might just do that," Professor said.

Seth put his duffel bag on the floor. Jana did the same. They joined the others staring out the observation window. The ship was now entering an orbit around Alenia. The moon filled the window's view.

Alan said, "Wow, it's bigger than I imagined."

Seth agreed. "It's a full-sized planet, even though it's a moon of this gas giant."

The freighter was slowly moving into a lower orbit. Below them was the western edge of the continent, the coastal plain richly green with vegetation. The mountains separated it from the featureless, bleak land rightly called the Great Desert that covered more than half the continent.

They passed over the mountains that defined the eastern edge of the Alenian coastal plain. The land looked arid, the only vegetation growing along the banks of rivers flowing on both sides of the eastern mountain range.

The Alenian coastal plain was boxed in at each end by tall, rugged mountains and the ocean. Seth estimated it varied between fifty to seventy kilometers wide and approximately a hundred kilometers long.

Gunther was fiddling with the third monitor, the one without a label that was turned off. He pulled a remote from behind the monitor. Pressing a few buttons, the screen lit up. It showed a zoomed-in image of what they saw out of the observation window. Gunther moved a joystick on the remote that directed the camera to move over the landscape.

Alan pointed to the upper portion of the monitor's screen. "I see Quonset huts, and there's a runway."

Gunther moved the camera to zoom in to where Alan was pointing.

They'd read that the runway and Quonset huts were part of the human compound. Thousands of box-shaped structures were arranged in a regular pattern south of the human compound.

"Those must be the Alenians' dwellings," Professor said as he studied the screen.

Everyone was engrossed looking at the zoomed-in image of the Alenian dwellings. Suddenly Seth had a feeling that something was wrong. A feeling like the one he had when Reilly was in trouble, but came without a vision, more a presentiment that something was very wrong.

Seth asked Gunther to shift the image back to the colony. He did. "Keep panning across the plain."

Gunther did what Seth asked. As the image panned across the plain, Gunther finally stopped it at the ocean's edge.

"There!" Seth yelled. "Zoom in on those towers."

There was a row of conical towers spaced evenly along the entire coastline. The two towers closest to the human compound had wispy clouds coming from their tops. Seth watched the two towers until the ship's orbit took them out of sight.

Twelve minutes later, the freighter passed over the colony again. Seth had Gunther zoom in on the two towers. The clouds above them had grown significantly larger. Seth knew what this was. He was sure this was the reason he sensed something was wrong.

Chapter 30

S eth ran out of the observation deck to the ship's bridge. The Major was talking to Captain Hollinsky. Seth ran up to them. "There's a problem!" Both men turned to look at him.

"They have what looks like Habitation Engine towers next to the colony. If I'm right, they have been set to the Initiation Phase."

Both men gave Seth a blank stare.

"During normal atmosphere maintenance, habitation engine towers will generate gases like oxygen with some water vapor. You will see small clouds above the towers that may produce some rain. However, these towers are emitting heavy outputs that are rapidly increasing. It should only happen during the early stages of transforming a planet's atmosphere, called the Initiation Phase. It's a brutal process that generates tornado force winds."

"Are you saying these machines are malfunctioning?" The Major asked.

"I'm saying an Initiation Phase has started down there. It only runs when you want to dramatically change the atmosphere. It's supposed to be human breathable. There is no reason an Initiation Phase should be running now unless someone wants to change the atmosphere to something other than human breathable."

"Assuming you are right, how long will it run before it has that effect?"

"It can take decades to change the atmosphere. That isn't the problem. Soon these towers will generate strong winds followed by tornadoes. Unless you have a runway that we can use far from the human compound, soon it won't be possible to land a shuttle on the runway near these towers."

"There is only one landing strip on the moon," the Major said.

The freighter's orbit had taken it over the human compound again. Seth asked Captain Hollinsky to focus his ship's scanner on the towers.

"See those clouds?" Seth pointed to the ship's view screen showing the two conical towers emitting a mist considerably larger than it was on the last orbit. "The output is intensifying. Soon the clouds you see will change from white to black. When that happens, it will create an intense storm. The storm will grow. Before long, it will be impossible to land anything on that runway."

"You say it will not end soon."

"It won't end for decades.

The Major was watching as the white clouds began to turn black. He addressed Hollinsky, "Get a shuttle ready. Tell your pilot he needs to get down to the ground fast."

He turned to Seth. "Do you know how to turn off these machines?"

"If it's anything like my father's Habitation Engine, I can turn it off."

"Then get to the shuttle bay now."

CHAPTER 31

S eth sat in the copilot's seat as the pilot guided the shuttle out of the freighter. The pilot was a member of the freighter crew. Three armed Marines dressed for combat sat in the back of the shuttle. The Major told Seth the Marines were there to protect him from the insane colonists.

The shuttle left orbit as it began a powered glide to the moon. The shuttle began to bounce about from atmospheric friction when it entered the atmosphere.

Seth could see the conical towers were now spewing large plumes of black clouds from their tops. These clouds would be highly ionized. Once the atmosphere around the towers was fully ionized, it would begin generating storms. It wouldn't be long before the storms increased in intensity that would become too strong for the shuttle to land.

The pilot began a circular descent approaching the colony from the ocean. Seth thought this was a mistake. The storms would first start over the water. He said nothing, believing the pilot knew what he was doing.

They were at an altitude of 800 meters when the shuttle began rocking violently. A lightning bolt hit the shuttle causing the instruments to go out, but they came back on in a second. The pilot struggled to maintain control as the wind buffeted the shuttle. Lightning raged around them, generating thunderclaps, that along with rain pounding on the shuttle's hull, were deafening.

The pilot turned to Seth, "I've never experienced anything like this. I don't think the shuttle can take it. We better go back."

"The Initiation Phase is still in its early stage. If we go back now, we'll never be able to land."

"You mean it's going to get worse than this?" The pilot's fear clearly showing.

"We have to get below the storm. It means flying as low as possible. It's the only place where the storm's effects will be minimal. It's our only chance to land before the storm becomes too intense."

"I'm not flying any lower with this much turbulence. It will crash us into the ocean. I'm getting out of here."

"You have to believe me. We still have a chance to land if we do it now. Let me fly the shuttle."

"I won't die because you think you can land the shuttle in this monster storm."

The shuttle gained altitude as the pilot turned it around. The Major told Seth the Marines were there to protect him. He yelled back to them, "I'm relieving the pilot! Get him out of here or he will ruin our chance to stop this." The Marines didn't hesitate. Two of them came up to grab the pilot. They ignored his protests and dragged him to the rear, setting him between them.

Seth moved into the pilot's seat. He leveled off the shuttle as he flipped on the autopilot. His first job out of university was piloting a shuttle to ferry crews and parts to the sites on a planet where they were installing Habitation Engines. He hadn't flown a shuttle in three years, and never in anything like these conditions.

Seth surveyed the shuttle's controls to reacquaint himself with them. Everything was as he remembered. He turned off the autopilot. He brought the shuttle around towards the land. The shuttle began to bounce as he reentered the storms generated by the towers. The closer he got to the land the more the shuttle acted like a leaf in a hurricane. The towers generating these conditions were between them and the runway. There wasn't time to go around the storm. By then, the storm would spawn tornados making it impossible to land the shuttle on the runway. His only chance to shut down the towers was to fly directly through the storm.

He had to reduce the turbulence by flying under the storm. He pushed the steering yoke down, diving the shuttle towards the ocean. From the back, he could hear the pilot screaming, "Great Klatan, he's going to smash us into the ocean!"

Seth ignored the pilot's screams. He hoped the Marines would too. The altimeter indicated they were at 1000 meters. The growing intensity of the wind bounced the shuttle around as it dove. He watched the altimeter read 900 meters, 800 meters, 700 meters, the shuttle continued to be tossed about by the wind. At 600 meters, lightning began hitting the shuttle every three seconds. The lightning didn't affect the instruments this time due to the shuttle's adaptive electronic system kicking in.

Things didn't improve at 500 meters. At 350 meters the lightning strikes stopped. However, the wind grew stronger. The shuttle bounced about violently as it fell through 200 meters. When the shuttle fell below 100 meters with no change in the ferocity of the wind, Seth feared he made a mistake believing he would find calmer conditions low to the ground. At 80 meters the wind suddenly died. Seth pulled up on the shuttle's yoke to stop its descent. The shuttle's momentum carried it down to 20 meters above the ocean's surface before it leveled off. Storms were raging above them. Here, there was calm.

Seth continued to skim the ocean's surface as he flew towards the land. Ahead were cliffs 100 meters tall. Towers on the cliffs were spewing huge black clouds laced with lightning strikes.

He checked for a transponder signal to guide him to the runway. There was no signal. He focused on what he'd seen from the freighter's observation deck. The human Quonset huts were south of the runway. There were only two towers active. The northern tower was even with the runway, the southern tower was south of the Quonset huts.

In the Initiation Phase, the least turbulence would be near the ground halfway between the two towers. It would grow stronger once the tornados formed. Before the conditions made that impossible to and, his best chance to get to the runway was to fly low between the towers.

The shuttle was approaching the cliffs. It was still skimming the ocean's surface 80 meters below the top of the cliffs. He pulled the shuttle's nose up, increased the thrust, and aimed for a spot just above the cliff and between the two towers.

He flew over the cliff, leveling off just eight meters from the ground. The wind was still light here. It would get stronger once he passed the towers. He flew in between both towers. Once past them, he brought the shuttle up to 30 meters.

His visibility went to zero. He was flying through a thick layer of moisture-laden fog. He expected there would be a layer of clear air between the ground fog and the raging storm above the towers. He brought the shuttle up to 50 meters. The shuttle burst through the fog into the clear layer above it.

The air was clear, but the wind here swirled and began to bounce the shuttle about ferociously as lightning strikes streaked across the sky in the black clouds above. Seth could make out the Quonset huts of the human compound ahead of them. The runway was north of the human compound. He banked the shuttle to the right.

He looked for a landing signal from the runway that would guide the shuttle's angle and speed of descent. There was no signal. Without the signal, Seth had to land the shuttle manually. If he came in too low, dropped too fast, or came in at the wrong speed, he would crash the shuttle into the runway.

The runway was ahead of him. He brought the shuttle up to 80 meters as he prepared to land. At this altitude, the wind was changing directions erratically. He fought to keep the shuttle on course.

The storm was intensifying. He had to land now, there wasn't time to wait. He brought the shuttle around to align it with the center of the runway. As he did, a gust of wind pushed the shuttle ten degrees off center. He increased the thrust to bring the shuttle back in line with the runway. He was going too fast to land. If he reduced the shuttle's speed, another strong gust of wind could crash it into the ground. He had to land the shuttle going this fast. There was nothing else he could do.

Seth ran through what he knew about the runway. The supply ship's hauler had landed here. A hauler required a least 1400 meters to land, while a shuttle only needed 1000 meters. There might be enough runway to stop the shuttle even if he came in this fast.

Seth yelled to his passengers, "Hold on to something, it's going to be a rough landing!"

Seth kept the main engine thrust high as he flew the shuttle close to the ground. As he crossed the end of the runway, he was still three meters above the ground as he cut the main engine. The shuttle fell out of the air. It bounced twice on the ground before it began rolling down the runway.

Seth could see a building at the end of the runway. They would crash into it if he couldn't slow down the shuttle. He tapped the shuttle's brakes. Hard braking would strip the brakes, making them useless to stop the shuttle, or worse, cause the shuttle to spin.

The brakes weren't slowing the shuttle enough to keep it from crashing into the building. Seth remembered the shuttle's hull rockets. They were used to maneuver in space when landing on the freighter in orbit, a place without gravity. He fired up the forward-facing rockets hoping they would slow down the shuttle. It began to slow, but not enough. There were also maneuvering rockets on top of the shuttle. He fired them to put more pressure on the tires to help the brakes. The shuttle bounced as the top rockets came on. It still wasn't slowing the shuttle enough to stop in time.

Seth had one more idea. It was dangerous and possibly crazy, but it was all he could think of doing to stop them before they crashed into the building. He fired the left-side maneuvering rockets as he applied the brakes on the shuttle's right wheel. It had the desired effect. The shuttle went into a spin. Timing was everything. The shuttle spun around 180 degrees. Seth released the brake and kicked on the main engine. The shuttle bucked as it reacted to the main engine's thrust. The shuttle wobbled, its nose dipped before it stopped spinning and began rolling backwards. The thrust of the main engine began to slow it. Ten meters from the building, the shuttle slowed to a stop. With the main engine firing, the shuttle began moving back up the runway. Seth cut the power to the main engine. The shuttle rolled to a stop.

The Marines began to clap. Seth turned to look at them. They were smiling at him. The pilot wasn't clapping. He was pale, looking as if he were about to throw up.

CHAPTER 32

Seth ignored the Marines' praise as he checked the gauges to make sure the outside air was breathable. The habitation engines might be changing the atmosphere to be less hospitable for humans, however the gauges confirmed the outside air was still breathable. He yelled as he ran past the Marines, "We have to shut down those towers!"

Seth opened the shuttle's door. The wind whipping into the shuttle almost blew him off his feet. The wind was reaching hurricane levels. The thick, moisture-laden air made it difficult to breathe. There wasn't much time to stop this before it became too dangerous to be outside.

Head down, he fought his way out of the shuttle with the Marines following him. The pilot closed the shuttle's door as they left. Seth led the Marines towards the north tower. They walked bent over, struggling against the wind. The Marines held their snub-nosed Plasma rifles at the ready as they scanned for insane colonists.

The north tower was 200 meters from the runway. The shortest distance to the tower was along the runway and through a field. Once they left the runway, they found the dirt in the field was clay. The growing pools of water on the clay made it slippery to walk.

The storms were strengthening. The constant barrage of lightning followed by thunder was high in the atmosphere, but the sound was deafening. The rain swirled with ever growing intensity. It felt like metal projectiles as it hit their eyes.

All they could do was use their hands to shield their eyes. They walked looking down at the feet of the person in front of them.

Seth continued to lead. He took quick glances up into the punishing rain to keep them going towards the tower.

The wind was reaching the level of a moderate hurricane. Soon it would begin spawning tornados. Once that happened, it would be impossible for them to reach the tower, even more impossible to fly the shuttle off the moon.

The increasing wind began picking up pieces of dirt from the ground. The dirt hit them like a boxer's punch. A Marine was hit in the head knocking off his helmet. When he retrieved the helmet, he found a stone embedded in it. If not for the helmet, his head would have received the full force of the stone.

They were drenched and exhausted by the time they reached the tower. They huddled against the tower's base where the wind was the weakest. The tower's surface was smooth, there was nothing for them to gain a handhold. The sound of the wind here was so loud it was painful. They needed to cover their ears with their hands as they pressed themselves into the tower's base.

Seth looked for some way to get inside the tower. He couldn't see an opening or a door. They were on the inland side of the tower. The way in must be on the other side of the tower. The wind would reach its maximum force in minutes. Once it reached that level, without anything to hold onto, they would be sucked off the tower's base.

Seth concentrated on what he'd seen of the towers from space. They were on the edge of the cliffs, with huge pipes coming up from the ocean to supply water to them. The door to get in the tower must be on the ocean side. He had only seconds to guess whether it was to their right or their left. If he guessed wrong, the pipes might stop them before they reached the door. If that happened, they wouldn't have enough time to go around to the other side of the tower before the increasing ferocity of the wind would suck them off like ragdolls.

Seth guessed the door was to their right. He began sliding along the tower with his face pressed against its surface, eyes closed to protect them from the blowing rain, as he felt blindly for a door. The Marines slid along behind him. He could hear the ocean waves crashing against the cliffs as they came around the ocean side of the tower. He still hadn't come to a door. He could feel the wind beginning to pull him off the tower. He opened his eyes for an instant. He could see a huge pipe directly in front of him. He'd guessed wrong. The door must be on the other side.

Just then, his hand touched a door frame. He opened his eyes again. The rain immediately assaulted them. Ahead of him was the door. He slid across to grab the door's handle as he pushed to open it. It wouldn't move. The door opened inward, but the wind suction kept the door from opening. Seth pushed on it with all his weight. It still wouldn't move. One of the Marines joined him. They both began pushing on the door. The door moved only a fraction. A second Marine slid next to them. All three of them put their weight into the door. It flew open.

The four of them staggered into the tower, shutting the door behind them. There was no wind inside the tower, but the roar from outside, coupled with the sound of the tower's equipment, was even more deafening.

It was dark inside the tower until one of the Marines turned on his flashlight. Two other Marines followed with theirs. The tower was enormous compared to his father's Habitation Engine. Seth had the Marine's use their flashlights to look for a control panel. They found one on the wall just inside the door.

Seth studied the controls. It had strange symbols next to an array of levers, buttons, and gauges. However, the more he studied it, he recognized it had all the elements of his father's invention. One gauge showed the volume of water being drawn up from the ocean, another the mixers that added the compounds needed to change the atmosphere, a third the levels of ionized gases being released. What he didn't see was a lever to shut the system down.

There wasn't a master power shutoff on the control panel, but he found an unmarked red lever just on the side of the panel. That had to be it. He could hear the tornadoes beginning to form outside the tower. If this wasn't the way to shut down this tower, they would be stuck in here until he found a way to turn it off.

Seth pulled the red lever. Immediately the giant turbines bringing water up from the ocean began to slow. They continued spinning from momentum as the deafening sound they made began to decrease. The sound outside began to lessen as well. After several minutes, they could hear the storm beginning to abate outside.

The Marines were smiling.

"We're not done. We have to shut down the other tower," Seth said.

He led them out of the tower. The door opened more easily in the diminishing wind. It continued raining, but the rain fell straight down, which didn't make it necessary to shield their eyes as they walked along the coast to the second tower. The second tower continued to spew dark clouds.

When they reached the second tower, the wind was less than half as intense as it was when they'd left the first tower. Inside the tower, Seth pulled its red lever to shut it down. The hum of the turbines grew quieter as they left the tower.

They were all soaked and exhausted. The rain was abating. The sky overhead had black clouds still laced with lightning followed by loud cracks of thunder. One of the Marines pointed to the lightning, "Is that dangerous?"

"The lightning comes from the ionized molecules generated by both towers. It's not likely to hit the ground. Now that the towers are shut down, it will stop soon. The dark clouds will dissipate in a few days."

They were southeast of the human colony. The shortest path back to the shuttle was through the Alenian dwellings south of the human compound. The air inland was thick with fog limiting their visibility. The Marines said it would be safer to return the way they came, along the coast. The fog was lighter there, easier to see if they encountered any insane colonists. Seth insisted they take the shorter path. He wanted to see the Alenian structures. The Marines finally relented. Most likely they felt they owed Seth for saving the mission, not to mention their lives.

As they walked, the fog began to lift. The Marines walked ahead scanning for signs of trouble. They came to the Alenian structures. They were identical one-story structures made of adobe with flat roofs. Each one was ten meters square and three meters tall. The buildings were closely spaced in parallel rows. Between the long rows of buildings was a narrow dirt path.

Seth walked up to one of the structures. It had a green wood door with windows made of a transparent cellophane-like material. He began to open the door when one of the Marines stopped him. "I'd like to see what's inside," Seth told him.

The Marine signaled for the other two to check out the building. The two Marines cautiously entered the structure with their guns up. The third Marine stood in front of Seth. After a couple of minutes, the Marines came out of the building. They said it was safe for Seth to go inside.

Seth entered the adobe structure. It was a living unit. There was a living room with woven mats for seats but no tables. There were two bedrooms with neatly rolled up sleeping mats with a cylindrical piece of green wood that served as a pillow. It had a kitchen with a ceramic cooktop, which meant they had electricity in their dwellings. The shelves were neatly stacked with dishes, serving pieces, and cookware made of fired clay. A table in the kitchen was made of the same green wood as the front door. The table was low to the ground with woven grass mats on the floor for seats.

It had a bathroom with a clay basin for washing, a large clay bathtub, but only a hole in the floor for a toilet. Seth could see that their furnishings would support the assumption the Alenians were human sized creatures.

When Seth came out of the building, the fog had lifted enough for him to see down the road. There were identical living units as far as he could see. Thousands of them. It substantiated the assumption that tens of thousands of Alenians once lived here.

Seth wanted to check out more of the living units, but the Marines said they should get back to update the Major on the situation. Seth reluctantly agreed. They walked up the dirt road between the living units with the Marines watchful for any insane colonists.

North of the Alenian living units was the human compound. Several Quonset huts faced each other across a large open area. The huts were made of semicircular cross-sections of prefabricated galvanized steel. Each hut was twenty meters wide, forty meters long, with a door in the front and a half-dozen windows along each side. Quonset huts like these were commonly used by the Empire when temporary buildings were needed in outlying planets. From their weather-discolored shells, the Quonset huts must have been constructed shortly after the first humans arrived thirty years ago.

One of the Quonset hut doors was open as they walked through the compound. Seth peered in. Two rows of bunk beds were overturned, as was a ping pong table. Along one wall, a holographic game player was smashed into pieces.

One of the Marines followed Seth's gaze. He said he had been stationed here several years ago, and this is where he bunked.

They continued north to the runway. The clouds generated by the towers had dissipated enough for Seth to see the mountain that boxed in the coastal plain to the ocean. The mountains were tall, their surfaces jagged, indicating they were a young mountain range. They may not be young. The minimal rainfall in the region would not have done much to smooth them.

When they approached the shuttle, the door was open. The Marines crept up to the door with their weapons raised, as Seth followed closely behind. As they reached the door, they overheard the pilot saying the landing was rough, though he managed it. The Marines shook their heads at Seth, then fanned out to guard the shuttle.

Seth entered the shuttle. The pilot looked guilty as he saw that Seth had overheard his conversation. He handed Seth the comm mic. "The Major wants to talk to you."

"Yes, Major. This is Seth."

"Tell that pilot we know you landed the shuttle. Now, what are the conditions down there?"

"The pilot heard you. We shut down the towers. The storms they created are dying. The dark clouds you see will take some time to dissipate. The lightning is being generated by the ionization from the towers. With the towers shut down, the lightning will end soon. Once it does, you can fly a shuttle through the dark clouds. It will be a bumpy ride, but it will be safe."

"What about the colonists? Are there any alive?"

"We haven't seen anyone."

"Stay by the shuttle. We will be down soon."

CHAPTER 33

Prime was walking to her office when one of the communications officers ran up to her. He bowed quickly, then straightened and said, "I have news of the Alenian mission."

Prime glared at him. She had ordered a blackout of all communications from those on the Alenian mission.

The man hesitated, aware she did not take bad news well. "The rebels attacked the fleet meeting the freighter. Three of the escort cruisers were destroyed. The fourth cruiser was heavily damaged, and their captain was killed."

"What happened to the scientists?"

"The First Officer of the cruiser said the freighter was unharmed. They left without telling him where they were going. He is unsure where they are."

"Have you contacted the freighter?" Prime said, keeping her anger under control, as she had to pull what was happening out of him bit by bit.

"We tried to contact them but received no response. We are not sure if the rebels captured it or if the freighter proceeded on the mission on its own."

Prime stared at the communications officer with an intensity that scared him. "Send two of our fastest scout ships to the wormhole. Have them send a signal through it. If the freighter is at Alenia, they will respond. What happened to the cruiser that escaped?"

"They made it back to Imperial space safely."

"I want all the officers aboard that cruiser imprisoned on charges of criminal negligence of duty. I want them court-martialed, then hung within the week."

The communications officer stood there stunned.

"Do you understand!"

"Yes—yes," he stuttered.

"That's all."

He bowed deeply before backing away quickly.

As he left, Prime feared that if the rebels captured the freighter they would learn of the wormhole. If they gained access to Alenia, it could mean the end of the Empire.

CHAPTER 34

Seth waited outside the shuttle for the Major. The pilot stayed inside. Seth estimated it was late morning based on the angle of their sun, though it was barely visible through the black clouds.

After an hour, the freighter's second shuttle landed. It taxied up to the first shuttle. The Major came out followed by the rest of the Marines. He surveyed the area. Seeing everything was calm, he walked up to Seth. "Stay by the shuttle while we look for the colonists."

One Marine stayed with Seth and the two shuttle pilots. Three hours passed before the Major returned.

The Major addressed Seth, "We didn't find any colonists."

"Did you find any bodies? I didn't see any dead bodies when we walked through the human compound or the Alenian village. From the description of the mayhem that took place here, I would expect to see the area littered with them."

The Major looked concerned as he answered, "We didn't find bodies or anyone alive." He turned abruptly and went back into his shuttle. Seth could hear him having a long radio conversation with the freighter Captain. When he came out, he announced the rest of the team would be coming down with supplies.

Two more hours passed before the freighter's hauler landed. The hauler was five times the size of a shuttle. It stopped on the runway ten meters from the two shuttles.

The rear hatch opened. Six members of the Cauloten Six's crew exited followed by the team. As they left the hauler, all of them scanned the area apprehensively. The team caught sight of Seth. They walked over to him as the crewmen began unloading supplies from the hauler.

"We watched your difficult landing from orbit. We began a small pool at your odds of succeeding. I have to say, I was the only one who bet you would. I won forty Imperial Crowns," Doc said, a big grin plastered on his face.

The Major walked up to them. "We've checked and found no signs of the colonists. You can begin your work." He waved a hand towards the Quonset huts. "You can stay in the barracks hut in the colony."

Professor spoke up, "I understand the colonists lived in the Alenian living units south of the colony. I would prefer finding a suitable Alenian living unit than living in cramped barracks."

The others agreed. They were happy Professor spoke up. Spending three weeks sharing barracks with the Marines wasn't appealing to any of them.

The Major said nothing. His face was tight, as if he were about to deny Professor's request. Instead, he said, "You can use the colonists' living units."

He ordered five Marines to accompany them as they searched for suitable living units. The boxlike Alenian houses began 400 meters south of the Quonset huts. The first Alenian building they encountered was larger than the one Seth had inspected. A Marine checked it was safe before allowing the team to enter. Inside they found rows of tools lined up in racks. There were rakes, hoes, and other hand farming tools.

"These tools support the premise they farmed the land by hand. From their appearance, they are tools humans could use," Professor commented as he surveyed the tools.

Seth remembered the comment in the database about hands or tentacles and smiled.

Outside the shed, Doc pointed out the outlines of a field that went north from where they were standing. "This shed is on the south end of a field. It looks like they built the human colony on Alenian farmland."

They continued down the dirt road to a set of Alenian living units with poles next to them and wires that ran back to the human compound.

One of the Marines spoke up. "I was stationed here a couple of years ago. Those wires bring electricity to the shacks the researchers lived in." Their confused looks hastened the Marine to add, "We called the Alenian houses shacks. The Alenians used small cylindrical power cells that powered the ceramic cooktop and the ceiling lights. The science guys couldn't figure out how the power cells were turned on or off. There were no switches on the power cells or anywhere else in the shack. When they broke open one of the Alenia power cells, all they found inside was some strange looking goop. They had no idea what that was. That's why they ran lines from the compound to bring electricity to these shacks."

Professor said, "Primitive farming tools but sophisticated energy devices. The more we learn about the Alenians, the more interesting they become. The name shack seems a bit antiquated, however, I like it."

They wanted to inspect the shacks. The Marines checked each one before they let the team members enter. These were different from the Alenian living unit Seth had investigated. They had human furniture in the living rooms, regular beds in the bedrooms, kitchens with ovens and ranges, modern cookware and dishes, and full-sized tables and chairs in the eating area. The bathrooms even had showers and a proper toilet.

The one surprising thing in the colonist shacks was their disarray. Some had overturned chairs or tables, some broken dishes, others had the remnants of rotted food on plates as if the occupants left suddenly before finishing their meal.

The team continued further down the road to inspect some of the Alenian living units the humans hadn't occupied. These were identical to the one Seth inspected. Simple and primitive.

Professor commented, "The remarkable thing about the living units the Alenians occupied is how neat they are. They may have lived simply, but they are a very orderly species. It looks like the Alenian occupants of these living units expected to return to them soon. Only a thick layer of dust covering everything contradicts that thesis. As interesting as this is, I think it's time we pick out our shacks."

They agreed and returned to the colonist shacks. They picked shacks closest to the human compound and across the road from each other. As each person selected their shack, Alan gave a pleading look to Seth.

"Do you mind if we share a shack?

Seth said, "Sure, why not?" He could see the relief on Alan's face. Seth had gotten used to being around Alan. He realized he was filling the role of Alan's big brother, like it or not. It was strange to be this close to someone, but not stressful.

The Marines stood guard outside as each team member began to clean up their selected shack.

CHAPTER 35

They hadn't been in their shacks for more than a few minutes when they heard the Major order them to come out. The Major was standing in the road. Once everyone on the team was there, he said, "I'm going to show you around the colony. Remember, you only have three weeks to learn what happened here. You need to work quickly. The sooner you find out what happened, the sooner you can leave.

"These shacks you picked to live in are at the northern edge of the Alenian village. There are 22,000 buildings in the Alenian village, all but a few of them shacks. Most Alenian shacks have two bedrooms, some have three, apparently as family units. It was estimated that over 30,000 Alenians once lived here."

"Are there any other Alenian sites?" Seth asked.

"These are the only Alenian dwellings on the planet. Nothing exists in the Great Desert, and there are no Alenian settlements on the west coast."

"They didn't live there despite the western coastal plain having ample vegetation?" Seth asked.

"This is the only Alenian settlement!" The Major said, as he gave Seth a hard stare.

"Major, you seem to know things about this colony that wasn't in the freighter's files. How is that?" Doc asked.

The Major shifted his hard stare to Doc, "I was the security officer here six years ago." He didn't expand on that. All he said was, "Follow me."

He walked north toward the human compound. He led them to a large oak tree in the compound's center. The tree was surrounded by a few benches giving it a picnic-like setting.

"This open area is called the Common," the Major said. He walked to the east side of the Common as they all followed him. Three Quonset huts on the east side were mirrored by three on the west side. He stopped at the northern most Quonset hut.

They were in front of the one had looked into through the open door.

"The Marines and I will use the racks here," the Major said.

Alan gave Seth a quizzical look. Seth said, "A rack is a bed. This is a barracks."

Alan nodded with a smile.

The Major walked to the next Quonset hut just south of the barracks. "This is the mess hall. We are fortunate the Cauloten Six was carrying food. The ship's crew brought down enough food for the three weeks we will be here. I expect everyone to come to the mess hall for meals. This way we can be sure you are safe." They nodded, knowing when he said safe also meant they hadn't gone insane.

Walking to the last Quonset huts on the east side. "This is the Communications Center. It will serve as my headquarters."

They followed the Major as he walked across the Common. He stopped in front of the northern most of the three Quonset huts on the west side. "This is the medical facility." He addressed Doc, "It should have most of what you will need."

Doc immediately walked to the door. He went inside, the team following him. Cabinets were overturned, some of their glass doors smashed, shards of glass scattered across the floor, drawers from chests had been pulled out and emptied, testing equipment was lying on the floor, some of it broken. Doc shook his head sadly as he came out of the hut. He faced the Major. "I hope I can work here. We will have to clean up the mess before we can determine what still works."

The Major ignored Doc's concerns as he said impatiently, "We need to go on." Everyone filed out. He walked a few steps south before stopping in front of the next building, "This is the Biology facility. It has equipment in there that will aid in learning what happened here. Anyone going in there to ascertain its condition needs to use a bio-suit. There are several protective bio-suits stored in the Communications Center."

The Major walked the group to the last Quonset hut facing the Common. "Alenian artifacts were stored in here."

Alan opened the door. He stood there a second before turning around and saying, "It's a bigger mess than Medical."

The Major waived his hand to draw the team's attention to a group of smaller Quonset huts behind the ones on the west side of the Common. "These were used for storage and equipment maintenance. You can check them out on your own."

The Major faced the team. "There is one building marked with a Do Not Trespass sign. You are not allowed in it. I assure you, nothing in it would have caused the colonists' affliction." He paused as if he was going to field questions, but then he continued, "One more thing you should be aware of. This area is over an active tectonic plate. You may feel small tremors from time to time. There has never been a significant earthquake in the thirty years since this colony has been here–"

The Major was interrupted when a Marine approached carrying a duffel bag. He laid it on the ground in front of the Major. The Major reached into the bag and pulled out a holster with a Stinger pistol. "I have a weapon for each of you. I recommend you always carry it. There is still the possibility some of the former colonists are alive. If you come across one, remember, they are dangerous. Don't hesitate to use lethal force. Is there anyone here who needs training to use a pistol?"

Everyone shook their head except Alan, who said, "I do. I've never used one."

The Major said, "I'll have one of the Marines show you."

"Don't bother, Major. I'll show him how to use it," Seth said.

The Marine who brought the duffel bag began handing out a Stinger pistol to each team member. Alan held the holster with its pistol as if it were a snake about to bite him.

The Major asked, "Any questions?"

"Have you found out what happened to the bodies of the dead colonists?" Seth asked.

"We believe the colony robots may have removed the bodies. We haven't yet found what they did with them."

Professor said, "You mean robots are roaming the grounds?"

"There are a few maintenance robots that maintain the colony. They do most of their work at night."

"Isn't it dangerous to have these robots roaming around when you consider the mayhem that went on here?"

"I doubt the robots had anything to do with what happened here. They are housed in one of the storage buildings. My men will check them before we allow them to continue their duties. Are there any more questions?"

They heard the hauler taking off.

"The hauler is returning to the freighter. A few of the freighter crew will stay here to help guard the colony. One of them is a cook who is preparing a meal for us. It will be dark in two hours. Go eat. After you eat, return to your shacks before nightfall. Tomorrow the Marines will search more extensively for any colonists who might still be alive."

The idea the night might be dangerous played on each team member's mind as they followed the Major to the mess hall.

The eating area in the mess hall had a dozen tables, each seating eight. One end of the hut was walled off with a door leading to a kitchen and a food storage pantry. The team selected a table near the front of the mess hall close to the kitchen. The Marines went to the far end of the mess hall and pulled two tables together. The Major joined the Marines.

Doc went into the kitchen to make sure the cook had followed his orders not to serve any colonist's food or water until he told him it was safe. Returning, he sat down with the team.

Alan asked, "Did the cook follow your instructions?"

"He did. He is in there with two other freighter crew members preparing our meal."

The meal was served in large bowls. It was a stew of synthetic protein with a few real vegetables. The cook did a decent job making it palatable. It wouldn't have mattered though since the team was famished, none of them having eaten since breakfast the day before.

No one spoke while they ate, but when they'd finished, Doc said, "Cleaning up the Medical hut must be a priority. Once we have it working, assuming that's possible considering the mess it's in, Jana and I will begin testing for agents that could have caused what happened here. For now, we need to only drink the bottled water we brought. Even forgo bathing until we have tested the colony's water supply."

Professor spoke quietly so only those at the table could hear, "Despite the Major demanding we concentrate on what happened to the colonists, I have to learn all I can about the Alenians. Once they destroy the wormhole, everything about them will be out of reach. I want to bring back as much as I can about these beings, despite the Major's prohibition we cannot. I may need your help in doing this."

Professor stopped talking as the Major walked up to their table. "It is time to go to your shacks for the night. Remember to adjust your clocks. Alenia has a 32-hour rotation. It is twenty eight hundred five hours Alenia time now. We will meet back here at six hundred hours tomorrow morning. That is one hour after sunrise. Get a good night's sleep."

Two Marines walked the team back to their respective shacks. Seth walked with Doc as they brought up the rear. Seth said, "Do you think Professor is overly optimistic that the Major will let him bring back things from here?"

Doc shook his head and said in a hushed voice, "My friend is caught up in the excitement of finally realizing his life's greatest ambition. He isn't focused on the politics of this situation, or what I perceive as the Major's inflexibility. I still feel this adventure will not go well for us, but I hope I'm being overly pessimistic."

Seth didn't think Doc was.

As they approached their shacks, they passed three of the freighter's crewmen. From their bored, unhappy expressions, they had been pressed into guarding the team's shacks tonight.

CHAPTER 36

The sun was setting. A cool breeze blew through two open windows as Seth and Alan entered their shack.

The two-bedroom shack they'd chosen had a flowery print sofa in the living area. The kitchen was fully equipped with dishes, eating utensils, and cookware, plus it had a cooktop with an oven. However, the refrigerator was mostly empty. It contained a wedge of cheese, an uneaten salad, and two unopened bottles of wine, one red, the other white.

If the pattern on the sofa wasn't enough to tell them they were in a unit once occupied by women, the female clothes in the bedroom dressers were.

"Do you think something here, like in the bedding or the kitchen, caused them to go mad?" Alan asked as he inspected the living unit.

"I hope not. Remember they lived here for a long time without problems," Seth said as he picked up his duffle bag. "Which bedroom do you want?"

Alan chose the room next to the kitchen. Seth went into the other bedroom. The bedding had been slept in and left unmade. He found a small closet in the living room with clean linens. "Change the bedding," he told Alan. "It might keep the crazies from getting us," he said with a grin. Alan returned his grin, before fetching new linens from the closet for himself.

Seth took off his Stinger pistol. He turned to find Alan looking worried.

"What's the matter?"

"This business of carrying a weapon. I detest them." Alan gingerly removed his holster and set it down on the table in the living room.

"Let me show you how to use it."

Seth picked up Alan's weapon. "A Stinger is a compact, lightweight weapon designed to be easy to carry. However, it is a lethal weapon. Only point it at something you want to shoot, not at your friends." Seth smiled as he said it. Alan didn't take it as humorous. For that reason, Seth did not mention that the energy within a Stinger could make a sizeable explosion if its power cell was breached. No need to worry Alan any more than he was already.

Seth checked that the safety was on. It was. He pointed to it. "This is the safety. When it is in this position, the Stinger won't fire." He flipped the safety switch. "Now the safety is off, allowing the weapon to fire." Alan was staring at the Stinger as if it were about to fire on its own.

"I'm putting the safety back on. Now, I want you to hold the pistol in your hand. Remember, never aim it at anything you don't want to kill."

"Isn't there a stun setting?"

"No. This is a lethal weapon. It shoots a plasma beam of charged particles that will make a sizable hole in most things it hits."

"Why is it called a Stinger?" Alan said, still not reaching for the weapon.

Seth held up the pistol. He pointed at the muzzle. "See the small opening in the muzzle. It shoots a single burst of plasma, like the lead bullets old-fashioned gunpowder weapons used to fire. Someone some time ago called it a sting of plasma. I guess to differentiate it from the plasma stream from weapons like the snub-nosed plasma rifles the Marines here have. The plasma rifles can fire single plasma bursts or bathe something in a stream of plasma, whereas the Stinger fires a single burst of plasma each time you pull the trigger. Don't think this weapon isn't as lethal as the Marines' rifle. Even a single plasma burst from a Stinger can go through a person or anything short of an inch-thick steel plate."

The concern on Alan's face didn't change as his eyes panned over the weapon.

Seth smiled. "It's a powerful weapon, but it won't hurt you or anyone else unless you intend it to. Here, take it." He held out the weapon.

Alan took the Stinger pistol, holding it gingerly but pointing it at the floor.

"Now aim it. Remember, the safety is on. It won't fire."

Alan slowly lifted the Stinger as he aimed it at the wall.

"I want you to press the trigger."

Alan gave Seth a worried look.

"It won't fire."

Alan pressed the trigger. Nothing happened.

"That's about what you'll feel when it fires. The Stinger doesn't have a recoil when it fires. That's it. No need for more training on the Stinger. I hope you will never have to use it. If you do, switch off the safety, aim carefully before pulling the trigger. Remember, only point it at something you want to kill. One more thing, if you are holding the weapon while walking, never keep your finger on the trigger. It's too sensitive, you might fire it by mistake. Put your finger along the side of the trigger guard until you are ready to fire. Are you good?"

"As good as I want to be. Thanks for the lesson."

"Then let's get some sleep. I think we'll need to be rested for tomorrow. See you in the morning."

CHAPTER 37

Even after all the day's physical activity, Seth had trouble falling asleep. He had a headache. He couldn't remember the last time he had a headache, at least not as painful as this one. It must have come from walking through the storm to shut down the Alenian towers. He tried to ignore the headache as he attempted to drift off to sleep. As he struggled to sleep, the image of the woman in white came into his mind. He thought of her after Jana kissed him, but before that, he hadn't thought of her for a long time. He didn't know why she was in his thoughts now. He didn't know who she was, or if she was a real person. He assumed she was someone he once saw. If she was, he couldn't remember where he saw her, but her image had been in his mind ever since he was a youngster. When he reached puberty, she became the picture of his ideal woman. She had silky blonde hair, a beautifully featured face, but what struck him was her iridescent blue eyes. Lying in bed, he could see her in his mind as clearly as if she were standing before him. Her image lingered in his thoughts as he finally drifted off to sleep.

Seth woke before his alarm rang. It was 0510 hours. He went into the bathroom. The shower was inviting, but he remembered Doc's warning not to shower or drink the water. The toilet worked. That was good enough for now.

Seth went back to his room to dress. When he came out, he heard the shower running. He yelled at the closed bathroom door to stop the shower. Alan came out of the bathroom in his shorts. He wasn't wet.

Seth said, "Remember what Doc said about avoiding contact with the water?"

"Oh, yeah." Alan showed his embarrassment at forgetting. He returned to the bathroom. Seth heard him turn off the shower. A few seconds later, Alan came out, still looking sheepish at his mistake. He went into his bedroom, coming out dressed minutes later. "Thanks, that might have been bad."

"Better safe than becoming a crazed killer," Seth said with a grin.

It was 0540 hours when they left their shack for the mess hall. Outside, the three bored freighter crewmen guards had been replaced by two Marines. They nodded to the Marines as they passed them.

The sky was still filled with dark clouds. Alan said, "It looks like it could storm any second."

"Those are residual products of the habitation process. They don't have much bite in them. They'll dissipate in a few days."

"Do you think there are more crazed colonists?"

"I don't know. Right now, I'm more interested in what happened to the dead ones. Where are their bodies? For that matter, according to the ship's database, they never found an Alenian burial ground. Does something happen to dead bodies on this moon?"

"You know you can freak me out with a lot less," Alan said.

Seth smiled. "Didn't mean to freak you out."

Doc, Professor, and Gunther were already in the mess hall at the same table they sat at last night. A second later, Jana joined them.

Alan said, "Do I smell something good cooking?"

Doc answered, "The freighter cook has been pressed into service again. He just finished feeding the Marines. We're next. I understand he has real powdered eggs."

The idea of real eggs, powdered or not, was far better than synthetic protein. As they began discussing what to do for the day, the Major entered the mess hall. He walked up to their table. "I have assigned three of the freighter crewmen to guard you today. I want you to stay close to the compound until I tell you it is safe."

"What will you be doing?" Doc asked.

"I am taking the Marines with some freighter crewmen to search the rest of the area." With that, the Major left the mess hall.

He hadn't been gone for more than a minute when three crewmen from the freighter entered the mess hall. Each wore a Stinger like those given to the team, except the crewmen seemed more comfortable wearing them.

One of the crewmen walked over to the table. "My name is Karlson. We were told to make sure nothing happens to you today."

"Good," Doc said. "Have you eaten breakfast?"

"We haven't," Karlson said.

"Then eat. I understand your fellow crew member is making eggs."

They sat at a table a discrete distance from the team. Shortly, everyone was eating a tasty meal of scrambled eggs.

CHAPTER 38

When they'd finished breakfast, Doc said to Karlson, "I want to begin cleaning up the Medical Quonset hut. Is there any problem with that?"

"We were told to keep you safe. No one said we have to keep you in here, so I guess it's okay."

Doc smiled. "One of the best ways to protect us is to come to the Medical hut where you can help us put it back together."

The crewmen looked to Karlson. He shrugged.

"This way." Everyone followed Doc out of the mess hall to the Medical hut.

Under Doc's direction, they swept the glass off the floor, refilled the drawers with their contents, eventually putting everything back in its proper place. With the entire team plus the three crewmen working, they had the Medical hut in order in an hour.

Doc was beginning to check the medical equipment to see what would still work when Gunther walked up to him. "I am good at fixing machines. Let me have a look at them."

"Be my guest," Doc said, pleased at the offer.

Doc took the opportunity to collect blood samples from everyone, including the freighter crew. He even had them fetch the cook from the mess hut to take a sample from him. While Doc was collecting samples of everyone's blood, Gunther completed his inspection of the medical equipment. He identified which pieces of equipment were broken beyond repair. Fortunately, most still worked.

Doc said, "The next thing is to test the colonists' food and water. I'll begin setting up the tests. Jana, I want you to get water samples. Take samples from the mess hall kitchen and any drinking fountains or other water sources in the colony. Also, get water samples from the adobe village. Professor, I want you and Alan to bring back any recent samples of all the original colonists' food from the mess hall. Seth and Gunther, I'd like you to go through the garbage. Bring back what you can find of recent meals they've eaten. All of you wear protective suits, masks, and gloves." Doc pointed to a cabinet containing the protective gear.

Gunther was about to balk at going through garbage, but Seth put an arm around him and said, "We might find a weapon there."

Gunther grunted he wasn't happy, but he followed Seth and put on a protective suit.

The next two hours a procession of team members brought in food and garbage to the Medical hut. One of the freighter crewmen accompanied each team member, but they avoided doing any of the collecting. It didn't take long before they'd filled several tables in the Medical hut with samples of food and garbage. Jana returned with test tubes filled with water.

Doc turned to Professor. "Jana and I have enough here to keep us busy for a long time. Is there something Seth and Gunther can help you with in the Artifacts Quonset hut?"

"Alan says it is more of a mess than your Medical hut. We definitely could use some help. We're going there now."

CHAPTER 39

Gunther and Seth followed Professor and Alan to the Artifacts Quonset hut. Professor suggested the freighter crew could stay outside to guard them. They were happy to comply. Under his breath, he told the team members he feared they would be like bulls in a china shop.

Alan was correct when he said the Artifacts Quonset hut was more of a mess than the Medical hut. Shelves that once stood on the outer walls had been tipped over. The Alenian pottery they held lay scattered on the floor, much of it now broken. Tables in the center of the hut had been overturned, their contents strewn on the floor.

There were free standing cabinets in the rear of the hut for binders containing the researcher's handwritten notes. The cabinets were empty, the binders in them removed, their pages dumped in a large pile in the center of the room.

"I think someone intended to set this on fire," Professor said.

"Fortunately, they hadn't," commented Alan.

There was a large machine at the far end of the hut. Professor walked to it. "This is used to date the artifacts they found." The machine was battered, the sledgehammer that had been used to do it lay next to it on the floor.

"What level of insanity would have made them do all of this?" Professor asked, his anguish was unmistakable.

There was one cabinet with its doors closed. Alan opened it. Inside were several undamaged VID cameras. "I guess these were overlooked."

Professor assigned tasks. He would work with Alan to collect the researchers' notes. Since Gunther had gotten most of Doc's machines working, Professor asked if he could determine if the dating equipment could be salvaged.

Professor asked Seth to begin putting the clay-fired pottery artifacts back on the shelves. For those objects that had been smashed, he asked Seth to collect the pieces he thought belonged to a single object before carefully grouping them on a shelf.

He warned everyone to step carefully to not further damage the pottery scattered across the floor.

Seth righted the overturned shelves. He began picking up the few undamaged pieces. There were vases, plates, cups, other serviceable everyday pottery, and a few decorative objects.

Once he returned all the undamaged pieces to the shelves, Seth began picking up the pottery shards. Besides the pieces of serviceable, everyday cookware, there were decorative pieces that looked like art objects. All these had brightly colored geometric designs. None of them had images of the Alenians. Seth speculated they may have had a religious prohibition against displaying their appearance or were so ugly that they didn't want to display their likeness. He grouped what appeared to belong together on the shelves.

Seth didn't know what to make of these aliens as he gathered the pottery. Did they have hands or tentacles? They had a spaceport and an advanced genetics laboratory. They used power cells in their living units, power cells the researchers here couldn't figure out how they worked, and this was supposed to be a penal colony.

Seth doubted the team would learn much to clarify the mysterious Alenians in three weeks unless the researchers left them the answers. From the state of the Artifacts hut, Professor would have a big job sorting out this mess before he would learn more about the Alenians from these researchers' notes than what was on the ship's database.

Several hours passed as they made progress straightening up the hut. Gunther said the dating equipment was ruined beyond repair. He came over to help Seth collect the pieces of broken Alenian pottery. Eventually, they had all the pottery pieces off the floor and some semblance of continuity on the shelves.

Alan helped Professor put the tables upright in the center of the room. They transferred the pile of researcher's notes from the floor onto the tables. They had begun collating the notes into their original order when a freighter crewman announced it was time for lunch.

They were the first ones in the mess hall. Doc came in with Jana a few minutes later.

Professor asked Doc, "Have you solved what drove the colonists into a killing frenzy?"

"Nothing we've tested so far shows any dangerous bacterium or viruses, nor has Jana found anything with a toxin. We still have a lot more testing to do, though we know the water is safe. We can drink and shower with it." The idea of taking a shower was welcome news since they hadn't had showers in three days.

The cook came out with a bowl of food. It was the same meal of synthetic protein with vegetables in a stew he served last night. No one complained about the tasteless food as they ate in silence.

After lunch, Doc left with Jana to continue running their tests. Professor said he would continue organizing the research papers, and Alan offered to help. Gunther said he was going to the Communications hut to see if he could help them fix the broken equipment. The freighter crewmen said they would continue to guard the colony from the benches in the center of the Common.

Seth followed everyone out of the mess hall. As the freighter crewmen headed to the benches, he ducked out of sight around the corner of the mess hall. There was something he needed to check.

Chapter 40

Seth walked through the field to the first tower he'd shut down. He was ignoring the Major's warning not to leave the human compound. It might be dangerous, but he had his Stinger for protection if he encountered any insane colonists. He had to check something inside that tower.

The tower was quiet except for water dripping down its sides from the vents at the top. The conically shaped tower was over forty meters tall. From a distance its outer shell looked silver, giving it the appearance of a large rocket. As Seth approached, the light hitting it reflected a spectrum of colors. Seth knocked on the tower's shell with his knuckles. It made a dull thudding sound. It could be made of a thin metal, or it could be made of something that wasn't metallic at all.

Seth walked to the door they had forced open. Now it opened easily. Without a flashlight, the dark cavernous interior was unnerving, especially thinking there might be an insane colonist hiding there in the dark. He found his way to the control panel. Enough light was coming through the open door to just make out the controls. Seth searched for a switch that might turn on lights. He found it next to the red shutoff lever.

Once the lights were on, Seth could see the pipes that brought water up from the ocean. They were connected to large tanks. The water would be mixed with chemicals in these tanks to transform the atmosphere. The tanks were connected to a chamber that ionized the water before it was sprayed out the vents at the top of the tower.

In every way, this was identical to the Habitation Engine his father invented. The difference was in size. His father's Habitation Engines were small compared to this. To transform a planet's atmosphere required many of his father's Habitation Engines. The few towers that ran along this continent's eastern coast were huge enough to alone transform the atmosphere of this moon.

The reason Seth wanted to inspect this tower wasn't just to learn how much it was like his father's invention, it was to learn how two of the towers went into an Initiation Phase. This moon had already been transformed into a human breathable atmosphere by the Alenians. For an Initiation Phase to be run in only two towers wouldn't be an attempt to change the atmosphere, it was done by someone who wanted to create enough localized turbulence to stop a shuttle from landing. The only other explanation for the Initiation Phase to run was by accident or due to a mechanical failure, but for it to happen in only two towers was an unlikely coincidence.

Seth studied the controls of this alien habitation engine. He couldn't read the Alenian writing, but the controls were similar enough to his father's Habitation Engine he could ferret out how it operated. His father's system had a timer that automatically ran to maintain a human breathable atmosphere. This system didn't have a timer. It meant it had to be run manually. His father's system had separate controls for the Initiation Phase. Here the controls were integrated. When he shut the power down the operating controls were not changed. They were set to full-on, that would be the Initiation Phase setting. Manual controls meant someone had set the Initiation Phase in the two towers. They had to have done it when the freighter entered orbit. That meant, at least one of the colonists was still alive.

Seth continued to study the control panel settings when he heard a sound outside. He could hear footsteps approaching the open door. He turned the lights off and hid in the shadows. He pulled out his Stinger pistol as he watched the door. A figure stepped into the doorway. All Seth could see was a silhouette, but he recognized it by its stance. He turned the lights on, making sure to first holster his pistol.

The Marine turned quickly towards Seth, aiming his plasma weapon at him.

"Slow down, Marine. It's just me here."

The Marine lowered his weapon. "The Major is looking for you."

Seth turned off the lights before following the Marine out the door. Jana was waiting outside. She walked up to Seth. "The Major came into the Medical hut looking for you. He said he couldn't find you, and Doc guessed you might be here. I tagged along with the Marine to make sure you were safe."

"Thanks for the concern. I wanted to have another look at the habitation engine."

Jana poked her head in the door. "This is impressively big. Is it similar to your father's?"

"It's a lot larger, but basically, it's the same mechanism. My father's towers are smaller, rectangular towers. His towers use a fusion reactor for power. I have no idea what the Alenians used as an energy source. The towers here are almost identical to my father's Habitation Engines. They both discovered the same system to rapidly transform a planet's atmosphere, maybe it's the only way."

The Marine interrupted, "The Major wants to see you. Now!"

They began walking back toward the colony. The Marine walked ahead of them cradling his weapon.

Seth told Jana, "Until today, I wasn't sure why they included me on the team."

"Well, we know someone made the right decision to include you, otherwise we would still be on the freighter. Without you, coming here would have been a waste of time."

"They couldn't know someone would try to sabotage our mission using the habitation engines."

"Is that what happened? Did someone deliberately do that?"

"That's what I found. The habitation engines had to be manually set to the Initiation Phase. Someone didn't want us to land."

"You better tell the Major we aren't alone."

"I intend to."

Jana tugged at Seth's arm to slow him down. Once the Marine was far enough ahead that he couldn't hear her, she whispered in Seth's ear. "I overheard the Marines talking about you. One of them said they had orders to watch you. Do you know why the Marines would be so interested in you?"

Before Seth could react to what Jana said, the Marine stopped. He turned to face them. "You better stay close," he said. He waited until they walked past him before following close behind. It made having a private conversation impossible.

They walked in silence. Suddenly they heard a groan from the Marine. They turned to see him standing there with an odd look on his face. He stood there for a second with this strange look. Then he fell forward. There was a hand pickaxe sticking out of the back of his head.

CHAPTER 41

A man was standing behind the dead Marine. He was holding another pickaxe in his hand. The wild look in his eyes made it clear he was one of the insane colonists. He began to run at them screaming as he waved a pickaxe above his head.

Seth reached for his Stinger. But before he could pull it from his holster, he heard a shot. Jana had fired at the charging man. He had a hole in his side, but he continued charging. Jana fired again. This one blew a hole in the middle of the man's chest. He fell forward, his outstretched hand with the pickaxe hit the ground centimeters from Jana's feet.

"One of the insane colonists," Jana said.

Seth said nothing but agreed as he slid his Stinger back into his holster.

"Do you think this is who set the habitation engine?"

"I don't know. But if one of the colonists is alive, there may be others."

"We have to tell the Major," Jana said as she holstered her Stinger.

They ran back to the compound. They found the Major in the Communications hut. He was watching a Marine and Gunther work on a piece of damaged communications equipment. Three other Marines sat watching them.

The Major turned around to face them. "Mr. Harthset, it seems you can't follow orders even when they are made to protect you."

Jana cut in, "We encountered one of the insane colonists. He killed the Marine who went to find Seth. I killed the colonist."

Seth had never killed anyone. It could explain why he was slow reaching for his Stinger. The terrifying feeling of seeing the Marine die at their feet as the man charged them was still pumping adrenaline through him. Jana looked relaxed as she told the Major what had happened.

"Where was this?"

"In the field not far from the northernmost tower," Jana said.

The Major barked at the Marines, "You three go check the bodies, then bring them back here." They ran out of the hut.

The Major turned on Seth, "This wouldn't have happened, if you hadn't gone off on your own!"

"I needed to check how the Initiation Phase started. It has to be set manually. It meant someone set the tower to go into the Initiation Phase. Someone wanted to keep us from landing."

"Was that this insane colonist?" he asked Seth.

"I have no idea."

"Maybe they go insane when they see other people, the rest of the time they are more rational," The Major said.

Seth didn't think the man who killed the Marine could have been rational enough to set the controls of two habitation engines.

The Major turned to the Marine working with Gunther.

"Where are the freighter crewmen?"

"They're about to return to the freighter," the Marine said.

"Is this equipment working?"

"Voice only," Gunther answered.

"Connect me with the freighter."

In a few seconds, Captain Hollinsky's voice came over the speaker. "This is Hollinsky."

The Major grabbed the microphone. "I am keeping your six crewmen here for a while longer."

Hollinsky began to protest. The Major cut him short, "I will tell you when they can return." He ended the call.

"Get the rest of the research members here," the Major said to the last Marine.

He ran out. A few minutes later the door of the Communications hut opened. The rest of the team came in followed by the Marine.

"Your Marine told us we had to come now. I was in the middle of a critical test that I will have to redo. I see that you've found Seth, so why have we been summoned with such haste?" Doc said, not hiding the frustration he was feeling.

The Major bristled as he scanned the group. "Whenever I summon any of you, I expect you to come immediately. It seems there was at least one surviving insane colonist. He killed a Marine before Ms. Walkner killed him. That means more colonists might be alive who have evaded our search. I am leaving the freighter crew here to guard you while we search for more colonists."

"I thought you checked the area when we first arrived," Doc said.

"There are thousands of shacks. We cannot search them all."

"We need to continue our work. If we must stop each time something happens, we will never learn what happened here. Please bring back the dead colonist. An autopsy might help explain how they became insane."

The Major gave Doc a hard stare, "You can continue your work, but be watchful. If you see any colonist, don't hesitate to shoot them."

With that, the Major left the hut, followed by the Marine.

CHAPTER 42

The team sat in the Communications hut asking Seth and Jana about their encounter with the colonist. It continued to bother Seth that Jana seemed unphased by what she did as she talked about killing the man.

The three freighter crew members who guarded them earlier came into the hut looking unhappy.

"We're here to guard you, again," Karlson said.

"Good," Doc said. "While the Major continues his search for insane colonists, I want to investigate the other Quonset huts not on the Common. I need some supplies for the Medical hut. One of the Marines told me there were medical supplies in those huts. I want to see what is there that I can use."

Karlson checked with his two companions. "Okay," he said.

The team filed out of the Communications hut. They went to the small Quonset hut directly behind the Medical hut. Seth went to open the door when Karlson put a hand on Seth, stopping him. "You better let us check it out first."

Seth backed away as Karlson drew his weapon and slowly opened the door. Looking over his shoulder, Seth saw a large machine in the hut's center. Karlson walked into the hut. A short time later he came out. "It's safe."

The team went in. Doc walked up to the large machine. "Now we have something," he said with a big smile. "This is an MTS machine. I was hoping they had something like this here." Doc sounded like he had just gotten a birthday present.

Seth remembered his mother was just as elated when they came to a planet with an MTS machine. That happened only twice. Both times had been planets with prosperous mining colonies that could afford an expensive Multi-wave-length Tomography Scanner. On most outer planets, the health facilities had old fashioned human diagnostic equipment like X-ray or CT scanners. The MTS was the gold standard. When Seth asked her why, she said the MTS could scan inside a person's body using different wavelengths. It could build a 3-D VID showing details within a body down to very small blood vessels.

The team fanned out to check the rest of the building. There were eight, one meter tall cylinders standing against the wall. There were undamaged cases of medical supplies in the rear of the hut. Doc found there were anesthetics, bandages, and other medical supplies. "This will be helpful," he said.

They went to the next hut. Karlson went in with another of the crewmen to inspect it. When he signaled it was safe, the team went in. It was a workshop with shelves holding spare parts to repair the researchers' equipment. Gunther showed a great deal of interest in it. The rest of them wanted to move on to the next hut.

The next Quonset hut had a sign on the door labeled Storage. Opposite the door was a row of cabinets. The backs of the cabinets were facing them. A sign taped to the center of the cabinets read Archive Research Materials.

Professor smiled at seeing the sign. "The researcher's notes in the Artifacts hut were only from the past few years. They had to have some place where they stored older material."

Jana asked, "Why does it smell like there was a fire in here?" She was right. It smelled like something had burned in the Quonset hut.

Seth walked around the cabinets. The cabinet doors were open, their shelves empty. The binders that once filled those shelves lay open on the floor. Paper from the binders had been used as fuel for a fire. A large pile of blackened ash remained in the middle of the room.

Professor came from behind Seth to see the burnt pile. He picked up one of the empty binders. Checking the writing on the binder he said, "Oh no. These are notes made by the researchers here from the earliest days of this colony." Professor looked disconsolate as he scanned the room. "Someone wanted to destroy all the work they did on Alenia. Thirty years of research. Why would anyone want to do that?"

Alan picked up an empty binder and began using it to sift through the black-ened ash. As he shifted the ash around, unburned papers appeared under the ash. He said, "They didn't burn it all."

Professor said to the team, "You go on. Alan and I will stay here to see what we can salvage."

One freighter crewman stayed to guard them while the rest of the team went to the next hut. This one was larger than the other service huts. It had a regular door plus a wide roll-up shutter door. Karlson opened the regular door. It was too dark inside to see what was there. He took a cautious step in. He was inside for several minutes before coming out shaking his head.

"Is everything all right?" Seth asked.

"It's a little weird in there, though safe," Karlson said.

The team walked in only to come face to face with a dozen robots. These were metallic bodied working robots. They varied in size from heavy lifters to smaller robots used for domestic chores. Some had wheels, others had legs, some as many as six. The larger robots had continuous band treads for propulsion. A few had claws for grasping, but most had articulated human-like hands to perform human applicable tasks.

One thing they all had were heads. It was found that humans related better to robots with heads that had eyes and a mouth. The eyes weren't usually their only visual sensors. The mouth was no more than a grill over a speaker for the robot to emit sounds, most of the time to acknowledge the commands it was given.

The robots here stood silently against the wall. Their eyes reflected the light in a way that eerily seemed to follow the team as they walked around.

"These robots are unsettling," Professor said. "The Major said they are safe, but they appear to be staring at us."

The robots took up a quarter of the Quonset hut. A door in the rear of the robot's section led to the other side of the hut. There they found several land vehicles. There were two trucks, an all-terrain car, a tractor, and one motorcycle. A large rollup door at the rear of the hut allowed the vehicles to exit.

The next hut had cables running from it to the poles that supplied electricity to the compound. Inside was a small autonomous nuclear reactor. Seth was familiar with this type of reactor. It was used to power his father's Habitation Engines.

This one could operate for thirty years without requiring maintenance. Since the colony had been here for over thirty years, Seth checked a tag on the reactor to see when it was installed. "This one was replaced twenty years ago, we have another ten years of electricity if we need it," he said playfully.

They moved on to the next Quonset hut. This one had paper goods, some canned food, toothpaste, trash bags, and other supplies to support the colony. Better still, the rear of the hut was filled with clothes. Pants, shirts, jackets, clothes of every size, even shoes, all outer planet working clothes.

Doc said, "I doubt any of you would mind if we got out of these coveralls and into something more comfortable." They enthusiastically agreed.

They sent one of the freighter crewmen to tell Professor and Alan of their find. Soon they joined them in the search for new clothes. In deference to the other team members who had no clothing of their own, Jana and Seth continued to wear the freighter's coveralls and not the clothes they had in their duffle bags. But they too found new clothes. Jana used the only changing room. The men changed in the main area of the Quonset hut. Everyone found something new to wear with Professor and Gunther being the happiest to have new, better fitting clothes.

Now in their new clothes, they walked to the last Quonset hut. It had a Do Not Trespass sign. The door had a chain with a lock securing it. Doc said, "I guess this is the one the Major told us we needn't consider as a cause for the insanity."

"Why should we believe him? What is in this building the Major doesn't want us to see?" Gunther said it more as a thought spoken aloud than seeking a response.

Finished inspecting the service Quonset huts, they returned to the Common. Before they did, Doc had them stop to collect medical supplies, which each carried back to the Medical hut. Since they were all in the Medical hut, Doc took his daily blood sample from them.

They went to the mess hall to wait for the Major. The cook was just beginning preparations for supper as they discussed what they'd seen in the outlying Quonset huts.

CHAPTER 43

They had just finished eating supper when the Major entered the mess hall followed by the Marines. The Major sat down at the table with them while the Marines went into the galley looking for something to eat.

"I see you've found new clothes. That means you've inspected the other Quonset huts," the Major said. He turned to Seth. "You're sure the habitation engine was set manually?"

"Yes. I'm sure."

"We checked as many Alenian dwellings as possible, but we didn't find any colonists. We did find the colonist's bodies. There is a grave site southwest of the compound. The ground was too disturbed to make an accurate count. The best guess is there are sixty-nine graves. Adding the fifteen colonists the freighter crew captured and the one Ms. Walkner killed today would account for the eighty-five colonists that were here."

"Who buried them?" Seth asked.

"There was a robot near the graves. One of my men checked it. He found it was programmed to bury a body. It is possible the colonist you encountered set the robot to bury the dead. It is also possible the robot did it on its own."

"This idea of a robot burying people is disturbing," Professor said.

"We put it in the shed with the other robots. All of the robots have been turned off."

The Major stood up to leave, stopped, and addressed Doc, "We left the dead colonist in the Medical Hut. I believe we have accounted for all the colonists. You can vigorously pursue your investigation to learn what happened here."

With that, the Major joined the Marines at the far end of the mess hall.

"A robot burying people on its own. It seems incredible, if not utterly dangerous. He says they guess all the colonists are accounted for. What if they're wrong?" Professor said.

Seth agreed with Professor. A guess wasn't an assurance that there were no other insane colonists. The more Seth thought about it, the more he believed the insane colonist Jana killed was too insane to set the habitation engines to the Initiation Phase. There was more going on here which begged for better answers.

Doc got up from the table. "Jana, will you assist me in autopsying the colonist?"

"I guess it's the least I can do after killing him."

Doc left with Jana. Professor said he was tired and needed to catch up on the sleep he lost on the freighter's lumpy mattress. Gunther said he needed a walk. That left Alan sitting alone at the table with Seth.

"Do you think the autopsy will tell Doc what drove the colonists insane?" Alan asked.

"If there is anything in the dead colonist that could tell us what happened here, I'm sure Doc will find it."

They decided to call it a day. As they walked back to their shack, only a few dark clouds were left from those generated by the habitation engines. This was the first look they had from Alenia to see the gas giant it orbited. The huge planet with its painted bands of orange, yellow, and red covered half the sky.

"Beautiful," Alan said, looking up at the gas giant.

"Yeah, it's quite a sight." Seth pointed to several small slivers of light next to the gas giant. "Those are other moons orbiting this big guy. I bet it has quite a few moons."

"Is there a chance we could collide with one of those moons?" Alan asked a slight tinge of fear in his voice.

Seth laughed. "Always a chance, but not likely. It seems more likely that this moon was once an independent planet orbiting the star that had the misfortune of being captured by the gas giant. My guess is it happened a long time ago. Maybe you can learn more about that from the researchers' notes."

Alan frowned. "Putting the notes back together in the Artifacts hut or finding anything useful from the burned papers in the Archives hut will take months. I doubt we will learn much in three weeks."

They'd arrived at their shack. Alan yawned. "I guess I'm more tired than I thought. I'm going to bed."

Seth watched as Alan went into his bedroom. Seth didn't feel tired enough to go to sleep. He sat on the living room sofa to consider what had happened. It bothered him that Jana showed no remorse in killing the colonist. He felt uncomfortable over the man's death. Maybe they could have subdued him, possibly returned him to sanity. He hoped the man didn't die in vain. He hoped Doc could find something in the autopsy explaining why these people became insane killers.

CHAPTER 44

Prime was at her desk reviewing reports on the rebel's activities. Their raids on Imperial shipping were increasing. In the past, they conducted most of their raids near the outer planets. Now they were attacking ships around the Core planets. They had elevated themselves from a nuisance to a more dangerous threat. It was increasing pressure on her to stop the rebels. It was pressure she didn't need.

The communications officer came to her desk and bowed. He retained the bow, waiting for her to acknowledge him.

"Yes."

He straightened up. "The two scout ships you sent to the wormhole encountered rebel ships. The rebels have been more active in the sector after the attack on our cruisers. While one of the scout ships drew the rebels away, the other sent a message through the wormhole. They received a reply from Major Krugar. The freighter Cauloten Six is orbiting Alenia. Major Krugar is on the moon along with the scientists. Communications with him are limited to voice only, he reports. Most of the comms equipment in the colony was destroyed. Here is Major Krugar's message." He handed Prime a note.

All members of the colony dead. Cause for their actions not yet identified. Widespread damage throughout the colony, but element secured. Not sure if element caused this, but I doubt it. Harthset proved useful, but not in the way we thought. We will continue to watch him.

"What of the scout ship that received the message?"

"It has been hiding from the rebel patrols."

"Tell them to continue hiding but return to the wormhole daily to get any updates from Major Krugar. Impress on them that their lives depend on not revealing the entrance to the wormhole."

He bowed and left quickly.

Prime drummed the pen she was holding on her desk. Knowing what killed the colonists could be extremely useful if it could be weaponized. Even more important was Krugar returning with the element. Her plans to destroy the rebels depended on it.

CHAPTER 45

Seth was up before Alan. He enjoyed having a shower, especially after finding a fragrant smelling soap and a bottle of shampoo in the medicine cabinet. The shampoo did a far better job cleaning his matted hair than the lye soap he carried. Alan was waiting in the living room to go in next when he came out. "Try the shampoo. It works well."

They were on their way to the mess hall before 0550 hours. The mess hall tables were empty except for one of the freighter crewmen taking a break from his kitchen duties.

"Where is everyone?" Seth asked the crewman.

"The Major with his Marines came in early to eat. They don't care about keeping to a schedule. We had to hustle to get them fed. They ate, then they left. They didn't tell me where they were going," he said in a snarky tone.

The mess hall smelled of something interesting. Alan poked his head into the kitchen. "Are those real pancakes?"

The cook looked up from the griddle where a dozen pancakes were cooking. "Doc said the colonists' food was safe to use. They had flour. Yeah, they're real."

Alan came out to tell Seth about the pancakes. Alan's excitement about having pancakes for breakfast made Seth think Alan might be a linguistic genius, but he was still a kid in many ways.

A few minutes later, the rest of the team came into the mess hall. Doc and Jana looked tired. Before Seth could ask, Doc said, "We were up all night conducting the autopsy on the dead colonist. We've taken a lot of tissue and blood samples that need to be tested to understand what made him act the way he did. The Medical hut doesn't have the equipment to conduct the tests we need. We will need to check out the Biology hut to see if it has testing equipment to evaluate these samples. But first we need to eat."

They feasted on the pancakes, as Doc and Jana had several cups of coffee. At the end of the meal, Doc said, "Now we need all of you to help us. Jana and I will go into the Biology hut wearing the protective bio-suits. Gunther, I want you to get disinfectant from the Medical hut. We have several gallons of it. You must spray us down as a precaution against bringing an infectious agent out with us. Seth and Alan, please work with Gunther to build a secure shower that will catch the disinfectant runoff. We can't have it running loose in case we encounter something nasty. Professor, will you please supervise?"

Gunther headed off to the Medical hut, but before Seth could leave, Doc pulled him close.

Seth told Alan he would catch up with him. He turned to Doc, "What's up?"

"I have some concerns about Gunther. I've never heard of a weapons expert who wasn't a member of the Imperial Guard. On our first night, I heard him come to his hut at 2 a.m. Last night, I took a break from the autopsy at 3 a.m. I saw Gunther walking through the Common. Maybe he is an insomniac, but it seems he was sneaking about rather than taking a stroll."

"Are you thinking he is a spy for the Major or Prime?"

"That's exactly what I fear. I suggest being careful what we say around him."

Seth didn't have time to think about this more as he left to join Alan in the Supply hut. They found materials to build a decontamination shower using plastic pipes to build a frame, plastic sheets to contain the spray, and a large tub to catch any runoff.

Gunther brought three two-liter containers of disinfectant along with the sprayer that came with them, then he Seth and Alan built the shower.

Jana and Doc put on the bio-suits they found in the Communications hut. The bulky suits were made even bulkier by the oxygen tank strapped to their backs.

All was ready. Doc and Jana lumbered into the Biology hut. The plan was for them to come out in twenty minutes. When there was no sign of them after thirty minutes, Seth began pounding on the door as he called to them.

Doc came out first. Gunther waved him over to the shower, but Doc pulled off his hood. "No need. The Biology hut is clean. It has an excellent environmental control system. It's as clean in there as the best cleanroom." Doc said.

Jana came out next. She pulled off her hood. "Doc, you're right. Someone was running tests during the attack."

She explained it to the rest of the team. "Someone had been running tests on blood samples for various toxic substances. Time stamps on the tests indicate they were being run about the same time the colonists were killing each other. Whoever was doing the testing didn't find any pathogens."

"Does that mean there are more colonists alive?" Professor asked.

"It means the person who ran these tests wasn't infected, or they were not infected at the time. However, if the Major's count is correct, they didn't survive."

Seth helped Jana out of her bio-suit. Gunther helped Doc remove his.

Once free, Doc said, "With the Biology hut available, we can begin testing the samples we collected from the autopsy. Along with the samples that were tested when the colonists were going insane, we should learn a lot about what happened here."

Professor said, "You won't need me then. I'm going to the Artifacts hut to continue organizing the notes."

"I'll join you," Alan said.

Seth asked Gunther, "Are you interested in seeing what's in the hangar?"

"I went over to check it out yesterday. The doors are locked."

"Let's see if we can find a way in."

"Might as well. There's nothing for me to do here."

CHAPTER 46

Seth considered what Doc said about Gunther possibly being a spy. None of them knew much about Gunther since he had kept to himself on the Cauloten Six and said very little at their meals in the mess. He wanted to see what he could learn from Gunther. If he was a spy, it wouldn't be wise to directly confront this giant of a man.

The hangar was two kilometers north of the colony, the building at the end of the runway Seth almost crashed into with the shuttle. As they walked to the hangar, they came across scattered puddles of water in the field. These were remnants from the rain generated by the towers. Seth crouched down over a puddle. He rubbed his hand across the wet soil and brought his dirt-smeared hand to his face. He smelled it, then he licked the mud. He stood up and stomped down hard with his heel on the ground. It didn't leave much of an impression.

"What are you doing?" Gunther asked.

"This was once a field where the Alenians planted their crops. This soil doesn't absorb the rainwater very quickly. From the smell of it, it is caliche. Caliche is a dense, slow water-absorbing clay. The fact I can't make much of an imprint stomping my foot on this wet dirt means the Caliche runs deep. The taste of this soil tells me it's very acidic and doesn't have many nutrients. If this is typical of the soil in this coastal plain, it would be difficult to grow much of anything here."

Gunther showed little interest in what Seth was saying.

"This is just me being a planetary engineer trying to understand this environment." He shook the dirt off his hand, and they continued walking to the hangar.

"You never said how you came about being on this mission," Seth tried to make it sound like a casual question.

"I said I was on Klatania on business when they came and brought me to the palace."

"What business were you conducting in Klatania?"

"Weapons business."

"Where you buying or selling weapons?"

"Just weapons business," Gunther said in a tone signaling he wasn't going to say more.

They reached the hangar. It was made of prefabricated steel like the colony Quonset huts, but it was much larger, with a peaked rather than semi-circular roof. It was three stories tall with a closed, two-story rolling door facing the runway.

There was a normal door on the side, but as Gunther said, it was locked. Seth found a heavy piece of metal lying in a pile of scrap. He used it to pry the door open. A row of windows running along one wall of the hangar provided enough light for them to see the hangar wasn't empty.

There were two Skimmers inside. Skimmers were two-person flying machines limited to atmospheric flight, typically used for observation.

Seth walked up to the first Skimmer. Its engine had been removed. It was lying on the floor next to the Skimmer.

Gunther pointed at the engine. "This looks like it has blown gaskets. It will be a job getting it to work again."

Seth went to the second Skimmer. It was intact. He crawled into the cabin. He turned on the ignition. All the dials lit up, indicating it was ready to fly. He turned it off.

"It looks like we can get an aerial view of this place," he said as he got out of the Skimmer.

Gunther grunted. "I don't know how to fly."

They walked back to the compound in silence. Seth was concerned that Doc might be right about Gunther being a spy.

CHAPTER 47

They were returning to the compound when Jana walked up to them. "Doc is busy analyzing the samples from the colonist's autopsy. He doesn't need me. Yesterday the Major told me the center of the Alenian village is not far south of here. It has buildings they used for commerce and a research facility. I want to see it, but I'd like some company."

"Sounds interesting. I'll come," Seth said.

"I was there yesterday. I didn't find it interesting. I have something else to do," Gunther said. He walked away briskly to the west side of the Common.

They hadn't gotten to the south end of the Common when Alan came running up to them. "Doc says you're going to inspect the Alenian research facility. Mind if I come along?"

Jana said, "By all means. Three guns might come in handy if we meet up with more colonists."

Seth didn't think Jana would need their help if they encountered more insane colonists.

They walked down a narrow dirt road between rows of Alenian shacks. Twenty minutes later, they arrived at a group of buildings larger than the shacks. They were made of adobe, only one story tall, but they were four to five times the size of the shacks.

The closest building had double green wood doors, apparently the only wood in Alenia. Inside was a corridor that ran down the center of the building with rooms on each side. The rooms didn't have doors. They did have low to the ground tables made of green wood. Around each table were woven mats identical to those in the Alenian dwellings.

Seth couldn't imagine a spaceship piloted by beings sitting on the floor on a frond mat. Maybe their culture required them to sit this way, or possibly, the Alenian bodies made sitting on the floor necessary. It also was possible they did it out of necessity. In this arid place, the green wood might be so scarce there wasn't enough of it to make chairs. That just added to the number of unanswered questions about the Alenians.

The hallway ended at an open area with several green wood filing cabinets. Alan opened each cabinet. They were empty. He shook his head sadly. "It's frustrating there are no written documents here. The researchers were here thirty years without being able to translate the Alenian's language. Looking at the few samples of Alenian writing they found, I understand why they couldn't."

The next building was an auditorium. The center of the building was a conical hole dug three stories into the ground. Benches made of adobe provided rows of seating to view the small stage at the bottom. Its only practical use would be to hear lectures or for village meetings.

"It can seat thousands," Jana commented. Seth agreed. The auditorium was large enough to seat the thousands of Alenians who once occupied this village.

They left to inspect the next building. They found a forge inside for making farm tools. There were racks of new hoes, rakes, and shovels. Seth inspected them. They were exceptionally well-made tools with smooth, even finishes. Far better than he would expect could be made by hand from a simple forge.

The last building was the smallest of the three. Jana said a Marine told her it was the Alenian's research facility. It had a central corridor with three rooms on each side. Workbenches were in the center of the rooms, with a few green wooden cabinets on the walls. Alan opened each cabinet. They were empty.

The corridor ended at a room larger than the others. They first noticed the musty, burnt odor coming from the room. Once inside, they found it had been heavily damaged by fire. There were floor to ceiling green cabinets along one wall. Most of them had been destroyed by the fire. On the opposite side of the room were two workbenches recessed into the wall with vent hoods.

A large machine took up most of the rear wall. Seth walked up to the machine. It was not only damaged by the fire, but someone had smashed it with a heavy object.

"Someone really didn't like this machine," Alan said, eyeing the damage.

"This is an Alenian machine. Look at the writing on it." Seth pointed to the written symbols on the machine.

"This machine has to have something to do with genetic research according to what we read in the ship's files since there isn't anything else in this building," Jana said.

"I wish I could read the symbols so I could maybe tell you what this machine did," Alan said clearly frustrated. Alan took out a notepad and began copying down the symbols on the machine.

Jana was checking out the cabinets. "I guess the insane colonists did this damage."

Seth went over to the workbenches with the vent hoods. His feet crunched on something on the floor. Shards of broken glass were scattered around the floor.

He ran his hand over a smudge of soot on the workbench. He crouched to eye the surface. "This happened long before the colonists began killing each other," he said.

Alan had been searching through the cabinets the fire hadn't completely destroyed. He came upon a pile of burnt paper. Most of it was ash, but he found a scrap of unburned paper. He pulled it out. "There is human writing on this. It says, 'Trial Seven Test Results.'"

Seth said, "It confirms my belief this lab was destroyed sometime when the humans were here, but not recently."

All three began searching for more scraps of paper that survived the fire. By the end, they found four unburned scraps with human handwriting, but there wasn't enough writing to be meaningful. Alan carefully put the scraps in his pocket.

They'd seen the entire commerce part of the Alenian village. South from here were more Alenian shacks. They started back to the human compound with more questions than answers.

CHAPTER 48

Jana was more talkative than usual on the way back to the compound. "It's strange the Alenians could dig out a huge auditorium. It looks impossible to do that only using hand tools. Then there is the laboratory. It has to be the genetics lab the ship's files referred to. The ship's files said the Alenians had a genetics laboratory, not that humans were using it."

"There isn't any doubt that humans were doing something in that laboratory based on the notes we found," Alan added.

"Maybe you'll find something about it in the colonists' notes."

"I'd have to be extremely lucky to find something like that. The notes are a mess. So many were destroyed, and the rest are in total disarray. It would take months, if not a year, to organize that mess. Maybe the answer to who used that lab was in the burned notes. In that case, we will never learn who used or destroyed it. Besides, there isn't much we can discover in three weeks."

Jana asked Seth, "Do you know what the humans were doing in the Alenian laboratory?"

"Not a clue," Seth said. He had some ideas about what they found but decided to keep it to himself. The notes with human writing plus the broken vent hood stations made it clear humans were working in that lab. The most logical reason they would be using that lab was the machine. Based on the soot from the fire covering everything, including the damaged parts of the machine, the destruction of the machine and the fire happened around the same time. It happened not now when the colonists went insane but in the past. If humans were using that machine, that meant the Alenians didn't destroy it. What they did in that laboratory, or why it was destroyed, was another mystery.

They were back at the compound. Alan said he needed to preserve the scraps of paper he found. He left for the Artifacts hut. Seth walked with Jana back to the Medical hut.

They found Doc standing over several Petri dishes laid out across a table.

"Learn anything from the autopsy?" Seth asked.

"I'm running tests here and also in the Biology Lab. They should finish sometime later tonight."

Jana said, "It's almost time for supper. I'm going to see what the cook is preparing for us." Then she left.

Seth rubbed his forehead.

"Are you alright?" Doc asked.

"I've had a headache ever since I got here. I thought it was from shutting down the towers, but it isn't going away."

"Do you often have headaches?" Doc asked in his professional physician's voice.

"I never get them. Before I was brought to Klatania, I was hit in the head so hard that I was knocked out. Our med guy on the project said I had a concussion."

Doc took out a small flashlight from his pocket. He shined it into Seth's eyes. "You don't have a concussion now. I'll give you some analgesic pills for the pain. If the headache doesn't go away, I want to check you out to make sure this isn't something serious."

Doc went to a cabinet and handed Seth a container of pills. "There's nothing else for me to do here. Let's go see what's for dinner."

CHAPTER 49

The team sat at their regular table as they discussed the day's events while waiting for the evening meal. Some of the freighter crew had left in the second shuttle. The cook and two other freighter crewmen stayed behind to prepare meals.

"Has anyone seen the Major or the Marines today?" Doc asked.

No one had.

Doc said, "If, as the Major says, all the dead colonists are accounted for, what would they be off doing?"

"Do you think something happened to them?" Alan asked.

"I doubt it. They have enough firepower that if a battle was going on anywhere nearby, we'd hear it." Seth didn't want to add if it was too far away, they might not hear anything.

Their speculation ended as the Major entered the mess hall with the Marines. The Marines went to their table at the end of the mess hall. The Major walked up to the team. "Did you find the cause?" he asked Doc.

"There is nothing conclusive yet. But we are running tests from the autopsy. I should have the results by tomorrow. There is one thing. We checked the Biology hut. We discovered someone had been running tests of blood samples at or around the time the killings were taking place. I assume they were of the colonists by the variety of the samples. I think someone was trying to figure out what was happening. I fear if you are correct about the graves, that person eventually succumbed to the insanity or was killed by another colonist."

The Major said, "I want the autopsy results as soon as you get them."

"Where were you and your men today?" Seth asked.

The Major glared at Seth before answering, "Mr. Voltig insists the colonists may have been attacked by an external actor using a weapon, or an external planetary pathogen, possibly introduced by a comet or meteorite landing near this colony."

The team members turned to Gunther. He nodded confirming the Major statement.

"We searched the surrounding fields for a foreign body that might have crashed into the moon, We found no evidence anything crashed recently into this moon anywhere near the compound. We also inspected the spaceport landing pad for recent activity. The single landing pad has not been used in a long time. We also didn't find any evidence of a weapon," he gave Gunther a hard look as he said it.

Professor said, "We found a researcher's log entry made only days before everyone went insane. It stated they found something of significant importance. This may very well have some bearing on what happened."

Everyone waited for the Professor to continue. He didn't.

"What did they find?" The Major asked sharply.

"We only found a single page with that entry. The rest of it is somewhere in that disorganized mess. If we had more time, we might be able to get the researcher's notes into some semblance of order to learn what they found."

The Major's frustration was apparent as he spoke to the team. "You have what is left of three weeks to learn what happened here, no more. If it appears you cannot learn what happened, we will leave sooner," then he left for the Marines' table.

"I can't let the Major do this. This is the only other advanced species we have ever come across. It is too important to abandon. It tears at every fiber of my being to not tell the Major what he can do with his orders to leave here and destroy the wormhole."

"We won't get anywhere confronting someone like the Major. Maybe he will listen to reason if we can find something of value that would be worth keeping us here longer, or saving the Alenian researcher's notes," Doc said to calm down his friend.

Seth agreed with Doc that they would need significant leverage to convince the Major to change his mind. He wasn't sure anything they found or learned would change the mind of the intransigent Major.

The two freighter crewmen came out of the kitchen carrying bowls of food. It was the same stew they served the first night. One bowl to the team, the other to the Marines.

Alan and Jana discussed what they found in the Alenian village's laboratory building as they ate. No one knew what humans would have been doing there, or when the room was set on fire. Seth could sense everyone was uncomfortable about this information. Still, since it had nothing to do with the recent killings or the Alenians, they decided there was no value in bringing it up to the Major. He may know what happened in that building if he was here then.

The evening ended when they filed into the Medical hut for Doc to take his blood samples. After, they all returned to their shacks for the night.

CHAPTER 50

Seth's headache worsened despite taking Doc's pills before the meal. The pain in his head was making it hard to fall asleep. He eventually did, but he woke in the middle of the night with an overwhelming feeling that something bad was about to happen.

He sat up thinking it was a bad dream, but the feeling of danger only intensified. It was a premonition, a warning, but this didn't come with a vision like the one he had about Reilly. This was only a feeling something was wrong. It was similar to him sensing something was wrong when they entered orbit around Alenia. He could sense it, but not what it was.

He swung his feet over the edge of the bed to focus. The feeling of danger was growing stronger. The headache was blocking his concentration. He shook his head to clear it when he heard the crack of a weapon being fired. He listened carefully, and then he heard another discharge. It was a Marine's plasma rifle. It was coming from the compound.

He jumped out of bed, threw on some clothes, and cinched the Stinger holster around his waist as he opened his bedroom door. Alan was standing outside his bedroom door in his underwear. He was clutching his Stinger and looked frightened. Seth was relieved that he was pointing the Stinger at the floor.

"Was that a weapon I heard?" Alan asked, panic in his voice.

"It was. Stay here and keep your weapon ready. Whatever you do, don't shoot one of us by mistake. I'm going to see what's happening."

Alan tightened his grip on the Stinger as Seth ran outside. Professor was standing on the road with his Stinger in his hand.

"Have the killings begun?" Professor asked anxiously.

Doc joined them. He patted Professor on the shoulder. "I don't think so, my friend. If what happened to the original colonists was happening, we would all be mad at this point. Though I suggest you holster your weapon before you startle the others into thinking you have gone mad."

Doc addressed Seth. "I thought I heard a weapon being fired. Do you know what's happening?"

"I have no idea, but I will find out."

Gunther and Jana joined them. "We're coming with." The three of them ran to the compound. The Common was empty, but they saw lights from flashlights behind the west side Quonset huts.

They found the Major standing over a dead Marine lying in a pool of blood. The Marine's skull was split in half, and his right arm had been torn out of his shoulder socket. The arm lay a few meters away, the hand still clutching his weapon.

"What happened?" Jana asked the Major.

"He was guarding this area. We heard weapons fire. When we got here, this is what we found."

Four Marines, weapons up, scanned the unlit area with their flashlights.

Gunther said, "To cave in a man's skull is one thing. To pull his arm from his body requires a great deal of strength. Unless we have huge, monstrous beasts roaming this moon, I think a robot did this."

The Major turned to the Marines, "Check the robot Quonset hut!"

The Marines panned their flashlights on the Quonset hut that contained the robots. One of them slowly opened the door as the others aimed their rifles into the blackness beyond the opened door. The Marine who opened the door panned his flashlight across the interior. His light reflected off the robot's metallic bodies and caused their eyes to shine eerily. Seeing no movement, he took a step into the hut and turned on the hut's lights.

The other three Marines followed him into the hut. One of the Marines began checking each robot to see if it had been activated. Another checked the larger robots for any signs of blood from the dead Marine. After inspecting all the robots, the Marines call back to the Major that they were all turned off, and none had blood on them.

The Major barked back at the Marines, "Lock the hut securely. Search the entire area for any signs of what did this." He turned to the team members. "Go back to your shacks. but stay alert."

They found Doc, Professor, and Alan standing on the road outside their shacks. Each of them holding their Stingers.

Seth told them what happened.

"This doesn't look good. Not only for that Marine but for the rest of us. It was dangerous enough thinking we might begin killing one another. Now it seems something else might be here to kill us," Doc said.

Two Marines walked up to the group. One of them announced the Major sent them to stand guard. With that, the team returned to their shacks for the unlikely prospect of getting some sleep.

CHAPTER 51

After a restless night, Seth was up before sunrise. When he came out of his bedroom, he found Alan fully clothed, sitting in the kitchen, his weapon on the table. "Did you sleep at all?" Seth asked.

"I couldn't. I kept seeing monsters creeping up on me. I figured I'd be safer staying awake."

"Let's see if the Major found out what killed the Marine."

The two Marines were still there guarding their shacks.

They found the Major in the Communications hut.

"Have you found out what killed the Marine?" Seth asked.

The Major shook his head. "My men have searched the area. They found gouges in the ground near the site where he was killed. The trail disappeared on the hard-packed ground outside the compound."

"Which direction were the tracks heading before they disappeared?"

"They were going west."

"There is an operational Skimmer in the hangar. Let me take it up. I can search the area west of the colony a lot faster from the air. Something big enough to do that to the Marine, either a robot or large animal, should be visible from the air."

The Major mulled over Seth's proposal. Finally, he said, "The Skimmer has two seats. You could use another pair of eyes to help search. Take a Marine with you."

"I volunteer to go," Alan said. "They used to call me eagle eye when I was a kid. I have exceptional distance vision."

The Major stared at Alan for a few seconds before saying, "All right. Mr. Daiton can accompany you in the Skimmer. I don't want you to land anywhere. If you find anything, come back. I'll send the Marines out to deal with it."

They left the Communications hut. As they did, they found Doc and Jana just outside the door.

Doc asked, "Where are you two going in such a hurry?"

"The Major agreed to let me search for the Marine's killer with the Skimmer. If you're looking for the Major, he's inside," Seth said.

"I want to report our findings from the autopsy."

"Did you find out what caused the colonists to go insane," Seth asked.

"I found something, but the Major insisted I tell him first. I will explain what we found when you return."

As Seth walked with Alan to the hangar, Alan said, "I didn't say that about my vision just so the Major would let me come with you. I really do have great vision. I can be more helpful doing this than sorting through that mess of the researcher's notes. The Professor is adamant he will learn something from those notes. But they are in such a mess, I doubt he will. I found one note that says they found a recording in the spaceport. They had no idea what was being said on the recording, but it repeated the word Alenian several times. That's the only reason we call these beings Alenians, and this moon, Alenia. For all we know, Alenian might mean don't land here."

They reached the hangar and found the controls to open the main hangar door. Seth went to check the Skimmer that still had an engine to see if it could fly.

Skimmers were designed for low level reconnaissance. It was a simple aircraft with a skeletal metal frame resting on three wheels, a single large propeller, and a plastic dome covering the two-seat cockpit. The usefulness of the Skimmer was its ability for low, slow flight. It could take off or land on a short runway, but it could also take off or land vertically. Five thrusters built into its frame could hold the Skimmer stationary in the air or land it vertically. This was ideal if it was necessary to land in a tight place. The wings could be folded into the body when the thrusters were engaged to accommodate vertical landings.

Seth popped open the cockpit dome and crawled into the Skimmer, then Alan wriggled into the right seat.

"Ever been in a Skimmer before?"

"No, I haven't. I like flying even though I can't fly anything. I love seeing things from the air. It makes me feel like a bird."

Seth turned on the ignition. The fuel gauge was full. The huge propeller began to rotate as he advanced the throttle. The Skimmer rolled forward as Seth guided it out of the hangar onto the edge of the runway. The Skimmer's wings were in the folded position. He cut the propeller before engaging the thrusters. The Skimmer began to lift. He killed the thruster and the Skimmer settled back on the ground. He unfurled the Skimmer's huge wings as he prepared to use the runway to take off.

He advanced the throttle once they were in place while keeping the brakes engaged. The propeller began to rotate. Seth checked the RPM. Once the propeller was moving fast enough, he lifted his foot off the brake. The Skimmer started rolling down the runway. The large wings caught the air almost immediately, as the Skimmer rose gracefully into the air.

Seth didn't believe the Major would let him use the Skimmer again, so he decided to explore as much of the area from the air as he could. He yelled to Alan over the engine's noise, "I want to see what things look like from the air. I'm going to fly north to get a look at the northern mountain range. After that, I'll fly over the Alenian village before we fly to the western edge of the colony to look for tracks from whatever killed the Marine."

Alan nodded eagerly.

Seth flew towards the northern mountain range. They could see the outlines of fields once cultivated by the Alenians. The mountain range was thirty kilometers north of the runway. As they approached the mountains, their jagged peaks towered above them, most over four kilometers tall.

"They look pretty stark," Alan remarked as they neared the mountains.

Seth agreed. The Major telling them there hadn't been a significant earthquake in the thirty years humans were here may have just been good luck. The tectonic forces that created these mountains could generate powerful earthquakes. He hoped they weren't here when a big one hit.

"Why does that mountain peak look so different?" Alan was pointing at one of the mountain peaks with an unusually flat surface. It was mirror smooth as if it had been cut at an angle.

"I don't know. Maybe it fractured leaving that smooth-looking face," Seth said, as he continued to fly along the edge of the mountains.

There wasn't much to see here, so Seth turned the Skimmer south, back towards the colony. He flew the Skimmer 600 meters above the center of the human colony. He continued flying south over the Alenian village.

The Major told them there were 22,000 living units in the village. Seth counted fifteen rows of living units that stretched south. All were single-story adobe shacks, separated by two meters, facing a three-meter-wide dirt road. The dirt roads between the living units were laid in perfect parallel lines. They were laid out with such precision it was hard to believe this was done by creatures that used hand tools to farm. The same creatures that had a spaceport as well as a sophisticated machine in what was described as a genetics laboratory. They were not that primitive after all.

They reached the southern edge of the village. Beyond the village were the outlines of fields the Alenians used to plant crops. The soil was a sickly gray, possibly from many years of neglect. The fields stretched to the mountain range that defined the southern boundary of the Alenian coastal plain.

"It looks like they irrigated their crops using the rivers from the western mountain range." Alan pointed to the outlines of canals from the west running along the edges of the fields.

"I did a rough check of the soil's quality. It's not good soil for growing much," Seth said.

"One of the researcher's notes says they believe the Alenians may have only grown a single type of crop here. If that's true, it must have been an extremely valuable crop."

It was time to stop touring. Time to see if they could find what killed the Marine. Seth turned the Skimmer to the western edge of the Alenian village. He flew north until they were over the just area west of where the Marine was killed.

"The Major said they found tracks going west. Look for any tracks," Seth said as he banked the Skimmer to the west.

Alan was already scanning the ground. "There. I see what looks like tracks."

He was right, there were gouges in the rain softened ground. The tracks were deep, indicating they were made by something heavy and it was heading west. The tracks continued until they disappeared on drier ground.

"Those were huge tracks. You think what killed the Marine made those tracks?" Alan sounded concerned.

"If it is, we are safe up here. I'm going to continue flying west. Keep watching for more tracks."

Seth slowed the Skimmer to just above stall speed as they scanned for more tracks. They didn't see any, so he brought the Skimmer down to thirty meters from the ground so they could see the faintest marks in the hard soil.

"There! I see scratches in the dirt."

Alan wasn't kidding when he said he had excellent vision. Seth could barely make out what Alan was pointing at. Alan was right. There were scratches in the dirt. Whatever made them continued to move due west.

They were approaching the western mountain range. The river along the mountain's base had thick vegetation growing on both sides. The grass was taller than a man. Interspersed randomly through the grass were trees measuring over ten meters tall with green bark and topped with fonds.

They could see tracks in the softer soil at the edge of the grass. The tracks disappeared once they entered the thick vegetation. Seth flew in the direction the tracks were heading, but he was forced to fly above the trees, limiting their ability to see what was in the dense grass below.

"I can't see anything in this jungle," Alan complained.

"I'll go around to come at it from the other direction."

"Look at that mountain top. It looks similar to the smoothed surfaced mountain top in the northern range," Alan pointed to the mountain directly in front of them. It had a flat, smooth face that was nothing like the jagged peaks surrounding it.

Seth's assumption the northern mountain top had cleaved creating its smooth face may have explained what happened to the top of one mountain, but not two.

Seth flew back and forth over where the tracks disappeared into the grass. It was too dense to see anything, and the trees were too tall to fly any lower over the area.

"I'm going to fly over the river to see if we can find more tracks."

The river was wide enough to allow him to fly just above the water. As he did, something caught his eye on the other side of the river. It looked to be a cutout on the side of the mountain. He was about to ask Alan to look at it when Alan yelled, "I see something under those trees!"

Seth strained to see where Alan was pointing. All he could see was light reflecting from something metallic. It was only a flash, but it was something that didn't belong in the grass.

CHAPTER 52

S eth turned the Skimmer around. He flew as low as possible over the river before he could see what Alan was pointing at. There was something metallic in the grass. It was forty meters into the vegetation and thirty meters from the edge of the river, but the grass obscured getting a good look at the object. The trees made it impossible to fly directly over it.

"Do you see any movement?" Seth asked Alan.

"I don't think so."

"I'm going to land to get a better look."

"You sure that's wise? Remember the Major told you not to land."

"We're not going to know what that is without getting a closer look. The only way to do that is on the ground. Besides, whatever it is, it isn't moving."

Seth flew 200 meters out into the field directly across from the object in the grass. Once there, he fired the thruster rockets. As they lifted the Skimmer, he cut the propeller. The Skimmer came to a stop as it hovered in the air.

The object was on Alan's side of the plane. Seth asked, "Has it moved?"

Alan, his eyes focused on the grass, shook his head.

Seth folded the Skimmer's wings. He reduced the rocket's thrust, and the Skimmer slowly descended until it gently touched down on the ground.

Seth cut the power. "Stay here."

As Seth began to leave, Alan said, "Wait. What if that is a killer robot or monstrous creature, won't it see the Skimmer. It might come out to attack the Skimmer, or me, if I'm in it?"

"It hasn't moved. I don't think you have anything to fear, but if you'd feel safer, come with me."

Alan stared at the tall grass. "Do you think there are snakes in that grass. I hate snakes."

"This coastal plain doesn't even have insects. I doubt it has snakes."

"But it might have giant monsters?"

"Come or stay, it's your call."

Alan got out of the Skimmer. "If something comes out to chase us, I warn you, I'm a fast runner. I think I can outrun you. That will leave you to deal with it."

Seth grinned. "Okay, you warned me. Now let's see what that is. Remember, if you pull your Stinger, only aim it at something you intend to kill."

They slowly walked into the tall grass towards the object. Seth fixed a reference on a mountain peak to make sure he would move parallel to the object. If this was what killed the Marine, it wouldn't be a good idea to boldly walk up to it.

They trudged through the grass until Seth estimated they were far enough in to be close to the object. The grass still obscured their view. Seth pulled out his Stinger. He looked behind him to see Alan already had his Stinger out and pointed at the ground.

Seth crouched down, so did Alan. Seth listened for a sound. All he could hear was the rustling of the grass made by a light breeze. He signaled for Alan to wait there.

He parted the grass as he crept forward. All he could hear was the swishing of the grass, but he couldn't see anything. He took another step forward. Parting the blades of grass, he could see something metallic. Slowly he moved closer. He could see a large cylindrical shape lying horizontal on the ground. He raised his Stinger as he crept towards it. It didn't move.

He was now close enough to see that the cylinder was the body of a large robot. There was a hole in the body made by a plasma weapon with scorch marks surrounding it. As he moved around the robot, he saw it had two arms with claws for hands. One of the arms was broken. It had a scorch mark where the arm had been broken. Seth inspected the robot's claws. He could see dried blood on the undamaged arm. This robot killed the Marine.

Alan crept up behind Seth. "Is it dead?" he whispered with a slight tremor in his voice.

"It's dead."

"Is this the robot that killed the Marine?" Alan asked, but seeing the blood stains, he added, "It is."

"It took two plasma hits, one to its arm, another to its body. It's surprising it made it all this way after receiving a direct plasma hit."

The robot's head was hidden in the grass. Seth moved the grass to get a better look at its head. Unlike anthropomorphized human robots with a head with eyes and a grill for a mouth, the head of this robot was nothing more than a small rectangular metal box.

Seth stood back and took in the entire robot. From head to foot, it would have stood over three meters tall. As he moved around the robot, its body reflected an array of colors. This robot was made of the same material as the Alenian habitation engine towers. This was not a human creation, this was Alenian.

Alan was standing beside him. "Where did it come from?"

"That's a good question. It's Alenian, not one of ours."

Alan looked at Seth before looking back at the robot. "The Alenians have killer robots!"

"Let's hope this is the only one, but we need to find out if it is. To do that, we need to learn where it came from. I believe it was trying to return there when it finally succumbed to the Marine's plasma blasts. There is something across the river. I saw what appeared to be a cut out in the mountain. I think that's where the robot was going. We need to see what that is."

"Do you think that's a good idea? What if there are more of these killer robots there?"

"If we encounter more killer robots, you can show me how fast you can run. Let's see if we can cross the river to find out where this robot was going."

CHAPTER 53

Alan reluctantly followed Seth to the river's edge. The river wasn't wide here, but it was too deep, the water running too fast, to safely cross. They agreed swimming across wasn't a good idea. They walked up the bank to look for a better place to cross.

Alan pointed to some large stones in the water. They were submerged just below the surface. They were round stones with flat tops large enough for someone to stand on. "This looks like a path of steppingstones to cross the river."

"Let's see." Seth stepped on the first stone. The stone didn't move, and it supported his weight. He stepped on the next one, the one after that, until in a dozen steps, he was across the river. Alan followed.

"That was convenient," Alan said, looking back at the stone path.

"Someone made it. I doubt it was a member of the human colony."

Seth walked along the riverbank looking for the odd cutout in the mountain. The grass was denser on this side of the river, and there were more trees.

"It was right around here. I'm sure it was a ledge cut into the face of the mountain."

From the ground, the face of the mountain appeared to be untouched. What Seth saw was at least twenty meters up the side of the mountain. Here the mountain was vertical, its face smooth. He looked for handholds where he might climb, but he couldn't find any.

Alan pointed to a tree that was a half-dozen meters from them. It was growing along the side of the mountain. "I think I see steps behind that tree."

Seth marveled again at Alan's exceptional vision. The tree obscured a set of steps cut into the face of the mountain. The tree had apparently grown here after the steps were made.

Seth said, "Stand back. I'm going to do tree removal." He pulled out his Stinger, aimed at the base of the tree, and fired. The flash from the pistol cut through the tree trunk with such ferocity the trunk exploded. The trunk, no longer attached to its base, bounced up once before toppling to the ground.

The Stinger's blast revealed this wasn't a true tree. It was a reed similar to the bamboo plants brought from Earth that were transplanted on several planets. It likely evolved from the grass on Alenia. Being the only wood-like product on the coastal plain, it was what the Alenians used to make doors, plus the few other things that required wood.

"I guess that will teach the trees around here not to get in our way," Alan joked.

"And that's why you don't point a Stinger at someone unless you mean business," Seth said in a big brotherly voice. "Now, let's see where these steps lead."

The steps ran up along the mountain face. They ended at a ledge cut into the mountain. The ledge was four meters wide, two meters deep, and three meters tall. Other than the ledge, the mountain looked untouched.

Alan scanned the area. The view from here was only of the river below. "There isn't anything worthwhile to see from here, so why would they make this ledge?"

Seth was checking the face of the mountain opposite the ledge. He agreed with Alan. This didn't make any sense as an observation platform, but maybe that wasn't what this was.

Seth saw a small hole that looked artificially made. It was just large enough to fit his hand.

Alan watched as Seth started to put his hand in the hole. "Are you sure you want to do that. No telling what might be living in that hole. What if some poisonous thing has made a home in it? I'm not strong enough to carry you back to the Skimmer. Besides, I don't know how to fly it."

Seth smiled, "This hole was cut into the mountain. No way of knowing why without seeing what's inside." He pushed his hand into the hole as Alan stepped back.

Seth felt around for something. He didn't feel anything. He pushed his hand deeper into the hole up to his elbow. His fingertips felt something. He ran his fingertips over it. It was a handle. He grasped it and pulled.

The face of the mountain began to slide back. It moved back two meters before it began to rise. When it stopped, it exposed an opening four meters wide by three meters tall. Whatever was inside was hidden in blackness.

CHAPTER 54

Daylight only illuminated a few meters into the opening. Beyond was darkness.

Seth took a step into the opening. Alan grabbed his arm. "We don't have a flashlight, and this is large enough for that robot to fit into. What if it leads to more robots?"

"We're not going to know if we don't go in," Seth said, taking another step.

"You're going to get us both killed!" But Alan followed Seth into the darkness.

Seth hadn't taken more than four steps before the area lit up. It wasn't a chamber. It was a tunnel. Lights in the ceiling lit up down its length. It was at least a hundred meters long, maybe longer, since the end of the tunnel curved out of sight.

Seth walked down the tunnel holding his Stinger ready. Alan followed, his Stinger out, too. Alan kept looking back to make sure the entrance to the tunnel didn't close. It didn't.

When they reached the curve in the tunnel, it continued another fifty meters to another curve. As they walked further through the tunnel, Seth had the feeling they were walking downhill.

They continued another twenty meters were the tunnel end at a stone wall.

Alan said, "This is nuts. Why build a lighted tunnel that leads nowhere?"

Seth didn't think the tunnel led nowhere. He studied the wall in front of them. The tunnel here was three meters across by three meters tall. The rock wall looked solid and natural. But so had the opening into this tunnel. Seth was sure there was a door here. He just had to find out how to open it.

Seth searched for a hole in this wall similar to the one where he found the lever to open the entrance to the tunnel. There were no holes or indentations, just a solid rock face. He studied the rock face for a seam. He found a thin line in the stone that ran from the ceiling down to the floor. It was so finely cut that it was barely visible. This had to be the edge of a door, but there was no obvious way to open it.

Seth ran his hand along the rock wall just outside the seam. It was solid. He continued running his hand along the wall. As he did, he pushed in on it. Something gave. It didn't look any different than the rock surrounding it. He pushed on it again. It moved a little more. He pushed hard. The piece of wall beneath his hand moved until it clicked. When it did, the end of the tunnel began to swing open towards them.

"Wow!" Alan yelled as he jumped out of the way of the opening door.

The door opened slowly. As the door opened, it swept away debris on the ground that had fallen from the ceiling. This created a bumping sound that echoed from the other side of the opening. It was too dark beyond the door to see anything. But whatever was on the other side of this door had to be large enough to create an echo.

The door finally stopped. They stood in front of the opening with their Stingers raised. Seth listened. It was quiet. He stepped gingerly into the blackness, inching his way forward, still unable to see what was ahead of him.

"Stop!" Alan yelled.

Seth turned to find Alan looking at the wall just inside the open door. "I think this is a power panel," Alan said. He was standing next to a panel of levers. One was larger than the rest. He pulled it down.

The ceiling began to light up. The light revealed they were looking into a cavern. It wasn't a natural cave. It had been hollowed out of the mountain. It was at least 300 meters wide with a ceiling 200 meters tall, and so deep they couldn't see its end.

Alan pointed to the ceiling, "It looks like a window to the sky."

It did. It was blue, the normal color of the Alenian sky, but this wasn't the sky. The real sky outside had patchy dark clouds, remnants from the habitation engine. This was mimicking a real sky. It supported a theory Seth had that the flat-faced peak on top of this mountain was the power source for the tunnel lights as well as this cavern sky. It had to be a solar collector. He filed the thought away to explore later.

Within minutes, the entire cavern was illuminated. They were standing on a cliff. Below them were buildings. Thousands of them.

There was no movement, no robots, nothing but stillness.

"This underground city is almost as big as the Alenian village," Alan said excitedly.

The air was stale with a damp smell, an indication no one had been here for a long time. "I don't think anyone would be living here in the dark, or that the robot came from here," Seth said as he holstered his Stinger. Alan followed, holstering his.

The cliff they were standing on had steps leading down to the floor of the cavern. At the bottom was a road. They walked down the steps. There were six buildings, three on each side of the road, some of them multi-story. Beyond the buildings were thousands of smaller, box shaped buildings. In size and shape, they were identical to the shacks in the Alenian village.

"It's a bit spooky. It is so much like the Alenian village yet it's different," Alan said.

Seth agreed. The smaller, one-story buildings were identical in appearance to the Alenian living units except in one respect. These buildings were not made of adobe mud. They were made of slabs of granite stone. Even the road was made of polished granite. Seth studied the workmanship of the buildings. The granite was cut precisely to fit together. He didn't see how anyone using hand tools could build these structures much less hollow out this enormous cavern.

They walked down the road past the larger buildings until they reached the start of the smaller one-story buildings. Seth said, "Let's look inside one."

Alan didn't object. Any trepidations he had were overcome by the sight of this incredible cavern village.

They entered the nearest small building. The decor inside was identical to those of the Alenian living units in the village. Here too they were neatly organized, ready for their occupants to return.

Seth ran his finger over a surface. It was thick with dust. He pointed to the mark his finger made. "No one has been here for a long time, just like the Alenian living units in the village."

They returned to the road. Alan said, "Let's look in the big buildings."

They walked back up the main road toward the stairs. On the left side of the road were three two-story buildings. On their right was a two-story building and two one-story buildings.

They entered the first two-story building on their left. There were separate rooms on each floor, some small, some large, all of them looked to be laboratories. Unlike the laboratories in the village, most of the laboratories here were not empty. They had strange objects in them made of Alenian metal. Some were half-meter diameter spheres, others were long, thin cylinders. They looked like they were solid. Their placement in the rooms would indicate they might be machines. If they were, they didn't have buttons or switches to turn them on.

They went into the next two-story building. This was clearly a hospital. There were rooms on the first floor with what could only be described as examination tables. Each room also had its own strange machine.

The second floor had four large rooms. There was a table in the middle of the room with overhead lights, which were off. Each had its own strange machine, but these were much larger.

"Are these operating rooms?" Alan asked.

"I bet they are. Which could mean these large metal objects might perform operations."

There was a another room containing cabinets filled with bottles of liquid, gauze, bandages, and other medical supplies. Everything here was also covered in dust.

"I bet Doc would love to inspect this stuff," Alan said.

They moved on to the third two-story building. Inside the outer green doors was a stairway leading up. It ended at the second floor, but it wasn't a floor, it was the upper entrance to an amphitheater cut into the mountain. The circular seats cut into the mountain faced a small stage five stories below.

"This looks like the theater in the Alenian village, although this one is larger. Considering how small the stage at the bottom of this theater is, I don't think the Alenians were into sporting events unless it was spelling bees," Alan said.

Seth agreed. This was a lecture hall, but lectures on what?

They left the amphitheater. Crossing the road was another two-story building. They found small rooms inside, dozens of them. Apparently, this was an administration building. Each room had a low table with woven mats for seats. It was identical to the administration building in the Alenian village though two stories tall. Like the village's administration building, this one had empty cabinets. Alan grumbled when he didn't find any documents.

The next building was only one story tall. The inside was one large open space. There were two-meter tall partitions jutting out every three meters along the outer walls.

"What in the world did they use this for?" Alan asked.

Seth smiled. "I think this was a market. The partitioned areas were stalls where merchants could sell their wares. I bet they set up tables in the center, too. It seems the Alenians were a mercantile society."

The last building was one story tall, smaller than the other one story building. Alan gasped when they walked inside. The walls were lined with racks of shelves made of Alenian metal. The shelves were filled with books. There were thousands of books here.

"It's a library!" Alan yelled as he ran to one of the shelves. He gingerly pulled off one of the books. He opened it slowly as if expecting it might crumble into dust in his hands. It didn't. He turned one page, then another. As he flipped pages, the gleeful expression on his face increased.

"It's all written in Alenian. If this is an Alenian library, with this much Alenian writing, it gives me a shot at translating their language!"

Alan set the book down on the shelf and went to the next shelf. He picked up another book. Each turn of a page made him beam with enthusiasm.

Seth watched Alan go from shelf to shelf, book to book. He was like a kid in a candy shop, unable to decide which of the treasured items was more valuable.

Alan was inspecting books on the other side of the building when Seth heard something. It was a low rumbling sound. "Alan, be quiet," he said. Alan looked up bewildered. Seth put his index finger to his lips. Alan fell quiet. They both listened as the rumbling grew louder.

Alan whispered, "Is something coming?"

"I don't know, but it might be a good idea if we get out of here."

Alan stared at the shelves. "Help me take as many books as we can carry. Please take some books from each of those six shelves. I don't know whether these are novels or something more valuable."

Alan ran down the length of the library grabbing books from different shelves until his arms were loaded. Seth took a book from each of the six shelves that Alan pointed out.

The rumbling sound was getting louder. They ran out of the library carrying the books. There was no killer robot outside. They ran up the stairs. At the top of the cliff, Seth stopped to see if he could identify where the sound was coming from. It was coming from everywhere. Seth pushed up the lever to turn off the lights. The fake sky immediately went black, but the rumbling sound continued.

Alan was already outside the cavern in the tunnel. Seth pressed on the mechanism that had opened the door. The door immediately began to close. They ran the length of the tunnel until they were outside again. Once they were out of the tunnel, the tunnel lights went out. Seth pushed the lever in the hole to close the door to the tunnel. The rock door slowly closed, hiding the tunnel's existence.

Lines of sweat dripped off Alan's face. "That was an adventure," he said, enthusiastically scanning the collection of books.

"We better get back before the Major thinks something happened to us," Seth said.

"I can't wait to tell the team about this."

CHAPTER 55

They walked down the steps cut into the side of the mountain, past the newly created tree stump, when Alan almost dropped the books from the unwieldy tall stack he was carrying. Seth took some of Alan's books to even out their loads. They crossed the river on the stone path, quickly walking past the robot, as if disturbing it might make it jump up and attack them, finally reaching the Skimmer.

Seth flew the Skimmer back to the hangar. As they rolled up to the hangar, Gunther was waiting for them.

"Alan, leave the books in the Skimmer. Don't tell Gunther what we found. Let's wait until we can tell everyone at the same time." Seth was thinking about what Doc said about Gunther. If Gunther was a spy, it might not be wise to inform this giant here, a place where he could stop them from revealing what they found to everyone.

Alan was bursting out to tell someone, anyone, but he agreed.

When they got out of the Skimmer, Gunther walked up to them. "The Major was angry you took so long. He was going to send the Marines out in trucks to find you or your dead bodies."

"Well, we are here now," Seth said. "We have some news. We need to have everyone meet in the mess hall. Alan, you go get Professor. Gunther, get the Major. I'll get Doc and Jana."

"News about what?" Gunther asked in a commanding tone Seth didn't like.

"Something interesting, but everyone needs to hear this at the same time."

Gunther grunted his displeasure as he watched Seth and Alan leave the hangar.

Seth was waiting in the mess hall with Doc, Jana, and the freighter crew when Gunther came in with the Major and the Marines. Alan and Professor were the last to arrive. Alan must have told him about the books because Professor looked as excited as Alan.

Seth stood in the front of the mess hall as everyone gathered around him. From the angry look on his face, the Major was about to complain when Seth cut him off. "We found what killed the Marine. It was a robot of Alenian origin, and it's dead. When the Marine shot it, the plasma blast didn't stop it immediately. It made its way back to the edge of the river about forty kilometers west of here."

The Major's face didn't soften. Seth said. "There is more. We found an Alenian city built under the mountain on the west side of the river. It's a hollowed-out cavern with buildings and Alenian shacks, and it's big enough to hold the entire Alenian population. Unlike the adobe shacks and buildings in the Alenian village, these structures were made of granite, demonstrating a technology superior to anything we've seen here."

The room exploded with questions.

Jana asked, "Were there more killer robots there?"

Before Seth could answer, Professor asked, "Was there anything that explained what happened to the Alenians?"

"Wait!" Alan yelled. "There is more. There is a library of Alenian books, lots of books. Far more Alenian writing than the researchers found in the past thirty years!"

Everyone in the room was excited hearing about the cavern city except the Major. He yelled over the clamor, "You are not here to study the Alenians. You are here to learn what happened to the colonists."

Professor said in a calm voice, "I remind you, before the colonists here lost their minds, they noted they made a significant discovery. They may have discovered this cavern city."

It shut up the Major, and the team continued to pepper Alan and Seth with questions. Each answer generated more questions.

What kind of medical facilities? What did the strange machines look like? A phony sky? How did they do that? It could hold the entire Alenian population, does that mean there were more Alenians than was estimated? How big was the Library?

Seth finally stopped the onslaught of questions. "We don't have answers to your questions. The only way we can learn more is to take you there."

"You're not going back there!" the Major shouted.

Professor spoke up. "Our mission was to find out what happened here. This caverned city may be an important clue in answering that question. Are you going to stop us from exploring every avenue that might give us the answers we seek?"

The Major's face, usually a stern mask, was showing frustration. Everyone expected he would repeat they weren't there to learn more about the Alenians. He didn't. He said, "All right. I will arrange for everyone to go there at first light tomorrow." Without another word, he left the mess hall, followed by the Marines.

CHAPTER 56

After the Major and the Marines left, the team continued bombarding Seth and Alan for details about the cavern city. They told them what they saw. There were more questions than they could answer. Finally, everyone accepted they would have to wait until tomorrow and see it for themselves.

Once the furor about the cavern city died down, Seth asked Doc, "What did you learn from the autopsy?"

"The autopsy gave an insight into why the colonists acted insanely, but it didn't show what caused it. We found the colonist's adrenal cortex gland was abnormally large, as well as his hypothalamus and his adrenal medulla. These enlarged organs would have put pressure on his brain. He also had abnormal hormone levels. His cortisol level was so low as to be barely measurable. His epinephrine was unbelievably high. That led me to measure his testosterone level. It was over 2200 nanograms per deciliter."

"Doc, could you translate that into layman's language?"

"Testosterone is one of the key flight or fight hormones. An adult male's testosterone level is typically under 700. This man had over three times the normal level. It meant his heart was beating so fast he might have died of a heart attack if Jana hadn't killed him. In short, if this man is any indication of what affected the rest of them, he was in a state of hyper aggression from the hormones in his body and swelling in his brain."

"Any idea what caused it?"

"I don't know of anything that could affect so many organs in this way, much less affect eighty-five individuals all at the same time. However, these results do explain the reason they were so aggressive. Now all we have to do is find what caused these changes in their bodies."

It was already late. Alan and Professor went to the Skimmer to get the books. The rest of them went to their shacks to get some sleep so they could be up early.

CHAPTER 57

The sun had barely risen when they began the journey to the cavern city. The Major had the Marines ready the colony's land vehicles for the forty-kilometer trip. There were two large trucks and an all-terrain convertible car, each of them driven by a Marine. The team piled into one of the trucks, the Marines into the other. The Major and Seth led in the convertible all-terrain car.

There were no roads to the river, only narrow footpaths. They had to drive over the fields, a jarringly bumpy ride. The trip took sixty-four minutes to reach the place where the killer robot lay. Seth led them to the robot. The Marines inspected it to ensure it was no longer functional. When they said it was safe, the rest of them came over to look at it.

"This is a very large robot. I'm not surprised it could do what it did to the Marine," Professor remarked, standing a little further away from it than everyone else.

"Humans didn't build this robot," Seth said.

The Major walked along the length of the robot. He stopped and said, "It is made of Alenian metal. This is not one of the colonist's robots."

After everyone had seen what they wanted of the robot, Seth led them to the stone path in the river.

"They will hold your weight, but make sure you step in the center of each stone." Seth demonstrated by crossing the river.

They crossed the river, followed Seth up the stairs to the ledge, and stood there amazed as Seth opened the mountain door. They followed Seth down the tunnel remarking at the lighting. When they reached the door that opened into the cavern city, Seth stopped before opening the door.

"He said to the Major, "We heard a rumbling sound and we left immediately. I don't think it's anything to worry about. But have your men ready when I open this door, in case I'm wrong."

The Marines had their rifles up as Seth opened the door to the cavern.

The huge block of stone scraped across the floor as it opened to the impenetrable darkness beyond. Quickly two of the Marines aimed their flashlights into the dark. They stepped inside, scanning the area with their flashlights.

"There is a control panel for the lights on the wall there," Alan pointed at it.

One Marine went to it and pulled the lever that turned on the lights.

There were noticeable gasps as the light revealed the city below.

"This is marvelous. In some ways identical to the Alenian village. In other ways, it is far more sophisticated," Professor said.

There were no alien robots roaming through the streets and no rumbling sound. But Seth noticed a difference. The air smelled fresher, and it didn't feel as damp.

"I think the rumbling sound we heard was a system of air handlers bringing fresh air into the cavern," he said to comfort Alan. But everyone relaxed, even the Marines, if only a little.

"It isn't possible the Alenians could have built this city with their primitive tools. They had to have access to more advanced technology, or someone else built this city," Gunther commented.

"This is definitely an Alenian city. The books here are written in the same idiographic symbol language as the few documents we have from the village," Alan said.

The team followed Seth down the stairs and stood on the main road looking at the large buildings on either side.

Gunther commented, "Look at the construction. It is beautifully engineered."

Alan grabbed Professor's arm. "You have to see the library."

They started towards the library when the Major stopped them. "I don't want any of you going off on your own without a Marine accompanying you. Do you understand that!" He stared at Seth when he said it. Seth responded with a acquiescent look.

The Major told a Marine to accompany Alan and Professor to the library.

Seth said to Doc, "Let me show you the hospital." A Marine accompanied them.

In the hospital, Doc roamed from room to room. "This is marvelous. I wish I understood what these machines do. It so strange that none of them have any visible controls, not even a switch to turn them on."

Seth took Doc on a tour of the other buildings finishing up in the amphitheater. As they came out, they found the Major standing at its entrance. Gunther, Jana and their Marine protector were just leaving the laboratory building and joined them.

Jana addressed Doc, "The laboratories in that building are fascinating. I have no idea what the machines in there do."

"The same is true of the hospital," Doc said.

He was about to say more when the Major interrupted him, "Where are Daiton and Howton?"

"They're probably still in the library," Seth offered.

The Major said angrily, "It is time for us to leave. I want everyone to stay together." He headed for the library, and they followed. They found Alan and Professor rummaging through the shelves. There were several large piles of books on a table. Alan turned when he saw them come into the library. "Great. We'll need your help to carry these books back. Professor has been helping me choose books I think I can use to translate the Alenian language."

Seth thought the Major would object. But he told the Marines to grab the books.

Everyone pitched in, and soon all of them were loaded with books as they headed out of the cavern city.

Seth was closing the cavern city's door when he heard Doc ask Jana if she collected the samples. She held up a bag with test tubes. "I've taken water samples from some of the living units and the laboratory building. I expect water from the other buildings will be the same. I couldn't find any food, so I collected some dust samples to test for sediment that might have come out of the air."

Dusk was approaching when they returned to the colony. No one had eaten lunch, and it was later than they usually ate supper. A procession of Marines and the team carried the books into the Artifacts hut before heading to the mess hall for supper.

The cook was miffed no one had been there when he served supper. He started to complain when the Major stared him down. He returned to the kitchen and brought out the meal. It was the normal fare of synthetic protein and vegetables.

It was dark by the time they finished their meal. Alan said he wanted to check out the Alenian books. Gunther said he needed to walk off the meal.

Doc stopped them, saying, "I want each of you to come over for your daily blood draw."

Grumbling, they followed Doc to have their blood drawn at the Medical hut before heading off in different directions. Professor said he was tired, and Seth decided he was too. They walked back to their shacks together. It was midnight Alenian time when Seth crawled into bed.

Seth found it difficult to sleep. His headache was getting worse, and Doc's pills were not helping. Finally, he fell asleep. He dreamt of the blonde woman dressed in white. Her image had always been static, a frozen picture in his mind. In this dream, she moved. She spoke to him, or at least her mouth was moving as if she were trying to speak, but there was no sound. He strained to hear her in the dream. She was saying something, but no matter how hard he strained, he couldn't hear anything.

Seth woke in the middle of the night, soaked in sweat, his first thought this was the start of the insanity that affected the colonists. The longer he lay in bed, the more he was sure it had only been a dream. The image of the woman lingered in his thoughts, making it impossible for him to relax enough to fall asleep again.

Chapter 58

S eth finally gave up trying to sleep despite only sleeping a couple of hours. He checked the time. It was two hours before sunrise. He came out of his bedroom and found the door to Alan's room open and the bed made. Alan was fastidious about making his bed each morning. Either he left extremely early, or he never made it to bed last night.

Seth showered and dressed. He went to the compound. When he reached the Common, he saw a light in the Medical hut. He found Doc bent over a table of samples labeled 'Cavern City.'

Seth sat on a stool and watched until Doc pulled away from the samples and acknowledged his presence. "Doc, I hate to bother you with this, but my headache is getting worse. The pills you gave me aren't working, and I'm having trouble sleeping. Is there something else you could give me?"

"I'd like to take a scan of your head just to see if there is something causing this headache."

"You mean something like the knock on my head I received before I joined you?"

Doc gave him one of his serious, doctorly looks. "It may be that. It also could be a tumor or something else putting pressure on your brain. We need to check to be sure."

Without saying more, Doc led Seth to the hut with the MTS machine. When they got there, Seth was surprised to see the hut door slightly ajar. "I'm sure I shut this door when we inspected this building a few days ago. Who else would have been in here since then?"

"It could be Gunther. He continues to wander around the camp at all hours, which worries me that his actions have a devious purpose."

Seth thought if he was a spy, he wasn't good at hiding it.

Inside the MTS hut, Seth noticed something was different. At first, he wasn't sure what it was. Then he remembered the large metal cylinders that had been lined up along the wall. They were gone. "Do you know if somebody removed the cylinders that were along this wall?"

Doc shook his head and walked over to the MTS machine. "I haven't worked one of these in years. Back in Klatania, we have technicians to do this. Give me a minute to refamiliarize myself with it."

He began fiddling with the controls while he asked Seth to lie down on the table in front of the machine. Doc put a brace under Seth's head to hold it still. He positioned the machine's emitter directly above Seth's head.

"Just lie still," Doc said as he went behind a shield to protect the operator from radiation emitted by the MTS machine.

Seth could see Doc standing behind the shield working the controls in his peripheral vision.

"All right. It is going. Just relax. It will be over in a minute."

Seth heard a soft repetitive buzzing sound. It was the beginning of the countdown before the machine fired. He and his mother were on a planet with an MTS machine when he broke his arm, and he remembered listening to the buzzing countdown while he lay under that machine, just as he was doing now.

Seth closed his eyes and relaxed as he waited for the machine to fire. Suddenly he heard Doc yell, "Get off the table! Get out of here!"

Seth opened his eyes and found Doc running out from behind the protective shield toward him. "Get out of here now!" Doc screamed.

Seth jumped off the table. He joined Doc as they ran out of the hut. Doc slammed the door closed. They heard the countdown buzzing stop, followed by a sound indicating the machine was firing.

Seth turned to Doc, "Why did you pull me out of there?"

There was a bead of sweat running down Doc's forehead. "It would have killed you. I set the machine to take a low-energy scan of your head. When I started it, instead of using my setting, the machine began following a program that was stored in it. I forgot these machines can be programmed. This machine was programmed to run an X-ray at its maximum level. If you were under it when it fired, it could have significantly injured you."

"Why would someone set an MTS machine to a high-level x-ray?"

"The only reason I can think of is to use X-rays to scan the interior of an artifact. That doesn't make sense since Professor told me all the Alenian artifacts were simple pottery."

"Well, I'm glad you saved me. Now can we look inside my head and find out if there's something seriously wrong with me?"

They went back into the hut. Seth laid on the table while Doc fiddled with the controls. Seth didn't understand why he didn't have a premonition warning him about the X-ray. He had one at the mine, another for Reilly, and even the one in orbit about the habitation engines set to their Initiation Phase. He even sensed something was wrong before the Marine was killed by the robot. But he didn't have one when the insane colonist killed the Marine who was in turn killed by Jana. And now, the X-ray machine could have killed him without a premonition warning him. Having premonitions was mysterious enough. Ones that only came when others were affected even more so.

Doc said, "I'm ready."

This time the MTS was done in a minute without any dramatics. Doc and Seth waited on a bench in front of the hut while the MTS processed the images into a 3-D VID so Doc could review it.

Doc commented, "The cavern city is incredible. The equipment there looks too advanced for the Alenians, considering how they lived and worked in the village."

"I agree, Doc. The cavern city seems more technologically advanced than the Alenian village dwellers. Alan says the books in the library were written in the Alenian language, the same as the samples of their language found in the village. I wonder if this moon had more than one species living here, or maybe two different cultures of the same species, one of them more advanced than the other. It's a puzzle. Just one of many open questions involving the Alenians."

"The Alenians' mysteries may remain unresolved. I doubt Professor will unlock their mysteries in the short time we have left on this moon."

They were interrupted by the timer buzzing indicating the VID was ready. Doc put the VID in a reader next to the MTS machine. The machine produced a 3-D representation of Seth's brain. Doc moved through the image of Seth's brain, layer by layer as Seth stood behind him anxiously watching.

After studying Seth's brain for a long time, Doc said, "It doesn't look like you have a brain tumor or an aneurysm. Your brain seems to be perfectly normal. I'd like to take another sample of your blood this morning. It might show nothing, but I think it's worth checking."

As they left, Seth made sure the MTS hut door was closed. Back at the Medical hut, Doc took a couple of blood samples from him. It was time for breakfast. They walked together to the mess hall.

CHAPTER 59

S eth and Doc joined Jana, Professor, and Gunther in the mess hall. The Major and Marines were not there, and when the cook brought out the food, he complained the Major forced him to feed them earlier.

Alan rushed into the mess hall, his eyes red, his hair tousled.

"Have you been up all night?" Seth asked him.

"Yes. That's not important. I've deciphered the Alenian language. I did it!"

Alan shook with excitement while looking like he would collapse any moment from exhaustion.

"Sit down," Seth commanded.

Alan plopped on the bench seat and began giving a rapid-fire description of what he found. "They were never able to decipher the language, not even after thirty years. I wasn't surprised, all they had were a few scraps of their writing. It turned out what they had were lists of farm tools. From that, gaining any insights into the Alenian's vocabulary or syntax was impossible.

"The books from the cavern city library had enough of their writing for me to get a handle on their language. The Alenian language consists of symbols followed by geometric squiggles. The symbols are things. They can represent objects, actions, or ideas. The squiggles add nuance to the symbol's meaning. I was lucky that one of the library books we brought back was a children's book. It had symbols with images. Some of the images were of their tools with the symbols for them. From that I could understand what some of their symbols meant, which led me to understand more of them. Once I understood the meaning of a few hundred symbols, I gained some insight into the syntax of their language."

He paused to take a needed breath because he was talking so fast. He continued at the same rapid pace, "I need to learn the meanings of more of their symbols. My best guess is they have between 20,000 and 30,000 unique symbols, and more than five dozen squiggles that enhance their meaning. Once I learn what more of their symbols represent, I will better understand how the squiggles differentiate the symbol's meaning."

Alan paused again to catch his breath. He looked like he was going to pass out.

Seth asked, "Are the books you have from the cavern going somewhere?"

"What?" Alan said, perplexed by the question.

"Are the books going to disappear?"

"No, they aren't."

"Then I think you need to get some sleep before you do any more with them," Seth said sternly.

Alan was going to protest, but he was too weak from exhaustion to put up an argument.

"First, eat something. Then I'm going to take you back to the shack so you can get some sleep."

Alan ate. As he did, he continued to explain his revelations of the Alenian language. "The Alenian picture book for children was my Rosetta Stone. With it, I gained a basic understanding of the Alenian language. I went through the other Alenian library books and the scraps of their writings the researchers found. I am a long way from understanding the Alenian language. I have learned so far that they have a complex culture."

Alan was breathless again and running out of the nervous energy keeping him going.

Seth stopped him. "Have you finished eating?"

Alan nodded.

Seth stood up and grabbed him by the arm. "It's time to go." Seth walked Alan back to their shack to make sure he got there. He watched Alan crawl into his bed and then instantly fall asleep. Seth left him expecting he would sleep for a few hours. He wanted to see if Doc had found anything from the blood sample he took before breakfast that would explain his headaches. They were getting worse.

CHAPTER 60

Seth found Jana alone in the Medical hut.

Seth asked her, "Have you seen Doc?"

"He's checking on something in the Biology hut," she said.

Seth found Doc in the Biology hut, intently staring at a monitor. As Seth approached, Doc had a worried expression as he pulled away from the screen.

"Find something, Doc?" Seth asked, becoming concerned by the look Doc was giving him.

Doc sat back in the chair. "Please, sit down."

Seth pulled up a chair and sat facing Doc.

"The MTS scan didn't show that a physical problem in your brain caused your headache. I took your blood sample this morning to see what else might be causing your headache. I've taken blood samples from each of us since we were on the freighter to look for any chemical imbalances in our blood that would signal a start of the madness."

Seth was confused. "I know this."

"What you don't know is how I test the blood samples. I put them in a machine that checks for differences from our previous samples. If the blood for each person matches their previous samples, the machine indicates that everything is fine and files away the details of that blood sample. If there is a difference in the blood from previous samples, it warns me."

Doc paused to make sure Seth understood. Seth indicated he did.

"The sample I took from you this morning registered no difference from your previous blood samples. I might have stopped there, but I ran your blood through this sophisticated Biolab machine. I wanted to see if it could give me any insight into the cause of your headaches. This machine does a deeper analysis of the blood chemistry and maps the DNA. I didn't need the DNA mapping, but it is part of the machine's analysis. The machine tests for chemical as well as genetic abnormalities. It found something unusual in your DNA."

"Doc, you're scaring me. What did it find?"

"If I'm interpreting this correctly, your DNA is like nothing I've ever seen."

"That sounds nuts. There must be something wrong with the machine."

"I've tripled checked everything. I even ran my blood through for a comparison. My DNA came out normal. I ran all the samples of your blood from the first blood drawn on the freighter to the one I took this morning. They all came out the same. The analysis from this machine shows parts of your DNA are dramatically different from a normal person's DNA. I'm not sure what I'm seeing or how to describe it. The machine indicates an anomaly in some segments of your DNA that it cannot analyze. Those segments have a chemical makeup so abnormal they don't appear to come from something human or even something living. I know that sounds ridiculous. I've checked and rechecked, and the machine comes out with the same results every time and for every one of your blood samples."

"That can't be. I wouldn't be alive. I wouldn't be human if that were the ..." Seth's voice trailed off. "It can't be. I was fine when I had my physical exam at Klatania University. You were in charge of those exams. You would have seen then if I was a freak."

Doc drummed his fingers on the table nervously. "I told you that your mother helped get you into Klatania University. I did something I shouldn't have done. I was overseeing the physical exams for all new students at the time. Part of the exam is a DNA analysis, much like the one I just conducted here. Each student must pay for this test, which is expensive. Your mother contacted me after you were admitted. She was aware we would require an analysis of your DNA. It was standard for every new student. She told me she didn't have the money to pay for it. She said she had performed this analysis on you recently to test out equipment in the new clinic she was working at. She asked if she could send these test results to me and if that would be sufficient. It wasn't policy, but she pleaded that she was only a poorly paid outer planet doctor, and this would be a big help to her financially. I gave in, and she sent the DNA analysis. It was normal, and I never ran our analysis on you. If I had, I expect I would have found the same results I found today. You were born with this anomaly. Your mother was aware of it and hid it by sending me results from someone else's DNA."

Seth hadn't told anyone about his telepathic ability except Tovar. The strangeness in his DNA must have something to do with this ability. Doc needed to know he was a telepath. "I am different. I'm a telepath. As a teenager, I fooled the EYE Corps Interrogator when he came seeking out telepaths, and I've been hiding it my entire life. I don't use my ability, and I don't want to use it. Do you think the fact that I'm a telepath has something to do with my strange DNA?"

"I'd like to know how you fooled the EYE Corps Interrogator, but the answer is no, and here is why I know that. The first telepaths appeared just over 20 years ago. They were only found on the outer planets, and only young children had this ability. The Emperor took a keen interest in them. He set up a team of scientists to study the telepaths. I was on that team. We studied them thoroughly, running every test on their body's chemistry and their DNA. As we were studying the telepaths, more telepaths began to emerge. Our research couldn't identify any differences between telepaths and non-telepaths except for their telepathic ability. Within a family, one sibling could be a telepath, the others not. Even between identical twins, sometimes both would become telepaths, but other times, only one. There was no chemical or medical predictor of who was a telepath or who would become one.

"The Emperor was unsatisfied with our results. When he pressed us to find a way to turn normal people into telepaths, we assured him we couldn't. This led him to collect all telepaths and to create the EYE Corps, where he trained the telepaths to do his bidding. I'm saying your strange DNA is neither the cause nor the result of you being a telepath."

"All this sounds nuts. Look at me. I'm like everyone else. I'm human. How can my DNA be that strange?"

"I believe you're a normal human male. I watched you flourish in your studies at Klatania University. I don't think you're abnormal, though I'm surprised to learn you are a telepath. Your unusual DNA is not in active genes. Many genes in a person's DNA are inactive. Some are from battles with ancient diseases long gone. Others are waiting to turn on when needed. In any case, your unusual DNA is inactive and should not affect you."

"Does it mean there isn't a problem, and I can relax?" Seth asked hopefully.

"Your blood isn't any different now than it was on the freighter, and I guess no different than when you were born. That brings me back to the issue I came here to analyze. I don't think your unusual DNA is causing your headaches. I don't know what is. All I can suggest is for you to continue taking the analgesic pills. When we return to Klatania, I want to thoroughly analyze your DNA."

Seth was about to argue he wouldn't become a lab rat when the door opened, and Jana walked into the Biology hut.

"Why the worried looks?" she asked.

Doc answered, "We were just talking about Alan deciphering the Alenian language and what that might mean. It's a great discovery. Unfortunately, we're running out of time. That said, we still don't know what caused the physical changes that drove the colonists into a killing frenzy. Enough of that. I have work in the Medical hut I need to get at."

Doc and Seth left the Biology hut as Jana began running a test. Doc said nothing more about Seth's unusual DNA as left.

Seth sat on one of the benches in the Common as he considered what Doc told him. "*You have strange DNA. It doesn't look like it came from something living or human.*" What did that make him?

CHAPTER 61

L unch was better than most of their meals. The cook found some real meat preserved in the freezer. Doc okayed he could use it, and he made a stew with real meat and real potatoes. It was their first tasty meal since the cook made them pancakes.

Seth continued to think about what Doc said about his DNA as he ate. He had accepted he was different when he learned he was a telepath. If, as Doc said, the differences in his DNA had nothing to do with him being a telepath, why did he have it? Was his strange DNA the reason he got precognitive visions? He didn't think so because Doc said his DNA wasn't active. What did it mean to have strange, possibly not human, DNA?

The thoughts swirled around Seth's mind until he couldn't handle it. He was human. Maybe the Biology Lab's equipment was malfunctioning. He wasn't going to let this get to him. For now, he had other things to deal with.

Seth turned his attention to the team's conversation. Gunther was pointing out once again that the Major and the Marines were mysteriously absent.

Professor asked Seth if Alan was alright. "I left him sleeping. I think he will be fine once he catches up on his sleep."

Seth asked Professor, "Did someone tell the Major that Alan had deciphered the Alenian language?"

"As far as I know, no one has. Discovering the Alenian library was a find of incalculable value. But to have Alan decipher the Alenian's language so quickly was miraculous. I can only imagine what we will learn about the Alenians once we read their books in the library."

Doc said, "I don't think the Major will consider learning more about the Alenians that important. He is focused on the single-minded goal that we learn what happened to the colonists, not the Alenians."

"Surely, he will let us take the books when we leave."

"I hope he does. I wouldn't be surprised if he doesn't."

"It would be barbaric if they don't let us take back what we've found here."

"Barbaric, maybe. The Major often repeats our primary objective here is determining what happened to the colonists. If that was his primary goal, he wouldn't constantly be off doing whatever he is doing. He would be here pushing us more aggressively to find answers. He isn't. He and the Marines are absent much of the time. I suspect the Major and the Marines have an agenda we are unaware of."

As Doc finished saying that, the Major walked into the mess hall followed by the Marines. The Major said nothing to the team as he walked to the table he and the Marines normally ate at. The Marines followed him like dogs trailing their master. All of them sat without speaking as they waited for their lunch.

The team had finished eating their meal, and they left together. Doc stopped them outside the mess hall. "We've tested almost everything there is to test in the colony. We will soon complete the tests on the samples Jana collected from the cavern city. So far, we've found nothing in the water, food, or in the air that is dangerous to humans, much less anything that would have caused the kind of anomalies we found in the autopsy. There must be something else, but I've run out of ideas what it could be."

"A weapon!" Gunther offered.

"At this point, I'm open to the idea it could have been a weapon, despite the Major saying they didn't find anything. Gunther's hypothesis of a weapon must be taken as a possibility. Assuming we can find this weapon, I'd like to know who wielded it and why."

Jana addressed Professor, "You said they made a significant discovery just before the killings began. It must be more than a coincidence. Do you think it was the cavern city?"

"I doubt they discovered the cavern city. If they had, I would have expected to find books from the Alenian library in the Artifacts hut."

"When Alan and I found the entrance to the cavern city, the area around the door was littered with fallen debris. The debris had been there a long time. When I opened the stone door to the city, it swept the debris away. It would indicate the colonists never found the cavern city, so it couldn't be their significant discovery. The question is, what was?" Seth asked.

"We need Alan to wake up and see if he can find out what it was," Professor said.

Doc added, "I think if we don't want to kill Alan, we need to let him get some rest. I suggest we return to what we were doing before lunch."

They agreed. Professor headed back to piece together more of the broken Alenian artifacts. He was biding his time until Alan would show him how to read Alenian. Jana and Doc went back to the Biology hut to recheck their tests. That left Gunther, who said he had nothing to do. It gave Seth an idea.

"Wait here," Seth told Gunther.

Seth walked back into the mess hall. The Major was eating lunch and looked up as Seth approached.

"Major, the Alenian robot didn't come from the cavern city. No one has been in that city in a long time. I expect you noticed that."

The Major said nothing.

"I might be able to find where that robot came from with another flyover of the area. We know what direction it was heading. Its final destination had to be somewhere near the cavern city when it finally died. If so, there may be other robots equally dangerous there."

If the Major agreed to his request, Seth was sure he would have one of the Marines accompany him. To avoid haggling over having a Marine babysitter, Seth quickly added, "I can take Gunther with me."

Seth waited to see what the Major was going to say. If Gunther was a spy, the Major wouldn't hesitate to approve having Gunther accompany him.

The Major took another bite of his food before he said. "I will allow you to take the Skimmer up one more time. Take Mr. Voltig with you. If you land it again, I will lock you up until we leave. Do you understand?"

"Loud and clear. No landings."

Seth left the mess hall. He walked up to Gunther. "I have something you might find interesting. Like to take a Skimmer ride?"

Gunther agreed he would, and they headed for the hangar.

CHAPTER 62

The Skimmer was low on fuel. Gunther refueled it before effortlessly pushing it out of the hangar.

Seth asked, "Can you fly a Skimmer?"

"I've repaired various flying craft, even Skimmers, but I've never learned how to fly."

It was the answer Seth was hoping for. This was an opportunity to test Doc's suspicion that Gunther was a spy.

Five minutes later, they were flying over the colony.

Gunther yelled over the engine noise, "So we are going west to find where that robot came from?"

Seth nodded, but this wasn't what he was planning. Gunther's giant body overflowed the Skimmer's seat. He was a head taller than Seth and at least forty pounds heavier, all muscle. He would be too formidable to confront on the ground. If he didn't know how to fly, here at 2000 meters above the ground, it should be a safe place to challenge him.

"You say you're a weapons expert, but you are not a member of the Imperial Guard. I've never heard of a weapons expert who wasn't in the Imperial Guard. They like to keep that expertise within their ranks. Were you put on this team to spy on us?"

Gunther stiffened. "You think I'm a spy?"

"Are you? Did Prime, the Major, or someone else put you with us to monitor what we're doing?"

Gunther said nothing as he stared at Seth. Seth thought he might have miscalculated. If Gunther could fly a Skimmer, challenging this giant in these tight quarters might not have been a good idea after all.

"I am not a spy."

"Okay, if you're not a spy, how is it you're not a member of the Imperial Guard?"

Gunther turned and stared straight ahead. Seth thought that may have ended the conversation, but it didn't.

Still looking straight ahead, Gunther said, "I work for the Imperial Guard. I build weapons, sometimes bombs, and fix their sensitive equipment, but I am not one of them."

That didn't satisfy Seth. "Why did they include you on this team?"

"You want to know why I'm here. I don't know why I'm here. This colony had few weapons, and it is unlikely a weapon exists that could drive eighty-five people insane at the same time. There is no reason for me to be here, but they made me come."

"I'll buy that you don't know why you're here. I don't know why I'm here, either. What's your story? How did you come to be working for the Imperial Guard but not be one of them?"

"You want to know my story. Alright, I'll tell you. I was born and raised on a backwater planet called Sidlon. It's a fringe outer planet, one the Empire considers of so little value that they allow warlords to rule it. There were constant battles as a dozen warlords fought over control of each other's districts.

"My parents lived in one of the larger districts ruled by a warlord called Vordrol. My father had a small repair shop, and I worked with him fixing machines. With the constant fighting, repairing broken equipment was a good business.

"I was a teenager and delivering a repaired machine on the other side of our district when warlord Regarland, our chief rival, exploded a bomb in a restaurant Vordrol usually ate at. The restaurant was next to my father's shop. The bomb destroyed the entire building, including my father's shop and the apartment we lived in above the shop. The blast killed my father in the shop, and my mother in the apartment. The bomb failed to kill Vordrol. He chose that day not to eat in the restaurant.

"I buried my parents and vowed on their graves I would kill Regarland. I fought in Vordrol's army against Regarland's forces for the next two years. I killed many, but my benefit to Vordrol was not as a soldier but to build weapons, especially bombs.

"It was the beginning of my third year in Vordrol's army when we won a significant battle against Regarland's forces. We continued moving on his stronghold until most of his men died or fled. Regarland died from one of my bombs. When I saw his mangled body, I thought it would make me feel better that I had avenged my parents. I realized in supporting Vordrol, I was helping someone who was just as evil as Regarland. Regarland's death changed nothing.

"I left Sidlon. At this point, the only thing I could do to make a living was hire myself out as a mercenary. I no longer wanted to fight, but my skill at making weapons, especially bombs, was known. I went from one conflict to another, making weapons and bombs for whoever would pay me. One day, the Imperial Guard captured me along with the people who hired me. They put them to death, but they had heard of my reputation for making weapons and gave me a choice. If I worked for the Guard, they would let me live. I chose to live. I made weapons and bombs for the Guard until I was brought to the meeting at the palace and put on this team. So, you ask me why am I here? I have no idea. The one thing I am not is an Imperial Guard spy or anyone's spy."

Seth didn't need telepathy to know Gunther was telling the truth.

"I believe you are not a spy," Seth said.

"Now that we've got that over, I can tell you something you don't know. A Marine watches your shack each night."

"You mean to guard us."

"I don't think so. I think he's there to see if you leave your shack during the night," Gunther said.

Seth remembered Jana saying the Marines were told to watch him. He had no idea why they would be doing that. But they weren't only watching him. Twice when he came back to his shack, he noticed his duffle bag was not exactly as he left it. Once the zipper was partly open. Another time, the duffle bag had been moved. He never left it that way, but since nothing was missing, he assumed he must have.

Gunther telling him this added to his belief he was telling the truth. Gunther wasn't a spy. He decided he could trust Gunther. He banked the plane.

"If the robot is west, why have you just turned north?" Gunther asked.

"The mountain peak above the cavern city has an unnatural flat face. I think it's a solar collector that powers the city. Alan and I flew the Skimmer to the northern mountain range and found a similar unnaturally smoothed peak. There might be another cavern city or something else the Alenians needed power for. It will be a short detour to see what's there."

Gunther grunted.

Seth took it to mean he approved of the detour.

The moisture from the brief rain had evaporated. The land below them was a sickly gray. This didn't look like a place where anything could grow.

They were approaching the northern mountain range. The mountains here were steeper, taller, and more rugged than the mountains in the west. No river ran along the base of these mountains. It was a stark, arid landscape, littered with boulders.

Seth pointed out the smooth mountain peak. "See the top of that mountain. It has a smooth face, just like the top of the mountain above the cavern city. If I'm right, it collects sunlight to provide power. I want to find out what it's providing power to. Look for something unusual on the mountainside."

"You mean, like the ledge entrance into the cavern city?"

"Exactly."

Seth flew across the mountain with the smoothed peak looking below for a ledge similar to the one for the tunnel to the cavern city.

"I don't see anything except boulders and mountain," Gunther said.

Seth didn't see anything that resembled the ledge he found in the western mountains, either.

"Maybe it's on the other side of the mountain. I'm going to see if we can get over the mountain to see what's on the other side."

Seth flew along the mountain range as he looked for a place low enough for the Skimmer to fly over. The mountain range was over four kilometers tall, with some peaks even taller. The Skimmer had a maximum flying altitude of three kilometers, but that was in dense air. The air on Alenia was slightly thinner, which meant he would have to find a place to cross over the mountains that was less than three kilometers tall.

He flew west from the smooth-faced mountain peak for ten minutes before he found a small gap between two jagged mountain peaks. The opening was no more than double the width of the Skimmer's wingspan, and only slightly less than three kilometers from the ground. It would be barely low enough and wide enough for the Skimmer to fly through, but it was the only place he could see where they might make it over the mountains.

"I'm going to try flying over the mountain here. Hold on. It might get bumpy," he yelled to Gunther over the engine's noise.

Gunther tightened his seat harness.

Seth spiraled up until he was at the Skimmer's maximum flying altitude. They were just thirty meters above the lowest point in the gap. Seth pushed the Skimmer's throttle to the maximum as he pulled up its nose and headed for the opening.

The wind was blowing in strong gusts coming down the face of the mountain. The Skimmer began to bounce up and down violently. Seth was afraid the wings might rip off from the stress. A strong downward gust forced the Skimmer to drop twenty meters. It came dangerously close to the bottom of the gap. Seth pulled up hard to lift the Skimmer's nose as he furiously worked the Skimmer's ailerons to keep it from crashing into either side of the gap.

When they reached the halfway point in the gap, the wind suddenly died. A few meters later, the wind began again, but it was coming at them, not pushing from behind. Seth could use the wind coming at them to gain lift. He pulled the Skimmer's nose up and it lifted above the gap. A few minutes later, they were through the gap and on the other side of the mountain.

Seth turned to Gunther to see how he dealt with their passage. Gunther returned a guarded smile. Seth could see a trickle of sweat running down the side of Gunther's forehead.

The north face of the mountain range was even steeper than the south face. Seth flew the Skimmer to the mountain with the smooth peak. The peak was also smooth on this side of the mountain. It was not a natural phenomenon.

"I'm taking it down so we can look for the entrance to a city."

Gunther said nothing but seemed comfortable with letting Seth do it.

Seth brought the Skimmer slowly down to 120 meters and flew along the mountain's base under the smooth peak. Gunther craned his neck to look out the side of the cockpit. "I don't see anything except the mountain." Seth didn't see anything either.

The steepness of this mountainside would make a ledge cut into it easy to see. He brought the Skimmer down to 90 meters. He flew east across the base of the smooth-faced mountaintop. Seeing nothing, he flew back across it from the other direction. Neither of them could see anything like a ledge cut into the mountain's face or anything else that might be the entrance to another cavern city.

Gunther yelled out, "There! It looks like a bulldozer."

Gunther was right. It was a bulldozer with Imperial markings like the equipment in the colony's Quonset hut. It was parked a short distance from the mountain with the smooth peak and partially hidden by large boulders. Seth scanned the area to see where the bulldozer could have been used. He couldn't see any of the ground disturbed near it.

"Why bring a bulldozer here?" Gunther asked.

"Good question. Another question is how did they get it here? A Skimmer couldn't lift a bulldozer, much less fly it over the mountains. That means there has to be a way to bring it to this side of the mountain."

Seth flew by the bulldozer. As he did, Gunther pointed to a spot a hundred meters from the bulldozer. "I see an opening in the mountain big enough for the bulldozer to fit."

Seth could see what Gunther was pointing at as he flew by it. It appeared to be the opening of a cave. It might not be a cave but a tunnel through the mountain. If the Alenians could hollow out a city in a mountain, they could build a tunnel through one.

Seth wanted to land and explore, but the Major would check the Skimmer's digital log to see if he landed, and he didn't like the idea of spending the rest of his time on Alenia locked up.

"We're going back over the mountain. This might be a tunnel. I want to see if there is an opening on the other side," he yelled to Gunther, who grunted his approval.

CHAPTER 63

S eth made a mental note where the opening was on the mountain's north face. If it was a tunnel, there should be an opening about the same place on the other side. He flew back to the gap they came through and circled to gain altitude. At three kilometers, he flew away from the gap. Knowing the wind came up the mountain's north face, he could use it to gain altitude beyond the Skimmer's limit of three kilometers. The wind obliged as it drove the Skimmer up. Once it was high enough, Seth turned it around and put it into a dive towards the gap.

They were approaching the gap from 3.8 kilometers. The added speed from the dive sent them through the gap so fast the wind didn't affect the Skimmer as much as before. Once the Skimmer reached the midpoint of the gap, Seth allowed the wind coming from the south to help push the Skimmer up and over the rest of the gap and through to the mountain's south face.

"Why didn't you do that the first time?" Gunther yelled.

"You live and learn," Seth yelled back with a grin. "Now, let's see if we can find the other end of that tunnel."

Seth brought the Skimmer down to forty meters and slowly flew it across the face of the mountain where he thought the tunnel would exit. He couldn't see an exit to the tunnel. Gunther shook his head to indicate he didn't see it either.

He brought the Skimmer around and flew back along the mountain's base. Gunther yelled, "There!"

It was an opening in the side of the mountain partially hidden by a jutting rock formation above it. The huge boulders around the opening would obscure it even at ground level. There was no way of knowing this was the entrance to a tunnel through the mountain, but the bulldozer on the other side was strong evidence it was.

"The Alenians must have made this tunnel," Gunther said, and Seth agreed. The question wasn't who, but why, they did it.

Seth checked the time. They'd spent too much time here. "We have to go look for where the robot was going," Seth told Gunther.

Gunther nodded.

Seth flew southwest until they were over the killer robot. It was still there. Seth didn't believe the robot was heading to the cavern city. The tree blocking the steps and the undisturbed door debris showed it hadn't come from there. There had to be another place the robot came from and was returning to.

Seth thought a robot that large could cross the river at any point, but it should have matted down the tall grass as it passed. To find where it originally came from, they should look for matted down grass or the robot's footprints on the mountainside of the river. He told that to Gunther, who agreed.

Seth took the Skimmer low and flew over the river as they searched for any signs of matted down grass or footprints. Pass after pass, they didn't find anything. As Seth took the Skimmer up to a higher altitude, he could see where the robot lay and where it must have come through the grass to reach that spot. The grass stood up and showed no sign the huge robot came through it. Even the grass where they walked through to inspect the robot wasn't matted down. This grass was resilient enough to spring back quickly.

The sun was getting low. Seth turned to Gunther. "There's no use continuing to look for where the robot came from or where it was going."

Gunther agreed. Seth headed back to the colony.

They landed as the sun set. Seth went to tell the Major they didn't find where the robot was going. He would keep the tunnel secret, for now. Gunther agreed he would say nothing about it.

CHAPTER 64

The team was eating supper when Seth and Gunther joined them. They told the team they didn't find the robot's origin but said nothing about the tunnel.

Alan had awakened an hour earlier and was rushing through his meal to spend the night translating the Alenian books. While they were eating, Doc said in a hushed voice quiet enough that the Major and Marines couldn't hear him, "I've finished running all the tests, and I've found nothing."

"Don't tell the Major, or he will make us leave," Professor begged.

"I can hold off telling him for a while, although not long. Whatever you want to learn about the Alenians, you had better do it quickly."

Supper was over, and Alan ran out of the mess hall to the Artifacts hut, followed by Professor. Doc said he would spend some time in the Biology hut, and Gunther said he was going for a walk. That left Seth and Jana walking together to their shacks.

Jana said, "You didn't find where that robot came from or where it was going. It seems strange it would travel to the compound, and all it did was attack a Marine. I guess it isn't surprising considering that they have a spaceport, they would have robots. The question is, where was this robot all this time?"

"It's one of many mysteries here. I might have learned more today, except the Major made it clear he didn't want me to land the Skimmer."

"I think he was looking out for your safety. You might have run into another killer robot."

Seth didn't believe his safety was the Major's primary concern.

They walked in silence for a while. Then Jana said, "One thing you didn't mention in your list of Alenian mysteries was the burned-out genetics lab in the village. The machine there appeared to be more advanced than any in the cavern city. Have you returned to that lab?"

"No, I haven't."

"You're pretty insightful. You understood the planet had habitation towers, and they would cause trouble for us before anyone else. You also said humans used that lab before Alan found notes confirming it. And you said the lab fire wasn't caused by the insane colonists but before. Do you have any idea what they used that machine for?"

Seth was surprised by the question. Why would she think he had insights into what they did in that lab? Did Doc tell her he was a telepath? He didn't believe Doc would reveal his secret. He was sure of it.

"The towers, by their number and location, could be habitation engines. Seeing the clouds rise from them confirmed they were. I've been around my father's Habitation Engines enough to recognize an Initiation Phase. The rapidly increasing clouds forming around these towers were just what an Initiation Phase looks like.

"The soot in the lab was covered in dust. That gave me a time frame long before the colonists went insane. The glass shards told me humans used the lab."

"Glass? What about the glass?"

"The Alenians don't use glass. Their windows are made of a cellophane material. The glass on the floor of the burned-out lab was from broken range hoods over the workbenches. The glass couldn't be Alenian, so it had to be put there by humans. You see, just simple observations.

"The machine in that lab had to be what the ship's files referred to as a genetics laboratory, hence it must have had something to do with genetics. How they knew that, or who destroyed the machine, is anyone's guess. But, why do you think I might have an idea what they were doing in that lab?"

Jana smiled. "Since your Sherlock is working well, I thought you might have figured out what they did in that lab."

They had reached their shacks.

"I don't have any idea what the humans did in that lab. Now that Alan can read their language, maybe we can learn why the Alenians had such a sophisticated lab in the village."

"Maybe," Jana smiled. "Good night."

Seth watched Jana go into her shack. Aside from taking Seth and Alan to the Alenian lab, he hadn't heard her speak about the Alenians until tonight. Was she more interested in what the Alenians had been doing or the humans who used the lab? He would try to remember to ask her.

Seth crawled into bed as he pondered the growing number of Alenian mysteries. The bulldozer on the north side of the mountain was another one. There had to be a reason the colonists brought the bulldozer there. It must have something to do with the solar collectors on the mountaintop. The questions were increasing for which there were no answers.

Seth tried to relax and fall asleep. Lying here in the quiet, his headache was at its worst. During the day, he could distract himself from the pain in his head. He tossed and turned until he eventually fell asleep.

CHAPTER 65

Prime's screen began flashing with an incoming call. Prince Victor was calling. She hadn't talked to or seen him since their clandestine meeting in the alcove several days before. She pressed the receive button, and the Prince's face appeared on the screen.

"Come to my quarters," he commanded. Commands from him irritated her. He held no power over her that the Emperor didn't grant, and since the Emperor didn't respect his son, the Prince had no power over her.

"I am busy now. I will come in an hour."

"We need to talk immediately!"

"I will be there as soon as I can get free," she said, forcing herself to keep a civil tone.

"I said, I need you now. Right now!"

The Prince's brow was furrowed from stress.

"Very well," she said. The line went dead.

Prince Victor showed that same level of stress the day his two brothers and mother were thought to have survived the crash. The stress changed to relief, for only a revealing second, when he was told it was confirmed they were dead.

She left her office and headed to Prince Victor's quarters. Another thought raced through her mind. What if the Emperor had learned the Prince was planning a coup? That would stress the Prince. She didn't want to be linked with him if that was so. That thought lingered as she entered the Prince's quarters.

Prince Victor was alone in the room, sitting on one of his overly gaudy colored sofas. He still had the stressful look she'd seen on the monitor.

"Finally, you're here," he said angrily.

"What is so important, Your Highness, that I needed to come immediately?" she said it in a non-complaining tone.

He checked to make sure they were alone. Of course, they were. He indicated he wanted her to sit on the sofa next to him. When she did, he leaned over and whispered in her ear. "It's today."

Prime realized he was talking about the coup. By summoning her here, it would connect her to it. She had to be careful what she did next. She checked her wristband. It showed there were no monitoring or recording devices in the room. She wasn't sure she could trust it. He was going to get her killed as well as himself.

"What is today?" she asked, putting all the innocence into her voice she could muster.

"The Emperor will end his reign today." He gave a quick, nervous smile as he said it.

She checked her wristband again. A passive listening device can turn on when certain words are spoken. The band still showed no hidden device recording their conversation. Her body relaxed, not her mind.

"I haven't heard anything about the Emperor stepping down." She would play this as safely as she could in case the coup failed. However, if it worked, she couldn't leave the Prince thinking she was his enemy.

"Stepping down! Are you kidding? I intend on relieving him of his life."

There it was, clear and to the point.

"How?" She wasn't sure how he could assassinate him when the Emperor was so paranoid and constantly vigilant against just that.

"I have been planning this for a long time. Let me say it will be swift and it will surprise everyone. All I want is your loyalty. If you wish to keep your position, I expect you to be as loyal to me as you were to my father, even more so."

Now, she had to be careful. What she said next might be the difference between dying or surviving. "I will do my job for the Emperor, whoever that is. Although what you propose will not be accepted by the Barons."

"I have three of the Barons on my side. The others will fall in line once it's done. I want you to make sure the transition has no complications, especially from the palace guards."

"As you wish." It was time to go. More time here would only compromise her. She walked out of the Prince's quarters. She'd better be ready for whatever happened next.

CHAPTER 66

Prime didn't return to her office. Instead, she went to the palace's command center where all activities in the palace were monitored. The room contained twelve small screens surrounding one large central screen. Every critical location within the palace was covered by cameras that could be viewed from this room.

A Captain of the Guard sat watching and controlling the cameras. When she entered, he stood and bowed.

"As you were," she said, walking up and standing next to him.

He sat back down, waiting for her to say why she was there.

"Is it time for the Emperor's walk?"

"In fourteen minutes," he responded.

"Put the camera outside the Emperor's quarters on the center screen."

The large screen showed the door leading to the Emperor's study. Two Zinder guards, as stiff as mannequins, stood on either side of the door. After twelve minutes, five more Zinder guards joined them. They were there to escort the Emperor on his passage to the gardens in the center of the palace. The Emperor enjoyed the garden's tranquility. At this time each day, the gardens were emptied so the Emperor could be there undisturbed. He once told Prime it was the only thing of beauty in his life. This despite the fabulous collection of art from Earth in his quarters.

The seven Zinder guards stood at attention waiting for the Emperor to emerge. The door opened, and Emperor Wuden stepped out. He was wearing a kaftan of blues and greens extravagantly embroidered with designs in gold thread.

The guards surrounded the Emperor as they proceeded down the halls to the garden.

"Keep following the Emperor on the center screen."

The image on the screen followed the procession. A Zinder guard stood at the door leading to the garden. He told the Emperor the garden was empty as he opened the door.

The Emperor had just stepped into the garden when a plasma blast from behind blew off half of his skull. The Emperor toppled to the ground. One of the escort Zinder guards had fired the shot. He stood unmoving with his plasma rifle still aimed where the Emperor had stood as the other Zinder guards fired their weapons at him. He died in a smoldering mass of burnt flesh.

The Captain monitoring the cameras froze. Prime shook him to get his attention. Taking off her wristband, she handed it to him. "I want you to play the recording on this device throughout the palace." She'd deleted anything that might incriminate her on the recording and edited what the Prince said as she walked to the monitoring room. She also deleted the Prince saying that three Barons supported him.

The Captain, still stunned, took the wristband and plugged it into the broadcast port. The speakers in the room came alive, with the audio now being played throughout the palace. The Prince's voice could be heard as he said, "I intend on relieving him of his life. I have been planning this for a long time. Let me say it will be swift, and it will surprise everyone."

She watched the Captain's reactions as he listened to the Prince's treachery. First there was shock, soon it was followed by anger. It was what she wanted and expected. After it played, she told the Captain to make a copy and send it to the People's Communications Council. The People's Communications Council was considered an independent public news organization, though it wasn't. Once they received this recording, they would put it on VIDs and send them to all the planets.

That done, Prime picked up the comm and ordered the palace guards to arrest the Prince for high treason.

CHAPTER 67

Seth was shocked awake with a vision of Gunther lying on the ground in pain. It was the middle of the night. This was a premonition as real as the one on the Beanie. As he tried to focus on the vision through his pounding headache, he heard the blast from a plasma weapon. Gunther needed help.

Seth quickly dressed and ran out towards the Common. Doc and Jana came out of their shacks as he ran by, and they ran with him. Once they got there, they came upon two Marines carrying Gunther. He was unconscious and bleeding.

"Bring him quickly!" Doc yelled at them as he ran to the Medical hut.

The Marines carried Gunther's large body into the Medical hut and put him on one of the beds. Gunther was unconscious. Doc grabbed his stethoscope and listened to Gunther's chest. "He's alive," he declared.

There was a plasma burn on Gunther's back. Seth helped Doc cut off Gunther's shirt. "Tilt him on his left side," Doc told Seth as he studied the burn. It went diagonally from Gunther's lower back to his right shoulder.

"He was lucky. A more direct hit would have burned through his shoulder," Doc said. He turned to Jana, "Get some burn gel and bandages."

She ran over to the cabinet and returned with the gel and bandages.

Seth held Gunther as Doc applied the burn gel over the wounds, before covering them with self-adhering bandages.

Seth continued to hold Gunther as Doc braced him on his left side with pillows to relieve any pressure on the burns on his back and right shoulder.

Professor came in. "What happened?"

"Someone shot him," Doc said as he finished bandaging Gunther. "Set him down slowly," he said to Seth.

"How serious is it?" Professor asked.

"It could have been a lot worse. He has third degree burns on parts of his back and right shoulder. He was lucky to have such a glancing hit. Either the shooter's aim was off, or Gunther ducked as he was shot."

Professor asked, "Why is he unconscious?"

Doc was looking at Gunther's head. "There's a contusion and a lump on his head. He must have hit it on something when he fell. He may have a concussion."

Doc lifted Gunther's eyelids to check his eyes with a small flashlight. "The pupils are dilating normally, which indicates if he has a concussion, it's a minor one. Barring any internal injuries, he should be alright once the burns heal."

As if on cue, Gunther stirred and opened his eyes. "What happened?"

"You were shot with a plasma weapon. Who did it?" Doc asked.

Gunther grimaced, trying to move his wounded right arm, now bandaged tight to his chest. "I remember hearing a noise behind me, and as I turned to see what it was, I felt a pain in my back. That's all I remember before waking up here."

"Where were you when this happened?" Seth asked.

"I was at the far west end of the Quonsets."

The Major entered the Medical hut. He looked at Gunther, before asking Doc, "Is he all right?"

Doc said, "He's been shot. Do you know who shot him?"

"We don't," the Major said.

Professor said anxiously, "Does that mean there are more crazed colonists?"

Just then, they heard shouting outside. Someone was yelling, "Stop or I'll shoot!"

Two Marines standing by the door behind the Major bolted outside, followed by the Major and Seth. A man was standing in the middle of the Common with his hands in the air. A Marine had his rifle pointed at him. The other two Marines joined him. One knocked the man to the ground and began binding his hands behind his back.

The Major and Seth ran up to them. The man wasn't a member of the freighter crew or a Marine. The man was lying face down on the ground, a Marine holding him down with a knee. The Major ordered, "Stay back, Harthset."

Seth backed away. As he did, the man on the ground strained to look up at him. It was more a look of curiosity than pain from the Marine kneeling on his back.

The Major ordered, "Get him on his feet.". Facing the man, he barked out, "Who are you?"

"I'm a scientist here. I mean, I *was* a scientist here."

"Where did you come from?"

"I was hiding in the mountains when I saw a Skimmer fly over. It meant someone was here."

Doc joined the group, asking, "Did you shoot our friend?"

The man said, "Shoot? I don't have a weapon. I didn't shoot anyone."

"Take him to the Communications hut for questioning," the Major ordered.

"Wait!" Doc said. "Were you here when the other colonists started killing each other?"

"Yes, I was. That's why I ran away and hid in the mountains."

"Major, this man may be vital in helping us learn what happened here. Let us question him."

"You can question him after I do."

Jana joined them. "Who is this?"

The Major ignored her question. Two Marines began half carrying, half dragging the man to the Communications hut.

Doc addressed Seth and Jana. "Go with them and learn what you can. I need to make sure Gunther is all right."

Chapter 68

Once in the Communications hut, the Marines forced the man into a chair. He appeared to be confused and fearful, not aggressive.

The Major walked up to him. "What's your name?"

"Ralph Thorndale."

"What did you do here?"

"I'm a biologist. I worked in the Biolab."

"You said you were here when the colonists went insane."

"I was."

"Why weren't you affected?"

"I don't know. I just wasn't."

Seth asked, "Did you run tests in the Biolab to see what was happening to the others?"

He stared at Seth for a long time before answering. "Yes, I ran tests on their blood."

The Major asked, "Do you know why they killed each other?"

"No, I don't. They just went mad and began killing each other."

"You said you were hiding in the mountains. Why didn't you come out when we landed?"

"I didn't know anyone was here until I saw the Skimmer fly over today."

"Are there any other survivors?" Seth asked.

"There was only one other, but I haven't seen him and don't know where he is. The rest of those who were here are dead."

The Major said, "How do you know they are all dead?"

"I buried them. They were my friends and I made sure they had a proper burial."

"We counted the graves. All the colonists were accounted for. That would include you if you are one of the colonists," the Major said.

"One of our people died long ago, that was the extra grave. There was a robot programmed to bury him. I had it bury the other bodies."

Jana said to the Major. "He may not know why it happened, but we can run some tests on him that might help us understand why he wasn't affected."

"Until we know we can trust him, I am putting him in the lockup. You can interrogate him there," the Major said, and walked away.

Seth addressed the Major's receding back, "We have a lockup?"

Jana answered, "There is a small cell in the rear of the Communications hut. I guess they thought it necessary to have one."

A Marine grabbed Ralph Thorndale, his hands still tied behind him, and led him to the rear of the Communications hut. Seth and Jana followed.

A door at the rear of the Communications hut opened into a small room. Inside the room was a single barred cell. The Marine untied Thorndale's hands and had him walk into the cell. He locked the cell door and left. Jana and Seth stood outside the bars looking at Thorndale.

"I don't know why you're treating me this way. I didn't do anything. I'm lucky to be alive."

"Once they verify your story, I'm sure they'll let you out," Seth said.

A Marine poked his head into the doorway and said, "The Doc wants to see Harthset. He says it's important."

Jana was left alone with Ralph Thorndale.

CHAPTER 69

Seth entered the Medical hut to find Doc sitting on a chair next to Gunther's bed and Gunther sitting upright with his legs over the edge of the bed. Gunther grimaced slightly as he turned to look at Seth.

"What's so important, Doc?" Seth asked.

"Gunther was telling me he doesn't know who shot him, but he believes it was one of the Major's men."

"Why would one of the Marines shoot you?" Seth asked Gunther.

"I've been watching the locked Quonset hut at night. I sit in the shadows to see who is going in and out of it. The Marines have been making a lot of trips there, and so has the Major. I thought I would get closer tonight to see what they were doing inside. That's when I was shot."

"You're lucky you only received a glancing blast and weren't killed," Seth said.

"Maybe a little luck. I was watching the hut when I heard something behind me. I was turning to see what it was when I felt the blast. It knocked me to the ground. I was trying to get up when everything went black. I think someone hit me on the head. I know I didn't get this wound from falling after I was shot."

Seth asked, "The guy they captured, Thorndale, could he have shot you?"

"Thorndale said he didn't have a weapon. And you notice the Major didn't have his men search him for one. I think the Major knows one of his men shot Gunther," Doc said.

"I've been watching that Quonset hut for a while. I was suspicious about why we weren't allowed to see what was inside. My suspicion increased when I saw the Marines carrying cylinders into the hut the night before last."

"Were they silver in color and about a meter tall?" Seth asked.

"Exactly like that."

"I think those cylinders were in the MTS hut when we toured it. I thought the cylinders were empty. Doc and I were in there yesterday, and the cylinders were gone. It makes me wonder what was in those cylinders, and why would they move them to the locked hut," Seth said it more to himself than to Gunther.

"That's not all. Over several nights, the Marines have been going to the Alenian village. I followed them and watched as they searched the Alenian buildings, especially the building with the burned-out lab. Whatever they're looking for, I don't think they found it. I've never seen them carrying anything out."

Doc gave a knowing look to Seth, *Now I know what he was doing all hours of the night.* He said, "If they are doing something they want kept secret, you're lucky they didn't kill you. Now I suggest you rest here so I can watch you."

Seth didn't think he could do much more here and was exhausted. "I'm going back to my shack. Let me know if you find out anything more."

Back in his shack, questions about what was happening kept him awake. Why were the Marines searching the Alenian village? What were the metal cylinders in the MTS hut, and why were they moved into the locked Quonset hut? What could they be doing in that hut that is so secretive they almost killed Gunther? And the biggest mystery of all was Ralph Thorndale. Why wasn't he affected by the insanity the rest of the colonists suffered?

He didn't need precognition to tell him all these things were bad omens.

CHAPTER 70

All ten Barons gathered at the palace the day after the assassination. They sat in the room reserved for their meetings with the Emperor. It was a large room with a single, round table in the center. The table was inlaid with the Klatan Crest in gold and highlighted with jewels. There were eleven chairs around the table, ten occupied by the Barons, the empty one, the Emperor's.

The Barons were there to decide who would become the next Emperor. Their responsibility was one of form and tradition more than purposeful function. There had always been a Klatan ready to ascend to the throne. With the only Klatan heir responsible for the Emperor's death, the problem was who would become their next Emperor. The Prince hadn't married or had any legitimate or illegitimate children. As repugnant as it was, they were discussing putting the Prince on the throne despite what he did.

There was another pressing problem. Immediately after the Emperor's death, the rebels escalated their attacks on Imperial shipping close to the Core planets. The rebels sent a message demanding independence for the outer planets to each Baron. The Barons were fearful if they didn't quash these rebel attacks soon, the push for independence would gain strength. It could even lead to some of the Core planets joining the rebellion and demanding their independence. The situation was getting out of control.

The discussion was growing more heated. It stopped when the door opened. Prime entered the room. Prime had only attended these meetings when the Emperor invited her, which had been infrequent. They watched as she walked over and stood behind the Emperor's chair. No one voiced an objection to her presence.

Prime looked at each of the Barons. She had identified the three who had conspired with the Prince. She talked privately with each of them before the meeting. She gave them a simple alternative that they could help her or be executed as traitors.

The Barons were silent as their eyes fixed on her. This was the way she wanted it.

She began, "The Prince killed his father. He reprogrammed one of the Zinder guards to kill the Emperor when the Prince gave the guard a cue. The Prince has admitted this in interrogation." She didn't expect the Barons to ask how that interrogation was conducted. They would assume it was done using an EYE Corps Interrogator. They would be wrong. Prime chose to use the old-fashioned method of torture. She was sure it would work on the foppish, weak-willed Prince, and it did. He had no tolerance for pain, and they didn't have to disfigure him much before he admitted everything.

She went on, "The Prince can never ascend to the throne. If he does, one of his first edicts would be to replace all of you. He wouldn't trust you because you had been loyal to his father. It would be easier for him to replace you than trust you."

She was right. They knew the Prince would not only replace the Barons. He would have them killed.

"By the Prince's action, the reign of the Klatan family has ended. This opens the position for someone new."

Each of the Barons secretly desired to be the next Emperor. If any of them tried, he would incur the wrath of the others, leading to civil war. Each Baron had a military force they used to maintain control over their planets. The military they had was assigned to them by the Emperor. In turn, the Emperor's military reported to one person in charge of all the Empire's military, Prime.

A Baron who plotted with the Prince began to speak. She controlled him now. "We need someone who is respected throughout the Empire. Someone who can command the loyalty of the military."

Another of the Barons who'd participated in the coup spoke up. "Only one person in the Empire has garnered such respect. She is standing here."

Prime stood there acting surprised, inwardly relishing as she watched the seeds of her plan blossom.

The Barons were considering if they could trust her. If she would allow them to continue in their positions, keep their wealth and their lavish lifestyles. More to the point, would she let them live?

Now it was Prime's turn. "I believe we have an Empire in peril. Without a strong leader, the rebels will convince all the outer planets to join them. Civil war is inevitable. If you decide to give me the reigns of control, I promise to keep the Empire as it has always been, safe and prosperous."

Subtle, but not too subtle. It should register in their small, greedy minds that she was offering them personal security under her rule.

On cue, the third Baron she controlled said, "Prime has all the qualifications we need to maintain a strong Empire. I say we vote for our first Empress of the Empire."

They asked Prime to leave so they could discuss it. Her plan had worked. She would be Empress of the Empire. Now she needed to decide what to do with the Barons. Three of them could never be trusted. They had to be killed soon. The other seven Barons she could replace with her people in time, depending on how well they accepted her rule.

CHAPTER 71

S eth was awakened by the sun shining into his bedroom. Alan's bed was unslept in. He hadn't seen Alan when Gunther was shot or even when they captured the surviving colonist.

Seth dressed quickly and ran to the Artifacts hut. He was relieved to find Alan sitting at a table surrounded by stacks of Alenian books. Alan was so engrossed in a book he didn't notice Seth approaching.

"Learn something important?"

Alan jumped at the sound of Seth's voice. "You startled me. I've learned something about the Alenian's history."

"Tell me."

Alan began talking excitedly. "The Alenians originated on the planet closest to their sun. They developed the ability to travel in space a long time ago, since I'm not sure how they measure time, I don't know how long ago that was, but based on what they accomplished, it was long ago. One of the first things they did when they became space capable was to check out the next planet from their sun. The two planets had nearly identical environments, the only difference was the second planet needed to have a slight adjustment made to its atmosphere to support the Alenians. Once it became hospitable, they colonized it. These two planets continued under a single governing body. I could only find one thin book that mentions this moon."

Alan stopped to take a breath. The lack of sleep and constant state of excitement was draining him. He continued, "The Alenians spent a long time transforming this moon to colonize it. The moon was in the final stages of transformation when a mutation began appearing in Alenian children. This is where it gets murky. Nowhere does it explain what that mutation was, but whatever it was, it upset the Alenians a lot. At first, they ostracized those with the mutation. Eventually there were so many with the mutation, the Alenian governing body decided to relocate them to this moon. The human researchers had it right. This was a penal colony. If I'm correctly interpreting it, the Alenians here were forced to work and live under harsh conditions. Many who were sent here initially died. The ones who survived were required to grow a single crop that only grew here. There aren't any details about this crop except that it was incredibly valuable and important to Alenian society. However, the Alenians who lived here only received necessities and food for growing this valuable crop."

Seth asked, "Did they change this moon to match the atmosphere of their other two planets?"

"From what I can tell, the two planets and this moon had the same atmosphere."

"Do these books say anything about what happened to the two interior planets? We've been led to believe they are uninhabited, but from what you read, they were their home planets."

"I haven't found anything more about that."

"Do you know if the Alenians remove their dead from this moon?"

"That's the strangest part. The Alenians refer to someone who died on this moon in the present tense. It's as if they continue talking with them after they die. That's pretty much all I've learned so far. I need to go back to the cavern city for more books if I'm going to learn more. Now that I can translate their language, I know how to identify the books I need. About half the books we brought back are novels. It turns out the Alenians like novels with happy endings."

"Did you hear what happened to Gunther and that we found a survivor from the colony?"

"Professor told me, and I went to see Gunther."

"I'll leave you to your translating. I'm going to check on Gunther."

Seth left as Alan returned to his books.

CHAPTER 72

Gunther was still lying in the Medical hut bed. His color was better, and he didn't grimace as he lifted himself to look at Seth as he walked in. Doc was standing in front of a machine studying its display.

"How are you?" Seth asked.

"I feel better. Doc gave me some pills, and I don't feel any pain. I'm going to ask for a large supply of these pills to take with me," Gunther replied, sporting a grin.

"Don't get carried away. Those painkillers are strong and addictive. They are only masking your pain. Your wounds are serious, and you need to give yourself time to heal," Doc said sternly.

Doc turned to face Seth. "Fortunately, the plasma burns are healing well. It is the wound on Gunther's head that bothers me, not due to its condition, but its source. I agree with him that he didn't get it from a fall. It looks like he was hit in the head with the butt of a rifle. That further supports Gunther's belief a Marine did this."

Seth checked the time. "Gunther, it's almost time for breakfast. I can bring you something to eat."

Gunther swung his legs over the edge of the bed. "I feel well enough to get my own food. Thanks for the offer."

Seth looked at Doc to see if he agreed with Gunther's assessment. "Yes, he's well enough. Let's all go."

When they got to the mess hall, Jana, Professor, and even Alan were waiting for them. They greeted Gunther enthusiastically. It turned out they had all visited Gunther earlier that morning.

Alan asked Gunther, "How are you?"

"Better by the minute," he said as he slid onto a seat at the table. "How is translating the Alenian books going?"

Professor answered, "I had to drag him away from the books. He will stay there until he translates all of them or dies of starvation and sleep deprivation."

Alan smiled faintly. "This is the most exciting thing that has ever happened to me. I can't wait until we return to the Empire, where I'll have more time to study these books in greater detail."

Doc said, "Yes, that will be excellent." The frown lines on his face made a different statement. Seth read it as *I hope you will have that opportunity.*

Neither the Major nor the Marines were there. The cook brought out the team's breakfast, and Seth asked, "Have you seen the Major or the Marines this morning?"

The cook put down the large bowl on the table. "They were here over an hour ago demanding I make breakfast for them. You can't argue with that Major, so I made them breakfast."

Inside the bowl was the pasty-looking, synthetic substitute for oatmeal.

The team began eating, and since they were alone in the mess hall, Doc and Gunther shared their theory that a Marine attacked Gunther. When they finished, Professor said, "I can't believe it. It begs the question what are they doing in the locked Quonset hut that is so secret they would shoot you from seeing what it was?"

Silence followed, until Seth asked, "Does anyone know anything about our prisoner?"

Doc answered, "The Major let me take a sample of Mr. Thorndale's blood this morning. He protested that he had done nothing to merit being imprisoned. He told me the Major's men had been interrogating him roughly, though I didn't see any obvious signs of physical abuse, but I wasn't allowed to examine him."

"Did you find anything in his blood that explains how he survived when all the other colonists went mad?" Professor asked.

"His hormone levels are normal, not the extraordinary levels I found in the autopsied colonist. I'm still running analysis on his blood for any abnormalities." As he said it, he gave Seth a quick glance before turning back to face the group.

Alan addressed Professor, "Since you have been acting as my father, can I now return to translating?"

"After all these years, I finally have a son. Yes, you've eaten, so go back and jump into your pile of Alenian books," Professor said.

Alan got up and ran out of the mess hall.

"That boy will work himself to death if we don't watch him," Professor said. He asked Seth, "Can I get your help with some of the artifacts?"

Seth agreed, and he followed Professor out of the mess hall.

CHAPTER 73

Professor pointed to the shelves containing broken pieces of Alenian pottery. "I'd like you to layout the pieces on the table and arrange them as closely as possible into their original objects. I want to photograph them so that when I return to Klatania University, I can use 3-dimensional imaging to reconstruct these fragments into an image of their original form. Whatever the Major says, I don't believe he wouldn't allow me to take a few VIDs from here."

Seth studied the piles of jumbled pieces of broken pottery. It was going to be a challenge. "Sure, Professor," he said.

"Start with those three shelves first and begin with the most decorative pieces. Call me when you have something I can photograph."

Seth smiled and said, "No problem," believing it would be a big problem.

Alan was in the rear of the Artifacts hut, his nose buried in one of the Alenian books and oblivious to what was happening around him.

Seth went to the first shelf and gingerly removed the broken pieces. He laid each piece on the table. The broken pieces were so small it was difficult to determine how the pieces fit together.

Seth studied the pile. It was a jigsaw puzzle without a pattern to follow. After moving the pieces around, it was apparent it wasn't one thing he was looking at, but three. Two decorative plates and a small colorful vase. He began arranging the pieces. Once done, he called Professor.

After taking several pictures from different angles, Professor asked Seth to return the pieces to the shelf and continue.

Seth decided to work on an object with larger pieces. He found a collection of pieces that came from a single decorative object that wasn't a plate or food serving piece but an emblem that was 20 centimeters square. As he began putting the pieces together, he saw it had a distinctive design. Eight overlapping circles intersected at one point in the center of the piece. A square enclosed the circles, and a diagonal line ran from outside the square on the lower left-hand corner to outside the square on the upper-right-hand corner. The line on the right side ended at a point, which gave the impression the line was a spear piercing the square.

Seth was about to call Professor over to photograph the object when he stopped and looked at it carefully. He thought it looked like a Coat of Arms. He remembered seeing a book with pictures of Coats of Arms that had once been used on Earth. They were symbols used in ancient times to identify wealthy and influential families. The more he looked at it, the more it reminded him of something familiar. He had seen this design before, not here in Alenia, but in the Empire.

"Professor, can you come here and tell me what this is?"

Professor came over and checked out the piece. "I've seen this same design in the cavern city. It was over the door of one of the buildings. I assume it is an official seal for the Alenians, although I haven't seen it in the village or anywhere else."

Seth said, "I'm sure I've seen this somewhere in the Empire, but I don't remember where."

Professor was surprised. "I would be extremely interested knowing where you may have seen it. This is a unique symbol. I can't imagine someone in the Empire having anything like it. Please tell me if you remember where you saw it."

A Marine came into the Artifacts hut and walked up to Seth. "The Major wants to see you in the Communications hut."

Seth told Professor, "I'll come back later to put more of these jigsaw puzzles together after I see what the Major wants."

CHAPTER 74

The Major was sitting at his desk in the Communications hut. He looked up as Seth approached. "The prisoner is refusing to talk to us. He said he will only talk to you." There was suspicion and anger in the way he said it.

"Why me?" Seth asked.

"We were able to verify he was a member of the colony. He won't tell us anything besides his name and profession."

Seth went to the rear of the Communications hut and opened the door to the cell room. Thorndale was lying on the cot, his back turned away from the door. Seth stepped up to the bars. He spoke loudly, "You wanted to tell me something?"

Thorndale turned on his cot and faced Seth. He got up slowly from the cot, wincing as he did. Seth thought Doc didn't look hard enough for signs of physical abuse the Major's men inflicted on Thorndale.

"The Major says you will only talk to me."

Seth hadn't gotten a good look at Thorndale last night. He could see now that Thorndale was in his late fifties or early sixties, thin, although not so thin as to look undernourished. He had auburn hair with wisps of gray, and a chin covered in scruffy stubble, also showing some gray.

The most striking feature on Thorndale's face were the scars crisscrossing it. The scars were deep, cuts too deep to be repaired by restorative surgery.

Thorndale got up from the cot and slowly walked to the bars until he was standing opposite Seth. He stood there silently, studying Seth's face.

"Is there a reason you're looking at me so intently?"

"Please close the door," Thorndale asked. Seth did.

"Do you recognize me?"

"I've never seen you before." Seth didn't know what Thorndale was getting at. Did the beating he received from the Major's men rattle him to the point he was delusional?

"I was looking to see if there is more of him or her in you. It's mostly her." Thorndale said.

"Him or her who?"

"You have your mother's eyes and her brow. The chin and the nose don't look like either of them."

"You knew my parents?"

"I worked with your mother years ago. I was there when you were born. I was there when, well, when it all fell apart."

"What are you talking about? What fell apart?"

"Them, your parents."

"You were there when they divorced?"

"Not the divorce, that happened later. I was there when they split up. They were such a tight couple, no one would assume anything could tear them apart."

"I was five years old when they separated. How long did you know them?"

"I was working with your mother before she got pregnant with you."

Seth wasn't sure if this man was crazy, or he actually knew his mother and father. "If you were friends with my parents until I was five, you might know the nickname my mother called me when I was a kid?"

Thorndale smiled, "She used to say you were greased lightning because you ran so fast it was hard for her to catch you."

"She never called me that," Seth said.

"She called you that when you were a toddler. When you were a little older, if I remember, she called you Speedy Rabbit."

Seth was stunned. That *was* what his mother called him. She called him that until he was seven years old, until he demanded she stop calling him that, and she did.

"If you worked with my mother when I was born, you must have been working with her on Digeria."

Thorndale grimaced as he took a labored breath. Thorndale told Doc the Major's men interrogated him roughly. If that meant hitting him, it didn't show on his face. It wouldn't because the extensive scarring on his face would mask a beating unless it bled, which it hadn't. Seth assumed the rough interrogation meant they used body blows.

Thorndale said, "I'm tired now. We can continue this conversation another time." He walked slowly back to the cot and lay down.

Seth wanted to shake Thorndale to get him to tell all he could about his parents. Questions that plagued him for years, *Why did they split up? What did his mother do that drove his father away? What was his father like?* He had dozens of questions for Thorndale about his family. Apparently, Thorndale was only going to answer his questions when he was good and ready.

Seth came out of the lockup. As he walked by the Major's desk, the Major asked, "What did he say to you?"

"He said he didn't shoot Gunther. He wants the Doc to look at him, he thinks he hurt himself." Seth didn't trust the Major, and he wasn't going to share anything with him.

The Major glared at Seth but said nothing. Seth left the Communications hut and headed back to the Artifacts hut.

CHAPTER 75

As she expected, the Barons voted to make Prime the first Empress of the Empire. She planned to have her coronation in two days, so there would be no time for the Barons to reconsider, or for the public to express their feelings about her becoming their first Empress.

There wasn't enough time to plan a grandiose coronation, the kind the Klatans held when one of them ascended to the throne. However, she wanted her coronation to be memorable. She sent the date and a description of what she wanted to the Communications Director. It was his job to make all the arrangements. She was told he gasped when he read the date for her coronation. Now she was going to see if he was up to the job, or if she needed to replace him.

She sent a message for the Communications Director to come to her. He had been the Communications Director for many years. He served the Emperor well by manufacturing VIDs of public appearances that never really happened so the paranoid Emperor could look like a man of the people when he was anything but.

It took ten minutes for him to appear. The heavyset man was red-faced and breathless. He must have run from his office on the other side of the palace.

He bowed deeply, almost bumping his head on the floor, still breathing hard. "You called, your..." His voice trailed off. Addressing her as 'your Majesty' was premature but calling her Prime didn't seem right. So, he just stopped talking and held the bow.

"Stand up. I don't want to talk to the top of your head."

He straightened and stood facing her.

"You have been told what I want done for my coronation. Is there a problem providing that?"

"The time is rather short. It might be difficult having everything you wish done in time," he said sheepishly.

"Then I will find someone who can do it."

"I didn't say I cannot do it. I will do it," he said, the ruddy color on his face from exertion hid any stress resulting from the conversation.

"Very well. I also want everyone in the Empire to know I am the Empress immediately after the coronation. Can you do that?"

He couldn't, but he said, "VIDs will be sent out to everyone immediately following your coronation."

"How long will it take to reach everyone on the outer planets."

He paused. If he lied to her, she might have him imprisoned or killed. She might do the same thing if he told her the truth. Better to be truthful. "The fastest we can deliver VIDs to all the outer planets will be ten days, Your Majesty." He was relieved she didn't immediately get angry hearing it would take ten days, and she liked being addressed by her future title.

She mulled over ten days. It was long, but everyone would know she was their Empress in ten days.

"I have a slight change to my plans. Arrange my coronation to be in the afternoon. That morning, you will arrange for the Prince's beheading. I want that broadcast to everyone on Klatania, and then I want it sent out as a separate VID."

The Communications Director said nothing, though the shock on his face, along with his complexion turning crimson, screamed volumes.

"Can you do this?"

"I can, Your Majesty."

"If you cannot, if you fail to deliver, I will have your head removed." She waved a hand dismissing him.

The man, almost quivering in fear, bowed and left.

As he walked out the door, she smiled to herself. His reaction when he heard about the beheading pleased her. She could expect the same reaction from everyone throughout the Empire. If she couldn't gain their immediate respect, she would make sure they feared her.

There was still something she needed for the coronation. It was a suitable crown. She had them bring her the crown the Klatans had used for generations. It was a simple gold crown with only a few jewels adorning it. Despite changing both the family and the sex of their leadership, she felt using the Klatan's crown would offer continuity with the past.

She summoned the palace jeweler. "Make this crown smaller to fit me," she said as she handed him the Emperor's crown.

The jeweler measured her head before bowing to leave. "Wait." She handed him a bag of precious stones she found in a chest in the Emperor's private rooms. "Add these to the crown. I want it to look spectacular."

The jeweler opened the bag and stared at its contents.

"What's wrong," she demanded.

"The crown might be unwieldy if I add all these gems to it," he said.

"I don't care. Make it work. Remember, you must have it ready the day after tomorrow. Now leave me."

The jeweler took the crown and bag of gems, bowed, and made a hasty exit.

It would be the same crown, but now it would be more fittingly adorned, a message to tell everyone she would be more than another Klatan ruler.

· · · ● · ● · · ·

Prime was up early. It was the day of her coronation. She was reviewing the details of the Communications Director's plans for the day. On the surface, he had the preparations in place she requested. Now he had to deliver. She would follow through on her threat to remove his head if he didn't.

The Prince's execution was scheduled in an hour. Prime went to the prison and had the Prince brought to her in a private room. His arms and feet were shackled so tightly that the guards dragged him into the room and set him on a chair. Prime sat in a chair opposite him. After the guards left, she said, "What do you think now of your plan to assassinate the Emperor?"

The Prince glared at her. "You said you were with me. You encouraged me to do it. And all along you were planning this, the first Empress of the Empire. Do you think that will stand? Do you think that you can hold the Empire together? The Klatan family has been the guiding light since long before the formation of this Empire. Do you think the people of the Empire, especially those on the outer planets, will tolerate you after the deaths you inflected on them?"

"You were a fool to believe I would support you in killing the Emperor. Before you came up with your half-baked plan for ascending to the throne, I was considering ways I might assassinate both you and your father. You made it a lot easier for me. And as far as the Klatan legacy is concerned, I believe the people will not be upset to see a change after centuries of Klatan rule. As for problems with the outer planets, our spies have discovered the location of the rebel's command center. I have a fleet of warships heading there as we speak. Once we destroy the rebel's base and their leadership, I don't think I will have much trouble from the outer planets."

Prime stood up. "Enjoy the next hour. It will be the last one in which your head and body remain connected."

When she was outside of the room, she told the guard, "Gag him. I do not want him to speak to anyone before his beheading."

She left the prison with a smile on her face.

CHAPTER 76

P rime was pleased with the events leading up to her coronation. It was just as she'd planned it. She watched the live video feed as the Prince was brought to the newly built platform. On top of the platform was a large block designed for chopping off heads. All of this was from an old Earth movie she once saw. She conveyed her desire to reconstruct the scene from the film to the Communications Director. She was concerned about his commitment to the task when he suggested using a guillotine for the beheading to make it less gruesome. After a look of dissatisfaction from her, he said he would, of course, do what she suggested.

The Prince was brought out, his leg shackles removed to make it easier for him to walk. He resisted, and the guards had to drag him to the top of the platform. She was pleased to see the makeup artist had successfully covered up all the physical torture marks on his face.

While the Prince was being held up next to the block, Prime's recording of the Prince saying he was going to kill the Emperor played in the background. When it finished, one of Prime's Captains stepped onto the platform. "It has been determined that the Prince reprogrammed the Zinder guard to assassinate the Emperor by ...." The Captain droned on with technical details of how the Zinder was reprogrammed. They'd learned this when they'd tortured the Prince. How they obtained the information was omitted from the public statement.

The Captain was followed on the platform by a spokesman for the Barons. He addressed the camera, "The Barons have voted that you, Prince Victor Klatan, be condemned to death by decapitation for your crime."

Behind the platform was a large screen showing the ten Barons looking somberly on as their representative announced the Prince's punishment. She told them they had to attend since it would be announced that it was their judgment to condemn the Prince to death. She could see them squirm at having to take credit for the Prince's execution. She said they had to show they were in charge of dealing with the Prince's crime. By now, she had them doing her bidding no matter what she demanded of them. But she offered them the alternative of not attending the beheading in person but being there via live feed. They quickly accepted the option of the live video feed.

The Barons' representative finished his announcement of how the Prince would be dispatched. Each of the Barons nodded to show they concurred with the sentence.

Prime was delighted. It had gone well so far.

The Prince, now limp, all resistance gone, was pushed to his knees, his head placed on the block. The Executioner, a hood hiding his identity, was the same one who'd tortured the Prince. He was a man without a conscience. Someone she felt would be useful to her in the future. The Executioner stood over the Prince, a giant axe in his hands. He raised the axe, and it fell. The Prince's head dropped into the basket beneath, and cheers erupted. The cheers were not from the few who attended the beheading. The Communications Director added the cheers from a recording. The entire effect made her smile.

The Communications Director had pulled off the beheading well. Now it was time to see if he could do what she wanted for her coronation.

The Great Auditorium had a thousand seats. They were filled with many of the Empire's most powerful people. Considering how little time the Communications Director had to gather such a large and influential audience, it surprised her. The threat of joining the Prince in losing his head had been sufficient motivation for him as well as those attending the coronation.

The stage glittered in gold. Behind the stage was a mural of a goddess floating above the planet Klatania. To no one's surprise, the goddess's face resembled Andraia Gretler.

The Communications Director suggested a simple and uncluttered arrangement on the stage. He suggested not having a throne, instead, having a simple pedestal holding the bejeweled crown with the Barons standing behind the pedestal.

She felt this would be too plain. He said it would appear basic, but that it would make a more powerful statement than any opulent proceeding could. She accepted his plan.

As she viewed the scene on video, she could see the Communications Director had been right. A spotlight on the crown with its many jewels bathed the stage in a rainbow of colors. The Barons standing behind it in their most ornate kaftans added to both the simplicity and power of the scene.

Majestic classical music from one of Earth's ancient composers played as Andraia Gretler walked slowly down the aisle to the stage. She was wearing a plain and unadorned white kaftan. Another suggestion by the Communications Director, who said it was not the time for extravagant dress.

She reached the stage and stopped in front of the pedestal holding the crown. One by one, the Barons walked up to the crown. They touched the crown, then bowed to her before returning to their original position on the stage. It differed from the traditional ceremony, a change the Communications Director suggested would be symbolically powerful to show the Barons' fealty to her. She liked it.

The last Baron, the oldest and the one who held the most powerful position, came last. He lifted the crown and placed it on her head. As he did, he proclaimed, "We crown you Empress Andraia, Empress of All Humans."

The auditorium exploded in loud cheers. She wasn't sure if the enthusiastic cheers were from those in attendance or provided by the Communication Director's soundtrack, but the effect was as she hoped it would be.

With the weight of the overbejeweled crown wanting to slide off her head, she turned to face the audience and, more importantly, the camera. She began, "I thank you for this great honor. I will make the Empire the greatest in history. One of the first things I will do is to provide the Empire with some recently found art treasures from Earth. The Klatan family lied when they said the art treasures from Earth were destroyed. They have been hidden in the Klatan family's private collection. I will put these magnificent treasures from Earth in a museum so everyone in the Empire can enjoy them."

The Communications Director had made a video panning the Emperor's study showing the paintings and statues from Earth. He played it on a split screen as she talked about the art treasures.

Newly crowned Empress Andraia walked back down the aisle, the Barons following her. She walked slowly and very straight. This was as much to look majestic as to keep the unwieldy crown from falling off her head. Once out of the auditorium and out of sight of the cameras, she pulled off the crown and handed it to a servant.

Now that was over, her first official act as Empress would be to eliminate the rebel threat by destroying their base.

CHAPTER 77

Seth spent the rest of the day in the Artifacts hut arranging pieces of broken pottery for Professor to photograph. He continued glancing at the piece with the eight circles as he worked. He tried to remember where he'd seen it before. It was late in the day when he remembered.

He ran back to his shack and pulled out his duffel bag. He rifled through it until he found the envelope that contained his mother's possessions. He poured the contents of the envelope out on his bed. Out came the VID and her necklace. She'd said the necklace was important to her and wore it every day.

The necklace had eight circles within a box with an arrow intersecting the center of the circles and extending outside of the box. It was identical to the design on the Alenian pottery. It meant his mother must have gotten this from someone who had been to Alenia.

It was time to confront Thorndale and demand he tell him about his parents. He jogged back to the colony and went to the Communications hut. A lone Marine was sitting at the comms terminal. The door to the lockup room was open, and Seth could see the cell was empty. "Where's Thorndale?"

"The Major released him. He's with the doctor."

Seth ran to the Medical hut. Doc and Thorndale were there alone. Thorndale was sitting on Doc's examination table with his shirt off and a bandage wrapped around his ribs. Doc was standing at a cabinet sorting through some drugs. He turned to face Seth as he approached.

"Doc, I want to speak to Mr. Thorndale in private."

Doc turned to Thorndale, who indicated it was okay. Doc handed Thorndale a container of pills and said, "Take one of these pills every six hours for the next three days. If you still have pain in your ribs or trouble breathing after that, come see me."

Doc could see Seth was agitated. He pulled Seth far enough away so Thorndale couldn't hear him. "He told me he directed the robot to bury the colonists, and I think he is still traumatized by what happened here. The fact that the Major's men beat him didn't help, so go easy on him." Doc said loudly, "I have some tests to check on in the Biology hut," and left.

Seth walked up to Thorndale and took his mother's necklace from his pocket. He showed it to Thorndale. "My mother wore this necklace her entire life. She died recently, and this was pretty much all she left me. This is the same design that is on some Alenian pottery. Do you know where she got this pendant?" Seth handed the necklace to Thorndale.

Thorndale stared at the necklace, his scarred face crinkling into sadness. "I'm sorry to hear about your mother's death. She was a wonderful person."

"What do you know about this necklace?"

Thorndale handed it back to Seth. "Your father gave it to her shortly after they arrived here."

The words "they arrived here" stopped Seth. "Wait. You're saying my mother and father were here on Alenia?"

"Your mother and father were with me in the first group of scientists sent here thirty years ago. Your mother was a geneticist and I'm a biologist, so we worked closely together. She was brilliant. It didn't take her long to figure out the Alenians were doing incredibly advanced genetic research. She studied the machine in the village lab, and despite being unable to decipher the Alenian's language, she figured out the machine was used for genetic manipulation."

"How long were my parents on Alenia?"

"Your mother was here over seven years. She left first. Your father left a year later."

"Before I was born?"

"No, you were five when she left with you."

"You're saying I was born here?"

"Your mother and I were friends. She told me she had been trying to get pregnant from the start of the marriage. A little more than a year after your parents came here, she did. Yes, you were born here."

The fact he was born here shook Seth. Here, not on Digeria. "I want to know more. But first I have to check something."

He ran out of the Medical hut and back to his shack.

CHAPTER 78

The last VID his mother made was lying on his bed. He put it into his portable VID player and fast forwarded to the end of the first recording. He waited for the question to come. Static showed as the mechanical voice asked its question, "Origin?"

Seth answered the question, "Alenia."

The static disappeared. A few seconds passed before his mother's face reappeared. She was as drawn and sickly as she had appeared in the first part of the recording. These recordings were made on the same day.

She spoke slowly as if gauging the weight of each word. "You now know where you were born. I don't know how much more than that you know. I will tell you what you've asked of me many times, though I would never answer. Let me start when your father and I were married. It was just before we graduated from Klatania University. Your father was already a brilliant engineer with several patents he obtained while still a student. I was beginning to establish a decent reputation as a geneticist. I think it was why they selected us to be on the first team of researchers to go to Alenia. We were excited to be the first to study another advanced species."

She coughed into a handkerchief she was holding. She closed the cloth quickly, but Seth saw blood on it. She continued, "When we got to Alenia, I discovered the Alenians had a sophisticated machine in their village. It took me some time before I realized the machine could conduct advanced genetic manipulation. I didn't understand how they could have such a sophisticated machine, far more advanced than anything humans had, when in every other way they seemed to be such a primitive culture. But the machine enthralled me."

She hesitated for a few seconds as if she were considering how to proceed, then said, "Your father and I tried to conceive a child from the start of our marriage. We were having no luck. We found that your father's sperm was very weak, it could not produce an embryo even if it were inserted into one of my eggs. I told him it wasn't important to me that we have a child. If he wanted a child, we could adopt after we returned to Imperial space. Your father was miserable over the possibility he would never have his own child. At that time, I was beginning to understand the incredible capabilities of the Alenian geneticists. I learned that the machine in the village could make genetic repairs to damaged cells. I felt sure it would repair the damaged DNA in your father's sperm and make it viable. Once done, I would artificially inseminate myself and become pregnant. It worked, and I became pregnant."

She coughed again, and Seth could clearly see she was coughing up blood.

She continued, "I didn't tell your father how I became pregnant, only that the analysis of his sperm must have been flawed. He was so delighted at the thought of becoming a father he didn't question my pregnancy. You were born, a healthy boy who we named Seth, after your father's father. Not long after you were born, I began to understand more about the machine I'd used to repair your father's sperm. I discovered the machine would not repair damaged DNA if it found the DNA too severely damaged, instead it would substitute DNA it constructed from its database. When I studied what it did with your father's sperm, I learned it decided that his sperm was not repairable. It replaced the DNA in his sperm. I immediately analyzed your DNA and learned you were different. There were peculiar parts of your DNA.

"I ran every test on your DNA I could. Each time the answer was the same. Some parts of your DNA are remarkably different from any living thing I am familiar with. Even with this anomaly in your DNA, in every other way, and by every measure, you are a healthy, normal human. I know this must come as a shock to you."

She paused as if she expected him to be overwhelmed by the news. He wasn't. It confirmed what Doc told him.

"Once I learned of these anomalies in your DNA, I decided to say nothing. If I told the other researchers on Alenia, they would begin to study you. I didn't want my son to become a test subject. I felt it would hurt your father knowing you weren't his biological child, so I kept it from him. I watched you grow up into a fine young man. After you left me, I believed you would lead a normal life. I felt you never needed to know you were born on Alenia or the nature of your conception."

She stopped for a few seconds and turned away from the camera as if she heard something or was listening for something. She turned back to the camera and continued speaking, "Things have changed. I decided that if you ever learned where you were born, I would tell you everything. That time is now. When you were growing up, you asked questions about your father, and later, about our divorce. I wouldn't answer them, and I know it drove a wedge between us.

"Here are some answers you've wanted from me. When you were five years old, you were listless, even unhappy. There were no children on Alenia for you to play with. Although I provided you with as many stimulating and educational activities as possible, you were lonely. One day, you told me you had a friend named Lena. When I asked where you met Lena, you said she was all around. When I asked how old Lena was, you said she was a grown-up. I thought you were talking about someone in the research colony. I soon realized Lena was a make-believe friend. I felt uncomfortable with this fantasy, however, I understood Lena was a coping mechanism for you, something to help you deal with the lack of playmates. I didn't try and get in the way of your fantasy friend. But Lena and the missing crystals changed everything in our lives."

She began coughing uncontrollably. It was so bad that Seth wondered if she could continue. She was now spitting up blood freely. Seth remembered his mother dealing with Boxtonaire disease patients. She was nearing the final stage of the disease. Soon her lungs would fill with blood, and she would asphyxiate. This was difficult for him to watch. All he could think of was that he had abandoned her, and it filled him with guilt.

It took some time before she stopped coughing. Grasping the handkerchief tightly in her hand, she took a labored breath, then another before continuing. "We discovered the crystals shortly before you invented Lena. It was by accident we found them in a false bottom of a cabinet in the Alenian genetics lab. They were ten perfectly round spheres, seven centimeters in diameter, made of a quartz-like substance. They had internal facets that gleamed brilliantly when placed in the sun's light. It was that reason we called them crystals. We didn't know what they were, only that they were from the time of the Alenians.

"One of our engineers took a crystal to the shop to see if he could open it. He began drilling a hole in it when it exploded. The explosion killed him. We returned the crystals to the cabinet where we found them and planned to have them taken back to the Empire to be analyzed in an Imperial laboratory. That never happened because the crystals disappeared.

"No one knew what happened to them. Before they disappeared, only one person had been near that cabinet with the crystals. He was my five-year-old son. It was reasonable to assume you might've taken these shiny objects to play with. I asked you if you had taken the crystals. You said you did. When I asked where they were, you said you couldn't tell anyone. When I pressed you to explain, you said Lena told you not to. I told you it was important that we find the crystals. You were reluctant to give up their hiding place. You insisted if you did, Lena would be hurt. I tried to explain that Lena was a make-believe person, someone only in your mind. You insisted she was real, and you had to save her by keeping the crystals hidden.

"The colony Commander was angry that we couldn't get our five-year-old son to divulge where he hid the crystals. He pressured your father to find the crystals. I want you to know your father was not a violent man. At the time this occurred, he was under great stress and not only about the missing crystals. He was working day and night to understand the workings of the conical towers that maintained Alenia's atmosphere. He was near a breakthrough when the crystals disappeared. When your father confronted you about the crystals, he hadn't slept in 36 hours. You wouldn't tell him where you hid the crystals, and he lost his temper. He slapped you. It was the first and only time he ever hit you. He began to scream at you, demanding that you tell him where the crystals were. You wouldn't, and he was about to slap you again when I screamed at him to stop. He said he was your father and had every right to punish you however he saw fit. It was then I made the biggest mistake of my life. I blurted out that he wasn't your father. He said

I was crazy for saying that, however I couldn't stop myself. I told him he had no part in making you, that I used the Alenian machine to repair his damaged sperm, but his sperm was so flawed the machine rejected it and built sperm constructed of DNA it synthesized."

She paused and took another labored breath. "I still remember the anguished look on his face when I said that. It quickly turned to rage. He ran to my laboratory and smashed everything before setting it on fire. He destroyed years of my work." A tear rolled down her cheek as she said it.

"The Commander said he couldn't tolerate our actions. He said we must return to Imperial space and answer for our crimes. He blamed me for the lost crystals and was furious with your father for destroying my lab. Neither of us wanted to leave Alenia, but your father had more to bargain with than I did. I had lost most of my work in the fire, while he had made progress understanding how the conical towers worked. He claimed he could use that knowledge to convert planets to habitable environments for humans in far less time.

"The Commander waited for orders about our disposition. When they came, they were exceedingly harsh. Your father could stay until he finished his work. I was to return to face Imperial justice. We were told that we could never tell anyone that Alenia existed. Your father would be allowed to pursue his work on what he called the Habitation Engine once he left Alenia. I would no longer be allowed to do genetic research. I could only work as a simple physician for the rest of my life. However, the most severe penalty was that you would be killed. They did not trust a five-year-old child to keep Alenia a secret. Your father said nothing. He was satisfied with their decision. I wasn't. I pleaded for you to be spared. I assured them you would never tell anyone about Alenia, but they would not budge on their demand for your death. I had only one thing I could offer to save your life. During my genetic research on Alenia, I was given an unusual substance they found there. The more I studied the substance, the more I was sure it had remarkable properties. It was a purple powder. I discovered mixing it with equal parts water and alcohol and then injecting it in a mammal, it had remarkable healing properties. But it did far more than heal. Daily injections of this serum prolonged the mammal's life. I believed it would have the same effect on a human, and I intended to do further research on it when I returned to Imperial space.

"I made a plea directly to the Emperor, offering this serum in trade for your life. The Emperor accepted my offer, but he said your life would be spared only if you underwent a brainwipe to remove all knowledge of Alenia. I invented the brainwipe machine with the help of a biology researcher named Thorndale. Selectively erasing memories had been a topic of conversation in graduate school. It was speculation since no one had any idea how to accomplish it. Once here and working in the Alenian genetics lab, I realized how it could be done. The Alenians were working on ways to alter their brains. I had no idea why they were studying this, but their work gave me insight into how I could do it in humans. I learned it was possible to erase and overwrite selective human memories. I intended for the brainwipe machine to be used on adults with emotional problems where erasing memories could be beneficial. The technology was new and unproven, and I never intended that it should be used on a child. The Emperor's decision was final, either perform a brainwipe on you, my five-year-old son, or you would be put to death. All I could do was agree and hope that it would not have a devastating effect on you."

Tears flowed steadily from her eyes as she continued. "They wiped out all your childhood memories of Alenia and replaced them with memories that you were born on Digeria. After we left, your father continued to finish his work on the Habitation Engine. He divorced me a year later, shortly after he returned to Imperial space. In our last conversation, he made it clear he never wanted to speak to either you or me again. I know I'm painting your father in a bad light. He was a good man, an honest man. By lying to him, I hurt him to his core. I can't blame him for his anger. I wish he could have seen that you loved him even if you were not his biological son.

"When you and I returned to Imperial space, I learned they had experimented with the purple powder and they verified my assumption it could extend human life, and the Emperor was using it. I wasn't sure how long the drug would work, or if it would eventually lead to serious and dangerous side effects. That fear made me stay as far from the Emperor's reach as possible. It was why I constantly moved us from one outer planet to another. The drug obviously is still working, and he has enough to last many more years. Now you know your origin and why I was afraid he would come for me. Once I am gone, I fear he might come for you, and I won't be there to protect you."

She leaned forward as if she was going to turn off the VID recorder. She stopped, then she leaned back and faced the camera again. "There is one more thing I should tell you. When I was on Alenia, I discovered why the Alenians were put on the moon. The moon was a penal colony for mutants, and their mutation was telepathy. Only some Alenians were telepaths. I believe the telepaths were moved to the moon to keep them away from the rest of Alenian society. I learned this by studying what they were doing in the genetics lab. They were researching ways to change normal Alenians into telepaths. They never completed their research, but I did. I discovered a way to give humans telepathic ability.

"When I returned to Imperial space, I perfected the process, despite the Emperor's restrictions I could not do genetic research. I developed a virus that if given to a young child, would give them telepathic abilities when they reached puberty. As the Alenians did, I believed it would make us better if we could perceive the world through each other's minds. I released the virus on the first outer planet we lived on after we returned to Imperial space, and I continued to release it on several other outer planets we moved to. I had also developed an antidote in case of problems, and I administered the antidote to you.

"Over time, and for reasons I didn't understand, the virus didn't work on everyone. Only a few developed telepathic abilities. When the Emperor began collecting all who had become telepaths, I feared my idea of a utopian society of telepaths was being corrupted. When the EYE Corps took your friend Tovar and later he died, I recognized the disastrous consequences of what I had done. My grand scheme for reducing conflict through telepathy became the EYE Corps, which instills fear throughout the Empire. I released the antidote to the telepathic virus by coating VIDs with it that I sent to each of the medical clinics on the planets where I originally released the telepathic virus. The antidote was undetectable, and eventually it stopped more telepaths from being created, although I could do nothing to change those who had already become telepaths."

She stopped to take a breath and then another. "These were my sins to you, your father, and the Empire. I hope you can forgive me. I only ask that you know what I did, I did out of love."

The screen went black, and the VID ejected. Tears flowed down his face. He was angry at himself for abandoning her, and for the first time, at his father.

Chapter 79

Seth sat on his bed holding his mother's last VID, trying to deal with the emotions welling up in him. He was sad, angry, and confused. Believing his mother was paranoid as she constantly moved them from one outer planet to another was wrong. It was her discovery of the purple powder's properties that kept the Emperor looking so young. She was justified in fearing the Emperor might come for her if the purple powder stopped working. Though, when they came for him, it proved her attempt at keeping them from the Emperor's grasp was pointless.

He had blamed her for driving his father away. He had put his father on a pedestal, but it was his father who would have let the Emperor kill him, who stood by when they erased his childhood memories, and it was he who abandoned them. He was touted as the great inventor of the Habitation Engine when he had stolen it from the Alenians.

Doc's analysis that his DNA wasn't normal and didn't look like anything human or even something alive was correct. An Alenian machine made him. Did that mean he was part Alenian?

If his mother gave him an antidote that should have prevented him from becoming a telepath, why was he a telepath. The Alenians were telepaths. Did they have premonitions? He wasn't sure he wanted to know.

When he finally pulled himself out of the well of these tortured emotions, he wanted to find Thorndale. He wanted Thorndale to tell him everything about his parents and what happened here when he was a child. He checked the time. They should be finishing supper. He wasn't hungry, but he would find Thorndale in the mess hall.

Seth stepped out of the shack and closed the door when the ground began shaking. The Major warned them to expect minor tremors. This wasn't a minor tremor. This was a full-on earthquake.

The dirt road in front of the shack began to undulate in meter high waves as if it had suddenly turned into water. The ground beneath him shook violently, knocking him off his feet. He was sitting on the ground with his back pressed against the shack's wall as the shaking continued to increase. He was fearful the shack would collapse on him. He struggled to crawl away from it as the ground continued to shake violently.

The quake continued for a long time before it stopped. Seth stood up and surveyed the damage. The dirt road was torn up with huge bumps and deep depressions. To his surprise, none of the shacks looked damaged, at least on the outside.

Seth's concern shifted to the others. He ran to the Common. When he got there, he saw sections of the Communication hut's roof panels were ripped off, as were some of the front panels on the Biology hut. The Medical hut's door was partially torn off its hinges and lying diagonally across its doorway. A table beneath the tree in the center of the Common was lying on its side, another was upside down.

Seth heard noises coming from the mess hall and ran to it. The door was jammed shut. He pulled it until it came off its frame in his hands. Inside the mess hall, several tables had shifted out of their orderly placement, otherwise the building was undamaged.

Seth found Doc, Gunther, and Professor under a table, and the freighter crewmen and the cook under another table. No one else was in the mess hall.

Seth ran to his friends as they crawled out from under the table. "Is everyone okay?"

"We're good here," Doc answered.

Seth turned to the freighter crew who had just come out from under their table. "We're not hurt," the cook said.

"Where are Jana, Thorndale and Alan?"

Gunther answered, "Jana left with the Major and the Marines before the earthquake hit. Thorndale said he was going to his shack, and Alan never came to supper. He's probably still in the Artifacts hut."

Seth ran out of the mess hall and across the Common to the Artifacts hut. He opened the door and found several of the shelves he'd put upright were tipped over again. The Alenian pottery Seth had worked to put together was scattered in disarray across the floor.

Seth called out for Alan but got no response. Stepping over the broken pieces of pottery and around the fallen shelves, he reached the middle of the Artifacts hut before seeing Alan lying on the floor at the rear.

Alan was unconscious, with a deep gash on his head bleeding profusely. Seth grabbed a towel that appeared to be clean and pressed it on the wound to stem the blood flow.

"Alan, wake up." Seth shook him gently. "Wake up!"

Alan's eyes fluttered open. He tried to move, but Seth held him tight in case he was more seriously injured. Alan turned his head. "What happened?"

"We had an earthquake. It looks like you fell and hit your head. We have to get you to Doc."

"I felt the beginning of the earthquake. I tried to stand up, but I fell. The next thing I remember is you leaning over me."

Doc came in and ran up to them. "I found him lying here unconscious," Seth told him.

"Pull away the towel so I can inspect his wound." To Alan, he asked, "What hurts?"

"My head, that's about all."

Doc felt around Alan's neck. "Move your arms. Alright, now move your legs."

Professor and Gunther came into the Artifacts hut.

"Help me get him to the Medical hut," Doc said to them.

Seth and Gunther helped Alan stand up. He was wobbly but protested he could walk on his own to the Medical hut.

Alan sat on the examination table while Doc checked him for a concussion. Doc said, "I think you have a minor concussion. I'll keep you here for a few hours to ensure you're all right. I want you to lie back and rest but don't fall asleep."

Professor asked if there was anything he could do. Doc said no. "Then I need to assess the damage in the Artifacts hut."

Gunther said, "I'll help Professor." They wished Alan well and left.

Doc pulled Seth aside and walked far enough away so Alan couldn't hear them. Doc whispered to Seth, "You noticed Jana was not with us in the mess hall."

"Gunther told me she was with the Major."

"She left with the Major and the Marines before the earthquake began. I've been wanting to say something to the team about Jana, but I haven't quite figured out how to say it without sounding irrational. You know I was suspicious of Gunther until you told me he was okay. You be the judge if I am doing the same thing to Jana. I don't believe Jana is who she claims to be. I know Kleinfeld, and he demands perfection from his students, and I would expect more from his First Assistant. When Jana was helping me test the food and water, she made mistakes. They were mistakes I would never expect one of Kleinfeld's assistants to make. She tried to hide her mistakes, which only made me more concerned that she isn't who she claims to be."

"You think she's a spy. It's what you thought Gunther was."

"I wouldn't put it past Prime to do that. It isn't just that she doesn't know what I would expect her to know. Gunther confided in me that he has seen Jana and the Major talking late at night outside the locked Quonset hut."

Just then, the Major came into the Medical hut. Doc and Seth joined him as he walked up to Alan. "Is anyone on your team hurt?" the Major asked Doc.

"Alan may have a concussion. The rest of us are uninjured. Are you or any of the Marines injured?" Doc asked.

"We are fine."

"Do you know where Jana is?" Seth asked.

"She was with me. She is not injured." The Major abruptly left the Medical hut.

Doc said, "Am I paranoid?"

CHAPTER 80

Doc and Seth stayed with Alan in the Medical hut. At midnight, Alan pleaded with Doc, "I'm feeling fine. I'd like to see how much damage there was in the Artifacts hut."

"I won't release you until you've had a good night's sleep. You can do it here or in your shack, but you'll do it before I say you can return to your work," Doc said firmly.

"I'll make sure he sleeps in his bed. I'll take him back to our shack now," Seth said.

"This is two against one!" Alan complained, as Seth pulled him towards the door. Seth walked Alan back to their shack, and a few minutes after Alan got in his bed, Seth could hear him quietly snoring.

Seth lay in his bed, but he couldn't sleep. The earthquake and tending to Alan had gotten in the way of him talking to Thorndale. Doc said that Thorndale had left the mess hut immediately after supper, saying he was tired and wanted to get to bed early. Seth would find him in the morning. He wanted to learn so much from him, but a good night's sleep would help him focus his mind on the questions he needed to ask Thorndale.

Seth lay in bed thinking about what he wanted to learn from Thorndale. He wanted to know if Thorndale was aware of the strange nature of his conception. Did he know about the purple powder, and that Seth's mother traded it for his life? Seth thought of dozens of additional questions, but they all boiled down to wanting to know about his childhood here. Seth wanted to know everything

Thorndale could tell him about his parents before this business of the crystals shattered their lives.

He slept restlessly, finally awakening when his room filled with light. He checked the time. It was just sunrise, but the light wasn't coming from the window, it was a bright white glow from the center of his room. The glow began to take shape. It formed into a woman with a young girl. The woman spoke to him. She spoke in a strange melodic language he didn't understand. Her voice sounded as if it was far away, as if it was a weak echo. He didn't understand what she was saying, but he could see fear in her eyes.

"I don't understand you," Seth said. She continued trying to speak to him as he could see her fear growing. The little girl with her began to cry. The woman continued trying to tell him something for another few seconds before they both disappeared along with the white light.

Seth shook his head to make sure he was awake and not dreaming. He was awake, and this wasn't a dream. He shifted his legs over the edge of the bed as his bedroom door opened, and Alan rushed in.

"I just had the most vivid dream. A man was standing in my room looking at me. Do you think this is from the concussion?"

"Did the man glow? I mean, was there an aura of light around him?"

"Yes, how did you know?"

"I saw a woman and a young girl in my room surrounded by white light. The woman was trying to say something to me in a language I didn't understand."

"You mean these were ghosts!" Alan said in a frightened tone.

"I wouldn't call them ghosts just yet." Seth wasn't sure why he said it, other than he didn't believe ghosts existed.

They heard raised voices outside. Seth and Alan came out to find Professor and Doc standing outside of their shacks.

"You didn't see anything?" Doc said to Professor.

"Were you tippling more brandy? I didn't see any ghostly images if that's what you think you saw," Professor said sharply.

Seth asked Doc, "Did you see people surrounded by a white light?"

"Just minutes ago, a man and a boy were standing in the middle of the living area in my shack. The man was beginning to say something. When I spoke to him, he stopped and gave me the strangest look before disappearing. I'm trying to convince Professor I haven't lost my mind."

"You haven't. There was a woman and a young girl in my bedroom. The woman spoke in a language I didn't understand," Seth said.

"There was a man in my bedroom," Alan added nervously.

"I can't believe that all of you are experiencing hallucinations," Professor said.

Gunther walked up to them. He was coming from the direction of the compound. "Why are you out here in your underwear?" he asked Seth.

"Did you see ghostly images?" Doc asked Gunther.

"Did I see what?"

"Did you see people surrounded by a white glow?" Seth asked him.

Gunther stared at Seth as if he had gone mad, but answered, "No."

Thorndale came up to them.

Doc asked Thorndale, "Did you see—."

Thorndale cut him off. "It's happening again."

They all stared at him. Doc broke the silence, "What do you mean it's happening again?"

Thorndale seemed unnerved as he said, "This is what happened the day the killings began."

Professor interrupted, "I'm confused. Are you saying we are about to begin killing one another?"

Doc ignored Professor as he focused on Thorndale. "I'm feeling disturbed, even a little frightened, but I don't feel an urge to kill anyone." He turned to Seth and Alan. "Do either of you feel like you want to go on a killing rampage?" Alan and Seth both shook their heads.

Doc faced Gunther.

"I'm not interested in killing anyone either," Gunther said stiffly.

Doc addressed Thorndale, "You said this happened the day the killings began. You've been keeping this from us. Tell us what happened."

"I didn't trust you. I thought you were working with the Major, but after talking to Seth, I realized I can trust you. The day the killings began, images appeared at dawn, just like today. I was getting dressed when I heard screaming outside my shack. I rushed out to find dozens of ghostly images surrounding some of my colleagues. They were speaking in a foreign language, but my colleagues were screaming and holding their heads as if they were in agony.

"The ghostly images saw me, and they came running at me. They surrounded me. They tried talking to me, but I didn't understand them. I could tell they were pleading with me, but that's when I began to feel pressure building up in my head. It was the worst headache I ever had. I thought it must be what was affecting my colleagues. I ran. The ghosts didn't follow me, but the pain in my head persisted. I ran to the vehicle hut, got on one of the motorcycles and headed west. As I got further from the colony, the pain in my head decreased, but it didn't stop until I reached the river."

Doc asked, "Were the ghostly images you saw people who lived or had once lived in the colony?"

"They were people, but not anyone from the colony now or in the past."

"What happened after you reached the river?" Seth prompted Thorndale to finish his story.

"I sat by the river for a long time. I didn't know what to do. I saw a hauler flying away from the colony, and I remembered we were expecting a shipment of supplies. I returned to the colony thinking the freighter crew might be there and maybe the mayhem had ended. The pressure in my head didn't return as I approached the colony. When I got there, there were bodies everywhere. I wasn't sure if everyone was dead or the hauler took those who were still alive.

"I began running tests in the Biolab to discover what caused this. I was waiting in the Common for the tests to finish when I saw Fredricks, one of our botanists. I called out to him. He ran towards me waving a hand pickax. I ran. The motorcycle was nearby. I got on it and raced back to the river. I feared Fredricks would follow me, so I hid in a cave. I waited for the hauler to return. I stayed there until yesterday when I heard the Skimmer flying over."

"You said you had a severe headache, but did you experience any feeling you might want to kill someone?" Doc asked.

"I never felt like I wanted to kill anyone, but when the ghosts kept coming, I was afraid I would go crazy."

"Kept coming? You mean they appeared again?"

"It was the second day I hid in the cave when they appeared. There were four of them. They were trying to tell me something, but I didn't understand what they were saying or what they wanted from me. That frustrated them. They continued showing up for days. When I considered what had happened just before the images first appeared, it led me to where they were coming from."

He had everyone's attention, even Professor and Gunther, who hadn't seen the ghosts. "Two days before the killings began, our people found a tunnel that ran through the northern mountains. On the other side of the mountain, they found a boulder cut perfectly to seal the opening to a cave. Our people removed the boulder from the mouth of a cave the day before the ghosts first appeared."

"Was that why they brought the bulldozer through the tunnel?" Seth asked.

Thorndale's scarred face bunched in surprise. "How do you know about that?"

"Gunther and I saw the bulldozer when we flew on the other side of the northern mountains."

"They used the bulldozer to remove the boulder. They were correct. It was blocking the entrance to a cave. The cave was filled with thousands of crystals, like the ones you hid." As he said it, Thorndale turned to Seth. Everyone followed Thorndale's gaze.

He turned away and continued, "The ghosts and killings started the next morning. I thought the cave must have something to do with what happened, so I went to the cave and used the bulldozer to replace the boulder to seal its opening. After that, the ghosts stopped appearing. Until today."

Professor said, "The notes I found stating they made a significant discovery. They must have been referring to that cave. Nonetheless, I did not encounter or see any ghosts this morning."

"Neither did I," Gunther added.

Doc asked Gunther, "Where were you just a few minutes ago?"

"I was walking through the Common."

"Did you see anything that appeared to be unusual?"

Gunther wrinkled his brow as he focused on his answer. "Jana was talking to the Major in front of the Communications hut. The Marines were sitting at tables under the tree playing cards. I didn't see anything that looked unusual."

Doc turned to Seth and Alan. "Were you both in your shack when you saw the ghostly images?" They nodded. He turned to Thorndale. "What did you see, and where were you?"

"There was a man and a woman in my shack."

"But the time before, you said they appeared outside your shack."

"That's true. Later, they appeared to me in a cave I was hiding in, not outside of it."

"You told me you were outside your shack this morning," Doc asked Professor.

"I awakened early and went outside for some air and to watch the sunrise."

Doc addressed Thorndale, "You said you had a headache in your previous encounter with these ghostly apparitions. Did you experience the same thing now?"

"I had a pounding headache then, nothing now."

"I'd like to run some tests on you to see why you weren't affected," Doc said to Thorndale.

"There's no need. I ran every test I could on myself. I couldn't find anything explaining why I wasn't affected like the others."

"It seems the ghostly images only showed themselves to those of us who were in our shacks. If their previous appearance triggered the insanity, I can't explain why we seem unaffected now that they have reappeared," Doc said.

"It's going to be difficult to explain this to the Major if he hasn't seen the ghosts," Alan added.

"I wouldn't tell the Major anything. There is something very dark in him. I remember when he was here years ago. He is cruel and dangerous, and he is not your friend or mine," Thorndale said.

"I agree we should keep this from the Major, at least for a while. And we should not tell Jana," Doc said.

"Why should we keep this from Jana?" Alan asked.

"Let's just say it would be better if this doesn't go any further than the six of us for now."

Seth grabbed Alan's arm as he was about to press Doc further. "Let it go. I'll explain about Jana to you later."

"Even if we don't tell the Major, he will eventually see them if they keep appearing," Doc said.

"They stopped when I replaced the boulder blocking the cave. I think the earthquake may have dislodged the boulder and reopened the cave. We need to replace it."

Professor shook his head. "All this talk about apparitions coming from a cave sounds insane to me. Have you considered you may all be suffering a mass delusion?"

"I doubt it is a mass delusion, my friend. For now, I can add nothing more to the events this morning, and I am getting hungry. You and I can go to the mess hall. I will tell you what I saw on the way, and you can try and convince me I am losing my mind. We'll see who wins that argument," Doc said, putting his arm around Professor's shoulder and directing him towards the mess hall.

As Doc and Professor walked away, Thorndale leaned over and whispered in Seth's ear, "Sorry I let it slip that you hid the crystals when you were a child here."

Gunther was explaining to Alan why Jana should be kept from knowing what happened when his head snapped in Thorndale and Seth's direction. "What does he mean when he says you hid crystals as a child *here*?"

CHAPTER 81

It seemed Gunther had exceptional hearing. "I'll explain it in my shack," Seth said.

Gunther and Thorndale followed Seth and Alan inside. Gunther and Thorndale sat on the sofa. Seth and Alan put on their clothes before getting chairs from the kitchen to join them.

Gunther began, "You can start by telling us about being a child here."

Seth decided to limit what he would reveal from his mother's VID. Thorndale might know more. The question was would he volunteer the information?

"What I'm going to tell you, I learned last night. Before she died, my mother made a VID to explain what she would never tell me about my childhood. The VID was encrypted, requiring a key I didn't have. Thorndale told me yesterday that my parents were among the first researchers to come to Alenia and that I was born here. That was the key I needed to unlock the VID. In the VID, my mother told me I was five when I hid some Alenian objects they found. They called these objects crystals. I wouldn't tell them where I hid the crystals. I had an imaginary friend called Lena, and I said if I revealed where the crystals were, it could hurt my friend. When I would not reveal where the crystals were, they returned my mother and me to Imperial space. But they didn't trust a five-year-old could keep the secret of Alenia, so they used a brainwipe to erase my memories of being here and substituted memories that I was born and raised on Digeria."

"A brainwipe on a five-year-old child! That's monstrous. They could have left you a blithering idiot," Alan said.

Gunther continued wanting answers, "Explain this business about crystals. What are they and why did you hide them?"

"I don't have any memory of the crystals. Thorndale was here then, maybe he can add some details." Seth hoped Thorndale would answer some of the questions he planned to ask him before the earthquake.

Thorndale began, "We found ten small spheres hidden in a compartment in the Alenian genetics lab. They were identical, seven centimeters in diameter with a semi-transparent shell. Their interiors appeared as crystals as you might find in a geode rock, hence we called them crystals. These were not natural. We had no idea what they were or how they were used. The fact they were found in the genetics lab could have meant the Alenians were experimenting on them. One of our engineers drilled into a crystal, and it exploded, killing him. The colony Commander planned to send the remaining nine crystals back to the Empire for further study. They disappeared before that happened. Seth admitted he hid them, but he wouldn't say where. We never found the crystals. When they opened the cave in the northern mountains, they were filled with the crystals."

"You believe the crystals in this cave have something to do with the ghostly images the three of you claimed to see this morning?" Gunther asked Thorndale.

"The ghosts continued appearing until I closed the cave's opening."

"All this business about ghosts and a cave filled with crystals bothers me. The crystals may be a weapon. That was why when someone tried to open it, it exploded. The ghosts may be the way they scramble our minds. Why seeing the ghosts didn't affect the two of you and Doc or Thorndale still needs to be explained," Gunther said.

"I don't know why I wasn't afflicted when the others here were. Maybe it didn't affect me since I was here from the beginning, over thirty years. I may have acquired an immunity to whatever happened to my colleagues. Seeing the ghostly images today wasn't the same as when they appeared before. I didn't feel the pressure in my head that I felt then," Thorndale said.

"You were here from the beginning?" Alan asked Thorndale.

Seth forgot that Alan had been so absorbed in the Alenian books he hadn't heard Thorndale's story.

"I came with Seth's parents. We were in the first group of scientists brought here."

"Holy Klatan!" Alan exclaimed. "You must have a wealth of knowledge about this place."

"I don't know why everyone went mad, if that's what you're asking."

"No, not that. I didn't understand why eighty-five colonists were here when the killings began. The researchers' notes said there were never more than thirty in the colony at any one time. When the colonists began killing each other, there were eighty-five here. Why?"

Thorndale seemed uncomfortable as he said, "Eight months ago, a ship brought fifty more people. They weren't scientists. They had an agenda they wouldn't share with us. What they did was search. They searched all the shacks. Since we'd been here, we only searched a handful of shacks. We saw no need to search all of them since each of them was identical. But they searched all of them. They also searched the mountains. This group found the tunnel and opened the crystal cave."

"Studying the Alenian books, I learned that the two inner planets in this system were Clanferion and Gorderion. The literature describes them as having large Alenian populations, which doesn't make sense. We were told the two inner planets were uninhabited and dangerous to humans. How could that be?"

Thorndale didn't say anything for a few seconds. He finally said, "We were warned never to repeat this. I mean warned under penalty of death. What I'm going to tell you must stay between us."

They sat there waiting for him to continue.

"We named the planet closer to the star A1, and the one further out A2. Observations from orbit determined they had a human breathable atmosphere, much like Alenia, and large cities capable of holding sizable populations on both planets. The strange thing was there was nothing moving on either planet or any detection of transmissions.

"The military sent a shuttle team to A2 to investigate. Although the atmosphere was breathable, the shuttle crew wore breathers as a precaution. The shuttle commander sent a message that they landed successfully. It was the only message we received from them. After trying repeatedly to contact the shuttle, another shuttle was sent to find out what happened to them. They did a fly over. They found that the first shuttle had landed safely, but there was no sign of the crew, nor could they raise them on comms.

"The commander decided to send a rescue shuttle to find out what happened to the first crew. He had the rescue shuttle crew wear Self-contained Environmental Suits. Another shuttle accompanied them and remained in orbit to monitor the rescue shuttle's activities.

"The rescue shuttle landed. When they exited the ship, they found everything was covered with a white powder. The first shuttle was empty. There was no sign of the first shuttle's crew. The second shuttle's crew reported seeing no movement. Not the beings that built the city, not any animals, nothing, not even the first shuttle's crew. After searching for a while, they found the uniforms of the first shuttle crew. Only their uniforms, nothing else. There were no blood stains or signs the suits were forcibly removed from the crewmembers. Based on what they found, it looked as if the first shuttle crew just took off their uniforms and laid them in a pile on the ground.

"An hour after the second shuttle landed and began exploring, the crew began complaining that something was eating into their SEV suits. The last they heard from the ground crew members were screams that they were being eaten alive. The orbiting shuttle recorded the gruesome sight of those on the ground frantically running back to their ship. None of them made it before they collapsed. Soon, the only visible signs of the second shuttle crew were their deflated SEV suits. No one made it out alive.

"Back here there was a lot of speculation about what happened to the two shuttle crews, but no one had any answers. The Commander discussed sending a third crew until Seth's mother suggested there was a safer way. She said they could send a survey robot that she could modify to detect any lethal substances on the planet. They agreed, and they parachuted a robot onto the planet. It roamed around transmitting a video feed. It found the breathers and SEV suits from the crews. The suits were empty, and there was no sign of the crewmembers."

"What happened to them?" Gunther asked.

"The analyzer Seth's mother built into the robot identified the white powder covering everything on the planet as an enzyme. This enzyme could digest anything alive and carbon-based. As it consumed, it reproduced itself. The robot's readings indicated the powder could digest a person in less than ten minutes, and it was acidic enough to eat through the seals of the SEV suit. It meant the crews were eaten alive by this enzyme."

"I've never heard of such a thing. It would be the ideal weapon if you wanted to kill everything on a planet. The only problem would be to ensure it didn't kill those wielding it," Gunther said.

Thorndale continued with his story. "Both the two inner planets were covered with this white powder. It killed every living thing on them. We were ordered never to mention this to anyone. Only a half-dozen of us, including myself, Seth's mother, and a few members of the military, knew about it. This information has stayed secret. Until now."

"I'd like to hear more about this white powder and the two Alenian planets, but our immediate problem is what do we do about the ghostly images appearing now? We can't keep that information from the Major for long. Eventually, he will see them, and what happens then?" Gunther said to no one in particular.

Thorndale answered, "If I'm right, the earthquake uncovered the cave's entrance, and that's the reason the ghosts returned. We have to re-block the cave's entrance to stop them from appearing."

"Thorndale is right. We need to stop these apparitions until we better understand what they are. I'll go to the cave and move the boulder back. Thorndale, you're coming with me," Seth said.

"I am coming too," Gunther said.

"Me too," Alan piped in.

"We can't all go. The Major will be angry once he finds I'm gone. He warned me that if I caused him more trouble, I'll be locked up in that cell they put Thorndale in. I don't want or need more company in there."

"I have an idea how we can pacify the Major," Alan said. "I told the Major that I was translating the Alenian language. He scoffed at it at first. When I explained what I was learning, he became interested. I'll tell him I asked you to bring me more books from the cavern's library. It's true, I need some specific books, and if you get some of the books I need, I can sell him on that's where you were."

"Okay, we can get some books. What do you want us to get?"

"Look for books with a symbol in the title that looks like an inverted letter 'V' with two horizontal lines crossing the center of the "V" and a single vertical line coming up through its center. Here, let me draw it."

He pulled out a piece of paper and quickly sketched the symbol. "It looks like this. It's their word for history. I only have two of their history books that have an overview of their history. Find all the books you can with this symbol in the title." He handed the sketch to Seth. "But before you leave, tell me why we are keeping secrets from Jana."

"Doc is suspicious she isn't who she claims to be. He says she doesn't know what Professor Kleinfeld's assistant should know. He thinks she might be a spy," Seth said.

"I can't believe it. That can't be true."

Gunther added, "Maybe it isn't so incredible. I've been watching the locked Quonset hut, and earlier tonight–."

Seth cut him off, "You were just shot doing that. Do you want to give them a second opportunity to kill you?"

"I was more cautious this time. I stayed in the shadows and at a distance. I saw Jana, the Major, and the Marines enter the locked Quonset hut. One Marine stayed outside as a guard."

"With all this spying, did you learn what they're doing in the locked Quonset hut?"

Gunther shook his head as he answered. "I can't get near enough to see inside. They were in there a long time last night. When they came out, they locked it before going to the Commons. I could break the lock, but that isn't a good idea if they're willing to kill anyone just watching what they're doing."

Thorndale looked like he was going to say something but didn't.

"Whether Jana is a spy or not, it's safer if we keep her from knowing what we're doing now. We need to leave now to block the cave's entrance before the Major stops us," Seth said.

Alan watched as Seth, Gunther, and Thorndale left for the vehicle Quonset.

CHAPTER 82

Thorndale watched to ensure they weren't observed as Seth and Gunther entered the Vehicle hut. Seth decided to use the all-terrain convertible that he and the Major rode in to the cavern city. Gunther filled the car with fuel. They pushed it out of the hut far enough away from the colony that Seth felt it wouldn't be heard when he started the engine.

Seth got in the driver's seat, Thorndale sat in the passenger's seat to navigate, and Gunther filled most of the rear seat.

Seth started the engine and headed north, driving as quietly as possible until they were a kilometer north of the compound. The terrain to the north had been plowed fields. There were no roads, just narrow walking paths between the fields. The fields were even more uneven due to the earthquake. The car bounced along, giving them a jarring ride as Seth drove over the field's furrows and irrigation canals. He had to be watchful to avoid obstacles that might tear out the bottom of the car. He couldn't drive any faster than 25 kilometers per hour.

Seth turned to Thorndale, "How did you get up here?"

"I used the motorcycle. It's a lot smoother riding on the footpaths."

Seth estimated the tunnel was thirty-six kilometers from the colony. At this speed, they wouldn't have time to close the cave's entrance, get to the cavern city to get Alan's books, and return to the compound before dark. The Major would know they were gone if they got back that late. Despite Alan's ruse about sending them out for books, he would have their heads.

The fields ended fifteen kilometers north of the compound. The uncultivated land beyond was flatter and Seth could drive faster. They arrived at the base of the northern mountain range just over an hour after they'd left.

Thorndale gave Seth directions, "Drive slowly west along the edge of the mountains. The tunnel's entrance is well disguised. Even riding slowly on the motorcycle and knowing there was a tunnel, I had difficulty finding it. It's the reason no one found it in thirty years until the additional fifty Searchers came. I call them Searchers because all they did was search for something, though they wouldn't tell us what it was. They found the tunnel and the crystal cave. My people might still be alive if they hadn't found it."

As Thorndale said this, Seth could see those events still shook him. All of his friends and coworkers suddenly became crazed killers, and he had the unenviable job of burying them.

Seth drove the car slowly over the rocky terrain along the edge of the mountain range as all three looked for the tunnel's entrance. The ground was covered with rocks that had tumbled down from the mountain, many large enough to seriously damage the all-terrain car if he drove over them. After fifteen minutes of weaving around the fallen rocks, Thorndale yelled, "I see it!" Large boulders hid the tunnel's entrance from anyone not directly in front of it.

Seth drove the car to the tunnel's entrance and stopped. It was over three meters tall and twice as wide, and cut straight through the mountain, since he could see light coming from the other end. Seth drove into the tunnel. The interior walls were smooth. It was cut with precision, like the cavern city's cave.

It took four minutes for Seth to drive slowly through the tunnel. Once they emerged on the other side of the mountain, he pulled up next to the bulldozer parked a short distance from the end of the tunnel. Fifteen meters from the bulldozer was a hole in the side of the mountain, the cave's entrance. Lying on the ground in front of the cave was a large boulder that had been used to block the opening. Thorndale was correct that the earthquake had shaken it loose.

They got out of the car and walked to the cave. The early morning sun was at a low angle that allowed sunlight to pour into the mouth of the cave. When they approached the cave, they could see a glow coming from within. Peering inside, they could see a structure filled with crystalline spheres.

Seth estimated the cave was at least ten meters from floor to ceiling, forty meters wide, and close to a half kilometer deep. The crystalline spheres were around seven centimeters in diameter, matching his mother's description of the crystals Seth hid. Floor to ceiling vertical poles were spaced a meter apart throughout the cave. Each set of two poles were connected by cross members that went up the poles from floor to ceiling at half meter intervals like rungs of a ladder. Facing cross members on two pairs of poles had ten pairs of wires strung between them, and on each pair of wires sat ten spheres.

"This is incredible. There must be tens of thousands of these spheres. Are these the same as the ones you found in the village, the ones you hid?" Gunther addressed both Thorndale and Seth.

Thorndale answered, "The crystals we found in the village looked exactly like these."

The crystals near the mouth of the cave were bathed in sunlight and glowed brightly. They weren't just reflecting the light, they were intensifying it. The light they were emitting was so bright it was painful to look at them.

Gunther approached one of the glowing crystals and touched it. He quickly pulled his hand back, saying, "I got a shock!"

"Since the one blew up when its shell was punctured, we thought they might be an energy source, like a battery, but we never learned much more about them before Seth hid them," Thorndale said.

Seth frowned. He felt guilty for that act, despite having no memory of what he did or why.

As sunlight hit more of the crystals near the mouth of the cave, the crystals that were not directly in the sun's light also began to glow. As they did, Seth's headache grew more intense. The pain increased until he couldn't concentrate on anything but the pain in his head. It continued to grow more painful until he couldn't take it. He fell to his knees in agony, holding his head and writhing on the ground in pain.

Gunther bent over him. "Thorndale, this is doing something to him. Help me get him out of here!"

They grabbed Seth under his arms and dragged him toward the cave's opening. They hadn't gotten more than a few steps when a faint glow appeared in their path. The glow grew into hazy-white swirls of light.

"This is them," Thorndale said, letting go of Seth and stepping back.

Gunther still holding Seth up, said, "Them who?"

"The ghosts."

The light grew in intensity. Gunther pulled Seth back from it.

Seth was still holding his head in pain, and then, suddenly, the pain stopped. The headache he had had since he arrived on Alenia was gone. Seth stood up and pulled himself free from Gunther's grasp. He watched as the swirling light began to take form.

The image of an elderly man appeared. He had a gray beard and hair and was dressed in a white tunic. His image was surrounded by glowing white light. The man began to speak. His voice was faint. Seth didn't understand what he was saying. It was the same language spoken by the woman who appeared in his room this morning.

"I don't understand you," Seth said.

Thorndale said, "It's the language they spoke to me when they came to the colony after everyone died."

The ghostly image of the man stopped speaking. He stood there with a confused expression on his face. His image faded and disappeared along with the hazy white aura surrounding him.

"Now I see what this business of ghosts is about. If this is an Alenian ghost, why does it look like a human? Too bad Alan isn't here, maybe he could understand what the ghost was saying," Gunther said.

They were still looking at where the old man appeared when a new glow began forming. The glow solidified into a different image. A young woman appeared dressed in a similar white tunic. She had blonde shoulder length hair, incredibly bright, almost iridescent, blue eyes, and a thin well-formed body. Seth recognized her. This was the vision in his dreams. The woman he had imagined for years. This was Lena.

"Lena?" Seth said.

She stood there looking at him. Her lips didn't move, but Seth could hear her. She was speaking to his mind in human language. "*Help us! We are trapped. Restore the power.*"

Seth asked aloud, "How do we do that?" She didn't reply. Her image began to fade and was gone.

"Lena? Is that your imaginary childhood playmate?" Gunther asked.

"I don't know how I know it, but she is. She is asking for our help."

Gunther said, "I don't understand. She just stood there. She didn't make a sound, not even move her lips." He faced Thorndale. "Did you hear her?" Thorndale shook his head. "How could you know what she said?"

"I could hear her in my mind. She said they are trapped. They want us to restore the power. That was all she said."

"Maybe what caused you to collapse a few minutes ago made you hallucinate she said something. Even assuming you did hear her, what power does she want us to restore?"

"I don't know," Seth said. The sun had moved on and was no longer shining into the mouth of the cave. The crystals had stopped glowing.

Seth touched one of the crystals that hadn't been glowing. He got no shock. He grabbed two of the crystals and took them outside the cave. He placed them in the sunlight and stood over them watching for something to happen. They didn't glow, and no ghostly images appeared.

Gunther and Thorndale followed Seth out of the cave, watching him as he stood over the crystals.

"I think the crystals absorb energy from the sunlight, but it doesn't seem to be having any effect on these two crystals," Seth said.

"When the cave was first opened, the sun was at a lower angle, more light would have been shining into the cave. Maybe they need to be on those wires in the cave before they can convert the sun's energy," Thorndale said.

Seth carried the crystals back into the cave and replaced them on the wires. "I think you're right. They must need this structure to convert energy from sunlight. It might mean the wires are carrying a current. It explains why Gunther was shocked when he touched one, and it may explain why the crystals that weren't directly in the sunlight began to glow."

Standing in the cave's opening, Seth pointed to the top of a mountain across from the cave. "See that mountain peak. Early in the morning, the sun's light can reach the mouth of the cave on that side of its peak. Shortly after, the mountain blocks the sun from the cave until the sun passes to the other side of the peak. If I'm right, the sun's energy powers the crystals, and the crystals produce the images. It explains why the images appeared early this morning in the compound and now again here. It also explains why blocking the cave's opening stops their images from appearing.

Gunther and Thorndale agreed that made sense.

"When we saw them here, would they have appeared again in the village," Thorndale said.

"I'm sure they didn't," Seth said. He was sure they hadn't returned to the village, but he didn't know what made him so sure.

"How do you know the image of the woman was your childhood friend Lena? Didn't you say your childhood memories were erased with a brainwipe?" Gunther asked.

"I don't know how I know, but this is Lena, the Lena I protected by hiding the crystals when I was a child."

Gunther checked his watch. "As much as I'd like to pursue this mystery, it's past noon. If we don't leave soon, we won't make it to the cavern city and back to the compound before dark. Without the books for Alan, we won't convince the Major we were doing that and not this."

"We have to cover the entrance to the cave, or we'll have more ghosts appearing in the colony," Thorndale said.

"We don't need to cover the cave's entrance. Their images won't appear in the village again," Seth said.

"How can you be sure of that?".

"I just know. Trust me. Gunther is right, we have to go now if we want to keep the Major in the dark about this." Seth wasn't sure if it was a premonition that told him the ghostly images wouldn't reappear in the compound, or something else, but he was sure they wouldn't.

One thing was apparent. Seth's headache had something to do with this cave. His headache was gone for now, and they were running out of time if they wanted to stay out of the Major's lockup.

CHAPTER 83

S eth drove the car west along the edge of the northern mountain range. This land hadn't been cultivated and was flatter. It allowed him to drive faster. On some stretches, he hit speeds of 50 Km/h. When he reached the western mountains, he drove along the edge of the grass that grew along the river. He slowed and scanned the area for the place where they'd previously crossed the river.

Thorndale and Gunther spent the time discussing what they experienced in the cave. The ghostly images still frightened Thorndale, but it was Gunther's first encounter with them. He was intrigued as he speculated on what they had seen. They argued if it was an image projected in space, or something only in their minds.

Seth didn't participate in their conversation. All he could think about was seeing Lena. How did he know who she was? The brainwipe had erased his childhood memories, yet he knew this was Lena. The Lena his mother said was his childhood friend, the Lena he hid the crystals for, an act that changed everything in his life. He never knew who she was other than fantasizing she was his ideal woman. He told himself she was either an acquaintance of the family, or a woman he met once but forgot where or who. Now, after seeing her, he knew this was Lena.

Seth's musings about Lena stopped when he came to where they could cross the river.

Gunther and Thorndale followed Seth across the river, up the steps cut into the mountain and through the tunnel. They stood back as he opened the door to the cavern city, stepped inside, and turned on the lights.

Thorndale was just outside the door when the lights came on. He walked in and stood on the cliff, his eyes roving over the city below. "It's spectacular! We determined the Alenians were prisoners in a penal colony, forced to live as primitive, simple farmers. That may still be true, but this city proves there was much more to them."

"We don't have time for a tour of the city. We need to find Alan's books quickly," Seth said as he led them to the library.

Once there, Seth pulled out the sketch Alan gave him. "We need to gather all the books with this symbol in their title." They studied Alan's drawing before going in different directions to search for books with that marking. Seth found four books with the symbol on one shelf. Gunther found two more books and brought them to Seth, then went to search for more on the other side of the library.

When Gunther was far enough away that Thorndale was sure he wouldn't hear him, he came over and whispered to Seth, "I think I know why they sent you on this mission. They want to see if you remembered being here as a child."

"You mean they didn't think the brainwipe removed all my childhood memories? It did, and it made me believe I was born and raised in Digeria," Seth said angrily.

Checking that Gunther was still far enough away not to hear him, Thorndale said, "Yes, the brainwipe."

"I want you to tell me about my mother and father and everything you can tell me about my childhood here. I want to regain some of the memories they stole from me."

Thorndale's scars exaggerated the frown forming on his face. "They didn't erase your childhood memories. I did."

"*You* conducted the brainwipe on me!" Seth snapped at Thorndale.

"Your mother and I were the only ones here who understood how to use the machine properly. After she built it, she had me check that it had no unintended side-effects. If one of us didn't do your brainwipe, she was afraid the Commander would have someone who didn't understand how to use the machine correctly do it. She never intended for her machine to be used to conduct a brainwipe on a child. It was a dangerous process to use on anyone, and potentially more dangerous to a child. She couldn't make herself erase your memories, so she asked me to do it. We didn't know if it would work on you or if it would destroy your brain. I would have faked it if I could, but I couldn't. The Commander was watching me as I did it, and he told me he would ask you questions about your childhood when I finished. He would kill you on the spot if you gave the wrong answers. I did it to save you."

Seth couldn't control his anger. "You succeeded! I have no real memories of my childhood. You stole them from me. What memories I have are fake!"

"That isn't true. You still have your original memories. I didn't remove them. I just planted new memories over yours. The machine works in two phases. The first phase erases the memories. The second phase inserts new ones in their place. I only performed the second phase. I was born and grew up on Digeria. I mapped my childhood memories over yours. When I finished, the Commander asked you where you were born. You answered, "Digeria." He asked you what you knew of Alenia. You said you didn't know what that was. He was satisfied and let you live. That is all your mother wanted. I hoped over time you would regain your original memories. It appears you haven't."

"If my childhood memories are still there, can you reverse the process?" Seth asked, trying to calm down.

"After your mother left, the Imperial Guard took the brainwipe machine and all the research. Even if I had the machine, I wouldn't know how to repair what I did. Your mother was the expert on using the machine, not me."

Gunther yelled across the room, "I found two more here."

Seth yelled back, "Keep looking."

Seth turned to Thorndale. "I want to know about my father. Before my parents broke up, what was my father like?"

"Your father was obsessed with discovering how the Alenian atmospheric engines worked. I didn't see much of him. He was an upright guy, maybe a little too much so. One of the researchers found something here that he planned to make a fortune with when he returned to the Empire. It was forbidden to bring back anything we found here. Your father learned what the researcher was planning and reported him to the Commander. They removed the researcher and confiscated his notes. Your father as someone who always followed the rules. Some years after he left, one of the new arrivals said your father was a genius for inventing the Habitation Engine. I was surprised he was passing off the Alenian's invention as his own. That didn't square with the man that I'd known. That man would never have taken credit for something he didn't invent. I finally realized the Alenian atmospheric engine was too valuable not to be used by the Empire. We were not allowed to bring anything back from here. They must have made an exception, but only if your father claimed the invention to be his own to hide its real origin."

"Were you the one who set the two towers to keep us from landing?"

"Yes, I did."

"Why?"

"I expected that the military would come to see what happened here someday. They would take me back with them, and I would become a lab subject as they tried to figure out why I didn't succumb to the mass insanity. I've lived here most of my life and have no desire to return to Imperial space, especially under those conditions. I would sooner die here alone than suffer that fate. The oppressive environment created by the Emperor is why I've stayed here for so many years."

Seth understood how Thorndale felt. He didn't want to return only to have them probe into his DNA to learn why he was different.

"Tell me what it was like working with my mother."

"I was busy in the Biology Lab and only worked with your mother occasionally before you were born. After you were born, I spent more time with her. Most of that was to help her with the brainwipe machine. She wanted to be sure it didn't have any damaging biological effects on the brain. Other than erasing selected memories, of course."

Thorndale fell silent as Gunther approached them carrying four books. "That's all I could find."

"That makes ten in all. It should keep Alan busy for a while. Now we need to get back," Seth said.

Seth grabbed the six books in front of him as Gunther carried the other four, a lot, considering he still had one arm bandaged and in a sling. They left the cavern city.

He was angry at Thorndale for replacing his childhood memories, despite knowing he did it to save his life.

CHAPTER 84

Admiral Wilson's fleet entered the asteroid field that surrounded the rebel base Liberty. He brought twenty of the most elite ships in the Empire's fleet to destroy the rebel's command center. There were fifteen Heavy Cruisers, four bombers, and the Viper prototype, the Delaigo. The Viper was fitted with an ion cannon, a weapon that could quickly render useless any anti-ship ground defenses they encountered.

Wilson watched his ships carefully maneuver through the field of rocks. He applauded the rebel's ingenuity for choosing a base on a moon orbiting a dead planet surrounded by an asteroid field. Few would ever think to look for it here. It was only when Prime ordered him to destroy it that he learned where it was. She said an EYE Corps spy learned of its location. Prime gave him this assignment the day before her coronation, but he would be reporting his success to the Empress. Wilson hoped it would please her that he was able to bring this fleet together in two days, and now they were about to wipe out the rebel scum's command base. He pondered what rich reward the new Empress might bestow on him. Possibly he would become the new Prime. The thought was tantalizing.

It had been slow and dangerous getting through the asteroid field. He smiled, envisioning the rebels trying to flee as his ships opened fire on their base. Those that weren't destroyed by his fleet would be smashed to bits as they tried to flee through the asteroids.

"Have all our ships cleared the asteroid field?" Wilson asked his Communications officer.

"Not yet. But very soon," came the response.

The rebels wouldn't see the fleet approaching. All twenty ships were stealth ships. The rebel's scans could only see the heat signatures from his ships' rockets. For this reason, he'd had the fleet enter the asteroid field with the system's star behind them. The star's energy would mask their rocket's exhaust allowing them to traverse the asteroid field undetected.

The Communications officer announced, "Sir, the last ship has cleared the field."

"Is there any activity from the base?"

"There is no movement on the moon, nor is there any sign of defensive artillery targeting us, and no ships launching."

Wilson smiled. His plan was working. They hadn't yet detected the fleet. This was going to be easier than he expected. The Empress would be elated. He recalled an old Earth saying, 'if you cut off the head of a snake, its body will die'. Once the rebel's command was destroyed, support for the rebellion would end.

"Put the moon on the screen."

The large screen on the bridge filled with the image of the moon.

He ordered, "Tell them to begin the attack!"

A smaller bridge screen showed his fleet ships beginning to fan out. They had clustered together in a tight formation to be undetectable as they threaded through the asteroid field. Once they fanned out, they could attack the moon from all sides.

"Sir, I have contacts approaching from behind the moon!"

"Contacts?"

"Thirty, no forty ships!"

The bridge screen showed the ships coming from the other side of the moon. They were smaller than his fleet ships, but there were a lot of them.

Wilson ordered, "Have the Heavy Cruisers engage those ships! The rest of the fleet continue with their attack on the moon."

The Communication officer didn't have time to pass along the order when he said, "Sir, there are ships coming through the asteroid field behind us." He didn't wait for the Admiral to ask. He flipped the bridge screen to a rear view showing a dozen ships approaching.

The Admiral was in a trap, and he was outgunned. His ships were faster, but the asteroid field blocked their escape and nullified their speed advantage.

In less than an hour, only the Viper was still fighting. The other ships were floating bits of broken metal. A well-placed rocket hit the Viper's power plant, causing multiple explosions that tore the Viper apart.

From the bridge of his ship, Commander Freedom surveyed the destruction in front of him. Twenty of the Empire's most elite ships were destroyed, their crews dead, a waste of so many lives to attack an abandoned base.

"Commander, you were right, they were no match for us." Commander Nightmare was on the comm from his ship, crowing over the victory.

Freedom responded, "We won this battle. We've made them aware that we won't be easily put down. Don't be too confident. This is only the opening salvo in our fight for independence. They will come at us with more ships, and the next time, they won't be as gullible."

"We'll be ready," Nightmare said confidently.

Freedom said under his breath, "I hope so."

CHAPTER 85

Seth drove the car back to the Vehicle Quonset hut. There was no need to hide their return. A Marine stood waiting for them. He didn't look like he was there to give them a friendly greeting, especially when he raised his gun and waved it at them. "The Major wants to see you."

Seth replied, "No problem. Let me park this first, and we'll be along shortly."

The Marine's eyes narrowed, and he pointed his gun directly at Seth. "Now!"

"Fine." Seth and Thorndale jumped out of the car. Gunther grunted as he slowly eased himself out, giving the Marine a challenging look.

"Bring the books," Seth said to them. Thorndale turned back to the car, reaching in to grab them and pass them to Seth and Gunther.

"I said now!" The Marine barked.

Gunther tensed. Before he could respond, Seth grabbed him by his uninjured arm and pulled him towards the Communications hut.

The Major was sitting at his desk when they came into the hut. Anger spread across his face as he yelled, "Where were you?"

"Collecting books for Alan from the cavern city," Seth said, selling it with a smile on his face.

"I did not authorize this," he growled while his eyes took in the books they were carrying.

"We need to find out what the Alenians were doing with two cities. Understanding what happened to them might explain what happened to this colony. Since Alan has learned how to translate their writings, he said he needed more books from the cavern city. We didn't need a Marine babysitter. There were three of us, two of us were armed because you didn't arm Thorndale. He came with us to see the cavern city. After over thirty years on this moon, I thought he deserved to see it. As for the books we brought back. If you'll let us take these books to Alan, you might get some of the answers you've been looking for." Seth said it, putting as much gravitas into his voice as he could muster.

The Major seemed to be ready to jump up and pummel Seth. But he slowly regained control, and his anger faded. Finally, he said, "Go! Give him the books. But if you ever pull another stunt like this, I am going to have you shot."

Seth, Gunther, and Thorndale hustled out of the Communications hut and headed to the Artifacts hut to drop off the books.

"He's dangerous," Gunther said.

"You don't know the half of it. When he was stationed here, he was a brutal ass. He left the researchers alone, but he would take it out on his men if they incurred the slightest infraction. One of them fell asleep at his post. The Major had him publicly flogged. Besides being humiliated, the man was recovering in sick bay for two weeks. I suggest you stop testing him," Thorndale told Seth.

Walking to the Artifacts hut, Seth thought, why hasn't the Major come down harder on me? I've crossed him twice, and he's backed down both times. Something must be protecting me from his wrath.

CHAPTER 86

They found Alan sitting at a table with three opened books in front of him. He didn't look up as they entered. When he noticed them, he pulled his gaze out of the books revealing his bloodshot eyes with drooping lids. But seeing they had more books, his face lit up. "You got them!"

He cleared off a section of the table in front of him. "Carefully, put them here."

He began inspecting the books. A broad smile filled his face when he found the upside-down 'V' symbol on each of the books. "You did it. These are all history books." He opened one of the books and began studying it.

Seth checked the time. "It's time for supper, we'd better get moving." Gunther and Thorndale started for the door.

Alan continued studying the book, oblivious to them leaving.

Seth raised his voice. "Alan, it's time for supper."

He still didn't have Alan's attention. Seth put his hand over the book Alan was looking at and pulled it down. "Have you eaten anything today?"

Alan seemed confused by the question. He finally said, "I don't think so."

"It's time for supper. I'm taking you to get something to eat. After, you are going to the shack to get some sleep."

Alan didn't resist as Seth guided him out of the Artifacts hut and into the mess hall. As he walked, he rattled off what he learned from the books. "This moon is called Demeerite. It's named after one of the Alenian ancient gods, but I haven't found a description of that god. I'm just beginning to read about ..."

Alan continued talking as Seth brought him to his seat in the mess hall. To everyone's surprise, Alan ate three helpings of the now all too familiar synthetic stew. Finishing the last one, he said, "I feel better. Just let me go have a look at the new books you brought."

Seth smiled as he grabbed Alan's arm and gently pulled him out of the mess hall and back to their shack. Alan grumbled he didn't want to go, but he didn't put up a fight.

Seth pushed Alan onto his bed, pulled off Alan's shoes, and was about to have him remove his clothes when he saw that Alan was already asleep. Seth covered him with a blanket and shut the door as he left Alan's bedroom thinking this was like having the brother he always wished he had.

Seth sat in the living room as he considered what had happened today. Learning Thorndale erased his childhood memories angered him. He reminded himself Thorndale did it to save him from being killed. Even so, he couldn't forgive Thorndale.

His thoughts drifted back to Lena. The brainwipe hadn't erased her from his memory, only who she was and where he saw her. She hadn't changed in appearance. The image that appeared to him today was the same one he had had in his mind all these years. The image of a beautiful woman. Now he knew where that image came from. Was she real? Of course, she wasn't real. She was a projection in his mind. Lena was like the other ghostly images they saw. The fact he could understand her, that she could speak into his mind, may have something to do with his strange DNA. His mother said the Alenian genetics machine made the sperm that created him. Did this mean he was part Alenian?

Another question was how he knew the ghostly images wouldn't appear in the compound. He was sure of it, but why was he so sure? Where did that come from? Was it a premonition? The other question was Lena saying, 'Help us! We are trapped. Restore the power.' What was she asking him to do?

Seth fell asleep on the living room sofa as these thoughts rambled through his mind.

He was awakened when he heard someone talking to him. A hazy-white glow was forming in front of him. It was Lena. She stood there with unmoving lips as she spoke to him in his head.

"*Are you the child Seth, the one I met long ago, the one who saved me and my friends?*"

"My memories of that time have been erased, but yes, I am."

A smile spread across her face as her eyes glowed ever brighter blue. "*Yes, I can see, you are Seth. You moved the Life Spheres, the things you call crystals, and saved my life and the lives of our best scientists who were with me. I need your help again. The power to the Lattice, the cave you and your friends were just in, is weak. If their power is not restored, they will die.*"

"Lena, how do I restore the power to the cave?"

"*You must reconnect the...*" She began to fade then she disappeared. Seth reached out and grabbed for the space where she had been standing. The movement awakened him. He'd been dreaming. Or *was* it a dream?

Alan was standing in the doorway of his bedroom watching him. Sunlight was filtering in through the windows. "I heard you speaking to someone, and you said the name Lena. Were you talking in your sleep?"

"The images we thought were ghosts, aren't ghosts. I think they are Alenians, and they're still alive."

CHAPTER 87

A lan wanted to know more, but Seth insisted they shower and dress first. As they walked to the mess hall, Seth told him about the crystal cave, seeing an old man, then Lena. That Lena could speak directly to his mind, and then seeing Lena again this morning.

"Wow! Is this the Lena you said was your childhood friend, the one who made you hide those crystals?"

"In spite of the brainwipe, I remember her. She is Lena from my childhood."

"She is asking you to restore the power, and you think that means power to the crystal cave."

"She told me it was the crystal cave this morning."

"In your dream?"

"Yes, if it was a dream.

"You think the ghostly images of Lena and the others are Alenians?"

"I know, it sounds incredible, if not impossible. But yes, I believe she and the others are Alenians. I believe they are alive. Until I know more, I'd like to keep all of this a secret." Alan agreed not to say anything.

As they walked to the mess hall, Seth thought what she must be referring to was the solar collector on top of that mountain. He had to return to the cave and talk to Lena again and clarify what she wanted him to do. The only thing stopping him was the Major and nine Marines.

They arrived at the mess hall to find the team had finished eating and was about to leave. As usual, the Major and Marines were absent. Doc said Thorndale was going to show him and Jana how to use one of the more sophisticated analyzers in the Biolab. Gunther, his arm no longer in the sling, said Doc asked him to get some bandages and sutures from the Medical Supply hut. Professor was off to take more VID pictures of the Artifacts. They all left, and Seth and Alan were alone.

The cook came out to collect the serving bowl and used dishes. Seeing they were late for breakfast, he grumbled, but he brought another bowl of the breakfast gruel for them.

"I'm having trouble understanding why the ghostly images we've seen look like humans if they are Alenians. If somehow their consciousness is in those crystals. They are projecting their images into our minds. They might be able to make themselves appear in any form that is pleasing to us. I think they might be tricking us into believing they look human. They could be dangerous beasts. Look what happened to the colonists the first time these Alenian ghosts appeared," Alan said.

"They might be projecting themselves as humans, but I don't think they're dangerous."

After they ate, Seth and Alan went to the Artifacts hut. "I'm going to start translating the new Alenian history books you brought," Alan said, going to the rear of the Artifact's hut.

Seth didn't know what he should do. If he tried to go back to the crystal cave, the Major would find out. He might not shoot Seth as he warned, but there would be no way he could help Lena if he were locked up in a cell.

Without having a way to get back to the crystal cave, all Seth could do was wait for Lena to contact him again, if that was what happened this morning.

He walked up to Professor. "Do you want me to continue reconstructing the pieces of broken pottery?"

"Only do it for the best-preserved pieces. We need to hurry to get all we can done before we are forced to leave."

The Artifacts hut had been cleaned up from the damage caused by the earthquake. The shelves were back up against the wall. The pieces of pottery large enough to be easily identified were on the shelves. The pottery the insane colonists or the earthquake had broken into small pieces were swept into a pile in a corner, apparently no longer relevant or worth the bother.

Seth spent the rest of the morning waiting for Lena to contact him as he reconstructed the pottery. He asked Alan to tell him if he learned anything about the crystal cave from the books they brought back. Alan said he would. Seth would interrupt him asking if there was anything about the cave. He said there wasn't.

Professor was taking pictures of the pottery Seth assembled. In between, he was learning how to read Alenian from Alan's notes.

It was just before noon when the door to the Artifacts hut opened, and a Marine came in. "The Major orders you to report to the Communications hut."

"We are busy. Can't you tell us what the Major is going to say?" Professor said, frustrated by having to stop every time the Major wanted to make an announcement.

"I don't know why the Major wants you."

"We will come when we have time."

The Marine waved his rifle at them. "You will come now!'

Reluctantly, they filed out of the Artifacts hut.

CHAPTER 88

Thorndale and the rest of the team were walking to the Communications hut with their own Marine escort.

Seth asked Doc, "Do you know what's up?"

"I have no idea, though I have a bad feeling about this."

They entered the Communications hut and found the Major sitting at his desk. He watched as the Marines moved the team to stand in front of him, in the way a shepherd might watch his dogs herd sheep.

They stood there waiting for the Major to say something. Finally, he said, "You were sent here to learn what happened to the colonists. I have observed that you are more interested in studying the Alenians than doing what you were sent here to do."

He focused his gaze on Doc. "Do you know why the colonists killed each other?"

Doc stared straight back. "No, I do not."

The Major shifted his gaze to each of the other members of the group before stopping at Thorndale. "Do any of you know why the colonists went on a killing rampage?"

No one answered.

"I am terminating this mission. Tomorrow we will return to the freighter. You will only be allowed to take medical samples for further testing when we return to Klatania."

Professor said anxiously, "You can't mean we are not allowed to take the books we found or the colonists' research notes. The Alenians are the first advanced beings we've encountered in the galaxy. There is a wealth of information that will be lost once you close the wormhole."

The Major stood up. "Only medical samples, nothing else. Get ready to leave at first light tomorrow."

Professor was about to continue pressing his objection when the Major signaled for the Marines to move them out. The Marines were not gentle as they pushed everyone out of the hut.

Seth was the last in line. He stopped at the door trying to decide if he told the Major about the crystal cave, it might buy him time to do what Lena asked him to do. Before he could speak, the Marine sitting at the communications panel said, "Sir, there is an urgent incoming message." When the Marine saw that Seth was still in the hut, he looked uncomfortable seeing Seth had heard him. The Major gave the Marine a stern look, before telling the Marine standing next to Seth to get him out of the hut. The Marine shoved Seth out the door so forcefully, Seth struggled to keep his balance and not fall on his face in the dirt.

Doc ran up to him. "What did you say to the Major to get tossed out like that?"

The rest of the team joined them. "I was about to complain about the early departure when the comms guy said there was an urgent incoming message. I doubt the freighter is sending him an urgent message. I think they must be in contact with the other side of the wormhole."

Thorndale said, "That's what we did. We would get messages through the wormhole to the Empire by having a scout ship pass by the other side of the wormhole on a regular basis. The scout ship would convey the message to the Imperial command, and the command would send messages back to us by the same means. Initially we did that a lot until the rebels got more active in that part of space. They stopped doing it, afraid the rebels would discover the wormhole."

"If they are in contact with Prime, this could be bad for us," Gunther said.

Doc added, "Very bad."

CHAPTER 89

The rest of the day, Doc, Jana and Thorndale prepared the medical samples for transport. Seth and Gunther worked with Alan and Professor to photograph pages of the Alenian books. If they couldn't take the books back, Professor felt the Major wouldn't stop him from taking a few VIDs. Seth wasn't so sure.

Suppertime came. They ate quickly, then immediately returned to what they were doing. They worked through the night. It was nearing sunrise when Professor surveyed the pile of VIDs filled with images and threw up his hands. "This is pointless. I have only recorded a fraction of the pages from these Alenian books, and there is an entire library we will never have a chance to study. How can we leave all of this behind?"

"What else can we do?" Alan said.

"I'm old, and my days at the university will soon end. Finding an intelligent, alien species is what I've wanted my entire life. I have no one to go back to. I will stay. They may not be able to close the wormhole, but even if they do, I have everything I have ever wanted here. I can't leave it."

"Then maybe I'll stay here, too," Alan said.

"No. You're young. You have your entire life ahead of you." Professor said, sounding more fatherly than normal.

Alan sat there pensively as he weighed the decision of whether to stay or go.

Seth hadn't planned on saying anything to anyone. He wasn't going to leave, not now that he'd found Lena. She needed his help, and he was going to stay to help her. But since Professor was planning on staying, he said, "Professor, I plan on staying."

Professor was about to say to Seth what he just said to Alan, however the look of determination on Seth's face made him change his mind.

"I doubt I'll ever have another chance to study an alien culture if I return to Klatania. I'm staying as well," Alan said. "I guess we'd better tell Doc, Jana, and Gunther that we're staying. I'll go to the Medical hut and tell Doc and Jana."

Gunther had left a short time before to get something from his shack.

"I'll tell Gunther," Seth said.

Seth left the Artifacts hut and ran to the shacks. As he did, the sun broke the horizon. He was almost at Gunther's shack when Lena appeared in the road in front of him. He wasn't sure if he was seeing her with his eyes or only in his mind.

Lena spoke to him. "Help us. Fix the power grid."

"Are the crystals powered by sunlight hitting the top of the mountain?"

She hesitated for a second, as if she were searching for how to answer. "You are correct. The mountaintop no longer powers the crystals. It has..."

He felt a tap on his shoulder. It was Jana. "Who were you talking to?"

If Jana couldn't see her, Lena had only appeared in his mind.

Seth was standing in the middle of the road. "I was just talking to myself. I'm on my way to get Gunther."

"Gunther isn't here. He's with Doc. Doc told me to get you. He said there's an emergency."

"What's the emergency?"

"I don't know. All I know is that he said to meet him at the locked Quonset hut." She turned and began running back to the compound.

Seth was about to ask Jana why Doc was at the locked Quonset hut, but she had already begun running back to the compound. He had to run fast to keep up with her. As he did, he felt something was wrong. He wasn't sure if this was a premonition or just a gut feeling.

Before he could figure out which it was, they'd reached the locked Quonset hut. The door was opened. Jana entered and Seth followed her. Eight Marines were standing inside the hut with their weapons trained on Seth. The rest of the team and Thorndale were sitting on the floor along one wall, their hands and feet were bound. Seth was about to say something when the Major stepped out from behind him.

Two Marines grabbed Seth. One removed his Stinger pistol, while the other began tying his hands behind his back. Seth resisted. The Major said, "If you resist, I will kill one of your friends."

Seth let the Marine tie his hands behind his back. A second Marine tied his feet. They forced Seth down on the ground next to Thorndale, then they ran another rope through the bindings on his hands and his feet. They pulled it tight, forcing him into a kneeling position, then tied it.

The Marine threaded a chain through the rope that connected Seth's hands and feet. Seth could see the chain was threaded through everyone's bindings in the same way. The Marine pulled the chain tight, forcing everyone against the wall. The Marine attached the end of the chain to a ring on the wall, then he secured it with a lock. Doc was on the other end. The chain was attached to a ring and locked the same way on the wall next to him.

Jana was standing next to the Major. Seth said, "So you are a spy."

"I'm afraid so. I was sent here to observe. Specifically, to observe you. The Emperor was sure your mother hid more of his life extending purple powder here, maybe even its formula. Prime didn't think so. To satisfy the Emperor, we included you with this group. He was sure you would lead us to more of the purple powder, if you even know what I'm talking about. It was the reason I took you to your mother's burned-out lab. I'm satisfied you have no memories of this place, and we are sure there is no more life-extending serum here. We've searched. Oh, and if you're wondering about the kiss, that was real. I thank you for comforting me when my mother was injured." She smiled as she left the hut. It was a sarcastic, not friendly smile.

The Major watched Jana leave. He turned and faced his prisoners. "You would be correct assuming the plan has changed. You are not leaving today. The fact that Professor came to me and said a few of you wanted to stay was prophetic. I received orders that none of you are to return. There is a news item that might interest you. It will, after all, be the last piece of news you will ever hear from the Empire. The Emperor is dead. It seems Prince Victor couldn't wait to succeed his father, so he had him killed. That was not a good decision. The Prince followed his father to the grave when the Barons had his head removed. Since there was no Klatan heir, the Barons chose our new Emperor, or rather, Empress, the person you knew as Prime, Empress Andraia."

The Major watched as they absorbed the news. He wasn't sure if their look of discomfort was from the tight bindings or the news. He guessed the tight bindings. He continued, "Your new Empress has decreed you should stay here. Do not worry about being abandoned here. We have taken care of that."

The Major nodded to one of the Marines. The Marine walked across the room where a canvas was covering something large. He pulled off the canvas exposing a metal cylinder. Strapped to the top of the cylinder were two tubes wrapped with tape. Wires ran from the tubes to a timer sitting on top of the cylinder. Seth recognized the cylinder as one like those he'd seen in the MTS hut. The tubes and timer on top were a bomb.

The Major walked over to the cylinder. He smiled. "Inside this cylinder is a substance that killed everything on the other two Alenian planets. It is lethal to everything it touches. It is a marvelous weapon, though you will not have to take my word for it." He reached over and started the timer on the bomb. "You have two hours before this bomb blows the cylinder apart and lets you personally experience this sublime weapon."

Doc said, "This is insane. You're going to destroy the wormhole. If you leave us here, there is nothing we can do to escape. Why kill us?"

"Our Empress isn't sure we will succeed in destroying the wormhole. If it is left intact, the rebels might find it, and they might come to this moon. It is prudent in case they come here to make sure nothing is alive on the moon. If they do come, all they will do is die." A wicked smile crossed his face.

Thorndale spoke up, "There were other cylinders. What happened to them?"

"You were the one who was moving the cylinders." It was a statement of verification, not a question. "They are on the airstrip awaiting the hauler so we can take them back to Klatania," the Major said.

Thorndale said, "You know how dangerous this substance is!"

"Of course. The rebels are becoming a bigger problem, and our Empress wants to demonstrate the power of this weapon. Destroying one of the outer planets should bring the rest of them under control, and that will end any support for the rebels."

The Major faced Gunther. "Mr. Voltig, you are valuable to the Imperial Guard, and I asked to bring you back with us. It seems our Empress didn't think that would be a good idea."

"Why did you bring me here?"

"You were included in case we had trouble with the cylinders. We had no idea what the insane colonists might have done with these cylinders. Fortunately, they didn't touch them. Unfortunately for you, your services were not and are no longer needed."

The Major waved his hand, and the Marines filed out of the hut. As he got to the door, he said, "Professor, I grant your wish to stay here. Too bad you will not have an opportunity to further your investigations of the Alenians. I offer you one consolation. I will leave the door open to give you one last view of Alenia."

The Major turned to leave but stopped in the doorway. He turned back to face them. "If you need to put this in context, you didn't succeed in finding what killed the former colonists. Consider this your punishment." He smiled as he walked out of the hut.

CHAPTER 90

Seth struggled to loosen his tied hands. Everyone else was doing the same. The chain limited their ability to twist enough to untie each other.

"Hear that?" Alan asked.

Seth listened. "It's the hauler landing." Twenty minutes later, they heard the hauler taking off. They struggled with their bindings, but all they succeeded in doing was bloodying their wrists where the ropes cut into them.

"These ropes are made of nylon that gets tighter the harder we struggle. I don't think we can get loose from the ropes. Maybe if we all pulled on the chain, we could dislodge the hooks from the wall," Gunther suggested.

They struggled to get their feet against the wall. Holding the chain with their hands, face down, feet against the wall, they began pushing together. As hard as they pushed, the chain anchors would not give.

Thorndale spoke up. "We may not have to worry about what's in the cylinder. This cylinder may not have a live agent in it."

"What are you talking about?" Seth asked.

"After the fifty Searchers came, they locked this Quonset hut. We were suspicious about what they were doing in here, but they wouldn't tell us. After everyone died and I buried them, I picked the lock. I found several dozen cylinders in the back section of this hut just like this one. Somehow, they got the white powder that killed everything on the other Alenian planets, and they were growing it and storing it in these cylinders. The cylinders were biological bombs. I learned from the notes they kept that a heavy dose of X-ray radiation would kill the enzyme. I didn't want to be on this moon with this stuff, so I began moving the cylinders to the MTS hut and bombarding them with X-rays in sufficient quantity to kill what was in the cylinders. The problem was I didn't do all of them. Your arrival interrupted me before I could finish."

"That explains why the MTS machine was programmed to x-ray at such a high level," Doc said.

"How do you know if this cylinder has live stuff in it?" Seth asked.

"I marked an X on the bottom of those I ran through the MTS. I can't see the bottom of this cylinder to tell if it is one that's alive or dead. If it's a live cylinder, when that charge blows, we will be consumed by the enzyme. If the enzyme is dead, we should be okay."

Gunther interjected, "I doubt that. All this talk about whether the cylinder contains a lethal substance is not going to help us. Our proximity to the device will kill us when it explodes."

Gunther was right. When the bomb on the cylinder exploded, it would send shrapnel flying through the Quonset hut. They were tied up only three meters from the cylinder. None of them would survive the blast, and there were only fifty minutes left on the timer. There was no way for them to survive even if the cylinder didn't have the active enzyme in it.

As Seth considered what they could do to survive, he heard Lena's voice in his head. "Seth, there is a way to free you. Make Thorndale tell you about our robots."

Seth turned to Thorndale, "Tell me about the Alenian robots."

"How do you know about the Alenian robots?"

"Lena just told me. She says there is a way to free us, and it has something to do with the Alenian robots."

"You mean Lena from the crystal cave just talked to you?"

"I don't have time to explain. Just tell me about the Alenian robots."

The idea they needed to hear his story now was absurd, but Thorndale began telling his story. "We found a cave in the western mountain range three years ago. The cave was filled with robots built by the Alenians. They had no internal computer to control them or an on-off switch. Our engineers couldn't figure out how they were powered. Where there should have been a computer there was a container filled with a gooey substance. They called me in to see if I could tell them what the substance was. All I could tell them was that it wasn't a brain. It had nothing like synaptic connections, and it wasn't even biological material. It was a composition of heavy metals and inorganic chemicals. They studied the robots for a time until they gave up on them. No one understood how these robots worked or if they could work. They reassembled the robots they took apart and returned them to the cave. There was a request made for a robotics expert to be sent here, but one never came."

Lena spoke to Seth again. "Have him tell you about the robot that helped him. Reach out with your mind to that robot. I'm using the last of our reserves to contact you," her voice was weak.

"Tell me about the robots that helped you."

"You mean the Sphere and Big Boy."

Seth wasn't sure what he was talking about but added, "Tell me everything about the robots. We don't have much time."

"Very well, though I don't see what good that is now. I returned to the river after the hauler left. It was getting late. I didn't want to be outside once it got dark. I hid in the Alenian robot cave, figuring if any of the colonists were still alive, they wouldn't find me there. The robot cave was carved out of the mountain, and it was filled with robots of every size and shape. I didn't worry about the robots since they were no longer functional. I sat there all night unable to sleep. When the sun rose, I opened the cave door to let light in. Sunlight streamed in, and I noticed the bodies of the robots reflected the sunlight in a multitude of colors in the same way as the atmospheric towers. We were aware the atmospheric towers received their power from the sun, but I didn't give it any thought as I sat in the cave trying to decide what I should do next.

"I was starving. I hadn't eaten for over 36 hours. I contemplated returning to the colony for food, though I feared it might still be dangerous. As I thought of food, a sphere bathed in sunlight began to move. I didn't know it was a robot until it suddenly sprouted arms with claws and legs with wheels. It began to approach me. It was between me and the cave door. I was trapped. The robot stopped a meter from me and just sat there. If you can say a sphere without any facial features could stare at you, that's what it did for a few minutes. Then, it rolled out of the cave and disappeared. I wasn't sure what happened. I was about to leave the cave when the robot returned holding a package. It held the package out to me. Once I grabbed it, the robot rolled away. I opened the package and found it contained something that seemed to be food. It smelled good. My stomach was plastered against my backbone with hunger, so I ate a little of it and waited. After an hour with no ill side effects, I ate the rest of it. It was far tastier than anything the colony cook had ever made. The robot stood unmoving while I ate. I pointed to the bag and asked it if it could bring me more food. The robot rolled out of the cave and returned with another bag of food. For the next three days, the robot would sit in the sunlight and bring me food whenever I asked. Sometimes I would request it verbally, but there were other times I would just think it. Apparently, the robot could read my mind. Each time I either said or thought of food, it would bring me food.

"Now that I was sure the robots were energized by sunlight, I had the sphere robot help me drag one of the larger robots into the sunlight. After a few hours in the sun, the larger robot began to move. It also reacted to my thoughts. I named this robot Big Boy."

"What happened to the robots?"

"I left them in the cave. When I returned to the colony, I had the robot programmed for it, bury everyone."

Seth couldn't see how any of this could help them escape. He directed a thought to Lena. "*What should I do next?*" She didn't respond.

"Are you paying attention that there are only twenty minutes left before the bomb goes off," Professor said, as if Seth wasn't aware of it.

Seth asked Thorndale, "Is that all you did with the Alenian robots?"

Thorndale hesitated before he answered, "I was still afraid of running into one of my insane colleagues. I had Big Boy come back to the compound with me. I inspected the locked Quonset hut and found the cylinders. I used the MTS machine to destroy what was in them. Big Boy was a great help moving the cylinders, and I think his presence kept Fredricks away."

Gunther gave Thorndale an intense look as he asked, "Was it the robot Big Boy that killed the Marine?"

"It wasn't Big Boy's fault. I still had more cylinders to destroy after you arrived. I came back to the colony that night with Big Boy. I had the robot start processing the cylinders when the Marine heard us. We came out of the hut to find the Marine. He fired at Big Boy, damaging one of his arms. Big Boy was reaching for the Marine's weapon when he fired again. The blast hit Big Boy's body, throwing him off balance. Instead of grabbing the Marine's weapon, he grabbed his arm. As he did, Big Boy's damaged arm swung around, hitting the Marine in the head, which made Big Boy stumble, pulling off the Marine's arm. Big Boy wasn't dangerous. It acted in self-defense."

"You didn't get captured until days later," Gunther said.

"When Big Boy was shot, I ordered Big Boy to go back to the robot cave. I stayed and hid in one of the unused shacks. The night I was captured, I came out to finish destroying the cylinders."

Seth didn't understand why Lena wanted him to learn about Thorndale's experiences with the robots. How could the Alenian robots help them? Thorndale said the robot could read his thoughts. Seth didn't sense that Thorndale was a telepath, but Seth was. Did Lena want him to reach out to the robot with his mind? His mother determined the Alenians were telepaths. If they controlled their robots telepathically, it would explain why they didn't have on-off switches. Did Lena think he could communicate with a robot telepathically when it was so far away? Yet, Lena was communicating with him from a great distance. He had to try to contact the robot. It was their only chance to survive.

"What happened to the robot that was a sphere?" Seth asked Thorndale.

"I left the cave door open so the sun would shine on it."

"If you have a plan for saving us, there are only fifteen minutes left before the bomb explodes," Professor said.

Seth directed his thoughts to a robot he'd never seen and had no idea if it could sense him. He tried to visualize a spherical robot that had arms with claws and legs with wheels, but all he could envision was a childish drawing of this robot. He concentrated so hard sweat began rolling down his forehead.

"What are you doing?" Thorndale asked, watching the tight furrows across Seth's forehead.

"I'm trying to summon the Alenian spherical robot to help us."

Everyone's eyes were on Seth. He couldn't help thinking this was absurd. Lena said he could do it. He had to try. With his eyes closed, he focused on a message to the robot to come to him. All he could sense was the blackness of having shut his eyes.

"Whatever you're doing, it had better happen quickly. There are only eleven minutes left on the timer," Professor prompted, the tremor in his voice conveying his fear.

Seth could only sense emptiness. In that, the emptiness wasn't his feelings, it was something else. And then, the blackness lifted. He hadn't opened his eyes, yet he was seeing the color green. It was grass, the grass along the riverbank. The grass disappeared and was replaced by unplanted fields. He was moving very fast across the fields. He was heading toward the compound.

"Anything?" Thorndale asked.

"I think I'm seeing what the robot sees," Seth said, his eyes still closed.

The Quonset huts of the compound were visible in the distance and getting closer.

Professor said, "There are less than two minutes left on the timer."

Seth opened his eyes. The timer was ticking down to the last minute. He closed his eyes again, but all he could see was the cylinder. He was seeing the cylinder through the robot's vision. He opened his eyes.

The robot was in the doorway. It was a sphere on three-wheeled legs with two arms ending in claws. It had no head or anything that could be a camera lens, yet Seth had seen himself and the others as if he were standing in the doorway.

Seth hadn't told the robot what to do when it got here. He formed a mental image of the robot entering the Quonset hut, removing the bomb from the top of the cylinder, and taking it outside the hut. He hoped the robot could understand what he wanted it to do.

He closed his eyes as he formed commands for the robot. Seeing what the robot saw, it rolled into the hut and over to the cylinder. It reached up with a claw and cut the ties holding the bomb to the top of the cylinder. It then rolled out of the hut carrying the bomb outside and then stopped.

Seth gave it a mental order to toss the bomb far away. The robot swung the arm holding the bomb and threw it towards the fields west of the compound. Almost immediately, there was a loud explosion.

Seth mentally ordered the robot to free him, though he wasn't sure how or if it could do it.

The robot wheeled back into the Quonset hut. One of its clawed arms retracted into its body and was replaced by an arm ending with a spinning wheel. The robot rolled over to the chain and cut through it with the spinning wheel. It rolled up to Seth and cut the rope binding his feet. Using its clawed arm, it lifted Seth's hands and cut the rope around his wrists.

Seth projected a command to free the others, beginning with Doc. Meanwhile, he began untying Thorndale. In a few minutes, everyone was free. The robot stood immobile in the middle of the Quonset hut.

Thorndale walked up to the cylinder and tipped it on its side. He smiled, "I killed the stuff in this one. It wouldn't have harmed us if it had been released. Though the Major might have a problem. When your ship entered orbit, I was in the middle of x-raying one of the cylinders. I stopped partway through to turn on the Alenian atmospheric engines. The X-rays may have weakened the cylinder without killing everything inside. If the Major and his men aren't careful handling that cylinder, they might release some of the stuff in it."

Still shaken by the experience, they all left the Quonset hut. A short distance to the west was a large hole in the field where the robot had thrown the bomb.

Professor walked up to Seth. "How are you able to converse with the robot?"

Seth said aloud so everyone could hear, "I'm a telepath. I've hidden it my entire life. However, it seems that being a telepath here has its advantages."

Everyone seemed surprised but accepted Seth's revelation, except Professor. He seemed to be troubled by it but said nothing.

Doc was still rubbing his wrists when he said, "Well, gentlemen, we are the new Alenians."

Gunther was looking up at the sky. He pointed at a bright, moving speck. "There is the freighter heading to the wormhole."

"Do you think they'll succeed in closing it?" Alan said.

"We may never know. We have no ship. The only way we might know if the wormhole remains open is if someone comes through it. Otherwise, we will be stuck here forever," Gunther said.

CHAPTER 91

M ajor Krugar was standing with Captain Hollinsky on the bridge of the
Cauloten Six as they approached the wormhole. One of the monitors
showed the image of Alenia, now no more than a bright disk next to the gas giant.

Krugar said, "By now they should all be dead. I have never seen how this
enzyme works, but it killed the crews who visited A2 very quickly. I cannot
imagine a more interesting way to kill an enemy than by having them eaten alive."

Hollinsky cringed at the thought. To avoid imagining people being eaten alive,
he focused his attentions on the forward-facing monitor. "We will be at the
wormhole in a few minutes. You said you had a way to blow the explosives on
this side of the wormhole without having us caught in its collapse."

"You worry too much. I had my men install an electronic signaling device on
one of your emergency rockets. Once we clear the wormhole, the rocket will be
sent through it to trigger the explosives."

Krugar turned back to look at the monitor showing the moon. "I wish I had
installed a camera inside the Quonset hut so I could see what is happening. I
imagine it would be an interesting sight. I need to keep that in mind when we
use this weapon on a rebel planet." He said it gleefully.

Hollinsky didn't like the idea of abandoning the landing party on the moon,
but he said nothing. Nor did he say anything when he learned they were going to
release this horrible weapon on the planet. He couldn't, the orders came directly
from the new Empress. All Hollinsky could do was cringe at the ugliness of it all
and hope it stopped here.

Krugar enjoyed seeing how uncomfortable he made Hollinsky, as he continued talking about killing those left on the moon. The only important thing now was getting the cylinders they were carrying into the hands of the Empress.

The freighter slowly approached the wormhole's entrance. It passed by the explosive charges. Krugar turned to one of his Marines sitting at the Emergency Rocket control panel. "Fire the rocket on my command." The Marine indicated he was ready.

The freighter entered the wormhole, and the ship began to shake. The shaking continued for several minutes before it stopped. The only image on the monitors was that of the wormhole's milky interior.

"We won't see this again," Hollinsky said, with a feeling of relief.

"No one will, if the explosives close the wormhole," Krugar said, never shifting his gaze from the monitors.

They traveled through the interior of the wormhole until the shaking started again, indicating they were exiting the wormhole and returning to normal space. The view on the ship's monitor changed from milky white to normal space.

"Fire the rocket now," Krugar told the Marine. The Marine flipped a switch on the panel in front of him and the vibration of the departing rocket echoed through the freighter. The rear monitor showed the rocket disappearing as it entered the wormhole.

Krugar checked the clock, timing how long it would take to see a reaction. He didn't know what to expect. If the wormhole only collapsed on the Alenian side, he wasn't sure if it would close on this side. It was only a guess that the bombs would close the wormhole. He got his answer when the wormhole's invisible entrance disgorged a plume of its interior milky white, immediately followed by a much larger burst of red flames. It grew into a massive fireball before disappearing.

Krugar said to the Marine, "Test for the signal."

The Marine moved to another panel. He flipped a switch and then began rotating a dial as he focused his attention on a gauge above the dial. He moved the dial back and forth, eyes fixed on the gauge. Finally, he said, "Nothing, Sir."

Hollinsky looked at the Major. Krugar smiled at Hollinsky's confusion. "We put a transmitter outside the Alenian entrance to the wormhole. If the wormhole was still open, we should hear its transmission. The fact we didn't means we have successfully closed the wormhole. Now we have a rendezvous with a military ship. We cannot keep them waiting."

CHAPTER 92

The team went to the Common while Seth stayed behind to inspect the robot that saved them.

All five sat on the benches under the tree in the center of the Common and stared up at the sky. The fact they'd come so close to dying was playing on their minds, as was the realization they could be stranded on this moon for the rest of their lives.

"Do you think we'll be able to see the explosion when they close the wormhole?" Alan asked.

Gunther answered, "They've had enough time to get to the wormhole. The wormhole is far away, and I doubt we'd see much, if anything."

They all continued to look up at the sky.

Professor spoke up, "There was no one for me to return to, and my best years at Klatania University are behind me. I've spent my life speculating on what an advanced alien species might be like. Here was an alien civilization. It was everything I had ever wanted. There was no point in me leaving all this information about the Alenians behind to return to the university. I decided I wanted to be left here. However, there is a difference between volunteering to remain and not having a choice."

"There, I see something!" Alan said pointing.

They followed where he was pointing. There was a bright speck of light in the sky. The speck grew larger, more intense, as bright as the star. Suddenly it changed to an orange smear that quickly faded away.

"I guess that means the wormhole is closed," Alan said, with the finality of their situation each of them felt.

Gunther said what all of them were thinking, "What do we do now?"

Doc patted Gunther on his non-injured shoulder, "We survive as best we can. Let me say there are two things that make me feel good today. One, of course, is being alive. The other is being here with all of you. From the beginning I harbored a feeling that this would be a misadventure for us. Except for Professor, whose expertise made him an obvious choice, any number of people with abilities like ours could have been chosen for this mission. We were selected because Prime, now the Empress, was aware that no one was waiting for us to return. We were expendable."

"We're not expendable yet," Seth said, walking up to them. "We have a lot to do. The first thing is to inventory how much food we have. Thorndale said he was fed by the robot that saved us. Apparently, there is a supply of food somewhere near the Alenian robot cave. Doc and Thorndale, take the truck and follow the robot. I gave it orders to lead you to the food supply. Professor and Alan, do an inventory of what the Major and the Marines have left behind. Look for any weapons, comms equipment, anything we might find useful. Gunther, I need your help at the crystal cave. We need to find out what is causing the problem with its power supply and fix it."

"Wait!" Professor said angrily. "You're giving orders? Who put you in charge? And you can explain about being a telepath, and who is this Lena and what is the crystal cave!"

"I'm sorry if I'm presumptuous in giving out orders. There are things we need to do, and one of them is not to sit here feeling sorry for ourselves. Professor, I know you haven't seen any of the visions the rest of us have. And neither you nor Doc know about the crystal cave. I believe the Alenians are not dead. They, or what they've become, are living in a cave in the northern mountain range, and they will die without our help. Lena is more complicated to explain. She is an Alenian that I can communicate with. I only learned that yesterday. As for me being a telepath, Doc can fill you in. I don't have time now."

Seth turned to Gunther, "Will you help me find out how to fix the power to the crystal cave?"

Thorndale said, "Do you think it's safe to provide power to the cave? I mean, look what happened to everyone who was here the last time they had an ample supply of energy, and that was just from sunlight. What will happen if you reconnect them to a full power source?" The scars on Thorndale's face accentuated his fear.

"I believe nothing bad will happen. The Alenians are crying out for help, and if none of you will help me restore power to them, I'll do it myself."

Professor stood up and faced Seth. "Why should we allow you to take charge? You have been hiding the fact you are a telepath. It may be that you, as well as Jana, were sent here as spies. For all we know that entire situation with the cylinder and bomb were a contrivance to gain our trust. Are you a member of the EYE Corps?"

Doc said, "My dear friend, I can vouch for Seth. I don't believe he is a spy or a member of the EYE Corps. As far as trusting him to direct our activities, he isn't telling us to do anything that isn't sensible. Any one of us might have come up with the same plan. It is just that Seth thought of it first."

Gunther offered his opinion, "Seth may not have been fully open with us, but I believe he is looking out for our interests." He turned to Seth. "Yes, I'll help you restore power to the crystal cave."

Seth said, "Professor, there is a lot about me you don't know. I will fill you in later. Right now, I suggest we all need to pull together to survive."

CHAPTER 93

Empress Andraia was beginning to feel the power of her new position. Within a day of her coronation, she put the wheels in motion to replace the Barons with people loyal to her. It would happen quickly so as not to give the Barons a chance to react.

She commanded architects to build a fabulous museum for the Earth's treasures the Klatans had kept for themselves. The Communications Director was sending out VIDs showing plans for the museum, reminding the Empire's citizens that she was fulfilling her coronation promise.

The Emperor had been paranoid about his safety, and that was the reason he'd created the Zinder guards. The Prince proved the near mindless creatures could be reprogrammed. She had the Zinder guards killed and replaced them with people who were thoroughly vetted for their loyalty to her. She would have them constantly checked by the EYE Corps to ensure their loyalty didn't change.

She planned to move into the Emperor's quarters. His living quarters, a place she was never invited into, were behind his study. When she went into the living quarters, she found them to be several spacious lavishly decorated rooms. It wasn't her style. She had the rooms stripped and the furniture replaced to accommodate her more utilitarian taste.

The Emperor's study, that long passage through his private art gallery, was barren now the art objects had been removed. She had the study reconfigured into separate rooms. Some rooms would be for her personal use, others to be used for official functions. At the same time, she had the Baron's' meeting room with its fine gold and bejeweled table dismantled and repurposed as a storage closet.

She was finding it difficult to get information on the Empire's wealth. There was a master accountant whose job was to keep all financial records for the Empire. She made repeated requests for him to come to her, but each time she got no response from him. After the third non-responsive attempt, she sent palace guards to hunt him down and bring him to her.

Two palace guards pushed the master accountant into the room she had made her office. He was a small man with a balding head, thin to the point of being emaciated, and displaying an irritating nervous facial tick. He didn't look like someone who would dare defy her request for the state of the Empire's wealth. So why had he resisted coming to her?

The small man stood in front of her focusing his eyes on the floor.

"You have been hard to reach. I want to know the value of the Empire's wealth." She expressed the question calmly, not as a command.

The little man didn't answer, but his facial twitching increased.

"Since you seem either not to hear well, or won't answer me, I expect I will need a new master accountant. Guards, show the master accountant to a cell."

"Wait, please! I'm afraid that if I answer you, you will have me killed."

"If you don't, you can be assured that will be the outcome."

The man blurted out, "The Empire is nearly bankrupt."

"Guards, leave us!"

He was more open after that. He told the story of the past two Emperors' excesses. Wuden's father lived lavishly. He spent money without regard to how much he spent or what it did to the treasury. During his time, the Emperor let the Barons have free reign. They took advantage by holding back some of the taxes they collected for themselves. When Wuden succeeded his father, he was neither interested, nor in his later years, capable of monitoring the Baron's activities, nor controlling his own expenses. He drove the treasury dangerously low. The master accountant's final assessment was that the Empire, although not yet insolvent, would soon be, unless drastic changes were made.

She didn't like hearing the disturbing news. She would let the accountant live. He couldn't be blamed for the Klatan family being spendthrift fools, or for his fear of reporting it to her. Besides stopping the Barons from stealing, there was only one thing she could do to bolster the treasury. It was to collect more taxes. She would start with the outer planets. They may not have the money, yet every Imperial dollar she squeezed out of them meant less they could use to support the rebels. Besides, once Major Krugar arrived with her planet killing weapon, she would release it on one of the outer planets. After that, they would do whatever she demanded.

She dismissed the master accountant and warned him never to ignore her requests in the future if he wished to stay alive. He bowed and scurried out of her office.

She had been waiting for word from Admiral Wilson about the attack on the rebel base Liberty. By now, it should be over. The most he would be doing was mopping up any rebel ships that escaped. She called her Military Communications Liaison. "Have you received news from Admiral Wilson?"

"No, Your Majesty. The only communications we received from the Admiral were before the fleet arrived at the rebel base. He was told to continue the mission in silence so as not to alert the rebels."

"Have you tried to communicate with the Admiral?"

"Yes, Your Majesty, we have tried. We have not received a reply."

"Send a scout ship to the site. I want to know what is happening there."

"I have already sent a scout ship that was in the area. I am expecting a reply from the scout ship or Admiral Wilson at any time."

"Report to me as soon as it comes in." She cut the call. Wilson and his fleet had better be celebrating their victory and too drunk to report. Anything else, and he would suffer.

The rest of her day was filled with trivial matters. These were only partially distracting her. Her real concern was not hearing news about the destruction of the rebel base. She sat in her private dining room, waiting for her dinner. She ordered the chef to make her favorite meal. It was not good to eat such rich food too often, however, this was going to be a day of celebration once she finally got word the rebel base had been destroyed.

The meal had just been placed on the table when a messenger boy ran up to her. She liked to have boys deliver her messages. The young women the Emperor employed were always an irritation to her. She was sure the Emperor used young women as messengers to titillate his libido, if not also to satisfy his sexual desires. She had them replaced with young boys, who were more obedient as long as they were young enough.

He bowed deeply and said, "Your Majesty, I have a call for you." He handed her a small comms device and left.

She turned it on. The screen lit up with the Military Communications Liaison officer's face. "Your Majesty, I have heard from the scout ship."

"What does the Admiral report?"

"The fleet sent to the rebel base has been destroyed. All the ships, including the Admiral's ship, were destroyed."

"That's impossible!" she screamed.

"I...I am just reporting what the scout ship reported to me. I have images of the fleet's wreckage I can show you."

She killed the call. *How can that be*, she thought? The rebels can't be that well equipped. I'll send in more ships. Then she remembered the accountant's assessment that the Empire's coffers were empty. She thought, *how can I build ships if the Empire is broke?*

CHAPTER 94

Seth and Gunther drove the all-terrain car to the northern mountains, through the tunnel, and parked next to the bulldozer. The sun was too high to shine light in the cave, leaving the cave very dark. Anticipating this, Seth brought two flashlights. He handed one to Gunther, and they walked to the cave's entrance.

"Since you think the power system is atop the mountain, why are we looking in the cave?" Gunther asked.

"I want to find where the power comes into the cave. It's possible the problem is inside the cave. Maybe the earthquake broke something."

They panned flashlight beams around the cave. The crystals were dark, none of them were glowing, and they produced eerie reflections as the light hit them.

"Do you think we'll see more ghosts?" Gunther asked as he scanned the area with his flashlight.

"Without the sun powering the crystals, I doubt we will."

The flashlight reflection from the frames holding the crystals gave off a rainbow of colors. Gunther walked over to one of the vertical poles on the frame and tapped it with the flashlight, "This doesn't look or sound like metal."

"Whatever it is, it's the same thing they used for the habitation engine towers," Seth said, as he continued walking down the aisle along the edge of the structure. "Walk down the other side of the frames. Look for anything that might be an external connection bringing power into the system."

Gunther walked to the other side of the cave as Seth continued checking his side.

Seth didn't see anything until he reached the end of the cave. Against the far wall of the cave, he saw six thick cables coming down from the cave's ceiling that entered a three-meter by two-meter metal box on the floor.

"I think I've found it!" he yelled to Gunther, who was still walking down the other side of the frames.

He inspected the box while he waited for Gunther. The six thick cables disappeared into the three-meter end of the box. He walked around to the opposite side and found hundreds of smaller cables exiting the box. They ran throughout the cave and were attached to the frames that supported the crystals.

Gunther came up. He pointed to the six cables coming down from the ceiling. "These must feed power to the system, and this box is apparently a junction where the power is distributed to the frames."

"Let's see if we can get the cover off the box and see what's inside," Seth said.

There were no bolts or other fasteners holding the lid down. Seth and Gunther pulled up on opposite sides of the box's lid. It wouldn't budge. They alternated pulling up each side, and it started to loosen and eventually came off. They set the cover on the ground.

Inside the box was a cube. The six thick cables were connected to one side of the cube. Hundreds of small wires exited the other side of the cube.

"This cube must act as a transformer to convert the power coming into something the frames can use."

Seth agreed with Gunther's assessment.

The cube had no seams and no apparent way to open it.

Gunther said, "I'll get the tester from the car so we can see how much power is being delivered to the frames."

Gunther went to the car to fetch the electrical test equipment they'd brought. Seth studied the cube. It was made of the same strange metal as the box it was in and the frames in the cave.

When Gunther returned, Seth pointed to the thick cables connected to the cube. "Let's see what current is flowing through these thick cables."

Gunther pulled out the leads from the tester. "I have no idea whether we have DC, AC, or Klatan only knows what. You'd better stand back. I don't want it to kill both of us if the tester explodes."

Seth stood a few meters away as Gunther put a lead on one side of a large cable. He touched the second lead on the other side. There were no sparks. Gunther checked the meter. "It's AC current, though it's very weak." He moved the leads to the next thick cable. "This one's dead. There is no current at all." He tested the other four thick cables and found none of them had current flowing through them.

"Test the smaller cables," Seth said.

Gunther tested several of the contacts of the small cables leaving the cube. They all registered some, though very weak, current. "They're all sharing the incoming current from the one power cable, and there isn't much coming through it."

"If my idea about where the power comes from is correct, it will be a challenge to get to it. Follow me," Seth said.

They walked out of the cave. Seth pointed to the top of the mountain. "See that peak. It looks different than the others. I think it's a solar collector supplying power to the crystals through the thick cables. Something up there isn't working. The only way to find out is to go up there."

Gunther craned his neck to see the peak with its flat, smooth black surface. It was four kilometers above them, and the side of the mountain was almost vertical. He turned to Seth. "If you are thinking of getting to the top, you are looking at one ugly climb."

It was already late in the afternoon. Seth would need some equipment to climb the mountain. As dangerous as climbing this almost vertical mountain might be, it would be infinitely more dangerous if he did it in the dark. "Let's go back to the colony. I'll come early tomorrow to see if I can reach the top and get back down in one day."

On the drive back to the colony, Gunther said, "You might kill yourself climbing that mountain. The face of it is almost vertically straight. Lena must be pretty special if you're willing to risk your life for a ghost."

Seth smiled. "She is."

CHAPTER 95

Seth and Gunther returned to the colony. Seth went to look for equipment he could use to make the climb, while Gunther headed for the mess hall.

Gunther found everyone eating. There was a large bowl of food which appeared to be a thick soup or pudding, but it smelled a lot better than either. Everyone had a small bowl and was eating this odd concoction.

"What is this?" Gunther asked.

Thorndale said, "It's a mixture of protein and carbohydrates. Doc and I took the truck and followed the robot to a cave where the food was stored. There are dozens of large, sealed drums there, each one containing bags of food. Apparently, the Alenians stored the food in these drums. Only one of the drums was open. Undoubtedly the one from which the robot brought me food. We loaded a couple of the drums onto the truck and brought them back. Doc checked them out, and the food is safe to eat. That's what we're eating tonight."

Gunther grabbed a bowl from the stack of dishes and scooped a ladle of the mixture into it. The mixture was stiffer than he expected, so he grabbed a fork instead of the usual spoon. He lifted a small portion of the food and held it to his nose. It had a pleasant aroma. He stuck the fork in his mouth and savored the taste. He said, "This tastes like something I had a long time ago at a friend's home. I believe it was called Italian Lasagna. This doesn't have the same texture, but it leaves the same satisfying taste in the mouth as that dish." He took another bite. "This is a lot better than what the cook was serving us."

Doc asked, "Where is Seth?"

Gunther took another fork full of food before he answered. "He's looking for climbing gear." The answer got questioning looks from everyone. "We found cables that bring power to the crystal cave, though not much power is reaching the cave. Seth thinks the power is coming from a solar collector at the top of the mountain. He thinks that's where the problem is, and he plans to climb the mountain to get to the peak and see if he can fix it."

"We flew by those mountains when I was with him. The peaks must be at least four kilometers tall, and the slopes are nearly vertical. I can't imagine anyone climbing to the top of that mountain," Alan said.

Seth walked in and joined them at the table. "Wow, the food smells good."

Alan addressed Seth. "You must be going insane. Gunther tells us you intend on climbing the mountain to restore power to the crystal cave. That mountain looks like it would be nearly impossible to climb."

"I'm not insane. At least not yet. And, yes, I do plan on climbing that mountain. I think something on that mountain is stopping the crystal cave from getting power."

"I still think it's dangerous to give the ghosts in the crystal cave more power," Thorndale muttered.

Seth gave Thorndale a stern look. "You need faith. Or call it intuition. I believe reconnecting power to the cave will result in something good. Now let me try some of this great-smelling food. I'll need my strength for tomorrow."

CHAPTER 96

S eth awakened at first light. He dressed quietly, not wanting to wake Alan. He planned to get the car and drive to the northern mountain. He thought about the problems he would face scaling the mountain. No matter how difficult it was going to be, he was going to do it. Lena was depending on him.

Seth came out of his bedroom and found Alan already dressed and sitting at the kitchen table. "You're not going to climb this mountain without me. If nothing else, I can help blot up your smashed body when you fall," Alan said, humorlessly.

"You're welcome to come along, although don't expect to see any spectacular falls today."

They walked to the Supply hut where Seth had collected all the rope he could find and a small hand pickax. He'd also found a couple dozen five-inch metal spikes that could serve as anchors as he scaled the mountain.

Alan helped carry the equipment to the Vehicle hut. Doc, Professor, Gunther, and Thorndale were waiting for them. Next to Thorndale was the little round Alenian robot that had saved them from being blown up.

Seth smiled. "A sendoff. How nice of you."

"We aren't here to see you off. We're going to come with you. In fact, we're here to make sure you don't kill yourself making the climb," Thorndale said.

"I thought we worked that out last night. I'm going to fix the power to the crystal cave whether you like it or not," Seth said.

Thorndale grinned. "We're not here to stop you from fixing the power to the crystal cave if you can. We'll deal with what happens after that. We're here to suggest there may be another way to climb the mountain." He patted the shell of the robot. "I named my friend here Charlie. It turns out Charlie can climb. I know it can. I watched Charlie do it outside his robot cave. Since you can see through Charlie's eyes, I think we can get Charlie to do the climbing while you guide him."

Charlie was rocking back and forth slowly on its wheels. Seth was about to say the idea was absurd until he was looking at himself. He was seeing through Charlie's eyes. He hadn't done anything, it just happened. Maybe it would be a good idea to have some help making the climb, even if it came from a robot, although he was suspicious that the spherical robot with wheels could climb.

The sun had cleared the horizon. "We better get moving. If all of you are coming, we're going to have to take one of the trucks," Seth said.

"I already put fuel in the truck," Gunther piped up.

Doc said, "I've brought something for us to eat. You will need your strength." He handed Seth a sandwich, then one to everyone.

"You found bread?" Alan asked.

"There was a loaf buried behind things in the freezer," Doc said.

Thorndale insisted on driving. He said he had a way of avoiding the bumpy route Seth had taken to the northern mountains by going west first. The ground there was partially uncultivated. It would take longer, but it would be a smoother ride, and it wouldn't break the backs of the passengers.

Seth sat in the passenger seat. Everyone else, including Charlie, climbed into the back of the truck. Thorndale drove west for fourteen kilometers before turning north. He was right, the land was smoother than the bumpier path Seth had taken. The smoother ground made for a more comfortable ride, although Thorndale still had to avoid deep holes along the way that could have caused the truck to roll over if they drove over one of them.

It took thirty minutes longer to reach the tunnel than it took by Seth's rougher, more direct route. Thorndale drove through the tunnel and parked next to the bulldozer. They all got out of the truck and walked to the mouth of the cave. Sunlight was beginning to shine on the crystals within the cave, and the crystals nearest the cave's opening were glowing brightly. Even some of the crystals not directly receiving sunlight were glowing.

"Thorndale told me about this, yet seeing it is incredible," Professor said, as he looked at the expansive cave with its thousands of crystals.

Gunther said to Seth, "No ghosts. By now the ghosts should have appeared."

"You're right. They should have appeared." Seth was wondering why he hadn't heard from Lena, especially now since he was here to restore power to the cave.

Thorndale stood outside of the cave with Charlie. "My friend is ready to start the climb."

Seth came out of the cave. "Let me get my gear out of the truck, and we can begin climbing."

"What do you mean *we* can begin climbing?" Thorndale said. "Charlie is here so you don't have to make the climb."

Seth walked over to the robot. Charlie was rolling back and forth energetically on its wheels like an excited child preparing to go on a fun trip. He looked at the three wheels it was rocking back and forth on. Its two arms were folded across its meter wide spherical shell. Seth closed his eyes. He could see himself through Charlie's vision.

Seth stood up and said to Thorndale. "I can see what the robot sees, but I can't see how it could climb, and it sure isn't going to roll up the mountain."

Thorndale grinned. "Not roll. Charlie, show this disbeliever what you can do."

The robot responded. The wheels folded into its body, replaced by six more arms. The new arms had claws, some large, others smaller. The robot used the new arms to move across the ground in spider fashion. Once it reached the side of the mountain, it began to climb. It moved quickly up the face of the mountain finally stopping thirty meters above them.

Seth focused. He was looking down at himself and Thorndale through Charlie's vision.

"Tell me, Seth. Can you climb that fast or that surefooted?" Thorndale asked, as a smile splashed across his scarred face.

Seth concentrated on his view through Charlie's vision. He thought *climb*. Charlie began to climb quickly up the mountain.

Thorndale watched as Charlie climbed. "Are you controlling him?" he asked Seth.

"I see what he sees, and he's following my mental directions," Seth answered, as he stared blankly in the distance, focusing his total concentration through Charlie's vision.

"It's a big mountain. Do you know what you're looking for?" Thorndale asked, turning away from Seth to watch Charlie climb.

Seth was about to answer Thorndale that he would keep looking until he found something when he heard a voice. It was a soft female voice. It said, "The western side of the peak with the flat black surface. Just below the summit is a connection point for the power cables that feed the cave."

Seth turned around to see where the voice was coming from. When he found no one was there, other than Thorndale, he realized the voice was in his head.

He projected a mental question, "*Is it you, Lena?*"

"*Everyone in the Lattice is contributing their energy to allow me to communicate with you. The sunlight hitting the crystals in the front of the cave is providing the energy, and they are transferring my thoughts to you. When the sun's energy entering the cave ceases, I will no longer be able to communicate with you. My own energy reserves have been exhausted, and I am using the reserves of my friends who are with me. You must fix the power to the Lattice cave, or they will all die.*"

"What's happening? You look like your thoughts are a thousand kilometers away," Thorndale said.

"I just got a telepathic message from Lena. She says the problem is below the summit on the western side of the peak. We have to hurry. They don't have much time left."

Thorndale noticed Charlie had stopped when Seth was conversing with Lena. He was about to tell Seth Charlie had stopped, but before he could say anything, Charlie resumed climbing, and was now moving up the mountain at a blistering pace.

Gunther was touring the others through the cave as they marveled at the number of crystals and the massive structure supporting them. They came out of the cave and stared up the mountain,   trying to see where the robot was. Charlie was already very high. It was hard to see the meter wide sphere against the rough granite surface of the mountain. Gunther went to the truck and returned with a pair of binoculars. He handed the binoculars around so they could get a better view of the robot.

An hour passed. Charlie was now so high up the mountain that even with the binoculars he appeared only as a moving dot. Professor complained his neck was sore from staring up, and he went back inside the cave.

Alan sat down next to Seth. Seth was sitting motionless on a boulder with his eyes shut. He sat with Seth for the next two hours. Seth said nothing, but if Alan could read anything from Seth's expression, it was worry.

Gunther was still watching Charlie. Charlie was approaching the smooth faced summit. Thorndale told him Lena conveyed to Seth that's where the problem was. Gunther could see Charlie had stopped moving. He asked Seth, "Has the robot found the problem?"

Seth shook his head to clear it. "I don't know. There is something there, but I can't see it clearly. Something is blocking Charlie's view. I have to move Charlie to a different angle." After a minute, Seth said, "There is a metal box. I see where the mountain fractured, and a boulder fell on top of the box. The boulder is blocking Charlie's access to the box. I'm going to see if Charlie can move the boulder."

Seth seemed to be straining, as if he was moving the boulder himself. There was a long pause, before Seth said, "Charlie was able to move the boulder away from the box."

Gunther asked, "What does this box look like?"

Seth continued his commentary on what Charlie was seeing. "The box is made of Alenian metal and about the same size as the box we found in the cave. It has six thick black cables coming out of its right side and going down into a hole in the mountain. These must be the six cables coming down the wall bringing power to the box in the cave. On the left side of this box are several smaller cables going up. The smaller cables must bring current from the solar collector to this box. I would guess there is an inverter in the box that changes the DC current from the solar panels to AC current for the cave.

"That sounds about right," Gunther said.

Seth continued, "The bolder smashed the latch on the box. I'm trying to get Charlie to open the box's lid."

Seth came out of his trance and opened his eyes. "Charlie can't do it. The lid is too bent to be lifted." Sweat dripped from his forehead, and his neck muscles were as taut as if he had been trying to lift the lid himself.

"I've got to go up there and get that lid off."

"You're in no state to climb this mountain now," Doc said. He had been watching Seth and could see he was exhausted from just directing the robot. "Maybe we can come back tomorrow and try again."

Seth shook his head. "I don't think the Alenians can last that long."

Seth returned his focus to the robot. Charlie was standing next to the box. Seth thought whimsically *Charlie, got any ideas how to get this lid off?* Charlie didn't answer, but it withdrew one of its arms and replaced it with the cutting wheel it used to free them. It began cutting into the smashed lid. Within seconds the latch was cut away from the box. Charlie grabbed the top of the box with two of its arms while using the other six arms to anchor it to the ground. It began pulling on the lid.

The lid didn't move. Seth was worried the robot wasn't strong enough to get the lid off. As he watched through the robot's eyes, he could see Charlie adjust its grip on the lid. It tried again. This time the lid moved a little. The robot changed its grasp again. It forced a third claw under the partially lifted portion of the lid. It began using this claw to pry open the lid as it pulled with the other two claws. Seth could almost feel the robot straining as it applied pressure to lift the lid. With one enormous effort, the lid popped off.

"He did it! The box is open! Charlie solved the problem by itself," Seth exclaimed to his audience.

Hearing Seth's excitement, Professor came out of the cave to see what was happening.

"What does the inside of the box look like?" Gunther asked.

Seth focused on what Charlie was seeing inside the box. In the center was a cube that looked identical to the cube in the cave's box. The smaller cables coming down from the mountain were connected on one side to this cube. The six black cables had connections to the cube on the other side. However, only one of the black cables was connected to the cube. The other four had been torn off the cube when the boulder hit the box.

Seth explained what he saw to the others.

"Can Charlie reattach the cables?" Gunther asked.

Seth studied what Charlie was seeing. The cube's connectors for the large cables had been severely damaged by the boulder. They were too damaged to reattach the cables to them. Seth had no idea how to reconnect the cables. He figured he had nothing to lose by asking Charlie if he could reconnect the cables to the cube.

Charlie didn't hesitate. It grabbed one of the cables, lifted it up and held it next to the connector it had been attached to. One of Charlie's arms withdrew into its body and out came a small, needle-like object. It held the needle next to the cable. Seth was shocked to see Charlie begin to weld the cable to the broken connector on the cube. Seth watched as Charlie did the same to the other four cables. Once it completed reattaching the cables, Charlie stopped.

Seth smiled and projected his thought, "*Charlie, put the lid back on the box and weld it shut.*" The robot complied.

To everyone's surprise, Seth ran into the cave. He stood there looking for an indication that the power had been restored. He watched to see if the crystals would begin to light up. The crystals remained dark. He walked out of the cave, "It didn't work."

Professor peered passed Seth into the cave. He began yelling, "They're lighting up! The crystals are lighting up!"

Everyone ran into the cave. Row after row, level after level, the crystals began to glow, not from the front of the cave, but from the rear. Slowly the crystals in the rear of the cave were giving off a warm glow, and it was spreading throughout the cave.

Seth heard Lena speak in his mind, "You saved my people. Now please help them live again. Our Elders will contact you soon."

CHAPTER 97

Thorndale reminded Seth to have Charlie climb down from the mountain. Seth sent the thought to Charlie, and Charlie began to climb down. Thorndale said he would wait for Charlie to get safely off the mountain.

Seth rejoined the others in the cave, watching as more crystals began to glow. The light they emitted was warm, not the intense brightness the crystals near the cave's entrance had emitted when they were immersed in sunlight. This glow was deep and golden in color.

As Seth watched the crystals, he projected a thought to Lena, "*What do you mean when you said, help them live again? And when will the elders contact me?*" He got no response.

Thorndale entered the cave. "Charlie is down from the mountain, and he's returning to the robot cave. I guess he is following some programmed rule that he must always return to the cave."

Seth noted that Charlie was now being called he and not it. Charlie deserved that much, and more.

Thorndale joined the others as they watched more of the crystals start to glow.

The sun was low. Thorndale said, "It's not safe for us to be driving back in the dark. We'd better leave now."

They agreed and got into the truck.

CHAPTER 98

They arrived at the colony just as the waning rays of the sun disappeared and headed for the mess hall to eat supper. Thorndale volunteered to be the cook, and he warmed up some of the Alenian meal packages and served them.

They were discussing the day's events when a hazy-white light began to form in front of them. It solidified into two men and two women wearing white tunics. One of them was the same gray bearded man who appeared to them in the cave, the one who had spoken to them in a language they didn't understand.

Seth was sure these were the Elders Lena spoke of.

Gunther commented, "These images are being projected in our mind. They could be making themselves look human to mirror how we look. It could be a trick to gain our sympathy. They may really be creatures with tentacles, or they could be gigantic insects."

The gray bearded man's image stepped forward as if he was going to speak. His lips didn't move but they could hear him. It was as if a ventriloquist was projecting his voice, but this voice was in their heads. "You are correct. We are projections in your minds. We appear to you as we once were in both form and size. The fact your appearance is no different than ours is surprising to us as well."

Alan said, "I can hear him, and he's speaking our language. Can you hear him?" Everyone could.

The gray bearded man continued, "We do not know your language. We find the words we need to speak to you in your minds. My daughter, Lena, showed us how to use your minds to find the meanings we wish to convey in a way you can understand. She learned this long ago when she was communicating with one of you who was only a child."

The team gave a quick look at Seth.

"We are the Elders of Demeerite. I am Ragonlar, Chief Elder." He turned his head to the older woman standing at his left. "This is Teila, our Administrator." He gestured to the young woman at his right, "This is Renola, our Head Scientist, and next to her is Monafar, our Historian. I imagine you have many questions for us. First, we thank you for reconnecting power to the Lattice. It is with this power we are able to communicate with you now."

Thorndale asked, "Are you Alenians?"

"We are, and once we lived on this moon."

"Something happened here that caused our people to begin killing one another. Was that your doing?"

Renola, the Head Scientist, answered Thorndale, "We are deeply sorry for that. To explain what happened to them, you need to know about the Lattice and our history. Our Historian, Monafar will explain."

Renola took a step back, and Monafar stepped forward. "Over seventy cycles ago, an enemy of unknown origin attacked the Alenian home worlds. The attack was unprovoked, and the enemy used a biological weapon we refer to as the White Death. It was a biological agent that consumed everything organic it encountered, and it multiplied from what it consumed. Everyone on our home worlds of Clanferion and Gorderion was killed by the White Death.

"The Enemy did not attack us in their initial attack, possibly because they didn't know there was a colony here. We were afraid they would return and dispense the White Death on Demeerite, it is what we call this moon. We have no spaceships to leave, and no weapons to defend ourselves from the Enemy. Our Chief Scientist, Renola, proposed a radical solution. She will explain it to you."

Gunther moaned, "They may never get to the point."

"Your history is interesting, though I don't see how that answers the question about what happened to our people," Thorndale said.

Renola had red hair, a thin frame, and, if she were human, appeared to be in her early twenties. She addressed Thorndale, "I ask for your patience. We have been trapped for over seventy cycles, which you call years. That is part of the answer you seek. To understand what happened to your people, you need to understand our Life Spheres, what you call crystals."

"Please continue," Thorndale said.

"The crystals were developed to preserve the essence of life after an Alenian dies. We discovered this process long ago and used it for those who lived on Demeerite. We never shared this process with our home worlds, the reason is a lengthy explanation that must be saved for another time. The essence of an Alenian is copied into a crystal, and when the Alenian dies, their crystal is added to the Lattice, which is the structure you supplied power to in the cave. The Lattice provides a simulated world that resembles life on Demeerite. Those who have died can communicate with others in the crystals, as well as those still living. In this way, we have given our people immortality.

"I worked with the crystals and began exploring the possibility of reversing the process. A crystal contains all the information of the Alenian within it, including the form of their original body and their essence. The essence is what you would call their conscious mind and their memories."

Seth interrupted, "When Lena asked me to help them live again, was she saying she wanted to return you to your bodies?"

"That was what Lena was asking. We gave up our bodies to save ourselves from the White Death. Shortly after the enemy attacked our home planets, I proposed a novel approach to save us. I proposed everyone on Demeerite be put in crystals. Since the crystals are not organic, the White Death would not affect them. I made this proposal based on the theory we could reconstruct a body from the information encoded in the crystal. A new body, one identical to the old one, but a healthy body. To provide the elements we needed to construct these new bodies, we broke down the bodies transferred into the crystals into their constituent elements. We stored these elements in hermetically sealed containers to secure them from the White Death. Once the White Death had passed, we would begin returning to our bodies using the stored elements."

Gunther grunted, "It's a bold proposal for anyone to choose to die with a vague expectation they might be made to live again."

"Faced with the prospects of being annihilated by the White Death, and after I demonstrated I could bring back one of our people in both their body and their essence from a crystal, the Elders agreed to accept this solution. We had been using the Lattice for our dead, now we expanded it to hold the entire population of Demeerite. I believed the White Death would dissipate quickly once it had nothing more to feed on. I estimated we would only need to be in the crystals a few cycles, years, before we could return to our original forms."

"The White Death was never released here. Why haven't you returned to your bodies?" Thorndale asked.

"My plan was both simple and flawed. We programmed one of our robots to begin the process of returning us to our physical forms after the White Death was no longer dangerous. We didn't anticipate what the enemy would do. They did not release the White Death on Demeerite, possibly because there was no one here to kill. They instead landed on Demeerite. They went to the genetics lab in the village. That they knew this lab existed, and what they did or wanted to do in the genetics lab, we can only guess. The robot that was in the lab was in contact with us, but once the enemy entered the lab, they destroyed the robot. Before the enemy left, they shut down all our robots and stored them in the cave where you found them. Without the robots, we were prisoners in the crystals with no way of escaping.

"Knowing this, I can explain what happened to your people. The Lattice was supported by two energy sources. One was the solar array you repaired on the mountain. It was intended as our backup power source. Our main source of power was a reactor in the basement of the Lattice cave. Thirty-five cycles ago, the reactor failed. We had only the solar array to power the cave. It could not fully power all the crystals in the Lattice. Many of our people's crystals had to go dormant to conserve power. For those who went dormant, it was as if they had really died. One day, not long ago, your people removed the boulder that hid the cave's entrance. Sunlight flooded into the cave and energized the crystals. Our people cried out for help. They projected their images and pleas for help into the minds of your people, thinking you were Alenians, you do look very much like us. We did not perceive the damage we were causing your people until they began to attack one another. All we could do was watch as your people committed terrible acts. Only one of you was unaffected."

"The images of your people continued after that. I know, I was the one who survived. It was me they continued to come to," Thorndale said to Renola.

Renola turned to face Thorndale. "We continued to try to contact you. We thought you were an Alenian. We didn't know why you couldn't understand us. The next thing you did was cover the opening to the Lattice cave. After that, we were left with only the power from the sun. When the ground shook, even that ended. Fortunately, it also loosened the boulder blocking the cave."

Thorndale felt embarrassed. "I didn't know what I was seeing or what the visions meant. I was frightened by what happened to my friends."

"We do not condemn you. The recent earthquake limited our power even more when the solar array failed. If it had not been for your help in restoring our power, we would have lost many. We are grateful to you for this. Now we ask you to help return us to our corporeal forms."

CHAPTER 99

"Where is Lena?" Seth asked Renola. Lena couldn't be on the Lattice. He was only a child, and wherever he put her crystal, it had to be somewhere in the human compound. Ever since he restored power to the cave, he kept sending Lena mental messages. She hadn't answered any of them.

"Lena and nine of our best scientists were the last to have their essences transferred to the crystals. This was done in the village's genetics laboratory, and the robot was there to take their crystals to the Lattice. The robot detected the enemy approaching and hid their crystals in the genetics laboratory. This was the robot the enemy destroyed. Lena and our scientists were on a powered rack, but it was not connected to the Lattice. We didn't know what happened to Lena after the robot was destroyed.

"Lena and our scientists' crystals remained in that cabinet for almost fifty cycles. During that time, our power source in the genetics laboratory failed, and Lena and the other crystals had to go dormant. When your people came to Demeerite, they discovered those crystals. A human child called Seth, moved Lena's and the others' crystals to safety after a human breached one of the crystals and killed the one in that crystal. Their crystals were put in a place where they could communicate with the Lattice since your people returned power to the village's genetics laboratory. This is how we know what happened to her and the nine scientists. They are there still, though we have lost contact with her."

"I'm the Seth who moved those crystals. I don't know where I put the crystals. All my childhood memories of being here were taken from me." As Seth said it, he couldn't see the image of Lena in his mind. Her image had been with him for years, but he could barely remember it now. Even the image of her in the crystal cave was fading. Something was wrong.

"Can you tell me where they are?" he begged Renola.

"Lena is in the vault in the village's genetics laboratory."

Gunther said, "The Marines cut all power to the village when they left. I restored power to our shacks, but I didn't reconnect the village's genetics lab."

"How long can the crystals last without power?" Seth asked, as he remembered Lena told him she was using the last of their power to contact him.

"There are power reserves in each crystal. Once that is depleted, the essence of the one in the crystal will die."

Seth turned to Thorndale. "Do you know where the genetics lab vault is?"

"I have no idea. We searched the genetics lab and everywhere else and never found where you hid the crystals."

Seth turned to Renola. "Please tell me where the genetics lab vault is."

CHAPTER 100

S eth ran to the Alenian village. Guided by Renola's directions, he entered the first small room in the genetics lab building. It was empty except for cabinets that lined one wall. She told him the vault with Lena's crystal was behind one of the cabinets, and where he would find a hidden release that would have the cabinet move away from the wall to reveal the vault.

He pulled on the release. Nothing happened. The release must depend on electricity. Gunther said the electricity to the village genetics lab had been turned off. Seth began pulling on the cabinet, trying to dislodge it from the wall. It wouldn't move.

Gunther came into the lab, saw what Seth was doing, and put his considerable muscles to the task. They both pulled on the cabinet that stubbornly resisted until it no longer could. The cabinet tore away from the wall. Behind it was a door made of Alenian metal. Seth opened the door. Inside were three rows of wires in pairs, and nine crystals resting on one of the wire pairs. A layer of thick dust covered the crystals. Seth rubbed the dust off one of the crystals. Its inside looked dull. There was no light coming from it. He sent a mental thought to Lena but got no response. He pulled off his shirt. He tied it into a sack, gently placing each crystal in it, before tying the top of the shirt to secure them. Carrying the crystals, he ran out of the lab.

He ran to the Vehicle hut and jumped into the all-terrain car. The fuel level was low.

Gunther had followed him. Seeing the low fuel level, he said, "I'll fill the tank."

Gunther was filling the tank when Alan came into the hut. "I saw you running here without a shirt. I ran to our shack and got one for you."

Seth put on the shirt as Gunther finished fueling the car. Gunther crawled into the passenger seat. "It isn't a good idea to drive to the Lattice cave at night. If you're going, you will need another pair of eyes."

"Two pairs of eyes," Alan said as he slid into the back seat.

Seth said thanks, started the car, turned on the headlights, and drove out of the Quonset hut.

Seth took the shorter, more direct route to the northern mountains. The ride was rough during the day. At night, when the headlights could barely see far enough ahead to warn of upcoming dips, ruts, and even deep trenches, it was hazardous to the point of death defying. The car bounced around wildly. Gunther cradled the shirt with the crystals in his arms to keep them safe.

Seth was driving so fast that he almost didn't see a deep ditch ahead of them. He slammed on the brakes, fishtailing the car, and only barely kept it from plunging into the ditch that might have ended their ride.

Alan yelled, "Hey, it won't help Lena if we die getting to the cave!"

Seth slowed down, but only a little.

He finally reached the tunnel, drove through it, and stopped at the cave's entrance. He grabbed the shirt with the crystals and ran into the cave. Gunther and Alan were on his heels.

The cave was lit with a warm glow from thousands of crystals. Seth ran along the frames looking for empty wires to put the crystals. He was three-quarters of the way down the cave's length before finding an open pair of wires. He carefully placed each of the nine crystals on the wires and waited.

The three of them stood watching the nine crystals. Seth projected his thoughts to Lena and waited for a response. None came. The crystals surrounding the nine were glowing warmly, but the nine showed no hint of a glow.

Hours passed. They sat on the cave floor below the nine crystals. The sun rose, and its rays entered the mouth of the cave resulting in the crystals near the cave's entrance lighting up brightly. Still, the nine crystals showed no sign of glowing. Seth made constant attempts to contact Lena telepathically but got no response.

Alan could see Seth's tortured expression, believing he had been too late to save Lena. "You did your best. With her help, you saved her people. It was what she wanted," he said, as he patted Seth on the shoulder.

Seth turned and faced Alan with tears welling up in his eyes. "She was my vision of the perfect woman. I know it's mad, but I promised myself that one day I would find her. I found her, and she saved us, but I let her down."

CHAPTER 101

Alan and Gunther stayed with Seth throughout the night. By mid-morning, none of the nine crystals showed any hint of lighting up, despite all the crystals surrounding them glowing with a golden hue. Gunther told Seth they weren't going to help the crystals by sitting there watching them, but Seth said he was staying. Gunther and Alan left, but Gunther said he would return later with food.

Two hours later, Gunther returned.

"Have you heard from Lena?"

The sad expression on Seth's face gave Gunther his answer.

"I brought you some food, a blanket, and a comms unit we found in the Communications hut, so you can call us if you need anything."

Seth looked half-heartedly at the packages of Alenian food, "Thanks."

"Thanks nothing, eat or I will force feed you," Gunther said.

Seth thought he might follow through with the threat, so he nibbled on the food.

Gunther said, "Renola contacted me. She said she understood I had some familiarity with reactors. I have no idea how she knows that. These Alenians can project themselves into our brains, maybe they can probe our minds, too. She asked me to meet her at the Lattice, what they call this crystal cave. I was coming anyway, so I agreed to meet her here."

Gunther hadn't finished saying that when Renola's image appeared before them. "Thank you for meeting with me. We told you last night the Lattice received most of its power from a reactor, and that reactor stopped working. Without it, the solar array barely supplies enough energy to support the Lattice. We will need more energy to return to our bodies. For that, we will need the reactor. Will you come and see if you can repair it?" Renola asked Gunther.

"I'll see what I can do." Gunther turned to Seth, "Come with me. You can use some time away from sitting here, and I might need your help."

Seth said, "I need to wait here for Lena to respond."

Renola addressed Seth. "The crystals that hold Lena and our scientists had their energy severely depleted. We have tried and cannot contact them. If the power within their crystals has been depleted to a level that cannot be reenergized, they are lost. If they are not lost, reenergizing their crystals with the limited power we receive from the solar array will take a long time."

Seth didn't like Renola's unemotionally clinical observation about the possibility that Lena was dead.

Renola added, "If you wish to help Gunther, I will tell you when Lena's crystal has been reenergized."

Seth wasn't helping Lena by sitting here watching her crystal. "I'll go with you to see if we can restart the reactor."

Renola led them to the rear of the Lattice cave. She pointed to a lever on the wall, and once Gunther pulled it, a part of the rock face in the wall opened, revealing stairs going down.

They followed Renola's ghostly image as it floated down the stairs. As they did, lights turned on to light their way. The stairs ended in an enormous room several times the size of the cave floor above. The room had thousands of body-shaped shells lying horizontally on stands. Pipes and wires connected the shells to a huge machine. The machine was also connected to large tanks at one end of the room.

"This is where most of our people were transferred to the Life Spheres, the crystals. This is also where the Transit will return us to our bodies if we have sufficient power." Renola led them along the wall to another door. This one opened automatically as Gunther approached, triggering a sensor that Renola's ephemeral body couldn't. Overhead lights came on as they entered the room. The room contained the controls for the fusion reactor. There was a large control panel with various gauges, levers, and buttons. On the wall behind the control panel were monitor screens. The screens were dark.

Gunther walked up to the controls and studied them for a few minutes. "There is nothing new here. Despite the markings I can't read, this is a typical fusion reactor."

He flipped a lever and checked the gauge above it. It flickered on. He walked down the length of the control panel, flipping more levers and checking the gauges.

Finally, Gunther stopped and turned to face Renola. "I know why your reactor isn't working. Everything is operational. There was no failure other than it ran out of gas."

Renola repeated, "ran out of gas?" It took her an instant longer to grasp its meaning, more than likely after seeing the meaning in Gunther's mind. "We have more fuel for it."

"What did you use to initiate the reaction when you first got it working?" Gunther asked her.

Renola's image froze. It stayed that way for several seconds before she said, "I have discussed this with the Elders. We paid a smuggler to let us use his ship to start this reactor. Our expert on reactors was the one whose crystal your people destroyed. We do not have another among us who understands reactors."

"I'm sorry for my people's stupidity. Do you have a power source comparable to a ship's reactor that we can use to restart this reactor?"

"We have no ships or other reactors. The only power source we have is the solar array powering the Lattice."

"What about the compound's autonomous nuclear reactor? Would that work to restart this one?" Seth asked Gunther.

"That reactor is too small. It doesn't have the power necessary to restart this fusion reactor," Gunther said.

"Maybe we could use the power source from the habitation engine. If I could dismantle one, I could bring it over to supplement the solar array."

Gunther shook his head. "I'm afraid even if you had fifty solar arrays, they wouldn't provide enough power to restart this reactor."

Without the reactor working, Seth feared there was no way of reenergizing Lena's crystal.

Renola listened with growing concern. "I will discuss this with the Elders. Thank you for your effort." Her image faded away.

Seth returned to continue his vigil at Lena's crystal. Gunther stayed with the reactor, double checking his assessment that it would need another reactor to restart it, all the time hoping he was wrong.

CHAPTER 102

G unther was still at the reactor when Renola reappeared. "There is something else you can do to help us. Our robots are stored in a cave. Two of the robots are programmed to run the process that will return us to our bodies. Can you see if you can restore our robots?"

"I'll do what I can. Where is this robot cave?"

"I have asked Thorndale to show you. He is waiting outside the Lattice cave to take you there."

Gunther found Thorndale outside the cave standing next to a motorcycle. "I understand you're going to take me to the Alenian robot cave," Gunther said.

"Renola asked me to do it. The cave is in the western mountain range. Jump on."

Gunther gave the motorcycle a skeptical look. Doc had driven him here in the all-terrain car before going to the cavern city to explore the hospital guided by Kamlanar, the Alenian who had been Head of Medical Research. Despite its name, Gunther still felt the bruises he received as the all-terrain car bounced through the fields. He could only imagine how much worse it would be to ride on the back of a motorcycle.

"Why did you bring this instead of a truck?" Gunther asked, with a scowl.

"We both know how difficult it is driving through the fields. This baby can use the footpaths. It's a much smoother ride."

Reluctantly, Gunther climbed onto the back of the motorcycle, and Thorndale started it up. They rode on the footpaths that ran alongside the fields, and not through the fields like a car or truck had to. Thorndale was right, the ride was smoother, and Gunther actually enjoyed it.

Thorndale drove to the riverbank and parked the motorcycle on the edge of the tall grass. He led Gunther across the river, this time in the opposite direction from the cavern city. After a short walk, they came to the cave. Gunther didn't see the cave's entrance until Thorndale led him to it. The door to the cave was made of the same green wood found in the Alenian buildings, but it was painted to look like it was part of the mountain.

Thorndale opened the door and picked up a flashlight he'd left inside the cave's entrance. Flicking it on, he used it to guide himself along the wall until he came to a lever. When he pulled it, the cave lit up.

Gunther could see the cave had been hollowed out of the mountain, just as the cavern city had, though tiny in comparison. A dozen unusual looking robots stood in the center of the cave.

"Is this where you found Charlie?"

"Charlie and Big Boy."

Gunther walked around the lineup of robots. Some were huge, others small, some had claws and legs for appendages, and others had hands with fingers much like Alenian or human hands. A couple of the largest ones had appendages with specialized tools like plow heads and cultivators for farming.

Gunther grunted, "I didn't believe the Alenians could tend all these fields only using primitive hand tools. It seems they didn't."

A couple of the robots were spheres like the robot Charlie.

"Is one of these spherical robots Charlie?" Gunther asked.

"Charlie is outside soaking up some energy from the sun."

"I don't see any visible sensors in these robots. I don't understand how these robots can see what they're doing," Gunther said.

"Seth can see what Charlie sees. They must have some kind of visual sensing device."

Gunther ran his hands over the body of a large robot. "Renola asked me to come here and see if I can get these robots working. I'm not a robot expert, and you said your people couldn't figure out how these robots worked. I'm not sure what I can do to get them working again."

"She sent me to help you," came a voice from a hazy-white glow forming in the center of the cave. It solidified into a young Alenian. By human standards, he appeared to be in his early 30's, clean shaven with thick black hair. "My name is Tomlenar. The Elders have sent me to guide you in restoring the robots. I was once responsible for these robots." His image faded and disappeared. Almost as quickly, it reappeared. "I may fade from view from time to time. It requires considerable energy to project my image to this cave from the Lattice. Even if I am not visible, I can hear you and respond."

"We'd be happy to have your help," Gunther said.

Tomlenar's image walked over to two of the smaller robots with cylinder-shaped bodies and arms ending in hands. "These two robots have been programmed to run the Transits. We expected they would be stored here for only a few cycles, I believe you call cycles years, before these robots would begin the Transits, the process of returning us to our bodies. It has been over seventy years. The power cells in these robots have been depleted, and with the moisture in these caves, there is a possibility of internal damage. It may not be possible to make them functional again."

Gunther joined him next to the robots. "We won't know until we try. How do we open them so we can see what's inside?"

Tomlenar showed Gunther where the release was to open the robot's body, and they quickly became engrossed in inspecting the robot's internal condition.

Thorndale hadn't spent much time with Gunther. From the enthusiasm on Gunther's face replacing his otherwise regular stern expression, this was his element. He and Tomlenar were deep into a discussion of the robot's condition and what they might do to get it working again.

Thorndale was a biologist. He wasn't handy with tools like wrenches and screwdrivers. His tools were test tubes and scanners. As he listened to Gunther and Tomlenar conversing about the robot's condition, he could see he wouldn't be of any help to them. He was about to announce he was leaving when Tomlenar looked up from the robot. "I sense you are not interested in this work. Renola informs me she has something to show you at the village's genetics laboratory. She asks you to meet her there."

"Are you all right if I leave you here?" he asked Gunther.

"I'll be busy for quite some time. Go and see what Renola wants."

"I will contact you when Gunther needs to return," Tomlenar said.

"Tell Renola I'm on my way."

CHAPTER 103

Thorndale rode the motorcycle back to the colony. He had no idea why Renola wanted to see him, and why at the genetics lab building. No one worked in this building after Seth's father destroyed the lab. That thought brought a wave of sadness as he remembered the time he spent in that lab with Seth's mother. Knowing she was dead, he felt her loss more deeply than he had when he thought she was working somewhere in the Empire.

He parked in front of the village genetics lab building and waited. Ten minutes passed before Renola's form took shape in front of him. "Thank you for coming," she said.

"I'm not sure why you want me to meet you here. This building has been abandoned for years. The only machine in it has been destroyed, and there is nothing of value in the building."

"Gunther has restored power to this building. We can now use it. Please follow me to show you."

Renola's image led him into the building. She floated through the doors as he opened them to follow her. She continued past the room Seth and Gunther had torn apart to find the vault with the crystals to another small room on the far side of the building. The room was empty except for one wall that had cabinets on the floor and more cabinets on the wall above them.

She pointed to a cabinet on the wall. "Pull the door of this cabinet open, then close it. Repeat that twice more quickly."

He did what she asked. A section of the cabinets on the floor began sliding away, as did the cabinets above them. They revealed an opening. Beyond was a stairway going down that disappeared into darkness.

Thorndale marveled that they had been on this moon for over thirty years and never discovered this.

"Walk down the stairs, the lights will come on as you enter them," Renola said as her ghostly figure glided down the stairs into the darkness.

Thorndale stepped on the first stair, and overhead lights came on. There were at least forty stairs. The bottom was dark, but as he reached the bottom of the stairs, lights lit up to reveal a very large room. In front of him were a dozen metal sarcophaguses mounted on horizontal stands. Each sarcophagus was connected by wires and pipes to a machine in the center of the room. Pipes from the machine were attached to several huge tanks at the end of the room.

"What is all this?"

"Before we built the facility beneath the Lattice to transfer our people into crystals, we copied our people's essence into crystals here. It was only used for those who died or were about to die, so we did not need many shells. It was here where I conducted the test to demonstrate the Transit process could restore someone from a crystal back into their original body."

The sarcophaguses, pipes and wires and the big machine connecting everything were impressive. Whether it could do what Renola said it could do was another matter.

"You're saying you can reconstruct your bodies using chemicals from those tanks and these metal shells."

"We could perform thousands of Transits in our facility under the Lattice cave if we had the power. Your people have supplied power to this building, and we can use this to perform a few Transits."

Dust covered everything. "This equipment hasn't been used in a long time, are you sure it will work?"

"With your help to get it ready, I believe it will."

"You said you brought someone back using this equipment. Once you proved your point, did you put that person back into a crystal?"

Renola hesitated before answering. "There was no need. The person who made the test Transit had died of old age before his essence was saved in a crystal. He volunteered to make the Transit. Once he was returned to his body, he only lived a short time before dying again."

Thorndale raised his eyebrows. "Why return a dead person if all they will do is immediately die again?"

"It was his decision knowing he would not live long. He allowed me to prove it was possible to reconstruct an Alenian's body. I have spent my years in the Lattice studying how to not only recreate a body but to make it healthy, even healthier than when it went into the crystal. I believe I can return all who are in the Lattice into healthy, living bodies."

"If it doesn't work, you can try again as long as you have their crystal, can't you?"

"Once the essence is extracted from a crystal, the crystal can no longer be used."

"You're saying you only have one chance to bring someone back. If that fails, they are gone forever?"

"That is correct."

Thorndale couldn't decide if she was being cold, or just stating a scientific fact. "What's the odds someone can't be returned to their body?"

"I calculate the Transit has a 94.6 percent chance of success."

Again, cold logic. Thorndale thought the Alenians might be concerned if they learned there was a 5.4 percent chance of dying instead of being returned to their bodies. If Renola's calculation of 5.4 percent was correct and not just her guess.

CHAPTER 104

Empress Andraia reviewed the fleet's status. The attack on the rebel's base was a disaster in every way. They had lost the best ships in the fleet. With the treasury as depleted as it was, the Empire lacked the funds needed to build new ships. Raising money by demanding more taxes from the outer planets would be difficult. She suspected most would not comply. In the past, she would have sent Imperial troops to collect the taxes. With the fleet already thin, the rebels brazenly attacking shipping between Core planets, even those with Imperial fleet escorts, it was going to be impossible to get the money she needed to rebuild the fleet.

A messenger approached her desk, interrupting these disturbing thoughts. The young boy bowed deeply. "Your Majesty, I have a message from Major Krugar sent via the scout ship."

"Leave it on my desk." At last, she thought. Krugar had what she needed to solve all her problems.

The messenger put the VID on her desk, bowed then left. She picked up the VID and inserted the VID into the player. She entered the code she gave Krugar to use. Krugar's face appeared on the screen.

"My greetings, Empress. The scout ship gave us the news while we were still on Alenia. My congratulations on your elevation to this exalted, though well-deserved, position. This is a report on what happened on Alenia. A biologist named Ralph Thorndale, one of the original researchers sent to Alenia, was the sole survivor of the massacre. He was unaffected by the insanity, though the people you sent could not determine why he was not affected, nor did they learn what drove the colonists into a killing frenzy. I am afraid the belief we might find a new weapon out of what happened on Alenia did not materialize.

"As per your orders, we watched Harthset. He did not lead us to more of the life extending substance nor to a formula for it. The Marines searched the colony extensively, however they found nothing. Of course, that is what you predicted. The Emperor would have been unhappy with this result if he were still alive." A rare smile crossed Krugar's lips as he said that.

"On a more positive note, the wormhole has been closed. The explosion sealed it as predicted. I am sure you want to know that we retrieved the containers with the enzyme. As you directed, I left one of the containers on Alenia with a bomb to kill the group you sent there. Anyone who might go to the moon in the future will die, although with the wormhole closed, it is unlikely anyone will ever go there.

"I am sending this message from the Imperial Cruiser Xanthle. We transferred the containers with the enzyme to the Xanthle. I had the Marines, along with Jana Walkner, remain on the freighter. As per your orders, the Xanthle destroyed the freighter. Everyone who went to Alenia on this mission is now dead except for me, your most loyal subject.

"The Xanthle is returning to Klatania. I will contact you when we enter Klatanian space."

Finally, some good news. With the enzyme in her hands, she wouldn't need a new fleet. Once she released it on an outer planet or two, the rebellion would collapse. She would be the most powerful ruler in human history.

CHAPTER 105

Commander Freedom was in the conference room at Focus, their new base of operations. Operations were moved from Liberty to Focus long before the Imperial Fleet launched its attack. The idea of luring the Fleet to Liberty came from one of Commander Hider's best spies, who called himself Graller. He was here lobbying the Senior Commanders to support his daring plan to attack Klatania.

A three-dimensional model of Klatania was projected above the conference table. Graller stood as he described Klatania's orbital defenses. "The blockade zone begins 1,200 kilometers above Klatania. All incoming ships are boarded in orbit, then they are thoroughly inspected before being permitted to land. Three ships conduct the inspections. They are supported by two Imperial sub-class-cruisers that are there to make sure all ships stop to be inspected. An Imperial Cruiser orbits at 500 kilometers to ensure no ship runs the inspection blockade."

"That is formidable. How do you intend on getting through it?" Commander Impulse asked.

"I will use six freighters. They will arrive at the checkpoint at the same time and line up in order to be inspected. The plan is to create a diversion to allow the last two freighters, ones armed with nuclear missiles, to get through the blockade."

Commander Nightmare shook his head as he said, "Six ships are a lot to sacrifice for this dubious mission. The fact there are six ships increases the odds that one will be discovered as not being legitimate. Once that happens, the entire plan collapses."

"That's possible, though unlikely. They should have no problem entering the inspection zone. I've obtained the transponder codes for six freighters that regularly come to Klatania. Our freighters will be the same class as the ones they are representing, each one has been painted with the same markings as the ship they appear to be. Each will have the code used by the real freighter. Oh, before you ask, the real freighters are far away. There is no chance they will show up unexpectedly."

Freedom prompted, "Please go on describing the rest of your plan."

"The six freighters will be lined up for inspection. As the inspectors connect to the airlock to board the first freighter, the freighter will send out an emergency call to say that it is having a problem. Immediately the freighter will explode. The blast will give our ships behind it an opportunity to fan out. Two of them will get next to the two subclass cruisers and then explode. This will create a chaotic situation that will allow the three remaining freighters to slip down to the 500-kilometer orbit. With the confusion, the last decoy freighter will slip down to get close enough to the Imperial Cruiser before it explodes. It was either destroy, or at least, disable it. The two remaining freighters should be able to continue to their target. One will fly directly to the palace, the other to the nearby space port. The freighter flying to the palace will encounter a barrage from the six batteries that defend the palace. It is unlikely it will launch any of its missiles before it's destroyed. Dealing with the incoming freighter should be a sufficient distraction to allow the freighter approaching the space port a chance to launch its nuclear missiles at the palace. Coming from that angle, the palace defenses will not be able to adjust to hit both targets in time."

"I'm not sure if I should call this an ambitious or foolish plan. We will be sacrificing six freighters and the lives of many of our men for a scheme that only has a marginal chance of succeeding," Impulse said.

"There is a chance it will fail, that no nuclear missiles will hit the palace. Even if it fails, it will drive home a statement that Klatania is not safe from our attacks. If it succeeds in destroying the palace and killing the Empress, the Empire will be thrown into chaos. We will be in a position to exert pressure on the Barons to grant independence for the outer planets."

Graller surveyed the table for challenges. No one voiced any.

Freedom asked, "When can you be ready to carry this out?"

"We can be ready in three days."

That ended the meeting. Freedom asked Graller to stay behind after everyone left. Graller took a chair next to Freedom.

"I've known for some time you are a rogue telepath. I expect you know that by reading my thoughts."

"I don't read the thoughts of my friends or members of the cause. I reserve that for those who support the Empire."

"We don't award medals for service, however the work you did on the Liberty trap deserves one."

"I'm just doing what I can for the cause."

"As you said, this mission may change everything. It may even achieve our goal. Assume you are able to kill the Empress, I'm skeptical it will be as easy to persuade the Barons as you believe. That question will have to wait to be answered if your plan succeeds. I wonder why you gave this mission such an unusual name?"

"The story of where I came by this name goes back a long time."

"Please tell me."

"I was hiding, a rogue telepath staying one step ahead of the EYE Corps. I was on an outer planet one day when I happened on a boy who was also a telepath. He told me he didn't want to be forced to join the EYE Corps. I gave him advice on how he might fool the EYE Corps interrogators. If the boy successfully hid his ability from the EYE Corps all these years, I thought I might persuade him to join our cause.

"I remembered his name, but I was unable to locate him. I found his family was still living on the outer planet where I encountered him. I contacted them saying I was conducting a survey for the Imperial Census. As part of the survey, they were chosen for a personal interview. They had no choice but to agree. In the course of the sham interview, I said our records showed they had a son. They told me he died. When I asked what happened, they became evasive. It was apparent they were hiding something, so I read their thoughts. I learned they had an overwhelming sense of guilt about his death. It seems not long after I met the boy, his parents discovered he was a telepath. They turned him into the EYE

Corps. He was only at EYE Corps University for a short time before he died. I have named this mission after that boy."

"Let's hope that Operation Tovar is successful," Freedom said.

CHAPTER 106

Seth stayed in the Lattice as he watched Lena's crystal for any sign that she was alive. The crystals surrounding Lena's glowed brightly, as hers and the others he'd returned to the Lattice continued to look lifeless. His repeated telepathic messages to her got no response. As the time wore on, his fear grew that she was gone, but he wouldn't let himself believe it.

Seth spent the time examining his feelings for Lena. He couldn't remember his own childhood, but the image of Lena had always been with him. When he was very young and unhappy as his mother moved them from one outer planet to another, he would see this beautiful woman in his mind, and it comforted him. When he transitioned through puberty, she became the image of his ideal woman. That now he had found her, that she was alive, his feelings for her only grew stronger.

All of this continued to play back and forth in his thoughts. He wouldn't let himself believe she was gone. Even if she could only be an image in his mind, he wanted her alive. His anxiety grew as his telepathic messages to Lena went unanswered.

Seth was lying on the blanket watching the sun's rays enter the cave. It was the morning of the fourth day since he brought the crystals to the Lattice. He thought he heard something, but was it real, or was he imagining it? After so many days and nights alone, each sound raised his hope it was Lena speaking to him telepathically. Each time it wasn't her, his fear grew that he would never hear from her again. It heightened the torment inside him that he could have saved her if he had acted sooner.

The sound came again. This time it was clearly not a cave sound, it was a voice. He focused on it, and it grew stronger. "Seth, my crystal is partially energized. I have enough power that I can talk to you."

Relief washed over him as he stood up and watched the crystals he brought begin to glow faintly. "Is everything okay? Did your crystal sustain permanent damage?"

"There is no permanent damage to my crystal, but it has taken time for my crystal to regain some power. The last time I contacted you, I had to use the power of my friends' crystals since there was no longer power in the village's genetics lab. It drained most of their reserves. We were all close to being fully depleted. You are Seth, the child I talked with who saved us then and again saved us now."

He felt uncomfortable that she was still thinking about the events that took place when he was a child. Was she still thinking of him as a child? "I'm glad everything is all right." He wanted to say more, to tell her how he felt about her. It wasn't the time. He buried his feelings deep so that, even if she could read his thoughts like the EYE Corp, she wouldn't see them.

"I don't remember my childhood. My memories were erased. Somehow, I remembered you but nothing else from that time. I don't remember hiding your crystals. Can you tell me what happened then?"

"We were in our crystals when the enemy came. The robot hid our crystals, but after the enemy destroyed the robot, we could not see what was happening. There was no power where the robot hid us. We had to go dormant to conserve the energy within our crystals. We did not know you humans had come to Demeerite. Humans removed us from the hiding place. They put our crystals in the sunlight, and it energized them. I could not sense the humans, but I could sense you. You were different, not like the others. I could see your thoughts. After a while, I learned how to use your thoughts to talk to you. You were no more than a child, but we became friends. When your people destroyed one of our crystals, I asked you to hide our nine crystals. I told you where you should put us, and you did. You put us in the vault. It had power and a direct connection to the Lattice. For the past years, we have lived with those in the Lattice as a result of what you did for us as a child. You saved our nine crystals then, and by restoring power to the Lattice, you have saved all Alenians."

"I'm glad I could help."

"You did more than..." Lena paused. "I see in your thoughts that saving us has caused you and your family great pain. I am sorry for this.

Seth was worried how deeply she could see into his mind. Could she see how he felt about her. "Can you see everything in my mind?"

"No, not now. As a child, you were open. Now your thoughts are closed. I can only see the thoughts you present to me, and a few a little deeper. It is difficult to read the minds of humans. What I can see is that you have memories of your childhood that are not your own. There is a block in your mind keeping you from seeing your own memories. I may be able to remove this block. It may not work, but if you wish, I will try. It would be small payment for all you have done for me and my people."

"I only recently learned my childhood memories were not mine. I will be extremely grateful if you can restore my real memories. What do I need to do for you to remove this block?"

"Simply relax your body and clear your mind. This will be painful, and I am not sure if I can return the memories. I might destroy them completely, and they will be lost forever."

"I'll take that chance. I don't remember them now. If they are no longer there, I won't know it."

Seth sat down on the ground next to the Lattice.

"Think of your childhood, of the memories you have even though they are false memories."

As Seth remembered the false memories of his childhood in Digeria, Thorndale's memories, each memory came with a flash like a strobe light going off in his brain. The memories began to come without him willing them, as did the flashes. They came faster and faster, and then came the pain.

CHAPTER 107

S eth had been absent for days from the compound. Gunther continued to bring him food, now using the motorcycle to go to the crystal cave. He told the others he didn't know how Seth was going to deal with Lena's death. Compared to the other crystals in the cave that were glowing, the ones Seth brought were dark, and they looked lifeless.

Gunther got the human compound robot working that had previously served as the colony's cook. Doc, with Thorndale's help, brought back three more drums of Alenian food. The cave where the drums were stored was large, the number of drums many, though this supply wasn't inexhaustible, nor was the human food they had. Once all the food was gone, they would have nothing to eat. To extend the food as much as possible, they limited themselves to two meals each day, only breakfast and supper.

Supper was the team's opportunity to share what they'd done during the day. More importantly, it was a time to share what they'd learned from the Alenians. Doc found an Alenian doctor who explained how the machines were used in the cavern city. Gunther spent much of his time with Tomlenar discussing what they could do to repair the robots or other non-working Alenian machines. Monafar regularly visited Alan and Professor to answer their questions about Alenian history.

Alan was telling about his visit with Monafar that afternoon. "I pressed Mon-afar to tell me more details about the history of this moon. There is very little in the library books about Demeerite. Most of the books we have are about their other two planets. Monafar was reluctant to say much. I guess my badgering eventually wore him down. He said that telepaths were feared by non-telepathic Alenians. The telepaths were isolated from non-telepaths on their home planets. The governing body over all the planets was called the Alenian Alliance. After Demeerite was made habitable for Alenians, they decided to relocate all telepaths to this moon. The telepaths welcomed this move. They thought they would have their own society, a place where they could be free. They soon learned that wasn't the Alliance's plan. The telepaths were put here to grow a crop called Gaylen, a plant that will only grow on this coastal plain. Gaylen was extremely valuable. According to Monafar, it could heal wounds and even extend life. Despite how valuable Gaylen was, the telepaths on Demeerite were not allowed to benefit from it. They were forced to grow it in exchange for food and basic necessities, nothing more. The Alliance also demanded they could only use hand tools to grow Gaylen. It was another way the Alliance exerted their control over the telepaths."

"You know the Alenian's didn't farm using the simple farm tools we found in the village. They had robots to do the work," Gunther said.

"Monafar said they had Overseers who controlled those living on Demeerite. The Overseers didn't live here. They only came to bring food and basic supplies in exchange for the harvested Gaylen. The Demeerites were required to give everything they grew to the Overseers. Despite having Alliance satellites watching them, they were able to hide some of the harvest. They used this to trade with smugglers for more sophisticated equipment that allowed them to build robots. It was in this way they were able to get a reactor to power the Lattice, the one Gunther said can't be restarted."

Alan took a bite of his food that had been sitting untouched as he talked. "The cavern city they call Glenna is important in that it allowed the Demeerites to increase their population. There was a population limit placed on them by the Alliance. Anyone born over the limit was killed. They carved out Glenna to hide their growing population. That population numbered forty-three thousand, not the thirty thousand the Major told us lived here. That number includes thirteen thousand who died but were kept alive in the crystals."

Alan stopped as everyone turned to see Seth walk into the mess hall. Doc was about to ask Seth if everything was okay. The grin on Seth's face answered the question before he asked it.

Seth walked up to Thorndale. "I forgive you."

Thorndale was confused. Before he could ask what he was being forgiven for, Seth said, "Lena restored my childhood memories."

This time it was Thorndale's scarred face that bore a grin. "I've been living with the guilt of doing that ever since it happened. If you have your memories back, do you mind if I call you Speedy Rabbit?"

"Don't you dare," Seth said, still grinning. "Minus Speedy Rabbit, I'm here to tell you all the details I can remember about growing up here, as long as you consider I was only five years old when I left."

Seth related what he remembered as a child. What he didn't say was how having his childhood memories restored also restored the emotions that came with them. Before this, he had no clear memories of growing up with his parents. With his own memories restored, he remembered growing up in a loving home with two nurturing parents. He also remembered the day his father slapped him when he demanded Seth tell him where he hid the crystals. Seth knew why he wouldn't tell them where he hid the crystals. He understood it could mean Lena's death if they found them. All those memories made him feel complete for the first time in his life.

CHAPTER 108

The humans agreed to help the Alenians return to their bodies using the facility below the village's genetics lab. It had sufficient power to make a few Transits, the term they used for the reincarnations. Since all the Alenians could do was instruct, it fell on the humans to make all the physical preparations for the Transits.

Renola described that a Transit took place in two phases. The first phase was to rebuild the body. That was done in the sarcophagus shell. A template of the Alenian's original body was contained in their crystal. A new body was built from the extracted template, a body that was physically identical, or even better than, the Alenian's original body. Rebuilding the body required five days in the shell. The second phase of the Transit began on the sixth day. The second phase was to transfer the Alenian's essence into the newly built brain. Renola described the essence as the Alenian's memories, personality, and brain-body connections. It was everything needed to make the Alenian feel their new body was their original one.

After the new body was constructed with the essence transferred into it, the shell would be opened. The brain would not have control of the body at this time. The body would be transferred to a recovery room where mechanical aids would be required to keep the lungs breathing, as well as the heart beating. In time, the brain would take over these essential functions. It would take time for the essence to slowly establish physical connections to the body. The entire process could take several weeks. In the end, the Alenian would emerge feeling as if they were in their original body, in some cases, a body healthier than the one they had before they were preserved in the crystal.

That was the theory Renola described. Thorndale was skeptical it would work. However, he did his part to prepare for the Transits.

Thorndale and Doc checked the biological elements needed to reconstruct the body were still viable in their hermetically sealed tanks. Seventy years was a long time to store these elements. If they were corrupted, the Transits would fail. Once they were sure the elements were good, Gunther reconnected the pipes connecting the tanks to the machine that would perform the Transit.

Gunther, with Tomlenar's guidance, repaired one of the robots that had been programmed to operate the Transit machine.

Everything was ready. Today they would run the first Transit.

Lena talked with Seth constantly as they prepared for the Transit. She said since she was the last to be put into a crystal, she should be the first through the Transit. Seth tried to talk her out of it. He discovered Lena was as stubborn as she was beautiful.

Seth asked Renola to talk Lena out of being the first to go through the Transit. She said it was Lena's choice. She would not interfere with her decision. Renola reassured Seth she checked every step of the Transit. In theory it should work. Seth was uncomfortable with the words *in theory it should work*. Thorndale told Seth about the test conducted to prove that the Transit worked. Knowing the first subject hadn't survived added to Seth's fear for Lena.

Seth didn't want Lena to be the guinea pig for the initial attempt. If it failed, she could die, or she could end up in a deformed body. Now that he could talk with her, be with her, he knew he was in love with her even though she was only an apparition, but at least in this state she was alive. If the Transit process killed her, he didn't know how he would deal with it.

Seth was sitting on a bench in the Common with Lena's image in front of him.

"Lena, please reconsider being the first Transit, I beg you. The Transit may be dangerous. It could kill you."

She smiled at Seth. "I know you are concerned for my safety. I also sense your affection for me. By our standards, it is an unforgivable intrusion into your thoughts for me to see these things, though we have shared more than most these past few weeks. I can still see you when you were a darling little boy. You saved me then. As a man, you have saved me again. I have difficulty fully embracing the fact that you are no longer that little boy. Know that I do have affectionate feelings toward you, though I am not sure if they are as strong as the feelings you have towards me. No matter what happens, my mind is set. I will be the first through the Transit. The Elders have agreed to let me prove to my people the Transit works."

Seth accepted he wasn't going to persuade her not to go through with it. As painful as the fear of losing her in the Transit, even more painful knowing if she survived, she might never feel towards him as he felt towards her. All he could do was hope that someday he could convince her to love him.

CHAPTER 109

Renola, Chief Elder Ragonlar, as well as the Head of Medical Research, Kamlanar, were in the basement of the genetics lab in their ghostly images with all the humans. The robot that would conduct the Transit was in place. Everything was ready for the Transit to begin.

Seth held his breath as the robot put Lena's crystal in a container that cupped the bottom half of the crystal. The robot closed the top half of the container over the crystal. Until the crystal was enclosed in the container, Seth could sense Lena. He could sense her fear, also her resolve to go through with it. Once the cover enclosed her crystal, Seth could no longer sense her. He had an overwhelming feeling of panic. He wanted to tear open the container and pull out her crystal. He focused on his precognitive ability to reveal the outcome. Nothing came. Seth stood there with the pit of his stomach tightening, facing the possibility that Lena could be lost to him.

The robot turned a few dials on the machine. It was beginning the process of extracting the design of Lena's body from the crystal. The robot opened a series of valves to the chemical tanks, giving the machine access to the elements for reconstructing her body in the sarcophagus shell. The process of rebuilding Lena's body had begun. All Seth could do now was wait.

• • • • ● • ● • • •

During the next six days, Ragonlar came with Kamlanar to observe. They only stayed briefly. Seth alone stayed around the clock watching the shell where her body was being built. Alan would bring Seth food and stay with him for a while each day. They sat in silence. There was nothing Alan could say to comfort Seth. Most of the time, his only company was the robot that stood unmoving in the corner, its work finished for now.

Nights were the most painful as he sat alone in the cold, empty basement with only an occasional sound coming from the machine rebuilding Lena's body. Seth would stare at the shell, unsure if the woman he loved was being rebuilt or dying.

On the third night, Seth heard gurgling sounds coming from the shell. He called Renola telepathically. She came, checked the dials, listened to the gurgling sounds, then said it was normal for it to make these sounds.

Renola would appear regularly to check the machine's dials. He watched her anxiously. Each time, she would assure him everything was going well. It didn't stop the nagging feeling he had that they weren't. He was afraid it was a premonition, but he couldn't be sure. It could just be his fear that he would never see Lena again.

At sunrise on the seventh day, it was time for the shell to open. Renola explained that even after the shell opened and the body was removed from it, it would be many days before Lena's essence was fully integrated with her new body.

Renola stood in front of the machine checking the dials. She turned to addressed the audience that included all the humans along with the ghostly images of the Alenian Elders, "The shell will open in a few moments."

Seth held his breath as he watched the shell continue to remain closed, showing no sign it was about to open. He heard a soft buzzing sound coming from the machine. The robot came alive. It walked to the machine, passing through the ghostly image of Renola who was standing in front of the dials. The robot checked the dials. Seemingly satisfied, it pulled down a lever. Slowly the shell began to open.

Seth ran over to the shell. Inside was the body of a fully formed woman. It was Lena, as he had seen her throughout his life, and as she had appeared in a ghostly form.

She wasn't moving. Renola warned him it would take time for Lena to gain control of her new body. But what he saw was a pale body that looked more like a corpse than something living.

Seth probed to see if he could sense Lena's thoughts. He sensed nothing. He turned to Renola, unable to keep the dismay he felt from his voice. "I don't sense her!"

Renola came over to look down at the body. She went over to the machine and quickly checked the dials. Worry filled her face. "It should have worked. All the equipment registers it did."

Seth turned to look at Lena's body. Tears began running down his face. He reached out to touch her when a sound interrupted him. It was someone talking to him telepathically, "You know it isn't polite to touch a woman unless she allows it." It was Lena's voice. Her thoughts sang in his brain. "I can make an exception for the man who has saved me twice." There was a twinkle in her voice.

Seth was oblivious to the shouts of excitement in the room behind him. All he could see was that the woman he wanted to spend the rest of his life with was alive.

CHAPTER 110

The plan was in motion. The freighters were entering Klatania's orbital inspection zone.

Commander Freedom monitored their progress from a live feed transmitted to Focus from the last freighter. The possibility of the plan killing the Empress, was unreasonably optimistic. Yet, if they somehow succeeded, it could be the turning point in their long quest for the outer planets' independence, possibly every planet's independence, from the tyranny of the Empire.

A messenger approached the Empress. "Your Majesty, you requested information about the Imperial Cruiser Xanthle. It is an hour away from Klatania."

"Has Major Krugar called in?"

"We are having trouble raising communications with the Xanthle. We have not received a response from them."

She had always counted on Krugar delivering on his promises. The last contact from him was three days ago. He promised to contact her when he entered Klatanian space. That communication should have come hours ago. She stood up from her desk. "I am going to the Communications Room. Tell the guards to prepare to take me there."

The messenger walked quickly out of the room to inform the guards. Although she had removed the Zinder guards, she wasn't foolish enough to think there weren't those with plans on her life. Guards she could trust were vital for her continued safety, even in the palace.

Six regular, human Imperial Guards were standing at attention to accompany her to the Communications Room. The Communications Room was down one level and halfway across the palace. Once there, she left the guards at the door. The communications officer on duty stood up. The look of surprise to see the Empress at his station didn't fade as he bowed.

"Get back to your station, then tell me why you can't reach the Imperial Cruiser Xanthle."

"Six freighters have entered the inspection zone. They may be causing interference as we try to contact the Xanthle."

"When did the Xanthle enter Klatanian space?"

"We picked them up on our scanners two hours ago as they came out of their jump," he said.

"Two hours ago! I left orders that I was to be informed immediately when the Xanthle made contact after it entered Klatanian space."

"They ... they never made contact. I haven't been able to raise them," the communications officer stammered.

"When will they enter orbit?" She was now angry at Krugar as well as the communications officer.

"That is hard to say. They have not slowed down. They should decelerate soon, or they will crash into Klatania."

"They are not slowing..." She had a frightening thought. If the enzyme had gotten loose on the Xanthle, everyone on the ship would be dead. If it crashed into Klatania, everyone on the planet would die.

She yelled at him, "Connect me with the orbital planetary defense commander!"

"But it is my job to conduct all communications."

"Connect me now!"

He did as she commanded.

The orbital planetary defense commander responded to the call. "This is Captain Koepel."

She grabbed the microphone out of the young man's hands. "This is Empress Andraia. I want you to destroy the Imperial Cruiser Xanthle. You are not to let it anywhere near the atmosphere of Klatania. Do you understand?"

"Wait, is this a joke? Who is this?"

She was about to tell Captain Koepel how he would die if he didn't obey her order immediately when the young communications officer said, "He knows me. Let me talk to him."

She handed him the microphone.

"Captain Koepel, this is Lieutenant Rogers of Palace Communications."

"Hi, Tom. Who was that giving me the absurd order to destroy one of our cruisers?"

"That was the Empress herself giving you the order. You better do what she says!"

Koepel said, "That was the...yes, Your Majesty." The line went dead.

She would spare the life of this young communications officer. Captain Koepel would not be so lucky.

CHAPTER III

T he first rebel freighter was told to prepare to be boarded for inspection. The other five rebel freighters were queued up behind it. Calvin Bristone was acting as Captain on the first freighter along with a minimal crew of three other rebels. He watched as his monitor showed the boarding craft approaching. The plan called for him to let them begin to board before he blew up the freighter.

He thought of his home on the outer planet Tavian, and of the girl waiting for him there. He couldn't tell her about his mission or that she would never see him again. He left a VID with his commanding officer to send to her afterward. His heart felt heavy knowing their plans to build a small house on some farmland and raise a family would never happen. He hoped she would have a happy life. That she would find someone to love her as much as he did.

Calvin shook himself out of the self-pity he was feeling. He'd volunteered for this mission. This was for the greater good. His life would be a small price to pay to free the outer planets from the Empire's subjugation.

He watched as the boarding ship slowly drew up to the docking port of his freighter. He went over to the controls. The bomb on the reactor was wired to a switch on the control panel. Once they docked with the freighter, he would flip this switch to blow up both ships.

The boarding ship stopped only a few meters from the freighter's docking ring. They were not calling him, nor were they docking with his ship. He had his channel open to them, but not to the general traffic channel that normally buzzed with chatter from ships in the vicinity. He flipped on the general traffic channel to see if there was something keeping the boarding party from docking with him.

"All ships in the vicinity of Gate Five, clear the area immediately."

Calvin thought, I'm in Gate Five. If they've discovered our plan, maybe I should blow up my ship now. He was unsure what he should do. They were told not to communicate with the other freighters, but he was desperate to have someone tell him what to do.

The general traffic channel repeated the message, this time with more urgency. "All ships, that includes you, Freighter 65591, leave the area immediately. Return to a higher orbit."

Freighter 65591 was Calvin's designation. What was happening?

"This is Freighter 49001. It's Luke. Calvin, do what they request. Go to a higher orbit."

That was his friend Luke calling from the sixth freighter. Calvin didn't need to hear the order twice. Setting the controls for his freighter he started for a higher orbit. He had just cleared Gate Five when he saw a ship was coming at him. It was an Imperial Cruiser coming in fast and too steep an angle to achieve orbit. It looked like it was going to crash into the planet. Calvin hit full thrusters to make sure he was far enough away to avoid the cruiser colliding with his ship. As he did, all the Imperial ships in the defensive perimeter opened fire on the Imperial Cruiser. They fired relentlessly at it, as if they were trying to obliterate it. The cruiser blew apart in a half dozen pieces as they continued to fire on it.

Calvin was still receding from the attack when he noticed that freighters five and six had slipped through the confusion caused by the attack. They were heading for their target. He received one more message. It was from his friend Luke on freighter six, "Go home."

Calvin watched as the two freighters deviated from the plan and both entered the restricted space above the palace. The palace anti-aircraft guns opened a barrage of fire at them. They were being torn apart as the two freighters continued flying toward the palace. Calvin didn't see the missiles fired until the two thermonuclear bombs exploded. His monitors were equipped with sensor shields that quickly darkened to keep from harming the cameras or those watching the screen. The image returned in two seconds showing two mushroom clouds filling the screen where the palace had been. Calvin set the course for his freighter to return to Focus.

Commander Freedom watched as the camera on freighter six showed it approaching the palace. The transmission continued long enough for him to see that the nuclear missiles fired from the freighter hit their target. The screen went blank. The freighter was gone. The tension Freedom felt from the start of this operation was finally released. He felt a wave of sadness for those who sacrificed themselves today. Maybe the rebel policy of not giving out medals for heroic acts needed to change. These brave souls deserved recognition as did Graller for the success of Operation Tovar. Now they would deal with the difficult job of negotiating for independence for the planets.

CHAPTER 112

They moved Lena's body to a hospital bed in the cavern city. Seth learned the cavern city was called Glenna. They had better equipment there to monitor her progress through the final stages of the Transit. Lena told him telepathically it was too exhausting to communicate with him. Renola said Lena needed rest. She would communicate with them once she was stronger. Seth was frustrated that, again, all he could do was sit by Lena's bedside. He sat there watching her motionless body now with an array of tubes and wires connected to it.

As the days passed, Renola came often to check on Lena's progress. She assured Seth it would take time for Lena to gain control over her new body. Her words were meant to reassure him. The fact they were holding off other Transits until Lena fully recovered continued to worry him.

Seth brought packages of Alenian food and never left her bedside. On the fourth day after she was moved to Glenna, Lena opened her eyes briefly. She blinked, then she moved her lips slightly. That was all. Though she could blink, there was no indication she could see.

On the sixth day, she moved her head slightly from side to side. On the tenth day, she wiggled one finger. Then on the eleventh day, she wiggled all her fingers and her toes. Still, she didn't answer Seth's attempts to communicate with her telepathically. Renola said this was expected since Lena needed all her energy to allow for her essence to gain control of her new brain.

On the twelfth day, Seth awakened from the cot he was sleeping in next to her bed. As he turned to look at Lena, she surprised him by shifting her eyes towards him. Then he heard, "I have been watching you as you sleep here by my side. I feel strong enough for us to talk telepathically, for a while."

Seth was overjoyed as they began to communicate. She could go for about an hour before she was too tired to continue. After an hour or two of rest, she was able to talk again briefly. Seth lived for those moments.

By the fourteenth day, Lena was stronger. She could talk telepathically with Seth for longer periods. After two hours of communicating with Lena, Seth's headache, which had continued to bother him, became unbearably painful.

"I'm sorry. I've had a headache ever since I landed on Demeerite. For some reason, it is worse now than it was before I began communicating with you telepathically."

"Your mind is not like that of the other humans. I can read your mind as if you were an Alenian, except there are parts of your mind that are different. Those parts aren't like other humans' minds or Alenians, either. I once served as a medical assistant. I was trained to analyze medical problems as well as psychological ones like fears, anxieties, plus other mental issues. If you wish, I can try to find out why you have your headache."

"If you can, do it."

She said, "Just relax. Let me probe your mind."

Seth could sense her presence in his mind. It was the same sensation as when the EYE Corps Interrogator probed him. He didn't resist her probes. He could feel her wander freely through his mind.

"I know what is causing your headache."

"What is it?"

"Your telepathic ability is powerful. For years, you suppressed your ability, which had the effect of directing it inward. Your telepathic ability is strong, much stronger than Alenians. It is also undisciplined. When you arrived on Demeerite, your telepathic ability was so strong you could hear the communications between those in the Lattice. We learn when we are children how to block out telepathic communications not directed to us. You don't know how to do that. You are sensing the conversations of thousands of Alenians in the Lattice. That is the source of your headache."

"What can I do about it?"

"I can train you as I would a child." There was laughter in her words.

Seth said, "You know how I feel about you. I can't hide it. You told me you were twenty-four years old when you were transferred to the crystal. Over seventy years have passed since. That makes you over ninety years old. Don't worry, I prefer older women." He laughed both in his mind and out loud.

"It is easy to love the man who has saved my life several times," Lena said.

At that moment, Seth had a vision of a future with Lena. They were together, they had a son, life was good. Was this a premonition or wishful thinking? He hoped it was a premonition.

CHAPTER 113

F our weeks after Lena's Transit, she could walk on her own. Renola was delighted at how well Lena had come through the Transit. In every way, she was as healthy as she had been before she went into the crystal.

The Elders agreed Lena's Transit had been a success. They began planning for other Alenians to go through the Transit. They were limited in that they could only conduct five simultaneous Transits in the basement of the village's building. By this time, the Lattice had built up enough energy to allow them to conduct three Transits there. Eight Transits for tens of thousands of Alenians in the crystals. It was going to take a long time to bring them all back.

Thorndale was becoming familiar with Alenian physiology. He made a startling discovery that he shared with everyone at supper. "I've been checking Lena's DNA. For now, she is the only Alenian we have. If she is a normal Alenian, as Renola says she is, then the Alenians are so close to being human it's astounding."

"I guess that answers the question why they look like us," Alan said.

"Maybe all advanced beings have the same DNA," Gunther added.

Professor said, "In my studies of life forms on different planets, there are marked differences in their genetics. The truth is that life evolves to match the planet on which it originates. The only exceptions are the planets humans have transformed to accommodate themselves."

Doc jumped into the conversation, "I concur with Thorndale. Besides a functioning appendix, their internal organs are identical to ours. The only other difference is a small organ in their brain we don't have. I assume that's what gives them their telepathic ability."

The ghostly form of Administrator Teila appeared before the group. Alenians only rarely appeared at the colony. The visitations drained energy from the Lattice cave, the energy they needed to perform the few Transits they could conduct there. When they did appear, it was to request help from the humans.

Teila's image stood there, mouth unmoving, as she projected her image into their minds. "I am here to express the Elders thanks to Gunther for all he has done to support the Transits by fixing the robots and seeing if he could repair our reactor."

Gunther had followed up on Seth's suggestion they might use the human reactor to restart the Alenian reactor in the Lattice cave. He wasn't sure it was feasible. Checking it confirmed his initial assumption that it wasn't powerful enough to restart the Lattice reactor.

Gunther nodded to Teila, "I appreciate your thanks. However, I haven't come up with a way of restarting the Lattice reactor."

"We accept you have tried. We have another request for your talents. As more people come through the Transit, we will need more food. We stored the food you have been eating to be used by those who came first through the Transits. As more will return, this supply of food will run out. I have been sent to request your assistance in restoring the robots used to farm the land. We have seeds for these robots to plant once they are operational. Given the time it will take crops to grow, this must be done soon before we run into a food shortage."

"It would be my pleasure," Gunther said.

"I will send Tomlenar to help you with the robots. When they are functional, I will direct them to the cache of seeds. I thank you ahead of time for your help."

Gunther acknowledged it with a nod and said, "We were told you have not built or farmed in the green areas on the other side of the continent. Why is that?"

"The Alenian Overlords banned us from living anywhere other than here. It was the only place Gaylen would grow. We did, once, send a team to explore the land on the other edge of the continent. They never returned. Since then, we have considered it too dangerous to send anyone else."

Alan spoke up. "I read that Demeerite was dependent on the home planets for goods you needed that you did not have here. What happens now that it is impossible to get these goods?"

Teila said sadly, "As you have told us, the White Death persists on both Clanferion and Gorderion. We will need to explore elsewhere to find what we need."

"It's too bad we don't have a spaceship," Gunther said offhandedly.

Teila smiled. "Alenians used their spaceships to explore many parts of this galaxy in the past. You are correct, we do not have a spaceship. Possibly, with your help, we can build one."

Epilogue

The story of Seth Harthset and the Alenians is just beginning. Their adventure continues in Far Star The Forest Land.

ABOUT THE AUTHOR

Nicholas Marselos fell in love with science fiction when as a child he first realized how much fun it was to read. The vastness of space, the potential that we are not alone in the universe, and the incredible adventures of traveling to distant and exotic places in the galaxy were intoxicating. He set a goal for himself to contribute to this genre. He has with his books Stories of the Strange, a collection of novellas and short stories, and Far Star Crystal.